THE COMPLETE WAR OF ROSES TRILOGY

XV, VII, AND I

LANA SKY

LANA SKY
LANA SKY
LANA SKY

The Complete War of Roses Trilogy

The Complete War of Roses Trilogy By Lana Sky

Copyright © 2019 by Lana Sky
All rights reserved.

No part of this publication may be reproduced, distributed, or transmitted in any form or by any means, including photocopying, recording, or other electronic or mechanical methods, without the prior written permission of the author.

This is a work of fiction. Names, characters, businesses, places, events and incidents are either the products of the author's imagination or used in a fictitious manner. Any resemblance to actual persons, living or dead, or actual events is purely coincidental.

XV: (FIFTEEN)

ACKNOWLEDGMENTS

Mickey, thank you so very much for taking the time to help me perfect this draft. As always, your feedback and expertise have been invaluable. Thank you, Charity for applying the final touches on this draft.

Thanks so much to everyone who supported this draft along the way, including the many beta readers who provided encouragement along the way! Please keep in mind that this story includes dark, graphic and explicit content matter that is not suitable for readers under the age of 18—or for readers who are uncomfortable with the following subject matter: explicit sex, mentions of sexual abuse, and graphic depictions of violence.

"You're going to die," my sister Briar tells me around a yawn while tucked beneath her embroidered blankets. "I saw it in a dream. You die. But everyone thinks you're me—hey! Why did you stop?" She tilts her blond head toward me expectantly.

I'm holding her brush. It's heavy and silver, so different from the cheap, wooden comb I use. Jealousy is a constant itch I have to smother. It's like Mother says: *Briar may have more material things, but things aren't everything. You have gifts too, Ellen, my Rose.*

My "gifts" aren't as obvious as the shelves of dolls and finery lining the walls of Briar's massive bedroom. Pink walls and buttery-soft carpet form a suite ten times as big as my room downstairs. Her bed alone is big enough for the two of us to lie outstretched on the center of it beneath a lacy canopy.

"Ellen?" Briar tugs on my arm. "Keep going."

Swallowing hard, I finger one of her golden curls and then ease the tangles from it. "No one would ever think I'm you," I reply, knowing exactly what she wants me to say.

"Of course." She giggles, wiggling her nose. "Because I'm prettier." And she is. Just nine years old—two years older than I am—and she already looks more like our mother than I could ever dream to. At least until, her pretty smile fades. "But everyone still likes you more."

"Nuh uh." My stomach drops. I hate when Briar gets this way, like when we play board games and I make the mistake of winning too many times. Everything becomes a contest.

And I always have to lose.

"You're so much better than me," I insist. "I have to be nice. That's all."

Because I'm not like her—not an heiress. If I pout, or scream, or throw a tantrum, I'll be punished and Mother won't be able to see me. Even the thought of it makes my heart ache, and I maneuver the brush more gently through Briar's curls. "Everyone loves *you*."

Her pink lips quirk into a lovely smile, and she shrugs me off to sit back against a wall of pillows. "I know that," she insists. "Even Robert is nicer to you though."

Robert. Her older brother who visits the manor sometimes. He's back now. Occasionally, I pass him in the hallway. Would I say he's nice to me? Maybe. But sometimes I think he looks at me the way Briar does her dolls once they're broken. Like I'm tiny, and plastic, and hollow.

"Ugh." Briar rolls her eyes. "Speak of the devil."

My cheeks grow hot. We aren't allowed to talk like that, not that it matters. Mother isn't the figure standing in the doorway, and Robert doesn't seem to care. Only Briar would ever dare call him unholy anyway; he looks like an angel. His hair is a brighter gold than his sister's, his eyes a deep shade of brown.

"It's late," he says, running his fingers along the collar of a pressed suit. He looks grown up wearing it. Like Briar's father, the master of the house, does. Like a businessman. "Shouldn't you be in bed? *Both* of you?" His eyes cut in my direction.

I cringe, jumping to my feet. "S-sorry—"

"She was getting me a glass of milk," Briar says over me. "That's why she's here. Don't you dare tell."

"It's dangerous to sneak around at night," Robert says, his voice soft. "Don't you know that's when the monsters come out?"

"There's no such thing as monsters," Briar declares, squaring her jaw.

But she's wrong. Monsters live right here in the manor. Sometimes I hear them if I stay up too late: faint scuffling noises from down below… Screaming.

It's why I'm never supposed to leave my room at night. Mother makes me promise I won't—but Briar is the only one worth breaking that promise for.

"Fine, then. If you insist on being a lazy brat, come, Elle." Robert waves his hand, summoning me closer. "I'll go with you."

A part of me wants to stay here with Briar—hide *behind* her if I have to. But Robert is sixteen, practically an adult. I have no choice but to shuffle after him into the hall.

Briar has a whole wing to herself. Even the walls are decorated in soft shades of pink to match the cream carpeted floors. We pass her playroom and the closet where she keeps her winter clothes. There's a servant's stairway back here too. Accompanied by the regal boy beside me, I notice all the flaws here that aren't visible in the grand hallway his family uses. The walls are painted white with cracks in the corners that draw his gaze.

"The kitchens are this way," I gather up the nerve to point toward a door at the base of the steps.

Robert shoots me an odd look. "I know. Your room is down here, isn't it?"

I force myself to nod, my eyes wide. I don't think I've ever seen him in this part of the house before.

Chuckling, Robert nudges my chin with the tips of his fingers and I shiver. He's smiling, one of the few times I've ever seen him do so. "Don't look so surprised," he gently scolds. "You aren't like Briar, are you? You don't act like a child. How old are you?"

Something squirms in my belly as I say, "S-seven."

"Seven." He nods like I've shared some powerful secret. "You seem older sometimes. Older than my sister, anyway."

I look over my shoulder just in case Briar snuck out of her room after us. My heart is pounding harder. My toes curl against the carpet, slick with sweat.

"That's a good thing," he insists. "You aren't naïve like her."

My tongue struggles to copy the strange word. "N-naï—"

"Silly," he says sternly. He leans down, bringing his face close to mine. "You aren't silly. I think you know what a real monster is. Don't you?"

I shake my head.

"Don't lie." Robert brushes my cheek again, forcing me to face him. "Tell me."

All the things Mother always warned me about gnaw at the back of my mind. *Never stay out late. Never come upstairs without permission.* She never told me not to talk to Robert, but…

"Sometimes I hear noises at night," I admit.

When he cocks his head, I realize I was whispering.

"What kind of noises?" he prods, his voice louder than mine.

"Shouting. Yelling. Screaming—"

"Shh!"

I jump as Robert presses his thumb against my lips. Noise echoes at the top of the staircase. Someone's coming.

Before they appear, Robert grabs my arm and steers me into the kitchen. "Here." Upon letting me go, the older boy rummages through a cupboard for a glass and fills it with water from the tap. When he hands it to me, I frown in confusion.

"I think she wanted milk—"

"Wait."

I stiffen at his playful tone, alarmed when he draws the cup beyond my reach. Robert is too serious for games. He doesn't even like to play checkers with Briar. He must be mocking me. Though why?

"You're smarter than Briar," he declares. "Aren't you?"

"I-I—"

"I'm going to show you a real monster," he says over me, leaning in close. "They aren't like they seem in fairytales. Are you brave enough?" He grabs my arm before I can decide and presses the cup of water against my palm, forcing me to take it. "Come on."

He leads me past the kitchen and down a narrow hallway, but my steps falter over the icy concrete floor. I'm not allowed this far, this deep into the basement. My stomach starts to hurt, like it does when Briar makes me bend the rules—such as staying in her room too late. If someone catches me, I might never be allowed upstairs again.

"In here."

Up ahead, Robert stops beside a door. Another man is already standing there and my heart sinks.

"Relax," Robert says, dragging me closer. He eyes the man, his head held high. "You won't tell anyone we were here." His voice rings with authority and the man nods. Then he opens the door and nudges me closer, his hand on my shoulder. "Look…"

My heart pounds as my eyes adjust to the darkness. Monsters have teeth and sharp claws. They thrive in the dark. They growl and prowl and…

They aren't small. Monsters aren't supposed to be hunched on the floor, with delicate limbs and pale skin.

I always thought Briar was the prettiest person I've ever seen, but the girl huddled in a dark room is beautiful. Long, dark hair falls over her like a cape, obscuring most of her tattered, gray shirt and jeans. She's young, maybe even the same age as Robert.

"Go on," Robert goads, pushing me closer.

My hand trembles and most of the water in the cup has spilled down the front of my nightgown by the time I reach her. Her face is bruised, and shiny ropes are wrapped around her arms—like the kind used to tie up the Rottweilers Briar's father owns: chains.

"Closer," Robert insists.

I have no choice but to take another step. Then another…

I jump as the girl lifts her head, her eyes huge in the darkness. "What's your name?" Her voice is so soft that I barely hear her.

"Don't answer," Robert snaps, but it's too late.

My lips are already moving. "E-Ellen," I croak.

The girl smiles. "My…my name is Anna-Natalia." She stares past me to Robert, meeting his gaze directly. But she doesn't tremble like everyone else does around the Winthorp heirs. She doesn't even flinch. "My *name* is Anna-Natalia."

"Go back upstairs, Elle," Robert says, shoving me toward the door. "Now, you know what real monsters look like. They look just like us."

Turning on my heel, I run, escaping the basement and sprinting back upstairs. I return to Briar's room panting, and she observes me from her bed, pouting.

"Where's my milk?"

I can't even speak. Instead, I grab the brush from the edge of her mattress and return it to her vanity. "I should go. Goodnight—"

"Stay with me tonight." She reaches out, and I marvel at her slim fingers. They look just like mine but softer. Cleaner. *Prettier,* like she said. "I don't want to be alone."

"But…" My eyes dart toward her bedroom door. I want to run to my room and crawl beneath my plain covers. I want to forget what Robert showed me. "If anyone else catches me—"

"They won't," Briar insists. "Come!" She pats the space beside her, and I reluctantly crawl onto the mattress, slipping beneath her silk sheets. "You see?" She runs her fingers along my stomach, tickling me. "We're just like real sisters."

"Real sisters," I echo, snuggling as close to her as I dare. Sometimes I forget that's exactly what we are: sisters.

"Ellen?" she whispers.

"Yes?"

"If monsters did really come for me… If I were going to die, you wouldn't let it happen. Would you?"

"No." I shake my head, my heart swelling with protectiveness. "I'd fight them for you. Always."

"Good." She closes her eyes and gestures for me to switch the light off. "Night."

Something is wrong. I know it the second my eyes open to darkness. Just a sliver of moonlight slips in between the curtains shrouding the windows but it's enough to illuminate the empty space beside me. Briar's gone.

As soon as I register that fact I catch a shadow drifting across the wall, ghosting over a shelf of porcelain dolls. Briar? No. It's too massive and terror descends like ice water.

This figure is bulky. Someone big. Too big to be Mother or one of the servants.

Too big to be Robert.

Their footsteps are heavy. Cautious. Paralyzed by fear, I crane my neck and find a figure hunched over the foot of the bed. The monster Briar feared. Just as Robert taught me, he looks *human*.

Blond hair peeks from the edges of a black woolen cap. That color makes my heart stop—he's wearing it from head to toe. Black slacks and a dark sweatshirt meant to disguise him in the shadows.

The second he meets my gaze, I know. He's dangerous, just like the men my mother warned me about. What he's holding proves it: something silver glinting in the dark, a forbidden object I'm not allowed to touch.

A knife.

He points it at me, his jaw clenched. "Get up. I said get up," he hisses. His voice sounds strange, with emphasis placed on odd syllables. "Now!" He adjusts the knife, but his hand wavers. His eyes are too wide. Fearful?

Suddenly, he stiffens, his head cocked. Behind him, the door is partially opened, and he cuts his gaze to it. When he turns back to me, he points the knife again, jabbing the edge toward the bed.

"Get under it," he commands. "Now! Don't think. Don't move. Just breathe. You hear me? All you do is fucking *breathe.*"

CHAPTER 1

Noise...
Chaos...
Briar...

The first thing I'm aware of is that I'm blindfolded —a fact that could be a blessing in disguise as my thoughts blur and jumble together. Only one coherent question escapes the fray: *Where am I?*

No answer comes to me immediately. My straining ears can make out only a few words muttered nearby in unfamiliar voices. Deep, *masculine* voices.

Various smells irritate my nostrils as well: sweat, body odor, male. *All* male. God, *where am I?*

I try flexing my shoulders only to wince. My hands are impossible to move, tied behind my back with something rough. Rope?

Oh, God.

Familiar terror gnaws at my belly as moisture gathers in my armpits and sweeps across my palms. At least, now, I have an inkling of my fate. I'm trapped in another one of his games. My nostrils flare with renewed purpose: seeking out *his* scent.

He must have hired lackeys this time; foreign body odor drowns out the stench of his cologne. I can't smell him.

But you can survive this. I fall back on the mantra that has gotten me through every day for sixteen years. *You can survive, Ellen. Focus, Ellen. Breathe, Ellen.*

Ten hours—that's how long I endured last time. My resolve had nearly splintered by the end. I'd almost given in. Almost.

But even psychological wounds eventually heal and leave tougher scar tissue behind. I can last another ten hours with Robert. My brain makes that distinction as the barrage of scents dissipates, revealing one that overpowers the rest: a man's. I taste the nuances in his stench rather than smell them—he's *that* potent, composed of a multitude of different things.

Cigar smoke.

Vodka.

One scent in particular makes my heart stop. Salty and sweet, it's almost as familiar as the flowery perfume wafting from my skin now. *Blood?*

Robert never smokes. He doesn't drink. Whenever he hurts me, he always washes his hands before and after. It is our routine, and he is nothing if not predictable.

No. This is someone new. Someone taller, whose shadow completely blots out what little detail plays across my blindfold. His footsteps are steady. Heavy.

"This her?"

I sense the outline of his fingers before the callused edge of one grazes my forehead.

"You made sure?"

His voice is deep. Almost *too* deep to be intelligible: a series of grated, rumbling notes. There's an accent tucked among them—something thick. Eastern European? Briar had a maid from there once. Sonja.

Sonja liked to read Jane Eyre. She liked scribbling love notes to Robert Sr.'s men before fucking them in the broom closet late at night when she thought no one was looking. Sonja liked a lot of things before Robert took a liking to her.

But another figure from my memory possessed this accent as well. Even though his words were hissed in a whisper, I still remember. *Breathe!*

"Bring her."

Those two words snap me back to the present. Unfamiliar hands grab my shoulders, cinching the soft silk of my blouse. *Briar's* blouse. She dressed me in it lovingly, remarking on how the color complemented my eyes. Our eyes, the same shade of light blue.

"Move!"

A tug on my shoulders hauls me upright and unseen hands shove me forward. Every sound echoes. Four footsteps, including mine. The biggest man takes the lead, I suspect, his gait rhythmic against creaking floorboards.

In contrast, the men holding me dig their nails into my skin and scurry toward an unknown destination. A rusty squeal seconds later conjures the image of an old door opening, and the footsteps trail off.

"Move!"

Something rams into my side and I stagger for balance until my cheek strikes a hard surface. It's warm. *Human.*

"Get her on the bed."

Those harsh hands return to my shoulders to fulfill the command.

"Sit her on the edge…like that. Cut her hands free."

A metallic hiss sends a shiver down my spine—then *pain!* Fire courses through my fingertips as circulation returns to them. I long to flex each one, but I know better. Instead, I keep them close, settling them onto my lap.

These men kept my skirt on, at least. Her skirt. The hem comes down past my knees, and I've never been so grateful for four inches of satin. It will buy me more time.

Ten hours. I've already lasted ten minutes. *You can do this,* the courageous part of my soul whispers. But then that voice dies in the wake of two more words uttered in that guttural cadence.

"Leave us."

The two smaller men scatter in the direction we entered— but it's all wrong. No. No. I don't smell Robert, and he'd never leave me alone with another man. Not his lackey. Not even his own father.

Most alarming of all, this man certainly is no Winthorp. His voice isn't familiar and this house doesn't smell like any property on the familial grounds.

They took me from the motorcade...

Fire sears through my skull as memories return in snatches. The clearest one is of her face. *Briar.* So beautiful, dominated by that pure, sweet smile. "I want you there," she insisted. "We're sisters, after all."

Sisters. I cherished how that word sounded in her soft cadence, tucking that moment inside myself like one of the trinkets hidden in my secret cache. Love was more precious than a button or rock I'd stolen away. Those four words meant everything. *I want you there.*

But the memory of that moment serves as a weak antidote to the terror paralyzing me now. More bits and pieces come back.

I was in the car—the beautiful limousine for once, instead of one of the servant vans that took up the rear. For part of the way, I was even sitting beside her while she braided my hair. "We look alike now," she wistfully remarked, beaming at our reflections in the polished windows.

We look alike. The phrase haunts me. As if I could ever look like Briar, with her lighter ringlets and her creamy skin. The only feature we truly share is our eyes. Our mother's eyes. Large, round, and blue. In every other respect, she takes after her father, with a beautiful aristocratic nose and a graceful neck. Every Winthorp possesses the same subtle characteristics—markings of the blood, they like to claim. Good blood. Blue blood.

I take after my father, whoever he is.

Briar loves to tout our tentative resemblance anyway— especially to her benefit. *I* am the one the maid saw sneaking out back two summers ago. *I* am the one who scurried out of the room of that visiting businessman one winter.

And now…

We look alike.

"Take off the blindfold." That voice…

I swallow hard, uneasy. Robert has found a new monster to play with. Someone who shares his flair for the dramatic. *But where is he?* My tormentor always relishes this part of the game. How he enjoys savoring my fear as I try to piece together where I am. Admittedly, it wasn't this hard before; he never strays too far from the property.

His favorite lairs are the boathouse, or the deserted crypt, or the east wing. I could always hear the bluebirds chirping throughout the grounds, no matter which corner of the estate he deemed my chosen cell.

My ears strain, searching for that faint, familiar song. This time of year, they're nearly deafening, able to be heard in even the farthest reaches of Winthorp Manor.

Two seconds. Three.

I hear nothing.

"Take off the blindfold."

The harsh rasp of syllables steals my breath away. I know anger on Robert. On Robert Sr. Even on Briar. They stutter. They shout. They scream.

None of them ever exude their impatience to the point where I can sense it in the air. Or taste it: copper on my tongue. This man isn't a Winthorp.

The realization coaxes my body into action. My sore fingers finally contort, trembling after what must have been hours of captivity. Whoever tied my blindfold snagged bits of my hair in the process and every tug on the knot at the base of my neck rips tiny strands loose from my scalp—comparable to my pathetic hopes being ripped from underneath me one by one.

I don't hear the bluebirds.

I can't smell Robert's favorite cologne.

When I finally get the knot loosened enough to uncover my eyes…

I see hell.

Mother used to say it was beautiful, forsaking the teachings of the local priest. "Hell is a rose," she used to murmur, her gaze turned inward, wistful and distant. "A flawless one, with all the life sucked out of it. The thorns have become knives. Its leaves have swallowed up the stalk. It's grotesque. It's deadly. But never forget that, underneath the violence, it's still beautiful."

He is beautiful. Or he was once. Blond hair draws my attention first—a sun-kissed gold in places, darkened with age in others. It's been clawed back from his face into a ponytail longer than mine was before Briar trimmed it. His eyes are that dangerous color between blood and brown. Like a flame, they catch the light filtering in through a sloppily boarded-up window beside him. His face is angular. Chiseled. Stone. Every feature is sculpted to convey just one emotion: determination. The way an owl might watch the mice scurrying underfoot in the stables. Or the way Robert used to look at me.

The way the devil looks, I presume, as if he has all the time in the world. More than ten hours.

An eternity to torture me.

CHAPTER 2

"Say your name." As the stranger issues the command, he lowers his eyes to fully take me in, and the coldness in them unsettles my every nerve. "Your name."

It should be a simple question with an even simpler answer. I'm Ellen. Just Ellen. I work as a maid in the Winthorp household—on paper. But papers can be forged, identities erased. Or mistaken.

I can't get Briar's last words to me out of my head: *We look alike.*

Wherever I am, I don't think she's here with me. This room must have been a bedroom once. Behind the man stands a rickety dresser, lopsided with age and disuse. Hanging on the wall above it is a mirror caked with dust. Only the hint of my reflection is visible, but the woman staring back at me is a stranger. Her brown hair is neatly coifed, half coiled into a braid and the rest cascading down her shoulders. Her blouse is silk, and—though it isn't visible from this angle— her burgundy skirt is satin. Her shoes are worth more than a Winthorp servant earns in a year. Her lips are a soft shade of pink.

"We look alike," Briar told me shortly before leaving the limo and taking another car to the airport. "I need to make a detour," she said. "We'll meet up later. I'm going to make sure you have the best time in London! You'll see."

Only London has never felt farther away. My chest has never felt so tight. This room is airless—I'm suffocating. For all her indifference to me, Briar has never played along in one of Robert's games before.

"I won't ask you again, Little One." The man strokes fingers caked with mud across my cheek, and I flinch. There's no gentleness in his touch. No malice, either. "Say your name."

"My name is…" My voice fails me as my gaze returns to the mirror and I finally identify the woman staring back at me. "My name is Briar Winthorp."

The man doesn't laugh at the admission. He doesn't squint as if to make out the pauper hiding behind these fancy clothes. He nods once, his eyes narrowing. "Your father has enemies, Little One."

I inhale sharply as more memories trickle back.

I was in the motorcade…

"I have to run an errand," Briar said. She left, only the procession continued as if she were still there beside me. The security remained, as did the four-man bodyguard detail lurking on either side of the main procession.

We look alike.

"Look at me," the stranger snaps, demanding my attention once more. He's closer now, but I still have to strain to take him in fully. He's tall, taller than Robert. Gray fatigues and a dark jacket shroud most of his frame. Muscle shapes him down to his massive hands. He cracks the knuckles on each finger one by one, aware of me watching. He's no businessman from the Winthorp industries. No, he's something else, a title that takes my brain nearly a minute to define. *Soldier. Mercenary. Murderer.*

"Your fiancé as well," he continues. "He has enemies. Can you tell me why that may be?"

Fiancé? He must mean Daniel. *Briar's* fiancé, a man who, to his own merit, has amassed a power almost comparable to Robert Winthorp Sr.'s.

"Answer me, Little One." The stranger strokes my hair this time, snagging loose strands as he does.

Robert used to touch me the same way—back when he still relished the thrill of hunting me down like cattle. Lately, he's been lazier in his endeavors, cornering me without even half the cunning he once employed. But that brief respite has made me weak against this method.

It's remarkable how much can be conveyed through someone's fingertips. Robert's are soft and maliciously manicured, and they bruised when he struck me too hard. *This* man's skin is callused and rough. From work. From brutality. From abuse. Scars mark him down to the base of his wrists, like the kind Briar disguises with long sleeves and silk blouses.

"I will warn you now." The stroking touch becomes a manacle of fingers latching onto my skull and forcing my chin upright. "Speak. Obey."

"He...he's a businessman, Daniel is," I stammer as his thumb grazes my lower lip, capturing each word.

"A businessman?" The stranger laughs. "That is one way to put it, Little One."

One way to put it. Criminal is another—a word only the most brazen of journalists dare to use in their headlines.

"What...what are you going to do to me?" I croak.

"Do to you?" His gaze roves downward, settling over the high neckline of Briar's blouse. Once again, he resembles Robert.

I know that look. *You can survive ten hours,* a part of me whispers. But it's cold comfort—this time, I'm lying.

"I am going to punish you, Little One," the man tells me, his tone a grating hiss. "Your father. Your lover. They took something from me."

Without warning, I'm shoved backward, my fall broken by the rickety mattress.

"I will take something from them."

The soles of his boots strike the floor in tandem. Closer. Closer. I can't make his expression out from this angle—just a circle of blackness where his face should be. His body doesn't disguise his intentions, however. His hands move to his belt. Leather kisses leather with a telltale hiss, followed by the hum of a zipper being undone.

Zzrrrippp…

I've heard that sound a million times before, yet it never ceases to steal my breath away.

"You will suffer," the man tells me, deftly undoing the front of his slacks, revealing a sliver of gray boxers underneath. "Unless…" He pauses, hovering on the edge of a question. Something vital. My answer will determine the next phase of this nightmare. "Unless you tell me what I need to know."

I nod. It's instinctive: a desperate jerking of my chin even though I know that salvation is a lie. I'm stalling, and he's merely prolonging this part of the game. Robert's decided to use a stand-in tonight—that has to be it. Cuckholding me wouldn't be the worst thing he's ever done.

I can survive. I can…

"Answer me, Little One. Believe me when I say that I do not want to hurt you." The stranger's voice deepens on the edge of a dangerous note. It's soft, almost like a whisper. Like a plea: *Don't fuck with me.* "Where is your father running to?"

My father? Oh. I blink, fighting to remember. Briar's father. Where is he running?

"I-I…"

Wait. Robert wouldn't write this script. There's no begging. No salacious words he likes to force me to say. No stripping me bare to give me a "taste" of what being his favorite saves me from.

And never, ever did he mention Robert Sr.

I read once that fear of a name only increases fear of the thing itself. In that case, the mere mention of his father must terrify Robert. He even avoids being called his full name. *Bobby*, he prefers his minions to whimper.

"I-I…"

"You do not have long to answer." The stranger cocks his head as if catching wind of a far-off noise. A slow smile shapes his mouth, chilling me to my very core. The hands at his waistband shift, and every deliberate movement makes my chest feel tighter, my heart beat faster.

"I don't know," I insist. "I…I don't know what you mean—"

Too late. The rotting floorboards broadcast his advance. My throat is too dry—I can't speak. I can't scream. I can only watch his hand descend before it snatches at the hem of

Briar's skirt. The garment was made especially for her from a designer in France—and he tears it right down the middle.

Weak, I flex my fingers at my sides. Not to cover myself, but to brace. Towering above me on a mass of sculpted muscle, this man will crush me. Experience warns me to arch my back as much as I dare, giving my lungs enough leverage to fill before he does.

Instead… The brunt of his palm grazes my upper thigh and my thoughts dissipate. Ice shoots through my veins, rendering me frozen. It's not his touch that alarms me. It's his expression. There's no lust. No fire. No thrill at the game.

Just anger smoldering in the thumb he draws across my right knee.

To tease?

No. To *feel*: the ropey length of a scar. One of the many Robert left behind.

My neck aches as I crane it in order to watch in horror as his touch continues to roam. He rakes his hands over them all. The cuts. The bruises. Some healed. Some not. He takes one of his fingers, long and callused, and traces a fresher cut along my hip. My belly roils at the slow, deliberate appraisal, and I can't swallow a gasp. Robert gropes me. He…studies me?

When I look up at his face, I'm forced to reckon with the realization laid bare over the harsh features. Within an instant, the hard veneer of a soldier is stripped away, revealing something much more terrifying: disgust. Then rage.

Tilting his head back, he seeks my gaze out and devours me whole. "Who the hell are you?"

*R*un! It's a new impulse, something I've never felt around Robert. He'd never let me escape, but this man…

He waits until I've rolled onto my side, flailing for the edge of the mattress, before he lunges, seizing a handful of my hair. One hard yank rips me from the bed, forcing me to my knees. I land hard, tasting blood but too stunned to scream.

"Who?"

The grated question rings out unanswered. With a hiss of irritation, he finds the truth himself by bunching the sleeves of my blouse and pulling. His first attempt knocks me forward and only my palms save my face from a nasty meeting with the floor. His second yank strips me bare. I'm not wearing a bra and instinct drives me to hunch over, which displays my back to the creature pacing behind me.

My face may have fooled him, but my body does not. Years

of abuse betray me. Hissing his rage, the soldier is forced to admit the ruse.

"Fuck. Vanya!" The door opens seconds later and two men race inside, stopping just short of where I'm kneeling.

"Look," their leader commands, his tone casual. As if this really were a game. Hide-and-seek, maybe? Only he's lost the round. "Does she look like an heiress to you?"

Air lashes my back as he moves. Seconds later, his fingers are in my hair and he tugs my head back, forcing my gaze to the ceiling. My eyelids flutter, shrouding the shape of him hovering on the outskirts of my vision.

"Her face is convincing," he declares begrudgingly. "But this bitch is no Winthorp. I know the mark of Robert's whores when I see them. She was a decoy."

He shoves me aside and I wind up facedown, tasting dust. *This bitch is no Winthorp.* Some small part of me snickers at that. It's like knowing a secret no one gives a damn about. A tiny, little detail that makes his statement a lie.

Not that it matters.

"Get out." He's not talking to me. No… This man and I are not through with our game.

His boot strikes my hip, knocking me onto my side. Blurred vision gives me a few seconds of reprieve. And even though I can't see his face, my imagination has no trouble conjuring an expression to match his coarse tone.

Eyes like fire and a fearsome scowl.

"I would have shown mercy to Briar," he admits while his shadow looms above, lacking all definition. "She did not ask for this. But you…"

He stoops to clutch my shoulders and drag me up to his level. I taste vodka on his breath, which perfumes the air as his features come back into focus.

"*You*. How much money did he offer you, hmm? What was your soul worth?"

My soul? Sluggishly, my brain pieces together what he means. Bought. He thinks Robert Sr. bought me to be his daughter's double. He thinks the man would be that kind. That generous.

The truth is much crueler. You don't buy a sacrifice.

"Whatever it was," the man continues, "I hope every penny was worth the pain you will suffer in her place." His nails graze my skull as he lets me go and stands. "Tell me what you know and I'll consider making your death quick."

"N-nothing." The truth spills out of me in a broken whisper. Nothing. I know nothing.

"We look alike," Briar told me. That was all. "Like sisters…"

I'm so lost in the memory that I don't register him moving until it's too late. Brutal fingers circle my throat and clench. Like a rag doll, I'm wrenched to my feet. Shoved back. I fall. Hit something soft…

And then unmovable steel pins me down. He's more than heavy. He's a battering ram, crushing me to the mattress.

What little air I suck into my lungs has no escape and forms a plug at the base of my throat.

He squeezes until stars appear, dancing through the air and obscuring his face. His *face*. For some reason, I force my burning eyes to refocus, seeking out as much detail of it as I can. I always thought Robert would be the one to kill me. Not a stranger, his gaze like midnight.

I'm dying. I feel it—my limbs jerk, controlled by instinct. Blood surges to my head. My pulse hammers against my eardrums. Right as my vision begins to fade, the pressure loosens a fraction. Just enough for me to suck in air again.

"I've been patient, Little One," he murmurs as I sputter. "Perhaps you need more incentive?"

My breast. He cups it, capturing the flesh against his palm, grazing my nipple. There's no ownership, like how Robert likes to caress me. Just rough, slow possession. I feel his nails, pinching and sharp.

"I will give you one more chance to tell me what you know," he says. "All of it."

He has no idea how dangerous a question he's proposed. What I know? Nothing. If anything, he's supplying more answers than I could ever deduce on my own. What was the word he used? A decoy.

We look alike.

"Robert knew I was coming for him," the man growls, flexing his grip until I gasp. "You will tell me how."

Nothing. I can't speak as terror crashes through my entire being. Even Robert couldn't reduce me to this state so quickly. My eyes prickle in warning before heat spills from them.

"I. Don't. Know."

He frowns at the pathetic syllables I manage to muster. With a shift of his weight, he mounts me fully, wedging his bulk in the narrow gap between my thighs. My feeble attempts to resist him are defeated by his knee. He uses it as a battering ram to gain enough leverage to draw his pelvis in close.

No man but Robert has *ever* been this close—and this newer creature is bigger. Crueler. Rougher.

"How?" The man recaptures my throat, caressing my windpipe. "How did he know, hmm? We were careful. Does he have a spy? An informant?"

My answering wheeze draws a chilling response: he sighs.

"Please do not test me, Little One." His touch leaves my breast and slides between my legs.

"N-no!" My hands hammer against unyielding muscle even though it's in vain.

I learned a long time ago that it's futile to resist. Admittedly, I've gotten better at it. Robert used to savor this reaction in me. He would ease a finger inside to prepare me for fucking.

This man…

He shoves me down, rearing back on his braced knee. "How many of my men do you think you can handle, Little One? Should I go first?"

The threat is real. His eyes reveal nothing but endless darkness. He'd do it.

I feel the evidence for myself, hard against my hip.

"How did he know?" He trails his fingers from my throat to my chin, cupping it so that I'm forced to meet his gaze directly. In it, I find only darkness. "Tell me and I won't touch you. I swear on your life."

But I have no answer to give him. No way to save myself.

"Your choice." The man's nostrils flare. Then, without warning, he climbs off the bed and redoes the zipper of his pants.

I can't help the frantic way my chest heaves, desperately seeking air. The places where he touched me burn as if scorched. I don't know if it's a trick of the light or if the dark strands of hair wrapped around his fingers really are mine, torn from my scalp. Still, I don't move. I lie there, at his mercy.

I seal my fate.

"I hope you are just foolish," the man laments, sounding almost genuine. "Because bravery won't serve you here."

He turns his back to me, adjusting his clothing with sharp, curt tugs on the fabric. Only from this angle do I catch the scars that riddle the base of his throat. Long, jagged, barely concealed by the fall of his hair.

As if sensing my reaction, he faces me again, giving my body a chilling appraisal. "I'm sure you've heard the rumors. What happens to those who cross me." He waits as if for me to confess.

But I wasn't lying. I know nothing, especially not of him.

"Fine. Perhaps not a fool, but reckless?" he wonders, shrugging. "If you won't talk, then you will serve another purpose."

He returns to my end of the bed and snatches my wrist. Pain sears through my arm as he drags me after him. I stagger, flailing for balance while the room blurs around me. He takes me into the hall and down a short flight of stairs. When we reach the bottom, I rush to piece together our newer surroundings. The smells register first.

Men. A lot of them. Their overwhelming stench chokes me, and I remember his threat. His promise. *How many do you think you can handle?*

It's darker here. The only light sneaks in through boarded-up windows. In the resulting shadow, I make out featureless faces. Shapes. At least ten figures are crowding this room, maybe twenty. All are suspiciously silent apart from a few laughs as I stagger in their leader's wake. There's an animal here as well. It growls as we come too close. A dog?

A large one, I realize, as I spot it crouched in a metal cage in a back corner. Without a word, the leader hauls me to it and undoes the latch with his free hand.

"Get!" he commands the beast, who skulks off, brushing my knee on its way past.

Before the animal has fully left the cage, I'm shoved in its place, forced onto my hands and knees to fit inside the enclosure. Metal clangs as the door is slammed and the latch engaged.

"Enjoy your new pet," the man announces before leaving the room. "But no one touch her. *Yet.*"

I've been a bone before: an object placed on display to be watched. Guarded. Coveted.

These men don't whistle and howl like Robert's. Even the dog does nothing more than sniff me. In the darkness, I sense a few searing gazes directed my way, but they're silent for the most part, focused on whatever task is occupying them.

We must be in a house of some kind. An old one. This narrow room with its faded wallpaper and sloped floors might have been a drawing room at one point, envisioned to entertain visitors or gatherings.

Now? Its purpose appears more nefarious. There are boxes dispersed in between the men. What they contain, I can't tell, but scents irritate my nostrils beneath the overwhelming stench of sweat. Chemical in nature. Gunpowder?

But when one of the men nearest my cage stands, hefting an object beside him, I realize they're all armed—with more than the small pistols Robert and his men carry. Long guns. Big guns. They prop them along the walls, always within reach.

This space must be a storeroom of some kind, containing materials that need fifteen pairs of watchful eyes to guard them at all times. Five men are sitting at a card table in the center of the room, conversing in snippets of a language I can't make out. Five more have taken various positions against the walls, while the rest are scattered in between, focused on packing something into the boxes. Something small. Round?

"Uh-huh!"

An object slams against the top of my cage. A hand? It belongs to a man who appears grotesque in the darkness. His eyes are the only feature I can clearly make out. They're narrowed, focused on my face.

"No peeking," he barks in accented English. "You want to keep that face pretty? Look at the wall."

I obey. The wallpaper in this corner is peeling in places, revealing dried, decaying wood underneath. As strange as it feels to admit, it's a slightly better view than what I'm used to. Ironic, considering that Robert's room is grand, as is the one he makes me sleep in. The walls are painted white. The floors are polished hardwood. Everything down to the bedsheets is of the finest quality. And every second I spent trapped within those four walls, I feared I might go blind.

I wished I would.

Darkness obscures the horror of my current surroundings. At the same time, it compounds it. There's nothing to distract me from my own thoughts and what they imply. Briar, beautiful Briar. Did she know all along what trap she was leading me into?

My eyes sting, and blinking doesn't keep the tears at bay. They spill, hot and burning down my cheeks. For the first time in ages, my initial impulse isn't to wipe them away. I let them fall and relish the bitter fear that leaves me trembling.

Fear. It's funny how such a terrible, awful emotion can be welcome. I once thought Robert had driven all emotion out of me—but he hasn't. I don't want to die here.

"Relax."

My cage is slapped again from above, this time decidedly more softly. The blow draws me farther back against the bars with my knees pulled up to shield as much of myself as I can.

"You don't have to fear rape," the man hisses. There's a roughness in his voice but no mocking. He's not lying. "Mischa can be cruel, but he never lets his men go that far."

The man jerks his chin toward the rest of the room as if to say, *See? Look.*

I sneak a glimpse from the corner of my eye, surprised by what I find. Minutes after my arrival and I still haven't drawn any more attention than a few guarded looks. Not out of respect, I suspect. More like...*disinterest?* Almost as if so many women have been locked within this cage that the novelty has worn off.

"You don't have that to fear from him. He is insane," the man beside the cage admits, "but not a monster. He will hurt you, though, if you do not give him what he wants. Do *not* make him angry." He stresses every word and taps the bars for emphasis. "He won't fuck you, but he'll still hit you."

My arm stings in memory. Oddly enough, I can't decide what I fear more: sexual violence or brutality? I've never had a choice between the two before.

"You want to ask something," the man prompts, hissing out the words. "Ask it now. Get it over with. You already know the answer."

"Will...will he kill me?" My voice trickles weakly in the shadow of his.

He's right though. I already know the answer, even before he nods.

"Yes. He will kill you. But, if you obey and keep quiet, he will make it quick. Try to make a scene or challenge him and..." He drags his thumb across his throat. Slowly.

My eyes drift shut as I fight to suck in air. *Keep breathing.* It's the one mantra that can save me when all else fails. *Keep breathing.*

But my ragged breaths are too loud, drowning out the muted noise coming from the rest of the room—and this is the one time when I need to focus. Gathering any and every clue I can is the only hope I have to... *What?* Perhaps just learn the motives of the man who will kill me.

"Y-your name?" I tilt my head back and strain my eyes through the dark, fighting to make out as much of my companion as I can.

He's old. Maybe fifty. The gray speckling his cropped hair catches what few flecks of light enter the room. I can't tell how well questioning him will go over. But I have nothing left to lose.

"What is your name?"

"Ivan." He scoffs. "They call me Vanya. However, it will be better for you not to—"

"M-Mischa?" *That* name tastes strange on my tongue. Two clashing syllables, one soft, the other violent and harsh. "Is that *his* name?"

Vanya scoffs again, shaking his head. The motion alone reveals that he didn't mean to let that detail slip. "I suggest you not use that one, either—" He breaks off suddenly, cocking his head. Then he curses and kicks the side of my cage. "Hush. Keep quiet and look at the wall."

He's gone a heartbeat later, marching toward the center of the room while two sets of footsteps approach from an outside hall. The heaviest pair belongs to *him*. Mischa. I know that even before I hear his voice, lashing like a whip that commands total silence in its wake.

"Out."

The room itself trembles as fifteen men lurch into action like a well-oiled machine. Not all of them leave, however. One set of footsteps lingers behind the rest—they're unsteady, betraying a slight limp on one side. From age or injury? I can't tell.

Apart from him and Mischa, there is one other man. He comes closer to my cage than his leader, his footsteps light and lazy. "Is this the decoy?" he wonders as the back of my neck prickles beneath his unfamiliar gaze. He too has an accent I can't place. "You must be slipping, Mischa. I didn't think even Winthorp could ever fool you—"

"You have a job to do," Mischa warns. "Do it."

"In front of her?" the other man asks.

"She won't live long enough to report anything of use to anyone." There's no malice in the threat. Mischa could be commenting on the weather for all the emotion his voice holds. Death must be that simple to him. That easy. "You have an hour. Vanya will watch you. I shouldn't have to remind you, Xavier, that if you short me, I will kill you."

"I wouldn't dream of deceiving you, *Pakhan*," Xavier simpers, but even I recognize the careful way he melds the taunt with a hint of respect. He knows which lines not to cross.

Apparently, the display satisfies Mischa enough to leave without reinforcing his brutality. In his wake, the air thins. I've been holding my breath all this time.

"Make it quick," Vanya says, apparently taking up the commanding role in his leader's absence.

Despite his warning, I can't resist the temptation to look. A furtive glance over my shoulder reveals that the two men are standing before the card table in the center of the room.

A light has been switched on. The weak glow casts enough illumination to make out the two men's features. One is gnarled, with graying black hair and a scar along his jaw. Vanya. The other is younger. A pair of glasses rests upon his Roman nose, and he's wearing a suit that does its best to convey wealth, but the fit is poor. It's not tailored. *Stolen*, a part of me suspects.

That man places a briefcase upon the table which he opens. Even from this angle, I recognize the stacks of paper contained within. Money. A lot of money.

A memory unfurls from the furthest reach of my consciousness, too quickly to fight. *Cologne. Silk. Copper.* That night Robert came to me, his face bloodied, a stack of bills clutched in his fist.

"Shall we play a game?" he asked, knowing full well that I couldn't refuse. "Tell me." He threw the bloodied cash in my face while I remained seated on the bed. "What is real and what is not?"

I learned a lesson then that remains with me to this day: Nothing is more important to a man than his money. Not women. Not drugs. Not family. Not even his soul.

This Mischa must hoard it at the expense of everything else. By selling something?

As Xavier removes stack after stack of dollars—American from what I can tell—Vanya approaches a cluster of cardboard boxes in one corner of the room. After assessing the cash, he hefts two boxes and brings them closer to the table.

"They're packed," he explains as he sets the second box down. "Ready to ship. You can sell them at the going rate with a little bit of interest for the inconvenience of having to accommodate you directly."

Irritation flits across Xavier's face almost too quickly to catch. "Fine," he says, still removing stack after stack from his briefcase.

As the growing pile continues to climb, I can't help but stare. It's more money than I've ever seen in one place. Even Robert never carries so much on him at one time. The obscene display betrays a more nefarious purpose, however. What on Earth could one box contain to be worth so much?

I shy away from the answer and face the wall. After a few more minutes, Xavier and Vanya seem to conclude their business. The former leaves, his briefcase in tow. I hear it swishing through the air at his side as he turns down that narrow outside hall. When he's gone, Vanya just sighs. There's a leathery hiss like that of paper being sorted, counted, and stored, though I never saw a safe.

Just when I gather up the nerve to peek again, he calls to me. "You'd do best to forget what you saw. If you want to extend your life for however long you can, anyway."

I don't dare turn away again. Instead, I study the wallpaper. The base is dark gray with leaves in a lighter print forming a simple design that crawls out in every which direction. Far, far away to the farthest reaches of the room.

"I have to go," Vanya says after a second's silence. Something unspoken hides within his weary tone. A warning: *Keep to yourself. Stare at the wall.* "When I return…if…I'll bring you something to eat."

But why? My welfare has to be at the bottom of his leader's list. For whatever reason, he made this offer solely out of kindness. Or perhaps pity. One word he used rings ominously. *If.*

If you are still alive.

"Th-thank you," I force myself to whisper regardless.

Without bothering to respond, the man leaves, switching the light off and drenching me in shadow.

I'm alone for barely five minutes before the other men return. With quiet efficiency, they take up their vacated positions, and I'm ignored once again. Heeding Vanya's warning, I don't move from my kneeling position. I stare at the wall and count the seconds. It's a familiar habit, though my surroundings differ from my room in Robert's suite. The basic gist of the game never changes.

Wait for the monster's return. How long will this one take?

Two hours? Four? By the sixth, biological concerns take precedence over psychological ones. My bladder aches, painfully full. Noises rumble from my stomach, clashing with the occasional murmured conversation from the men. The floor of the cage is lined only in crumpled newspaper that chafes against my contorted limbs. Using it for anything but padding is an uncomfortable dilemma to contemplate.

So I stall.

Breathe, Ellen. My lungs expand to obey my old mantra, and for the first time in years, my brain replays snippets of the creature who originally inspired it. Not Robert, though he is similar in shape. A man. A boy. Someone who didn't belong, his eyes catlike in the darkness.

"You breathe," he hissed to me. "You don't think. Don't feel. Just breathe…"

A noise breaks my concentration, dragging me back to the present. Night must have fallen. I can barely see the leaves on the wallpaper anymore when Vanya finally returns. I recognize his unsteady gait even before his hand slams against the top of my cage.

"If I let you out, you obey me. No questions. No complaints. Understand? Try to run and Mischa will be your least concern."

I nod. At the mere hint of freedom, my muscles throb in torment, and I unfurl my sore limbs the moment I hear the latch disengage.

"Slow," Vanya barks as I twist in the narrow space and pull myself through the cage's opening. "Slow…wait—"

I freeze, crouched at his feet while my eyes struggle to adjust to the shadow.

"Here. Put this on."

Something soft brushes my cheek. I reach up, trying to decipher the garment through touch alone. It's thin. Satin?

It sports sleeves like a shirt but opens in the center and seems long enough to cover me at least to my knees.

"It's the only thing I could find," Vanya adds almost apologetically. "Hurry up. Then follow me and keep your head down."

He shifts his weight, blocking me from sight—either on purpose or accidentally—as I scramble into what I quickly realize is a robe. After tying the thin sash around my waist, I rise to my feet, forced to cling to the wall for balance. Movement is painful, but I grit my teeth and face Vanya without swaying. He towers above me, almost as tall as his leader. After casting me an appraising glance, he heads for a doorway, leaving me to follow.

Mischa may be the leader here, but I suspect that Vanya isn't too far behind him in their hierarchy. There's respect conveyed in the fact that no one questions him as he leads me from the room and down a narrow hallway.

A bulb hanging from the ceiling illuminates a row of closed doors and more peeling wallpaper. Eventually, Vanya stops beside one door and opens it. "Use it," he says, jerking his chin toward the opening.

A bathroom lurks beyond, small and cramped, but containing a toilet at least and a rusted sink. I nearly collapse with relief, but when I attempt to close the door, Vanya shakes his head.

"Not all the way. I won't look," he adds when I stiffen. "Go on."

My body is in too much distress to give a damn if he does watch. Crouching as low over the toilet as I dare, I relieve myself. As my bladder empties, I have no choice but to face the woman watching me from the dust-covered mirror above the sink. She's pale, her hair hanging wild around her shoulders. A sheer black robe doesn't shield much of her body. Not its nakedness. Not its scars.

"If you're done, hurry up," Vanya warns.

Obediently, I wipe and flush the rickety toilet only to realize that the plumbing must have given out years ago. My waste just sits there, mingling with others I didn't notice in my haste. Vomit surges up my throat, but I manage to choke it down and stagger to the sink to wash my hands. There's soap at least. With my wet fingers, I slick the worst of my tangled curls back before tapping on the door to convey that I'm finished.

When I creep into the hallway, Vanya casts me a single glance before heading farther down the hall. We reach another doorway that opens onto a room that might have been a kitchen once. Now, there's too much clutter to tell. Boxes crowd the few countertops. The stove has been gutted, which leaves an empty space now filled with bags of garbage. The only item in working condition appears to be a stained refrigerator with duct tape on the sides to seal it. Vanya has to try twice to heave it open only to reveal that it contains just a pitcher of water and a loaf of bread.

"Here." He breaks off a slice and hands it to me. After rummaging through the chaos scattered over the counter, he surfaces with a glass and fills it with water.

I accept both, genuinely grateful. "Thank you—"

"Don't thank me," he snaps, jerking his chin toward the food in my hands. "Hurry up and eat."

I devour the bread in three bites and down the water just as quickly. Now that the shock of my predicament has set in, horror and familiarity slowly replace the fear. I've been a prisoner before. I know the role to play. I also know that most captors don't offer their prey a shred of dignity—as much as can be found in a robe and some privacy to use the restroom—or let them from their cell for a walk. Not without a reason.

Why? Guilt? I try to suss out his motives as I gingerly rub my hands together to scrape the crumbs from them. The old man is good at containing his secrets, however. I discern nothing from his stern expression. Just the cold knowledge that, as much as I'm trying to understand him, he's already unraveled me.

"What's your name?" he demands, catching my probing stare.

My heart races at the question. Common sense warns me to lie. But…kindness is such a rare gift, deserving of the same in return. Even Robert hasn't broken me beyond that point.

"My name is—"

"Here you are."

My body reacts to the dangerously soft voice before I turn and see him there, towering in the doorway. Mischa.

Slowly, his eyes flicker from me to Vanya, but the old man doesn't draw half of the rage building in his gaze. "I told you to bring her to *me*," he says. Strained politeness keeps his voice above that unsettling growl.

My brain scrambles to place it. Respect?

"You did," Vanya says, nodding in deference, but there's nothing at all submissive about his posture. He snatches the cup from my grip and refills it with water from the still open fridge. When he places it in my grasp, Mischa's irises darken, honing in on my throat and the black robe drawn tight around me.

"Bring her," he snarls, no longer sounding as composed as he did before. "Now."

"When she finishes," Vanya says calmly. To me, he crooks his fingers in the universal symbol for hurry up.

"Vanya—"

"She'll be better able to withstand your methods on a full stomach, don't you think?" It's not so much a suggestion as it is an insinuation of something.

Whatever it is makes the younger man flinch. "Are you challenging me, Ivan?"

My throat contracts at the lethality of those words. How he says them. *Challenge.* As if it's the ultimate crime.

"No." Beside me, Vanya stiffens, lowering his head. "Of course not, *Pakhan.*"

"Good." Two steps bring Mischa closer. Heavy, wide steps that rattle the peeling tiled floor. "Then she can *finish*."

It's a dare. One that haunts me as my gaze reconnects with Vanya's. He motions for me to drink and I robotically gulp from the glass. The moment I've drained it, Mischa advances. From the corner of my eye, I see him reach for me, but the ferocity of his grip catches me off guard. I stagger into the counter, knocking an unseen array of objects to the floor. The glass slips from my grasp. Shatters. Something pierces the sole of my right foot in a barrage of searing pain, but I'm dragged forward without mercy. Back down the hallway. Through the room with the cage. Beyond that. Stairs. Hallway. Silence. Room.

Shoved forward, I struggle to make out my surroundings. A bed is paces away, near a rickety dresser positioned by the window. Above, a naked light bulb casts pale light and flickering shadows. Behind me, the door closes.

And my tormentor advances as though he has all the time in the world to play this next phase of the game. Without warning, he runs his hand along my shoulder. His touch burns beneath the thin fabric of the robe and I jump back, preparing to withstand any assault. Anything but the callous swipe that dislodges the garment from behind.

"Have you thought about my offer?" he wonders as I stiffen.

I have: the "truth" in exchange for a quick death. How utterly used to violence he must be to think that those are tempting odds. And, to him, they *are*. There's no mistaking that.

He will kill you quickly, Vanya insisted as if that was somehow the preferable outcome to this nightmare.

Maybe it is.

Rather than speak, I say nothing. It's stifling in this room. The window is nailed shut, preventing any circulation. Sweat springs beneath my armpits and along my neck. He's perspiring as well. The stench of salt seeps from his pores, but it's not potent enough to reek.

I'm too busy trying to place his position that I miss the next move he makes. A shove to my hip nudges me closer to the bed. The mattress brushes my knees. The sheets covering it are bunched in the middle as if slept in. More salt wafts from them, and something else… Male. Musk. Has he slept here?

"I warned you once never to ignore me," he hisses against the nape of my neck before shoving me once again.

I manage to throw my hands out at the last second, catching my fall. The position gives me enough leverage to twist onto my side so that I can face him. It's a habit I learned from Robert. Watching him is always my only defense. Only then could I guess his next move.

But this man is unreadable. When he snatches at my hip, I don't fight, letting him wrench the fabric of my robe loose. My only action is to flex my shoulders so that he can remove the garment without tearing it—out of courtesy to Vanya for sparing it. Within seconds, the black satin is in his fist before being tossed onto the floor.

Again, he eyes my body with unabashed interest—but I can't help but notice that his gaze doesn't assault the places where I'm used to being ogled. He eyes my stomach, not my breasts. My arms. Thighs. I know why. I can feel the marks throbbing after the rough treatment of the past twenty-four hours, but I don't dare focus on them.

I watch him instead. His wounds are much older than mine, scarred over and silvery with age. Battle scars. Gunshot wounds. He reminds me of the target in the fields where Robert likes to practice shooting. Dinged and marred but still unbroken.

"What's your name?" he asks, flicking the words at me one by one. Language to him is a projectile, used to inflict damage.

I cower. Everything I would have spilled easily to Vanya sticks in my throat.

Mischa lets nearly a minute go by before he entertains the fact that I might have disobeyed him. It amuses him rather than angers. His lips quirk around the edges, his eyelids lowering. With one knee, he nudges my right leg, making the space between both of them wider. A lazy shift of his weight allows him to dominate that vacant space. But he's too big. My inner thighs chafe against the coarse fabric of his pants. The air catches in my chest.

Vanya's warning becomes a mocking taunt: *He won't fuck you, but he'll still hit you.* He sounded sincere, but I know men. I learned long ago how to recognize the subtle ways their bodies tense. How their breathing changes when logic ends and lust begins.

But it's not my body that excites him.

It's the silence. The longer it extends between us, the bigger he seems, towering above. Defiance in general is unacceptable to most men like him. But from a woman?

He laughs, almost to himself: an unstable, guttural sound. "Did you not hear me, Little One?" Again, his fingers come to dance the length of my hip, but this time, they don't inspect the injuries there. They fan out, pressing firmly. *Feeling.* "He's treated you roughly. I can tell."

His hand is big enough to circle my entire thigh. Sensing the danger enclosed in his palm, I flinch, and in retaliation, the tips of his nails rake a path to my knee.

"But trust me: I can be worse. Tell me your name."

My lips flutter, but nothing comes out. Inhaling, I try again. Again. My tongue frantically moistens my lips as my chest heaves, seeking air. *My name is…*

Before I can form the words, his knee strikes the mattress near my hip, rattling the bed frame. The way he's positioned brings his thigh overtop mine, crushing me down. Heat sears, mingling with the sweat slicking my skin. It's too hot. Can't breathe…

"Tell me your name, Little One." He hasn't fully mounted me yet, remaining crouched instead. "Tell me what you know of Robert's plans and this will end for you. I swear it."

He means it—as much as a man like him can mean anything. This is his idea of mercy: a painless death. "But if you don't…"

A gasp rips from my chest as he adjusts his knee, lifting it from the bed only to reposition it directly between my legs. He slams it forward, nudging my mound.

"I will make you wish I'd *only* killed you."

My vision swims as my lips struggle to part. My name is right *there*, wavering on the tip of my tongue. I try as hard as I can to spit it out. Ellen… Ellen…

But the only sound to reach my ears is the ominous creaking of the bed frame. The hand on my thigh becomes a razor, nails sinking deep. Scouring. Using that grip for leverage, he brings his weight forward, mounting me fully, lowering his chest against mine. My nipples scrape the cotton of his shirt while his breath assaults my cheek, scorching a trail down to my throat. He's too close. Too heavy. Too…raw.

There's no disguising the muscle straining beneath his clothing. Poor Vanya doesn't know his master as well as he thinks.

He's hard. Not hard enough to be of much use—at least not yet—but hard enough to feel against my thigh, too real for comfort. My thoughts scatter. Instinct kicks in. With Robert, there is only one way to survive his assaults: lie there motionless. Never react. Let him finish quickly. Lick my wounds in peace.

My body is already complying with the first step of that routine. I go limp, conforming beneath the stranger's body. My eyes focus somewhere beyond his head. I don't think. I don't feel. I just endure…

"Look at me."

An unexpected sensation disrupts my mental clarity. *Fire.* Unfamiliar heat trickles between my legs: his hand. Each knuckle traces the outlines of my mound. Once. Twice. I tense, anticipating brutality: for him to jam them in at once. Stretch me open. Prove his point.

Anything but another slow, teasing swipe that tugs on my spine like a string. Too harsh. Too sharp. Too soft.

"Look at me, Little One." He snarls the command into my ear, bringing his mouth so close that his teeth clip my earlobe.

The pain won't let me escape. It buzzes through my nerves like a fly until I have no choice. My vision refocuses, bringing his features into stark relief.

"You think I don't know?" he wonders coldly. "You think I can't see the abuse on you? You don't fear pain." He pinches my hip as if to prove it, rousing a deep, sharp ache that makes me shiver. "But there are some things worse than pain, Little One. Betrayals that only your body can commit against you. I won't just hurt you. I can make you *enjoy* what I do to you."

It's an almost cartoonish threat, but he never laughs. There's a sudden darkness to his features that wasn't there before. A harsh, knowing look that makes a part of me clench in despair. God, it's familiar. Understanding? The same expression worn by the boy who taught me how to endure agony in silence all those years ago.

He *knows*. What I've been through—or at least what he could discern from my scars. Even worse, he seems to think he can use that trauma against me. It's as laughable a boast as it is terrifying.

Breathe, Ellen. I make myself limp again, building an invisible wall between my body and my thoughts. I succeed. I feel nothing. Hear nothing. Just silence and…

Wet. Sliding along my breast, slicking the nipple. His thumb. While I watch, he brings the digit to his tongue and licks along the edge, wetting it further. Then he lowers it to my nipple again, letting his saliva merge with sweat. Disgust traps the air in my lungs, suffocating me during the long, deliberate journey he travels down the curve of my rib cage.

"W-what are you doing?" *No!* My own mental plea can't keep the words from leaving my throat. It's already too late.

He heard me, letting his fingers still against my torso. "So you *can* speak," he murmurs. "What a shame. I was beginning to suspect that your master had the perfect woman. Beautiful *and* quiet as a fucking mouse."

Vodka still taints his breath, but he isn't drunk. The look in his eyes is too hardened. Too steady. For the first time, I see the hint of real lust lurking in his heavy-lidded gaze. Chuckling, he slides his palm down to my hip and then underneath, cupping my buttock. My skin crawls. I can't look at him. The ceiling. *Feel nothing. Breathe, Ellen—*

"No." His free hand latches onto my scalp, forcing my face toward his and those soulless eyes. "You want to end this? Give me what I want. Or I'll just take it. "

He continues to touch me—and there is no blocking him out. Rough. Hard. Nails. Fingertips. My mind reels at how he interchanges brutality with…softness? Almost like a child flickering a light switch to disorient those trapped inside a locked room.

"I underestimated you," he proclaims, frowning as if disappointed by the fact. "Your master trained you too well."

Master. Trained. I can't explain the reaction those words set off in me. Heart stopping. Chilling. Mainly, they just trigger memories. Robert. Those awful nights. The hateful things he made me feel. Enduring him. Suffering him.

He never trained me to withstand him. All I had to cling to was one pathetic word. *Breathe.*

"Don't ignore me." My captor touches me again, grazing me more firmly with ragged nails. "I've been patient enough—"

"Stop." A stranger utters that plea—not me. I rarely say that word anymore. Only when Robert's at his worst. His cruelest. When I can barely think through the pain. But all I feel now is…

More heat prickling down my spine, fading between my legs. It's more alarming than pain. Too foreign to place. My hips roll of their own accord, desperate to escape it.

Unconcerned, the stranger continues to touch me, sliding his fingers from the curve of my hip, down between my legs. Each pass is bolder. Faster.

"S-stop!" My hand forms a fist without permission from my brain. Rises from the mattress. Strikes his shoulder. "Please—"

"Your name." The callous tone doesn't match the lazy sweep of his fingers against my flesh. Once. Twice. Again.

On the next pass, he curls his fingertips, teasing my entrance. Only the ragged tip of a nail breaches the barrier of my curls—but I feel the invasion deeper than just in my skin. In my heart, jagged and unwelcome like a rusty nail being jammed into a fortress I thought impenetrable for so long.

"S-stop." It's more than a broken whisper now. "Stop. Please."

His expression is unreadable, composed of fathomless eyes that watch me tremble without a shred of pity. Of mercy. "You want to end this, Little One?" he wonders, drawing his hand away. "Give me your name and all you know of Robert Winthorp."

My name. I try to remember through the chaos flooding my brain. The stranger has to compete with phantoms from memories. *Like sisters…like sisters…*

I can't find the answer in time. My punishment comes swiftly.

He presses more firmly with his finger, grazing flesh and nerves that shudder at the brazen display. Humiliation descends. My eyes burn. Tears gather, along with the knowledge that nothing I do can keep them from falling.

I can't even scream.

"Give me your name, Little One. Say it, or I will make you scream—"

"Misha! We need to move. Now." That voice…

Hope, the fragile thing, rises in my chest as I make out the figure who appears in the doorway, his face half in shadow. Vanya.

"Mischa," he prods in a cautious tone directed at the man on top of me. "We need to go. Now."

"Is that so?" Eyes narrowed, Mischa shoves me aside and backs off the bed. Something terrible unfolds across his face, but I sense that it isn't all directed at Vanya—or even me. He stares down at his hands, flexing the fingers. Then he shakes his head and his expression is cold again. "And what could have happened so suddenly that we need to move base now?"

Vanya doesn't shy away from meeting his gaze. If anything, his chin juts slightly into the air, almost as if echoing their previous standoff but in reverse. *Are you challenging me?*

"You told me you trust my judgment. My judgment is telling me not to trust that snake Xavier with our location for too long. Besides, it's dark. The men are ready. This shithouse could crumble beneath us at any moment. I say we move now, to another safe house. Before it's too late."

"And her?" Mischa cocks his head toward me, his mouth tilted in a dangerous smirk that's more snarl than grin.

Vanya shrugs. "We bring her with us. You can continue your questioning later. It doesn't make sense to kill her now—"

"Oh?" Mischa reaches into his pocket and withdraws what I *actually* felt against my hip during his torture: a knife, thick at the base with a tapered tip. Light plays off the honed edges of the metal, stinging my eyes to the point where I have to blink. At that moment, he turns toward me, raising the blade. He's nearly to the bed when Vanya takes just a step in his wake.

"We don't have the time to hide her body—"

"Really?" Mischa wonders, chuckling when he doesn't receive an answer. "Relax. I will let you keep your toy, Vanya," he taunts, growling another hollow laugh. "You only need ask."

"I…" Vanya shakes his head dismissively. "You can deal with her later. We need to move now."

"Fine." Mischa heads for the door, sheathing his blade. As he passes Vanya, he deliberately nudges the man's shoulder with his, knocking him off balance. "Do what you wish, Ivan. But she is *not* Anna-Natalia—"

That name. It tugs on another memory. A name so beautiful that I strived to remember it, even though I only heard it uttered once, by a woman with a gentle, quivering voice years ago.

"I *will* question her later," Mischa says, snapping my attention back to him. His eyes narrow. He noticed my reaction. "Until then, she's your responsibility," he adds, still speaking to Vanya. "Whatever she does, you do, Vanya." He slips through the doorway and marches down the hall, but his voice reaches back to us, assaulting my fragile skin one last time. "I suggest you keep her in the cage."

"Here." Vanya approaches the bed and stoops to pick something up off the floor nearby. My robe. He hands it to me and averts his gaze while I hurry into it. "Stay close to me," he warns as my cheeks flush. "We need to go—"

"Wait." I reach for his arm without understanding why. He doesn't shove me off, which gives me enough time to regain control of my throat. "Ellen… My name is Ellen."

Confusion flickers across his face. Then he just nods. "Right. Let's go."

I stand and follow him into the hallway. The floor feels strangely slick beneath one foot. On top of that, I'm limping, subconsciously avoiding any pressure on my right heel. A quick glance down reveals blood coating the side of it. I must have stepped on the glass in the kitchen.

"We'll get that fixed later," Vanya says, noticing the blood as well. "Come."

We return to the main room, where roughly five men are in the process of taking what little items remain and carrying them down the hall. It's organized chaos with an air of routine underneath. These men are used to being on the move.

Vanya takes my wrist, pulling me along after him before I can wonder why. "Come." He reaches the kitchen through a different hallway. There, a man exits through a rickety screen door and we follow him, leaving the house altogether.

It's dark out. A blanket of stars coats an ebony night sky while a cold wind nips at the naked skin beneath my robe. Before us, an empty yard stretches for what seems like miles, closed in on either side by a wall of trees. It's quiet here. Too quiet. Craning my neck, I realize there are no other houses nearby. Just wilderness and silence.

"Have you lost your mind?"

A firm body brushes mine from behind. Before I can turn, my eyes are covered by something warm. Flesh. A hand?

"Go," my captor snarls—presumably at Vanya. I recognize his voice. *Mischa.* "I will keep her before you let her escape with enough intel to draw a fucking map for Winthorp."

He drags me in a different direction, heedless of how I stumble as my sore heel is aggravated. I'm forced against him, a slave to the motions of his body, my vision obscured. We don't go far, just paces from the house, over rugged terrain that crunches underfoot. Other footsteps catch my attention close by. Someone mutters something, but I can't make the words out. The language isn't English.

Suddenly, heat tickles my ear and the stench of vodka floods my nostrils.

"Get in," Mischa snarls.

I have only enough sense to throw my hand out in front of me before he shoves me forward. My fingers catch the edge of something firm. Metal. It's curved with space underneath for me to duck. My knees hit a ledge, which forces me to climb onto it. The seat of a vehicle, I think. The suspicion is proven correct when Mischa climbs in beside me, his bulk backing me against what must be the opposite door. Only now does he let me go, taking his hand off my face.

I'm not foolish enough to look up. Instead, I use stealth to discern our surroundings. Supple leather gives way beneath me—I was right. We're in the back seat of a van. The windows are tinted, letting in little light, and only one man occupies the front seat: the driver. I can't see his face, but he's wearing the same faded fatigues the other men are.

"Drive," Mischa tells him, tapping his fist against the window on his end. "Take up the rear. I'll keep watch."

He leans back against the seat, propping his arm along the headrest so that his reach extends beyond my neck. The tightness to his jaw betrays the otherwise casual motion. He's done it for my benefit, to remind me just how quickly he could regain control should I run.

Aware of him watching, I place my hands on my lap and face ahead. My heel stings. There's no doubt that I've tracked blood all over the floor of the vehicle. I do my best to keep the wound from contacting anything else, but the best way requires that I cross my legs with the injured heel dangling in the air. The motion puts my foot in his domain, close enough to his knee that I'll brush it with one good bump in the road.

Which is worse?

"Do not think that Vanya's pity can save you," Mischa says as if to warn me from even an accidental touch. "I have humored him this long. Besides, it's not you in particular that he cares for. He does it out of grief."

I can't help but wonder if he said that more to himself than to me. When my gaze flickers in his direction, I find him frowning and my heart beats faster in foreboding. A man like him secretes anger like sweat. It slicks his skin and floods the car, drowning me beneath the scent.

Suffocating me.

"You haven't asked why," he remarks after seconds pass in silence. Something battles with the malice in his tone, catching me off guard. Approval? "Perhaps your master trained you, after all."

I shudder at the mention of Robert. My master? He has a different word for it. I am only allowed to call him one thing, apart from his name. My thoughts shy from recalling it and I turn to the window, desperate to piece together the scenery.

Breathe, Ellen…

A hand seizes my jaw before I can make out anything more than shadow, wrenching me around to face the man beside me.

"You remind him of his daughter," he tells me. His gaze traps mine, probing deeply without mercy. He sees the way I flinch and interest flickers across his otherwise callous expression. "She was murdered years ago. Butchered. I think you know by who—"

"Sir?" the driver calls as he wrenches on the wheel. Too fast.

The sudden shift throws me in Mischa's direction. In disgust, he shoves me off, twisting around to gaze from the back windshield. Whatever he sees makes his face fall flat.

"Shit. Get down!"

There's an eerie moment when all I hear is the roar of an engine. My gaze meets a pair of amber irises staring back, and for the first time, something other than hate is reflected in them.

Fear.

"Get down!"

Wham! Everything happens too quickly to decipher. Clanging noise. Shattering glass. Darkness. Pain.

A thunderous roar rattles through my being, and then…*slam!* Air wheezes from my chest—I'm being crushed. Whatever it is pins me into the sliver of space between the front and back seats. Metal?

No…a *body.*

A guttural voice snarls something into my ear, but only snippets register. "Down—stay down!"

Sharp noises cut the air. *Gunshots.* They echo in tandem. At least twenty right after the other.

Bang!

Bang!

Bang!

Then nothing.

"Vlad?" Misha shouts through the resounding quiet.

A groan comes from the front seat. "I…I'm alright."

"Good. Then drive!" Crouched beside me, Mischa rummages through his pocket, withdrawing something that he aims in the air. "I'll cover you."

Predatory. That's the only way to describe how he maneuvers swiftly into the seat, aiming at something unseen through the window. The *shattered* window.

Glass speckles the seat, glimmering in my hair and over the satin of my robe. Did we hit something? In the darkness, I make out the edge of what seems to be a dirt road. The windshield is cracked, but branches extend beyond it, casting shadows over the hood. A tree—we must have run into it.

When the driver tries to reverse, the engine squeals and then dies.

"Shit." Keeping low, Mischa nudges the door beside me open. Before I can even think to escape, his fingers clench my shoulder. "Move without my say so and I'll kill you." A cold, round object taps the side of my skull as a deadly reinforcement. "Go."

With him on my heels, I climb from the wreckage.

It quickly becomes apparent that we aren't alone. Three other vans are stalled up ahead. Each one sits askew, as if their drivers had to slam on the brakes to stop suddenly. Men exit them. When they see Mischa, one of them shouts words I can't discern.

Then…gunshots.

"Get down!"

I'm shoved to the earth and crushed once again. This time, I can hear the breathing of the man on top of me. It's steady despite the tumult of noise happening around us. More people shout. More gunshots ring out.

"Get up!"

The pressure lifts from off me, and I barely manage to suck in a breath before I'm being dragged into the shadows that line the roads. Grass prickles my feet. Shadows flicker in the darkness. Near. Far.

Another gunshot rings out, way too close for comfort.

And then a man appears from behind a tree up ahead. He's armed, pointing a gun squarely in my direction. His clothes stick out to me as fear grips my lungs—he's not wearing fatigues. Instead, a crisp suit clashes with the wilderness around us. His gun isn't large and bulky either but sleek. A pistol. His face…

I know it—the hazy kind of recognition that comes only from a glance.

And he knows me.

His eyes widen. Quickly, his free hand goes to his ear. "She's alive. I found her! She—"

Thunder roars nearby, deafening me as blood flies from the man's head. He falls and my brain belatedly names the reason why. *He's dead.*

"Move."

The grip on my arm turns brutal, crunching bone and twisting flesh. Changing direction, Mischa steers me to the road, keeping his gun at the ready. From the acrid smell tickling my nostrils, I know he is the one who shot the other man. If any more enemies are lurking nearby, they must have been dispatched. Only his men remain, their weapons drawn…

Or their bodies lying prone and lifeless.

"Fuck." Mischa spits on the ground, his face drawn tight. When we come close enough, he shoves me toward someone, and the man catches me, gripping my shoulders. "Go. Get her to the safe house."

The way he said it… My body trembles at the unspoken warning. He saw it too. He heard it. Those were not generic mercenaries.

"Go!"

My new captor steers me toward an open van and hastens in after me. Vanya. His face is drawn tight, and I stiffen when he reaches over me.

"Your seat belt," he prompts, shoving the bit of metal into my hand and nodding toward the base. "Put it on."

I obey and the van lurches into motion, presumably heading toward even more danger.

Whether by accident or intent, Vanya doesn't cover my eyes, and I'm allowed to witness the entire trip through winding fields and hills. It's desolate here, somewhere in the countryside, far from the airport. The thought makes my stomach clench in a way that has nothing to do with fear. Just pain. Just guilt.

As Mischa claimed, I was just a decoy. Though, assuming she was aware of the switch, would Briar fare any better in my situation? Sweet, playful Briar who couldn't even go five minutes without a friend to chat with or sycophants to entertain. I've seen her charm Robert Sr. in his foulest of moods, always getting her way. Could she enthrall this murderer with hell in his eyes and a million scars written upon his skin?

I have no shame in admitting that, yes, she probably could. Men always fell for Briar. Fought for her. Fought *over* her.

But there is one man who will fight for you, a part of me hisses. *Whether you want him to or not.*

Robert.

I cringe from the thought and turn to the window, desperate for a distraction. I find one. Hell stares back at me. Dark eyes meet mine coldly through the glass as the door is unceremoniously opened. He doesn't reach for my hand, but my *hair*, wrenching me out by my scalp. Through watering eyes, I can only assume we've arrived at the "safe house" by the gravel at my feet and the shadow of a building ahead.

The air here reeks of copper. There's little light to see by, and inside the structure, cold floors betray a sense of abandonment. I'm not sure how far we've traveled before he releases me so suddenly that I fall to my knees. A ratty, threadbare carpet beneath me coughs up dust with every movement made upon it. Only one other person occupies this room, pacing the length of the floor.

"Who are you?" His voice is low, but it somehow still manages to echo to the far reaches of the room.

A single light fixture illuminates the narrow space: another decaying cage of wood coated with brown wallpaper this time. The windows here aren't boarded up. Blurred glass displays my reflection: wide-eyed and trembling.

Who am I? I'm not sure the woman staring back at me even knows.

"Those were *Winthorp's* men," the man in front of me continues. "You are not Briar." He tosses me a calculating glance as if to make sure of that fact. "So who are you? Robert only has two children."

I can see him trying to put the pieces together on his own. When he looks at me again, his eyebrow is raised, but he shakes his head as if to cut off his own thought. Not a Winthorp by blood. So who?

"What is your name?"

"Ellen." The voice isn't mine, and I turn to find Vanya standing in the doorway. There's blood on his chin. His? Or someone else's, smeared there during the attack? "Her name is Ellen," he says again, the words rushed. "She—"

"Leave us," Mischa says sharply. He jerks his chin in dismissal but Vanya remains.

"Mischa." There's a plea tucked into the name this time. Something emphatic, more than just concern for me. *Don't do this.* "She's just a woman—"

"A woman who nearly got us all killed." Mischa reaches into his pocket and withdraws his knife, letting the blade catch the light. "I told you to leave us once, Ivan. Do not make me tell you twice."

Seconds crawl by until reluctant footsteps finally retreat down the hall. My heart aches in Vanya's absence, hammering against the wall of my rib cage. But I can't take my gaze off the knife.

As if aware of that fact, Mischa crouches on one knee and brings the blade near my jawline. Sharpened metal tickles my cheek, stinging. Slicing. All the while, his eyes stare into mine, hunting down the confessions I haven't voiced.

"Who. Are. You? Not an innocent after all? One of their spies?"

An answer is on the tip of my tongue. *No one.* My lips twitch to voice it. Too late.

Those amber irises darken with violent intent, but I only see his arm twitch before…*pain!* I instinctively clutch the side of my face with one hand as my brain struggles to process the sensations battling for attention. Burning. Searing. Wide-eyed, I watch scarlet drops dribble onto my chest. My thighs. The floor.

"I just lost three men because of you," Mischa warns, sounding miles away. His tone has changed in a heartbeat. There's no anger. Just grim acceptance that conveys the inevitable. He'll do it now. Kill me. "Answer me."

The knife grazes my throat next, biting deeper when I flinch.

"P-please." I don't recognize the plaintive voice that comes out of me. I don't know why I resist him at all. Dying would be easier than suffering him. Dying would be preferable to returning to Robert.

Though maybe not. Barely a day from Winthorp manor and something I thought I'd never feel again floods my veins. It's weak, hardly strong enough to outlast the fear, but still there. *Survival.*

"My name is Ellen—"

"I don't give a damn about your name," Mischa growls, and the knife cuts deeper. More burning. Stinging.

A whimper escapes my throat, but nothing registers over his features. No pity. No humanity. Nothing.

"Who are you?"

"My name is Ellen Winthorp," I stammer through the pain. "Ellen *Winthorp.*"

The blade stills. Withdraws. "How?"

Shaking, I force myself to meet his gaze directly. More tears sting my eyes and I let them fall, forsaking any attempts to hide the truth. "I…I am Robert's wife."

*R*obert's wife. I don't think I've ever said those words out loud. At least not to another person. In my old world, they would have been met with something akin to pity and decorum. A tight nod perhaps. Or maybe a sympathetic pat on my hand. Not disgust. Not revulsion so potent that I taste it on my tongue.

"His wife?" He mulls the title over, deciding within an instant that it must be a lie. His pupils constrict menacingly. "Robert Sr. has no wife—"

"Not him." I shake my head, too tired to specify.

"His son?"

I just nod.

"You're lying."

My body stiffens at his tone, but I'm not quick enough to cower beyond his reach. He grabs me, his fingers clenching the back of my scalp, twisting through my hair.

"*He* doesn't have a wife, either. And I doubt that he would let her be used as a decoy."

It's a question I haven't let myself think on. Has Robert grown tired of me? Or has his father finally sought to put an end to his son's obsession?

Both scenarios are equally alarming.

"You wear no ring," Mischa adds, jerking his chin toward my naked hand. "I know of every goddamn Winthorp for generations, and I've never heard your name before."

"I-I'm not…approved." It's the only thing I can think to say. The only explanation that doesn't require divulging the full truth. Perhaps I'm not that desperate to live after all? Some wounds aren't worth reopening. Some horrors can't be faced alone.

Regardless, the answer seems to satisfy my captor. He frowns, and I can tell from the grudging set to his jaw that he'll believe that much at least: that the defiant son of Robert Winthorp Sr. would take a wife without his notorious father's permission. After all, there is one undisputable fact this night has proven.

"He sent his men after you," Mischa says, obviously annoyed by what he can't explain. Something bright and terrible flits across his gaze, illuminating the irises. Before I can blink, the knife returns. "He's willing to kill for you. And you shall return to him in *pieces*."

Pain! Fire sears through my skull: the result of another cut slicing right through the first. Instinct takes hold of my body. I try to turn away, but his free hand grips my scalp tighter, holding me in place while he raises the blade again. He lets me see the tip of it, painted red with my blood. Then he lashes out, piercing the meat of my cheek, down my jaw.

"You are number fifteen," he tells me over my whimper.

Somehow, I'm still fully aware as he makes another cut, angled toward the first. God, it hurts—just like he wants it to. He takes his time, slicing through flesh bit by bit. And I see lightning. My eyes flood and overflow. I'm shaking in his grip as air escapes my lungs in a pathetic, wheezing gasp.

"The fifteenth martyr in a blood war," he continues, his voice wavering.

At first, I assume it's because I'm delirious. Dizzy. But no… I see his throat jerk as he swallows hard. There's an unsteadiness to his grip that I didn't notice before—I'm not shaking on my own.

"You may be an innocent in this, but I will kill you, Ellen Winthorp," he promises me, negating any suspicion that what he feels might be guilt. No. He's resigned to my murder. "But not yet."

He pushes me to the floor and leaves me here, bleeding over the carpet. I count his footsteps as they fade somewhere deeper inside the house. When that sound trails off...I count my heartbeat.

"*D*o not hate him." Vanya insists as he dabs at the blood from my face with a wadded piece of cloth.

Is he speaking to me or himself? I can't tell. I'm not sure when the older man returned to find me, bleeding and broken, either. All I know is partial relief as he treats my wounds.

"It's not you he hates. He wasn't always this way," he admits almost reluctantly. "There was a time when he'd never... Do not hate him."

Is hate what I feel for the newest monster to mutilate my body? I'm not sure. Maybe I just don't care enough to define it. Every man has a story to explain away the demons that eventually consume him. I've learned the history of one. I'm not keen to learn another.

But more than his violence troubles Vanya about his leader. Frowning, he draws the cloth away and reaches for a pack of gauze. Inside is a square piece of bandage, which he places over my left cheek and secures with tape. Then he sighs. "You are my responsibility," he says, changing the subject. "I do not want to bind you. Or lock you in the cage."

I can't swallow my sigh of relief. "Thank—"

"*But*," he says over me, "I will if I have to. What you do reflects on me. Do you understand?"

I nod.

"Good." He stands, wincing once he's on his feet. From this angle, it's not hard to see why. Blood cakes the side of his face near his ear.

Something soft strikes my fingers and I look down and find that I've reached for the cloth without realizing it. When I start to stand, Vanya says nothing. He simply watches as I raise the fabric in a trembling fist and dab it along his ear. He's too tall. I have to stand on tiptoe to clean the wound properly. Underneath all the blood is only a hairline scratch, caused by glass I presume.

Rather than thank me, Vanya snatches the cloth and tosses it aside. Then he gathers up the rest of his supplies and heads for the doorway. "You'll stay in here. I'll try to find you a blanket, but I suggest you make do until then. I'll keep watch outside the door. Get some sleep."

Gratitude renders me speechless. By the time I remember how to speak, he's already gone, closing the door to the room after him. Unless my ears play tricks, I hear the lock engage. Oddly enough, I feel safer here than at any other point in this nightmare. I don't care to decipher the reasons for his kindness. Maybe they're entirely selfish, as Mischa insinuated.

Still…

No matter how small, the mercy is rare enough to be cherished.

At least without wondering how long it may last.

*V*ibrations draw me awake. Footsteps? Gasping, I open my eyes to an unfamiliar ceiling and a chillingly familiar silhouette.

"I changed my mind," Mischa declares. "Get up."

He heads for the door, leaving me to follow. Limping, I struggle to keep up before he can issue a threat not to fall behind. Pale daylight spills in through the window, illuminating part of the narrow hall while leaving the rest of the house bathed in shadow.

It's older than the last one, with rotting floorboards and a smaller floorplan. The men seem to be spread throughout rather than grouped in one room. They keep their guns close and linger near windows. Searching.

Up a rickety staircase are two rooms. I spy a bed in one, but I'm herded toward another. Small and confined, the space contains a card table surrounded by mismatched chairs. Black sheets shroud the windows, and a single lamp in the corner casts dingy yellow light.

"Sit." Mischa nods his chin toward the metal folding chair closest to me.

Aware of him watching my every move, I lower myself slowly, keeping my gaze trained on my imminent surroundings. There is nothing else in this room. In fact, it appears to have no purpose other than this: silence, isolation.

"Look at me, Ellen Winthorp."

He's seated across from me. Shadows distort his features, making his eyes seem darker, his face narrower. Hollow.

Without warning, he reaches toward me, sliding a finger along the gauze taped to my cheek. "Have you seen your face?"

There's a taunt tucked into the question. Beneath the bandage, the wound sears, reacting to his nearness. One of his knuckles deliberately nudges the area that feels the deepest and I hiss in response.

"Take the bandage off."

My fingers shake as I obey, carefully undoing Vanya's handiwork.

"Look." He places something on the table and shoves it toward me. A mirror, small and round, with a crack in the glass.

I lift it, seeking enough light to make out my reflection. A haunted ghost stares back, her blue eyes wide and empty. Blood coats the left side of her face, running in rivulets down her throat. I swallow hard at the sight, but that's not what he wanted me to see.

It's the shape of the wound. Careful. Intentional. I have to tilt my jaw to make it out fully. From beneath my eye all the way down to my jaw, he carved an X. Beside it, extending toward my ear, is a jaggedly sliced letter V. The nonsensical doodles of a madman?

I almost assume as much until I recall what he said. *You are number fifteen.* XV. He marked my fate in Roman numerals. If I live long enough for the wounds to heal, they will leave scars proclaiming my fate forever.

"Look at me."

I lower the mirror and find him watching me. There's no hiding beneath his gaze. Heat wells behind my eyes and spills out. Each tear sinks into the rent skin, setting the flesh on fire. I don't turn away from him or try to disguise the pain, however. I let him see it.

And he should relish this moment. His jaw clenches as he tracks the descent of every drop of moisture. Every wince. Does it justify his hatred? Feed his rage? For once, I can't tell.

"How did you meet your husband?"

I look down, recoiling from that word. *Husband.* The action irritates my captor.

He seizes my chin. "Look at me." He jerks my face toward his, tightening his grip so that I have no choice but to meet his gaze. Emptiness stares back.

I always thought Robert had no soul, but even he could feign humanity when he wanted to. *What do you think I'd do without you, Ellen?* he'd growl every now and then. *You keep me sane. Don't you fucking see?*

"Answer me, Little One." My new tormentor has had to repeat himself. Irritation sparks from those fathomless irises, prickling my skin. "Your husband. How did you meet him? I know Robert has a fondness for whores."

I stifle my reaction to the insinuation. Whore. If only. At least, then, I would have earned something from my endeavor. I could have justified it.

"I grew up in Winthorp manor," I say. Speaking hurts. Even the slightest movement of my jaw triggers more wet warmth to drip onto my collar.

"As a maid?" Mischa questions.

Still restrained by his grip on my chin, I nod.

"Really?" He lets me go and rises to his feet, circling toward my side with effortless speed. He has the knife again and lowers the blade so that I can see it, cleaned from the night before and ready to inflict more damage. "Lie to me again, Ellen, and your pretty face will be nothing more than a painful memory. Understand?"

"Y-yes—"

"Then tell me who you are. Really."

"I-I wasn't lying," I insist. "I *did* grow up in the manor."

"But as a *maid?*"

"N-not officially—"

"Don't mince words with me." His fingers flex against the knife's handle in a warning. "If not a maid, then as what?"

I run through those memories, trying to put my role into words that don't sting. Something that doesn't require further questioning.

"My mother was…close to the Winthorps. When she died, they kept me around as Briar's companion." I hold my breath as he digests that explanation.

Relief renders me boneless when his hand finally withdraws.

"And?" he presses.

"When I grew older, Robert…noticed me." My throat tightens and I leave it at that. Not even the threat from the blade can draw out more.

Thankfully, Mischa doesn't seem to give a damn either way. Robert. That name acts as a trigger to whatever evil lurks within him. His face becomes that fearsome mask once again, reducing him to more monster than human.

"And you married him?" He stands back, watching me with an expression I can't decipher. Disgust?

Or something more terrifying: *suspicion.*

"Stepanov," he says quietly. "Do you know that name?"

I shake my head.

"Really?" The man lifts an eyebrow, unconvinced. "You've never heard your husband say it?"

"He doesn't talk about business around me."

"Oh?" Two heavy footsteps bring him closer. Slowly, he sinks to his knees, down to my level. "What about the *Mafiya*? The *Pakhan?* Do those ring a bell?"

The corner of his mouth quirks when I shake my head, but it's not a smile.

"What about…" He leans in close, allowing his breath to nuzzle my bleeding wounds. When I shiver, he trails his thumb along my cheek and withdraws it, painted red. "What about Anna-Natalia Vasilev? Does *that* name ring a bell?"

I jump instinctively. There's no hiding it. I'm sure the memory that name triggers unfolds across my face just as strongly as it does in my mind.

It was so long ago that I shouldn't be able to recall her so clearly. She was thin. Small. Her hair was long and dark, like Vanya's might have been once. Her upturned eyes were a delicate shade of brown.

And she was in chains.

"I only saw her once."

There's no point in lying to him. He knows. There's something predatory in him that hunts through my pain, drawing the truth out whether I like it or not. Maybe it's what I think I find lurking beneath all the hate and rage.

Desperation?

Do not hate him, Vanya insisted. *He wasn't always this way.*

"Where?" His tone makes me suspect he already knows the answer.

"Winthorp Manor," I croak through my pain. "Robert Sr. had her…in a basement. I was young. Maybe seven? His son had me bring her water—"

"Why?" He slams his fist against the table out of anger more than emphasis. *Again,* he already knows the answer.

Tasting blood, I tell him. "I don't know—"

"Did you see her die?"

I blink, thrown off by the question. Do you need to see the killing blow to witness someone die? Not necessarily. Death can be a slow process, tracked only by a steady change in your reflection day after day. Or a look in the eye. I picture the woman, Anna-Natalia. Was she dead then, huddled in chains at the mercy of the Winthorps?

"N-no—"

"Do you want to hear how they did it?"

My heart hammers against my chest as I shake my head emphatically. *No.* They butchered her, he claims. I've seen firsthand what Robert does to animals for sport. He hunts them. Guts them. He shows them no mercy.

Mischa comes in close so that his words slither directly into my ear. "They slit her throat. Then they cut off her hands and sent them to her father in a box. She was sixteen."

I gag at the imagery. Those beautiful eyes open and unseeing. Her pain. Her fear.

"Her body, they dumped into the river. Unlike you, she was an innocent in this. She was number twelve."

Twelve. A martyr in a blood war, he said. But the only wars I knew of were the internal ones raging through the Winthorp estate. Father against son. Brother against sister. Gossip. Intrigue. Jealousy. Anna-Natalia Vasilev never cracked the dinner table chatter.

In fact… The only figure to ever intrude upon the sanctity of the manor was a boy who snuck into my room in the dead of night. His eyes burned through the darkness, his voice a hiss. Even then, so young, I knew he'd kill me. There was a knife in his hand and murder in his soul.

Though, for whatever reason, *that* monster let me go.

But I don't tell Mischa that. Something he said keeps echoing in my thoughts, intriguing me enough to voice it. "T-twelve?"

He frowns at my pathetic attempts at probing. Still, he tosses me a bone. "Your husband's family has a long list of sins, Little One," he tells me. "A very long list. We keep track of the victims related by blood." Almost gingerly, he fingers a piece of my hair, lifting it for inspection in the dim lighting. I don't expect the moment he tugs hard, drawing a whine from my lips. "But his transgressions are nothing compared to mine." He returns to his full height and kicks the leg of my chair. "Get up."

The world spins when I do. Pain and exhaustion play a violent game for supremacy over my battered body.

I stagger on my feet when he takes my hand and drags me into the hall. Rather than head for the stairs, he shoves me toward the room next door. Oh, God. It's the one with the bed and another window, nailed shut. A mocking view of an empty field greets me beyond it. Outside, the sky is a dreary, stormy gray. How many days has it been so far? I can't tell.

"Don't get any cute ideas, Little One." Mischa cups my chin, forcing me to face him. "In fact...I *dare* you to run from me."

His eyes glow at the threat of a chase. Here and now, I make the decision never to take him up on that challenge.

"You *do* look like her. You're just as beautiful," he admits, almost to himself. His finger drifts up my jawline and comes away red. Meeting my gaze, he swipes his tongue along the pad of it. "But are you worth as much?"

His hands capture the ends of my robe. Aware of my terror, he takes his time, peeling the panels back, relishing how I shudder with every inch of skin revealed. When he finally undoes the sash, I don't resist. I lift my arms, letting him strip me down to nothing.

Then I watch him toss the satin onto the floor.

His gaze sweeps over my body, shamelessly logging every flaw and pore. Beautiful like Briar, he said? I'm not sure if he still has that opinion by the time our eyes reconnect.

"Lie down."

His voice seizes control of my limbs, and I take two steps back until my calves strike the mattress. Still facing him, I start to lower myself, but he frowns, irritated. Then he crosses the distance between us and shoves me down himself. Dazed, I blink up at the ceiling, tasting more blood on my tongue as wetness coats my neck. I'll ruin his sheets, but something tells me he doesn't mind.

He watches me bleed, nodding in satisfaction. "I want you to think about your husband, Little One," he says. "I want you to remember every twisted, sordid thing he's done to your body. Every way he's used you…"

It's a terrible request. My mind has more than enough ammunition to spawn a million nightmares. But does he know that? Looking at him, I can't tell. Maybe consent is such a foreign concept to him that he takes it for granted that most men ignore it altogether.

"Now…imagine me doing those things to you. All of them. Every last one." The malice in his voice doesn't match the involuntary way his eyes flicker across my naked chest. Quickly. As if nothing holds his interest—or he doesn't want it to. "Think about it until I come back and I hope you reconsider your silence."

Despair renders me boneless as he leaves the room, locking the door behind him. Then…something twisted enough to call amusement sets in. Imagine him as Robert? It's as easy as swapping out one monster for another. Or is it?

My eyes shut against the memories, but nothing short of unconsciousness can keep them at bay. My husband dishes out pain in exchange for his pleasure, and he *never* let me forget my role: *his*. When he touches me, I feel nothing but shame. Fear. Panic.

Never…fire. This man inspires a new terror I don't know how to fathom. I've grown so used to Robert. I can endure his routine. I can survive his games—Mischa is a dangerous anomaly. Were I given the choice between the two of them, is it really that hard to pick who I'd prefer?

No. I'd pick Robert. The known is always better than the unknown.

Always.

The lumpy mattress beneath me reeks of mold, but I can't resist its comfort for long. When my eyes flutter open to a darkened room, I'm not sure how much time has passed. An hour? Longer? The darkness beyond the window doesn't reveal any answers. Neither do my sore, aching limbs, which throb as though I never slept at all.

My face, however, feels stiff. Sticky. The wounds have stopped bleeding from what I can tell, but each laceration burns with a new kind of pain. Robert always took care never to scar my face. He'd strike me, but always with an open hand.

What would he think to see me so ruined?

I trace the wounds with my finger, following the jagged contours that form my new title. Fifteen. *XV*. Does the reality of a new scar sadden me? I can't tell. Every instinct in my body warns that I won't live long enough to care.

As if the thought of mortality is their cue, footsteps

approach the room. *His.* I sense him behind the door seconds later, lingering there as if aware of the unbearable anticipation building in my body.

He savors it. How it gets harder to breathe. How my nipples tighten in the still air, knowing that they'll be under his scrutiny soon. Humiliation is his greatest weapon, and he hones it for what feels like hours on my already frayed nerves.

"Get up."

I nearly sigh in relief when he finally kicks the door open and switches an overhead light on. Rather than smug, he looks...cold.

"This is my last offer of mercy: Will you tell me what you know of Robert Winthorp?"

I swallow down a lump of dread. "I know nothing."

"Fine." An expression distorts his mouth, which causes my heart to sink. Disappointment? "Then get dressed." He tosses something onto the floor near the bed.

Then I realize the position I'm in. How he finds me: twisted in the sheets on my side, my hair tangled around my shoulders. In sleep, my body forgot all about being a prisoner, seeking out the most comfortable position.

I have to take my time detangling my limbs before I can stand. My cheeks burn from more than just pain and I don't dare look up to see his reaction.

Instead, I stoop for the pile of fabric nearby. It's soft. Not a robe, but a thin negligee—though, where Vanya gave me clothing to preserve my modesty, this black creation of lace and silk is meant to entice. Or shame.

"Put it on."

I do without comment, surprised that the garment reaches past my knees. When Mischa observes me, I don't blush. Frowning, he turns away, shrugging his shoulder in a silent command for me to follow.

The cramped house is shrouded in darkness. I can hear other men moving throughout, but with Mischa in front of me, my vision is reduced to what little of the floor separates us. We pass through a doorway somewhere on the lower level and then descend a set of wooden stairs hammered into a concrete wall. A basement. My new cell?

There's little light here, but enough to make out another card table in the corner, where two men are sitting. One of them I recognize. Xavier, the man with the briefcase filled with money. He's wearing another suit and sitting tall, his hands folded neatly on his lap.

Sitting beside him, a balding stranger is wearing a black dress shirt and slacks. He eyes me boldly, drinking in the battered flesh beneath the hem of my shift. A pink tongue shoots out along his lips and he nods to no one in particular.

"I see what you mean, *Pakhan*," he says to Mischa. "They could be twins. But ah!" He tsks between his teeth and sadly shakes his head. "You've marred her already."

"Which shouldn't keep you from fucking her."

The words stop me dead in my tracks—not that my captor notices. He approaches the table while I shy back against the wall, pressing myself against the concrete.

"Name your price," Mischa demands, sending my heart into a frantic race against my thoughts. *Fucking her. Fucking her.*

The balding man smirks and casts another searing glance in my direction. Then he sighs, turning back to Xavier. "Business first. Tell your accountant here that my goods still sell for their going rate."

Mischa nods and Xavier lifts yet another briefcase from the floor and places it onto the table. This time, he sets something square, made of gray plastic, down as well. A scale of some kind? When he withdraws a stack of money, he removes the rubber band and sets the bills on the electronic device. He does that with five whole stacks and then looks to Mischa as if for approval.

"Take your goddamn blood money, Boris," Mischa snaps, but his voice lacks any real passion. When he cocks his head in my direction, my heart sputters. I make out only a sliver of his expression, the rest of his face is bathed in shadow. "Now, name your price."

For me.

Boris sits back and forms a steeple with his fingers as if thinking over the amount—but I can tell he already has a price in mind. "Just one night with Robert's bitch? Five thousand."

Mischa shrugs. "Done." There's something in how he says that word that sends alarm shooting down my spine. Distracted. Disinterested. There's no mocking ownership of his captive. No haggling. Like he's in a hurry to foist his cruelty onto someone else.

Someone who can do the job, a part of me whispers.

"Where can I have her?" Boris wonders as Xavier begins to reorganize his stacks of bills. Maybe focusing on him is the only way I can keep any sanity. His hands. How they shake…

"Upstairs," Mischa commands, his voice faint and distorted.

Blood rushes through my ears, counting the seconds that tick by. One heartbeat. Another. There's no time to think. Just survive.

Breathe, Ellen. Move, Ellen!

"W-wait!" I stagger forward, stupidly grasping Mischa's forearm.

His reaction is near instantaneous. *Wham*! I'm on my knees, enthralled by a million stars bouncing across my vision. They sparkle as my fingers clutch the right side of my face. It's numb. I taste blood. My ears ring.

"Take her upstairs," Mischa snarls. "Get her the fuck out of my sight—"

"No!" I move on instinct, following the sound of his voice with my fingers. They brush scalding muscle hidden beneath harsh material. His hip? "Wait!" The world swims around me as I stagger to my feet. Speaking is suddenly an ordeal. My jaw won't move the way it should, and every attempt sounds thick. Muted. "Wait. I can be of more use to you than—"

A hand clenches my throat, shoving me back against the wall. Mischa's. He pins me there without mercy, his face a terrifying snarl. There's no life in his eyes. Just darkness. Rage. Pain. "You're lucky I haven't killed you—"

"I can be more useful to you than as a whore," I rasp, fighting against my own tongue to sound intelligible. Human. He's reduced me to a creature that spits blood when she talks. My vision is blurred in my right eye. He's a smeared specter of light and shadow, but fear is a funny thing. It turns out to be no match against a deeper, more ingrained instinct: survival. "I can help you—"

"Shut up!" His fingers tighten, cutting off all air.

There's only enough left in my throat for two words. "He's…cheated…"

Confusion. It flits across his face so quickly that I almost miss it. But then his grip loosens and I don't wait for him to change his mind.

"He's cheated you," I croak, jerking my chin toward the table. "There's something wrong with the money—"

"Bitch." Mischa laughs, chuckling at the absurdity of it all. "You have permission to use force with her," he tells Boris from over his shoulder. "This whore has a smart little mouth."

"Just don't damage it too much," Boris replies. "You hit her again and I'll knock a grand off my price—"

"Listen to me!"

Shock registers across my captor's face, which is how I realize I screamed at him. Pleaded. *Listen!*

I've never said that to anyone. There was no use before. Ellen Winthorp was either a doll on display or a secret to be hidden. She had nothing to say and even fewer people who might care to hear it.

He has no choice but to listen to me now.

"I saw him," I blurt, forcing out the words as quickly as I can. "The bills. Ask him to weigh them—"

"Enough!" Mischa snarls. "I suggest you shut the fuck up—"

"Ask him to weigh the damn money!" I'm panting with the effort it takes to speak. My chest hurts. My face is a conflicting mixture of searing fire and throbbing ice. My eye must be swelling. It's impossible to keep it open, which gives me only a fraction of my normal field of vision to gauge his reaction from. By his side, his hand clenches into a fist and I stiffen in anticipation of the next blow. "Please—"

"Xavier," he snarls to the man at the table. "Do you have a different scale?"

The man fidgets, tugging on the collar of his suit. "Of course. Why?"

Mischa's eyes narrow into slivers. "Take it out."

When he turns, he drags me by my hair and shoves me against the table, rattling the bills stacked neatly there. "Show me."

Xavier recoils as my blood speckles the pristine rows of dollar bills. "What in God's name?"

Mischa doesn't answer him. He speaks only to me, twisting his fingers painfully through my hair. "Show me."

I reach for bills at random, searching for any clue as to their value. Something subtle… Or maybe I missed it? No, *there*. I lift a bill with a slight discoloration from the rest. Even through blurred, unfocused vision, I notice the abnormality. The green is a shade *too* bright, and the bill feels different from how it should. Brittle.

"Th-this one." I give the bill to Mischa, who hesitates only a second before snatching it.

"Weigh it," he tells Xavier, but the other man just laughs.

"*Pakhan*? Are you seriously humoring this—"

"Now." Mischa slams the bill onto the table so hard that the legs buckle, toppling over what precarious stacks of money remain. "Weigh. It."

Slowly, Xavier places it onto one side of an old-fashioned metal scale. He reaches for another bill, but I shake my head and fumble through the crumpled, blood-soaked paper myself.

Finally, my fingers find what I'm searching for. "This one."

Without a word, Mischa jerks his chin toward the scale, and I place the bill on the other end. Droplets of blood speckle both sides, but there is no mistaking the fact that one bill is obviously heavier than the other. The scale tilts a fraction of an inch.

And, suddenly, the air in the room loses all sense of stiff professionalism. Nothing riles men like money.

"Th-the bitch got them wet," Xavier says, his voice wavering only slightly. "Of course that will skew the—"

"Do it again." At his normal volume, Mischa sounds gruff. Dangerous. Now? Thunder resonates in every word, echoing down my spine. His fingers tighten around a chunk of my hair to convey a warning. *If you are wrong, I will kill you.* "Do it," he commands when Xavier hesitates. "But *she* chooses."

I blink my good eye and put all of my energy into focusing on the sea of green beneath my fingertips. Am I right? Have I just gambled my life away? The questions crowd my thoughts, nearly drowning out the senses that catch the irregularities in one bill. Another. Desperately, I point a shaking finger at them both and Xavier races to clear the scale before placing them on either side. Slowly. Reluctantly.

There's a heart-stopping second as the scale wavers. Up. Down. Balances…dips to one end. *Bingo*, as Robert would say. Both bills are fresh and clear of blood. There's no denying it this time.

As the revelation registers between the three men, the tension boils over. Spills.

"You thought you could steal from me?" Mischa shoves me aside and circles the table as Xavier backs himself into a corner.

"I-I don't know," Xavier stammers, desperate to find a narrative to save his life.

But it's too late. Mischa draws his knife…

And I turn away, stumbling in the dark until I hit the wall. Guilt. Fear. I feel all of it, inescapable even when I slam my hands over my ears and hum to drown out what happens next. La, la, la—it's no use. A high-pitched scream pierces my palms, followed by a sickening thud. A violent, choking gurgle.

Death smells like salt. It reeks in a way that extends beyond just stench. You feel it in your bones. You taste it: the bitter flavor of someone else's soul escaping on the air. They steal a piece of you along with it.

Though I doubt this murderer has anything left of his to lose.

"I didn't know," Boris says, still eerily calm despite the violence. In fact…I get the sense he enjoyed the gruesome show. "You should pick your accountants more carefully, *Pakhan*," he adds. "But, if the offer still stands, I'll take the girl. Of course, we'll need to send for a new accountant—"

"Get out." Mischa looms in the shadows like a specter. His chest heaves erratically as he callously swipes his knife along his pants to clean it while his gaze roves in my direction. "Leave!" he snarls at Boris. "We'll continue this later. You —" He never takes his eyes off me. The hue of them clashes violently with the red liquid splattered across his chest. Blood reflected in more blood. "*Upstairs.*"

Moving blindly, I make it up the basement stairs in seconds and find my way to the main staircase by feel alone. The darkness distorts my already limited vision. Every shadow morphs into the shape of a man chasing me up the steps and into that narrow bedroom.

Once inside it, I don't close the door. I creep toward the bed instead, intending to sit on the mattress. I miss and wind up on my knees, pressing my bleeding cheek against the cold floor. My stomach roils, but nothing escapes my abused, sore throat. I don't know what's more alarming. The terror I feel? Or how quickly my body is able to process it.

Breathe, Ellen…

I inhale noisily, aware of the blood flooding my mouth for the first time. My nose feels tender to the touch. My right eye aches, impossible to open. I can't tell if the thumping in my ears is my heartbeat or approaching footsteps. Then the light switches on with a hiss, illuminating the puddle of blood growing beneath me.

"How?" Every step Mischa takes echoes, alarmingly unsteady. He's lost that smooth, predatory prowl. All that's left are harsh motion and tension.

Through a tangled net of my hair, I watch him advance. In one hand, he's holding Xavier's briefcase, but the money's been hastily shoved back in, peeking through gaps in the seal.

"How the fuck did you know?"

I don't have the energy to stand. "Robert," I admit to the floor, watching my saliva mingle with scarlet. "He…taught me."

"He taught you to what? Inspect his money?" His harsh laugh proves he doesn't know whether I'm lying or not. Not that it matters. Logic means less to him with every passing second. He craves the rage and chases it with flared nostrils and a trembling fist. But curiosity wins out. "You really expect me to believe that?"

I don't. But again, it doesn't matter. "He only ever talks to me about money," I explain, even though saving my life is futile. I'm tired. Resisting him is too damn hard. Too fucking bloody. I want it to end. "He made a bad deal once.

His father nearly killed him. So he taught me to…" The words trail off, broken and worthless. I doubt he even heard me.

He wants to fight. He wants to kill again. He wants to justify whatever hatred has eaten him alive. He can't have that narrative ruined, not even for his own benefit.

But silly me. I nearly forgot the one constant of the world that has yet to prove me wrong: *money*. A man values nothing more.

"You want to make yourself useful?" he wonders in a hollow tone.

I sense his intention even before his shoulder tenses, but I'm too tired to move. He throws the briefcase at me. It bounces painfully off my hip and falls open, spilling its contents over the floor.

"Then count it. Every last fucking bill. If you're off by so much as a cent, I'll gut you and send you to your fucking *husband* in pieces."

He slams the door in his wake so hard that it jerks on its hinges. Loose bills flutter in the air, falling down softly to coat my body like snowfall. I'm tempted to ignore him. To let him kill me when he returns. Give up here and now.

I'm so tired…

But it would never end there. *Nothing* comes between a man and his money.

CHAPTER 10

It takes me hours to capture and count every last bill, but I do so carefully before tucking the final amount away in my mind. The series of numbers sits heavy and out of place there, like some foreign trinket I never sought to add to my collection. One my husband certainly wouldn't approve of. Picturing Robert's scorn, I'd almost prefer physical penetration—at least my new tormentor would have to leave my body eventually.

But this, I will never forget: He carries five hundred and twenty-five thousand dollars on his person. Or at least he *did.* Now, it's all nothing more than pretty paper, considering that few respectable institutions would accept bills quite literally stained with my blood...

Will he punish me? Retaliation would be the least of my worries, however. I've caused so much more than a stranger's death by blowing the whistle on Xavier's deceit. I've lost Mischa his *accountant,* which I assume is not an easy position to fill in his line of business.

And for good reason.

"No motherfucker worth his salt keeps shit written down anymore," Robert used to tell me, his words rushed with paranoia. "No. A smart man hides his secrets where no one would think to look. That's the key, Elle. Somewhere safe."

Like locked inside a woman's head…

Rotting wood creaks nearby, betraying footsteps. Rushed. I stiffen at the realization that someone's standing above me before I can even turn my head in their direction.

"God have mercy…"

The hunched shadow seems familiar. Vanya? Either he teleported to my side or delirium is stealing my consciousness bits at a time. I can't see his face, just a blur lacking any definition, but his voice rings out clearly.

"Sleep," he insists, prying the last bloodied stack of money from my grip. "You're safe… Just sleep."

His voice trembles with the grim truth that he has no way of honoring that promise. Not really, yet he chooses to lie anyway. Out of pity or denial?

I'm not sure.

I'm too tired to really give a damn either way.

*P*ain keeps me tethered to my body, pulling me in and out of wakefulness—too strong to ignore for long, but too intense to suffer at the same time. Like a toy ball, I'm bounced between consciousness and delirium, but terror is the tiebreaker.

It scuttles at the edge of my awareness, growing more potent the more I become aware of the scent flooding my lungs—and the voice in my head. Deep. Guttural. Merciless.

"Look at me."

I can't. My eyelids are too heavy to lift. Whenever I try, I only see indistinguishable smears of light and shadow. So I just feel instead. *Pain, pain, pain.* But, beneath it all…relief?

My fingers perform an agonizing journey to my jaw, brushing something stiff and dry secured there. Gauze? Someone must have bandaged the wound on my face again, as well as draped me beneath what feels like cotton. The bedsheets? They're warm against my throbbing skin—which is the only part of my body in any semblance of comfort. My skull is a fragile shell that barely contains my thoughts. They threaten to spill out at any moment, like so much blood already has.

Breathe, Ellen. Breathe…

"Look at me."

All I can do is tilt my head in the general direction of his voice. As if to betray me, my vision slowly returns, and his features come into stark focus before I'm ready. Cold gaze. Harsh expression. He's cleaned the blood from his hands and changed his clothes, at least. His hair hangs freely down his shoulders, contrasting with his hooded, empty eyes.

"You have five hundred and fifteen thousand dollars in real bills," I croak out before he can issue another command. "One hundred bills were fake—ten thousand dollars altogether."

He scowls at the deceit, but his anger lacks the fire it should. He already knew. Maybe he counted the money after I did, using my own tricks for his benefit? Whatever the reason, testing my skills isn't his reason for waking me.

"Get up," he says, proving my instinct correct. "You're coming with me."

My heart hammers a pathetic resistance. *No. No. No.* I'm too tired. I can't do this again. I can't be sold, but I can't fight him, either. My eyelids fall, trapping tears stinging beneath them. "Just kill me."

"When I'm good and ready." Again, his voice lacks any real emotion. Something's tempered his anger, allowing him to hone it, at least for now. "You will come with me. Get up."

My head pulses in torment as I haul myself upright. The room is devoid of anyone else. Judging from the stiffness in my muscles, I've slept for a few hours, maybe longer. An entire day? The blackness beyond the window offers no clues. I have to decipher what I can from the man staring down at me. His knuckles have bruised and my cheek smarts in sympathy. So it *has* been hours, at least. Was Vanya the reason for my long reprieve?

I don't find him lurking in the doorway, and disappointment joins the flood of emotions racking my body. So much for his promise.

"Hurry up," Mischa snaps, already near the door.

I bite back the agony moving inspires in order to stand. The room spins around me, distorted by the fact that I only have the use of one eye. When Mischa heads into the hall, I do my best to follow him, but my body sways unsteadily. Before I can regain my balance, both legs twist beneath my weight, and the floor rushes to meet me.

Only a grip on my shoulder keeps me from crumbling into an unceremonious heap. *Mischa.* Without a word, he pulls me after him, navigating the cramped floorplan.

It's either my imagination or fact, but he moves at a pace I can manage. When I falter, he uses his grip on me to keep me on balance. There's no cruelty in his touch for once. Just strength and a foreboding feeling I can't escape. We don't run into Vanya on our way to a wooden door that opens onto a decrepit porch. Near the steps leading to the ground level, a van is parked. Mischa steers me to it without explanation and climbs into the back seat after me.

This time, our driver is joined by another man who's quietly sporting a gun on his lap. The moment the door closes after us, the van lurches into motion, heading down a gravel road.

I'm not dumb enough to look back at the house we left behind, so I stare at my hands instead, noticing more signs of simple kindness. Someone cleaned the blood from my fingers. They bandaged my foot as well and treated the other open wounds on my neck. It's a show of mercy I'm not used to. Poor Vanya holds enough humanity for two households, and the thought is sadder than anything I've experienced up until this point.

If only he could share part of his soul with the man beside me.

As if sensing the direction my thoughts have taken, Mischa places one of his hands over his right hip, near his blade. A lethal reminder.

"You disobey me here, Little One," he begins harshly, "And—"

"You'll kill me," I finish for him. I don't know where the defiance comes from.

"So, your husband taught you to count his money," Mischa says carefully. When I gather the nerve to look, his expression is unreadable. "Why?"

I consider lying, but the answer spills over my tongue before I can craft a good one. "He said I was the only calculator he could trust." Parroting those words out loud sends a chill down my spine. It feels wrong. Like I've betrayed some secret hidden in Robert's madness. It feels…strange.

"Calculator? Did he have you do this for him often?"

I should lie. "No. Yes." Once again, the truth spills out against my will. My tongue burns, as if every word is poison being expelled from my system. Will I survive without an antidote? Who knows. "He kept an accountant, but—" *Enough.* I bring my hand to my mouth, pressing my lips closed.

Beside me, Mischa stays eerily patient. He waits long enough for me to hope that he'll let it go. "But?"

I don't recognize the sound that trickles from my throat. A groan? A laugh? Whatever it is sounds too distorted to recognize. "*But* you cannot fuck your accountants into submission, can you?"

In my right mind, I'd never say something so vulgar. So cold. In my right mind…

"How many 'numbers' did you keep for him?" Mischa asks. "Do you remember them?"

"N-no." The lie sticks this time, though not for Robert's benefit. "He only ever had me double-check his real accountant."

Does he believe that? I can't tell. Even in the close confines of the back seat, he takes care to avoid any contact between us. If I couldn't see him from my peripheral vision, he could have been light-years away. A distant shadow clawing its way through my past in search of something to feed on.

This time, he lets me huddle in silence for a few minutes longer, and I use the reprieve to gather my scattered senses and lock them up tight. It's the pain that makes me so reckless. My thoughts are harder to string together. My fear of Robert takes more energy to grasp. I need to stay silent. Silent…

But silence here sounds different than it did at Winthorp Manor. There's no fragile peace to be found. Just my racing heartbeat to count the seconds, and the sound of Mischa's knuckles cracking in a menacing fashion.

Then…

"Why do you hate him so much? R-Robert?"

At the sound of my voice, remnants of anger flare, igniting whatever calm he's maintained until now. *Poof!* There's no more eerie patience. "I suggest you focus on yourself, Ellen Winthorp."

I obey, facing straight ahead once again. I'm painfully aware of the fact that he hasn't covered my eyes yet, though I can't make out much of our surroundings beyond the van. Just flickering shadows, broken every now and again by an impenetrable sky.

I'm more than willing to play by his rules: *Shut up.* My teeth clench tight against disobedience.

But he ruins his own game. "You haven't asked to go back to him."

No. I don't like this line of questioning. It's far too dangerous. I turn to the window, but his palm finds my chin, reinforcing the fact that, at any second, he can make me look at him.

"You haven't pleaded," he adds softly. "When that man saw you in the woods, you didn't run. You didn't cry out. I *know* you saw him—"

"I'm of more use to Robert alive than dead," I say.

But that's not it. Once again, he's peered beneath my skin without permission, seeking what lurks below the surface. Secrets I can't name. Horrors I won't face—not again.

"You shouldn't worry about being useful to *him*..." He brings his mouth near my ear. "Most wives are willing to *barter* for their husbands."

Barter? I lick my lips tentatively. "W-what do you want?"

He lets me go and pretends to mull it over. But there's a reason why he brought me along to wherever he's going. One I'm not sure I want to discover in full.

"What I want is simple." He snatches my wrist and presses something against my palm: a stack of bills. "Count."

He doesn't mean by amount. Slowly, I flip through each bill, feeling the paper for imperfections. "They're all real," I deduce once finished.

For whatever reason, he doesn't take the money back just yet. Instead, the trip comes to a sudden stop in darkness. Near darkness, anyway. Faint light betrays the shapes of other vehicles parked nearby. A garage? Distracted by him, I missed any sign of civilization.

Or any hope of escape.

"Come on." Mischa shoulders the door on his end open, while his men wait in the vehicle. Jerking his chin, he indicates for me to follow, but not them.

I shiver as my bare feet hit the icy pavement. We're underground, definitely in some kind of garage. Up ahead, an elevator waits, opening its doors as if on cue the moment we approach. Mischa enters first, pulling me in after him. I sense that unnerving calm once again. He's determined.

To sell me?

I find myself staring down at my fist, desperate for a distraction. I'm still holding his money. At least a grand, maybe more. Is this my going price? My stomach clenches at the thought. Robert always claimed that I was worth diamonds, but what would he give to have me back now? Morbid imagery pops into my head: diamonds drenched in blood.

"Stay close." It's the only warning my captor bothers to issue before the elevator doors part, revealing a long hallway decorated with burgundy wallpaper and rich ebony carpet.

Faint music drifts from a pair of closed doors up ahead, where a man in black is waiting, his expression stoic. When we approach him, the man steps aside.

"*Pakhan*," he greets.

As the doors open, I'm suddenly self-conscious of how I must look: like a prisoner of war being paraded after her captor. I run my free hand halfheartedly through my hair, but it's no use. Blood and bruises can only be obscured by so much.

The room beyond contains at least five people, spread throughout a grand layout that resembles a casino. A luxury bar dominates one wall, while a poker table seats three of the five men. They are wearing suits and sharing a cigar between them. The atmosphere is light and friendly, while the remaining men linger on the periphery, their arms crossed, their eyes straight ahead.

One of the figures at the poker table spots us and rises to his feet. "Mischa! Welcome! Welcome!" He's tall. Maybe forty, with a thinning goatee and piercing, green eyes. Unlike Xavier's imitation, his suit is real and tailored to perfection. As we approach, he reaches out to Mischa and then firmly clasps his hand. "How kind of you to enter my humble abode. It's just a spare room, for me and the boys." He gestures to the two men beside him, and they aren't mirroring his charming grin. They're on edge.

"Nicolai," Mischa says, drawing his hand away. He's wary as well. Tension hardens his posture, disrupting the otherwise calm surface he projects.

"Well…" Nicolai smiles in a chilling display of ivory teeth. "I know you're a busy man, so best to get business out of the way," he says. "Now, tell me again how you cheated me out of *my* money?"

The words have the effect of striking a match near a pool of gasoline.

Whoosh!

"It wasn't intentional." Mischa stiffens and jerks his chin toward me. "My previous accountant made an error. But I have the full amount."

He snatches the wad of bills from me and places them down on the poker table.

Nicolai snaps his fingers and one of the seated men quickly counts the money. "It's all here," the man declares once finished.

"Excellent." As Nicolai claps his hands, his smile returns, but it never reaches his eyes. Chilling and endless, they hone in on me. "And who is this?"

"A new toy of Ivan's," Mischa explains. A lie. But why?

"I see…" Nicolai nods, rubbing his chin. "He always did have a soft spot for his women."

"Her old owner was an accountant," Mischa says, continuing his distortion of the truth. "He taught her to count. She's the one who noticed Xavier's *mistakes*."

"Hmph." Nicolai chuckles in amusement. "I assume he's been shown the error of his ways?"

"Permanently," Mischa declares so viciously that I shiver.

"Excellent." Nicolai clasps his hands together once again. "Now that that nasty business is taken care of, I suppose all that's left is for you to carry out that favor you owe me. For the inconvenience."

A slight narrowing of his eyes is the only clue to Mischa's confusion. "Favor?"

"After all, I've always supplied your family and organization with unwavering loyalty and support," Nicolai continues, still smiling. "You fuck with my money, even by *accident*, and you fuck with a domino chain that extends well beyond the *Mafiya*. My other clients don't like scandal, you see." He shrugs dismissively as if to say, *Can't be helped.* "As retribution for such an error, I will humbly accept whatever help you see fit to bestow, *Pakhan*."

"Of course." A muscle in Mischa's neck twitches, but his voice never loses that low, cautious cadence. "What do you need?"

"Nothing big." Nicolai snaps his fingers a second time and a door near the back of the room opens.

Two people enter, and it's almost like watching a mirror image. A small, ragged figure trails a man nearly twice her size. Her shoulder-length hair makes her childish features seem even larger—enormous brown eyes and a little nose. She's young. Too young. When they reach the poker table, her companion sets a gray duffle in the center and unzips it.

"The finest cocaine," Nicolai declares almost lovingly while eyeing the small, round packets the bag contains. Each one is no larger than a golf ball, rubbery in appearance. "Several uncut grams," he adds, "all ready to be consumed by one of the wealthiest men in the world. This client tends to be tricky to supply, however. He likes it brought to him directly, and let's just say he travels within a…select posse.

Tonight, they're at a hotel in the city. I believe you're familiar with the location?"

Mischa nods.

"Excellent. All I need you to do is escort my friend here to the rendezvous. There are clothes for both of you in the bag. Get her through security and leave the cocaine where my client can retrieve it discreetly. Then our debt shall be settled. Oh, and"—Nicolai lifts a packet for inspection—"my new chemist doesn't know his head from his ass. These packets will last only about an hour, tops, in the body, and that's roughly how long it will take to reach my client. So speed will be of the essence. Though, if the girl survives, you can have her." He reaches out, running his fingers through her blond hair. "I'm sure you can find some *use* for her in one of those clubs of yours."

"Where am I meeting this client?" Mischa demands, swatting the suggestion aside.

Nicolai rattles off what sounds like a random number. "Make sure she swallows the cocaine before you arrive. I'm sure there will be a blockade of some sort, searching vehicles. And, if by some bad turn of luck, you *do* get caught…"

"We were never here," Mischa says. Turning to the girl, he snatches up the duffle. "Come on."

In utter silence, she follows us back to the elevator and into the garage, where the van is still idling, ready to pull away the moment we climb into the back seat.

As the door slams shut, Mischa forms a fist and punches the window. "Damn it!"

Sandwiched between us, the girl doesn't react to the outburst, but I flinch. I can't take my eyes off the duffle. I can't stop hearing Nicolai's words echo in my head. *If the girl survives, you can keep her.*

Even the Winthorps weren't so callous when it came to human life. They killed their toys quickly, and when they were no longer of any use.

And, despite his own brand of cruelty, something tells me that even Mischa is balking at the logistics of this plan. Smuggling drugs in the body of a child so that some rich bastard can get his fix. I *almost* believe it.

Until I see his face. He's lost that fragile calm again. In its absence, darkness consumes all that's left. Poor Vanya was wrong: There's nothing human about this creature. Without a word of explanation, he unzips the duffle and rummages through it for a bottle of water, which he shoves aside. Then a packet he hands to the girl. "Put this in your—"

"No." My hand flies out before I can stop it, gripping his forearm. *No!* Some frantic voice at the back of my mind sounds a meaningless warning. But it's too faint to hear clearly. *Don't do this, Ellen…*

As if used to a routine, the girl obediently grabs the water bottle and tips it toward her mouth, but I snatch it away before she can even down a drop.

"Don't." Reaching across her, Mischa snatches my wrist. "Stay the fuck out of this."

My sore body throbs at the warning in his tone. Disobeying him is futile. I know that, but I hold my free hand out anyway.

"Give it to me," I demand, nodding toward the packet.

Words can't describe how rage distorts his features. His fingers clench, but if he hits me in such a narrow space, the girl will be caught in the middle.

Lunging toward him, I snatch a packet from the bag and shove it into my mouth. Only sheer force of will can override the instinct to spit it right back out. *Swallow, swallow!* My gag reflex triggers. Even the water doesn't help. I have to *shove* the packet down with shaking fingers, igniting my already tender throat in the process.

"Fuck!" A heavy hand swipes at my mouth in vain.

"It's too late," I somehow manage to croak as my throat struggles to down the foreign object. "I already swallowed it. Now, give me the rest before…"

Before time runs out.

I barely fit the dress meant for the girl—it's too damn big. Made of white cotton, its modest neckline is more conservative than anything else I've worn over the past few days. But that's about the only improvement.

The tailored suit Nicolai provided fits Mischa perfectly, however. *Unfairly.* With his hair slicked away from his face, he could almost pass for another person. Some rich, cold businessman with enough money to hide whatever secrets his scars might reveal.

In the right lighting, he could even pass for a Winthorp.

The only flaw in his ruse is that he drives himself rather than commands a chauffeur, as Robert would. After we changed, he left the girl with his two companions a few streets away from the rendezvous point. They were to call someone from the safe house and then Mischa would return later. If…

Well, I suppose that depends on how quickly my body digests the thin layer of material encasing the cocaine. An hour, Nicolai said.

Twenty minutes have passed already.

"You fucking idiot." They're the only three words Mischa has said to me since pulling off. "Do you have any idea what the hell you've done? I should kill you. I'll fucking make you suffer—"

"Like that girl would have suffered?" *Oh, God.* The vitriolic response spilled out of me before I could choke it down. Though I doubt there's any room left in my stomach for more suppression. More lies. More fear. So, for once, I forget my mantra. I don't breathe. I yell. "She's a child!"

"Is that so?" He laughs darkly while manipulating the steering wheel, cutting off an oncoming vehicle, the driver of which honks his displeasure. "You don't know a fucking thing about that *child*. You think she hasn't done it before?"

Because she has. Scars haunted her eyes, deeper and more violent than anything found on my skin. Scars like the ones haunting the boy who intruded into Briar's room all those years ago. Though their circumstances may be different, they both had no choice in the matter.

"So that makes it right?" I question. "Even Robert wouldn't—"

"Don't." With one hand, he grips the back of my neck in warning. "You don't know a fucking thing about what your Winthorp is capable of."

"He never cut my face," I counter, glaring through blurred vision. I couldn't hold my tears back if I tried. So I don't. I let them fall. "*He* never put me in a cage, and he's done… terrible, terrible things. But even he would *never*—"

"You think you know me enough to compare me to him?"

The vehicle slows to a stop. We're on a narrow street where lights flicker nearby. Flashlights? At first, I think he's stopped to threaten me, wasting precious time. But then a beam of light shines directly through the windshield.

"Shit."

Mischa lets me go, and I hunch over, hiding my face. It's the one little detail I didn't consider before sacrificing myself. The girl was clean and whole enough to play a role in Nicolai's charade without catching notice. Even Mischa excels at playing pretend. As an officer approaches his side of the car, he sits taller and lowers his window, resembling the guest of some important gala. Only I can see the gun tucked beneath his seat.

"Good evening," he greets while I observe his every move through the curtain of my hair.

"Where are you headed?" The unfamiliar voice belongs to the officer.

"We just came back from the opera," Mischa says, nodding toward me. "She fell asleep halfway and demanded we return to the hotel."

He chuckles warmly while the officer peers in my direction. "Oh? Can I see your ID and registration please?"

Mischa hands the documents over and precious seconds pass while the officer scrutinizes each one. Finally... He steps back and beckons us forward with a wave of his hand. "Move along."

As the officer passes by, Mischa visibly deflates. He's more cautious than nervous. Like he accused of the girl, he's done this before. Just how many times? With *how* many women, their bellies stuffed with drugs? I'm almost tempted to ask him, but then I notice the time on the dashboard.

There isn't much left.

To compound matters, Nicolai vastly understated the "exclusive company" his client must keep. Police cars are lurking near the front of the hotel when we draw closer, their lights turned off as officers scour those entering and leaving the elegant building.

"Shit." Rather than circle for the valet, Mischa takes a shortcut toward the employee entrance. He knows the way, parking in an empty, secluded space beside a dumpster.

I exit the van after him and realize, even before I see his jaw clench in frustration, that there's no way in hell we can go through the main security. Parking alone cost us three minutes.

There're barely twenty left.

"This way. Keep your head down." He takes my wrist and drags me across the parking lot and then through an emergency exit that opens into a laundry room of some kind. By some oversight, there's no security here—yet, anyway—and Mischa moves swiftly, navigating a maze of rooms and industrial-sized machinery.

Twenty minutes.

Nineteen.

I stop counting.

Past the laundry room, we take a service elevator that brings us to the main lobby of the hotel, but rather than head out in the open, Mischa shoves me into a stairwell. We climb two flights in seconds. Then five more. Ten. Twenty. Thirty.

I'm panting, dripping sweat, by the time he finally stops at a floor. My stomach hurts. *Don't think about it,* I try to tell myself. But running aids digestion, doesn't it?

How many minutes? I can't remember...

"In here."

We reach a hallway of closed doors, but he passes them all, heading right to one at the end. A potted plant rests beside the door. Crouching, Mischa rakes his fingers through the dirt and withdraws a keycard from the base of the plant before I can question. On the first swipe, the reader flashes red. No good. On the second attempt...

Green!

The door opens to a spacious suite. It's impressive, decorated in black leather and white accents, but I only have eyes for the bathroom. I race to the sink. Bent over it, I open my mouth and try to gag. Nothing. I cram a finger down my throat, but it's not enough.

"Move!" He shoves my hands aside, and three thick fingers trigger my gag reflex, causing my stomach to erupt in protest.

One bag comes up, still intact. Another. Another…

"That's ten," Mischa grunts after what feels like an eternity. "Five more."

His fingers continue to assault my esophagus, but minutes tick by without another packet. Too long.

"Shit."

He shoves me toward the tub. Before I can get my bearings, his hands form fists over my stomach, and with a grunt, he thrusts them both. Hard. One packet comes up. Another.

"Keep going! One more."

"I can't…" Horror steals the words from my throat. It's too late. The last packet's already dissolved. I know it has. Any second, I'll go into shock. Die. *Stupid, Ellen. Stupid—*

"Don't think about anything else," Mischa snarls, gripping me tight. "Just fucking *breathe.* Do it!"

Harsh fingers ram into my stomach. Again. Again.

"Ugh!" I double over and bring up the last packet, shaking with exertion.

He drops me there, slumped over the tub. I'm only conscious enough to hear him run some water, cleaning the acid from the packets before tucking them away. I can't move. I can't think.

I just breathe, fighting for air as the bathroom fades. I'm a child again, back in Winthorp Manor.

Something was wrong.

From the hallway, I heard footsteps. My mother's? But no. These were too heavy, and the figure appearing in my doorway was far too large. His blond hair peeked from the edge of a black woolen cap. The color that made my heart stop. He was wearing it from head to toe: black slacks and a dark sweatshirt meant to disguise him in the shadows.

The second he met my gaze, I knew. He was dangerous, just like the men my mother warned me to avoid. Something silver glinted in his hand. A blade.

He pointed it at me, his jaw clenched. But his hand wavered. His eyes were too wide. Fearful?

Suddenly, he pointed to the bed.

"Get under it," he warned. "Don't think. Don't move. You just fucking breathe."

Trembling and terrified, I had no choice but to obey, crawling on my stomach beneath Briar's silk sheets. I'd only just tucked my legs beneath the frame when I heard the soft thud of another stranger's approach—someone who sounded way too big to be a regular maid.

"Is she in here?" another man demanded, his voice thick. Guttural. He talked as strangely as the boy did, betraying a heavy accent. "Well, is she?"

"I don't know," the younger man replied as I inhaled raggedly, obeying his command. Breathe. Breathe. Breathe! *"But we should leave. Now. Before they return."*

They? Robert and his father. There was a gala that night. That's why Robert was wearing a suit earlier that day. It was his first time attending the grown-up parties.

"Leave?" the older man hissed. My stomach churned as thuds resonated through the floor: footsteps inching farther into the room. "You don't make the shots, boy. Check. She has to be here."

"I've looked." Lighter footfalls drift toward the opposite end of the room. "She's not here. We should be looking for Anna—"

"We are," the older man insisted, his tone harsh. "But I will not let this insult stand. I don't care if she's just a child. The little whelp will pay for her father's sins—"

"Did you hear that?" the younger boy interjected. "Someone's coming. We need to move!"

Silently, they crept back into the hall, but I couldn't move. Not even when my bladder protested and warm liquid dripped down my legs. Not even when a soft, small hand slipped beneath the mattress runner and brushed my wrist.

"Ellen?" Briar's face appeared through the darkness next, inches from mine. "Are you okay?" she asked, her eyes wide.

Only later would I learn that she heard the boy coming way before I had. Thinking quickly, she'd hidden in the closet.

Leaving me behind…

"Drink." Something cool brushes my cheek. "Drink!"

I blink as the rim of a water bottle presses against my mouth, but I shake my head. I doubt I'll be able to swallow ever again.

"No." For whatever reason, Mischa won't let me turn away. He grips my chin and grinds the rim of the bottle against my teeth. "Fucking *drink*."

I cringe with the first sip, surprised when it goes down with less pain than expected. Before I know it, I've drained the entire bottle.

And all that's left to do is face the wrath awaiting me.

"It was you," I croak, watching Mischa scowl at the confession from the corner of my eye. His gaze darts toward the sink as if counting the packets to ensure I really did expel them all.

But I'm not delirious. For the first time in so long, I see everything clearly.

"You were the boy," I add. "In Winthorp Manor. I saw you. You thought I was Briar."

Yet he saved *me*.

His eyes widen and narrow in quick succession. Remembering? Or suppressing. Gritting his teeth, he shakes his head, dismissing the accusation. "You dumb bitch," he hisses, tightening his grip on my shoulder. "I should kill you—"

"Better me than a child," I whisper. Vanya was right. Mischa wasn't always this way—but that knowledge only makes his fall all the more tragic. "I'd rather die than let you use her."

"Oh?" he laughs. "You stupid bitch. I wouldn't have made her *swallow* it."

Too breathless to speak, I stiffen at the confession, my eyes wide. There's a grim honesty to his words. Even I can't deny it.

"I know this fucking hotel," he adds. "All she had to do was hide them in the dress—"

"You'd still…use…a child as a pawn." It hurts to speak. My voice grates over the air, pathetic and broken.

He hears me regardless. Radiating hatred, his body cages mine from behind, trapping me against the tub and tile flooring. There's nowhere to run—not that I have the energy. I just press my bruised cheek against the rim and wait.

If silence alone were as far as his cruelty went, I could survive it. But no. His touch creeps along my injured cheek, aggravating the sore flesh.

I have no choice but to beg. "If you're going to kill me, just kill me."

"Kill you?" He growls out a terrifying imitation of a laugh against my shoulder. "I should. It would be fucking easier than keeping you alive."

He's still touching me. Rough fingers swipe at my cheek—to test the bandage, I realize. Next, he grabs my ankle to ensure the one on my foot is intact. There's a rehearsed familiarity to the motions. Almost as if…

"You cleaned me." My voice echoes off the basin of the tub, hollow with shock. "*You* bandaged me—"

"But maybe I *should* kill you," he counters, ignoring my accusation. All at once, his hands fall away. "Is that what your fucking Winthorp would do? *You* compared me to the bastard, so tell me how this ends. With you dead?"

I shake my head without bothering to reply out loud. Robert would never kill me. That would require that he give me something I actually want.

An escape.

"Then what?" Mischa wonders coldly. His fingers return to rake through my hair, softer than before. Alarm bells go off in my mind. Once again, he proves to be unpredictable. Wild. Dangerous. "You compared *me* to *him*," he reminds me, hissing into my ear. "So fucking tell me what I'm supposed to do next."

I tremble at the implications of such a question. What would Robert do? He'd play a game, of course. One of his favorites.

"He'd kiss me," I hear myself croak, naming the first stage of any twisted session. "He'd touch me. Make me beg…"

"Beg him for what?" His voice is too raw, scorching my tender skin. Anger on him is like wildfire; within the blink of an eye, it's too violent to be contained. "Don't feign you're mute now." He cups my sore throat from behind, sliding his fingers along my windpipe in a chilling caress, daring me to lie to him. "He'd make you beg him for what?"

The memories chase me. Haunt me.

"To stop…"

"He'd hurt you?"

My nerves cringe at the genuine curiosity in his tone as he hooks a hand beneath my waist and flips me onto my back with my head propped against the rim of the tub.

But I don't scream.

He's too heavy. His eyes are empty, the gaze of a monster. But his mouth…

Crushed to mine with no warning, there's no comparison. Robert bites, and licks, and takes. But Mischa just claims. His lips are too soft. Not possessive and unfeeling—but *fire*. There's no teasing buildup. No savoring of my fear. He slides his tongue between my lips and just steals what he wants. With hard, searing thrusts. With heat. With more fire.

He destroys every instinct before I can remember what emotions to salvage. In the resulting chaos, all I can do is feel. Everything.

"He touched you?" Mischa growls against my parted lips, remembering the second stage.

"Y-yes..."

With deft motions, he unhooks the back of my dress. His fingers still against my spine as if waiting for me to react. Scream. Run. When I don't, his fingers drift lower and my body quakes at the feel of his warm flesh molded over solid muscle.

"And then," he snarls into my open mouth. "What?"

I beg. Always. Without fail. Robert never heeds my pleas, but they come anyway. It's our tradition. My torment. His game.

My lips flutter, ready to play, but Misha takes his role of my husband too seriously. His hand descends between us, unzipping his pants to an erection straining against his boxers. His fingers capture mine, forcing me beneath the waistband to feel him for myself. Hot. Silken. Steel.

"Go on," he goads, bucking into my fist, testing my grip. "Beg."

Stop. He's bigger than Robert. He'll hurt me more than my husband ever could. I know it. I feel it. I...

Breathe, Ellen. Breathe. Breathe. Breathe!

"Come on." Frowning, Mischa meets my gaze directly, still throbbing against my fingers. "Play your part, Little One," he commands. "Beg me to stop."

My lips flutter, but when I say nothing, he laughs, throwing his head back.

"You can't take me. Admit it. I am nothing like him. I'll fucking *break* you."

It's a promise. One that adds a new level of danger I've never felt before to the game. No one has ever taken *anything* from Robert Winthorp.

Nothing.

I'm so sure of that that I can't stop myself from croaking, "Will you?"

I almost sound amused. Intrigued?

At the prospect, my captor growls in irritation, freeing himself from his boxers. To prove that he can. That he will. And as I stare down at what rises beneath a thatch of blond curls, a word comes to mind. Something terrifying. A term I'd never apply, even to Robert.

Beautiful?

Dusky flesh and glistening ridges form a cock as repulsive as it is impressive. He could break me.

And maybe there will be nothing left...

"Beg." He hammers the word into my skin with his teeth, nipping the flesh of my throat. He's too close. Flexing his hips brings him between my legs. Heavy. Dominating.

A moan dies behind my teeth as the slick crown of his cock bats against my entrance. Beg? But how? I can't get any air to go into my lungs.

Robert would take his time at this point in the game, stretching me with his fingers, telling me all the while that I want him. *We were made for each other, Elle,* he'd croon.

There is no such teasing with Mischa.

"Fine, Little One," he snarls, bracing his hand against my thigh. "I'll show you just how much like him I can be." One flex of his hips and he slams into me with a groan. A curse. A million fucking words hissed in English and whatever language he natively speaks.

I see black. Then white porcelain as my head falls back and a scream claws its way from my throat. He's too fucking big. I'm too tight. We just *don't* fit, and that natural deterrent demands one solution: He has to force his way into me. Thrust after thrust. Over. Over. Again.

I feel him in my skull, like a battering ram, fucking my body and not just the space between my legs. All of me.

"Say it," he grits out between clenched teeth. "Fucking...say it. I'll stop—"

An answering moan trickles from my lips. I can't contain it. Begging, finally?

But no. My ears catch my own voice whispering something far more dangerous. "M-more." I tremble, every nerve in an uproar.

This isn't part of the script. This isn't right. This isn't…Robert.

He's not Robert.

That fact is only solidified by how roughly he thrusts into me—not patient and unhurried. He's *frenzied.* Splitting me open. Ripping me apart.

Like he doesn't *need* to save me for another round. I'm not his toy to keep unbroken.

"What…what the fuck did you say?" he demands. But his body contradicts the anger in his voice. Even now, he's throbbing and thickening. So deep. Not deep enough. "Stop." Gritting his teeth, he starts to withdraw, hissing into my ear, "Tell me to stop." It's not a command as much as it is a plea.

But there are no rules anymore. My body has a mind of its own, taking control of my throat to voice it as my knees draw up around him. "M-more—"

"Fuck," he hisses in confusion, gripping my hips.

Before I can even register his absence, he's back. Deeper. Harder. Faster. Our lips fuse, grappling for leverage, and I finally feel the fear I should. It's hotter than fire. Than hate. Burning. Scorching. Desolating.

"Beg," he pleads, still on a vicious race toward his own release.

But my lips seal shut as a grim realization sinks in: *I won't beg…*

I don't want to.

It's like that single thought is the trigger to surrender. My body tightens, rippling around him, collapsing in on itself. He snarls at the reaction, still thrusting. Harder. Faster.

He fucks his rage into me without mercy. Everything. I feel him shuddering with release and sullying the shell of Robert Winthorp's "whore." Deflated, he slumps against me, knocking the air from my chest.

And I lie here, letting him crush me.

I hover on the edge of consciousness for what feels like an eternity. Any minute, I'm sure someone will kick, shake, or threaten me awake—but that moment never comes.

I'm left alone to suffer, and in the end, hunger is what finally rouses me. My stomach aches. So does my head. Between my legs… *No.* I ignore that pain and focus only on what I can fix now. *Food.*

Gradually, my eyes open to an unfamiliar ceiling and unease returns. I don't recognize the bed I'm lying on; it's too soft to be the one in the safe house. The sheets twisted around me feel clean, but the comfort they impart doesn't do much to negate the terrifying reality that someone stripped me naked. That *everything* hurts. The insides of my legs feel sticky…used.

Don't think about that, Ellen.

Groaning, I roll onto my side, trying to find a semblance of familiarity in the darkness. I track the twisting shadows and vague furniture-like shapes without recognizing much. There's too much space. I cradle my forehead against my palm and try to remember. *Hotel room.* Mischa must have kept me here. *Left* me here? I don't sense him nearby.

When I finally crawl from the bed, drawing a white sheet around me, he doesn't lunge from the corner and command me to stay. In fact, there doesn't appear to be anyone else in the suite but me. Beyond the bedroom is a small sitting area and then the bathroom. Someone left the light on in the latter area. The floor looks wet, scrubbed down. A chemical odor itches my nostrils.

Rather than inspect further, I aim for the mini fridge in the corner, tucked into a tiny alcove. Whoever bought this room must have paid for the complimentary mini bar in advance. It's already been stocked, and I grab a pack of crackers and a soda. The pain in my throat is enough to temper my hunger, however. I can only choke a few crumbs down at a time, and even hearing the soda hiss as I pop the top makes me set it aside. Instead, I hunch over the tiny sink above the bar and swap intervals of chewing with measured sips of water from the tap.

That's how he finds me: with my mouth upturned beneath the faucet and the last wet crumbs of cracker clinging to my fingers. I hear his approach rather than see it. His footsteps resonate in slow, steady waves. One step. Another. Pause. Another. Then something lands at my feet, startling me into spraying water down my front.

"Get dressed." Mischa's calm is a distant memory. *Now,* his voice is unsteady. His breathing… Only the thinnest thread of control seems to hold him together.

I sense it wavering the longer I stay hunched over the sink. Slowly, I shut the water off and gather enough nerve to face him.

It's a bad idea. His silhouette flung against the wall is more than enough for me to realize my stupidity for challenging him in the first place. His fingers flex at his sides. Opening and closing. Finally, his shadow flickers and fades as his footsteps head toward the bedroom.

When I crane my neck to look down, I find a pile of fabric at my feet. Clothing. The small white shirt and jeans are all he brought, but I gratefully accept them. Even in my hands, they feel better than a flimsy negligee.

From this position, I can't see the bedroom—or into it—as long as I don't turn around, so I muster what little bravery I have to creep into the bathroom and shut the door. My first action is to run the shower as hot as I can stand it. Then I climb in. *God.* It feels…

Like heaven. Like hell.

Blood and grime wash away from me to circle the drain, but the heat makes everything sting and throb at full force. Every bruise. Every cut. Every brutal "love bite" scraped into the flesh at the nape of my neck.

I feel them all no matter how much I scrub. Clean. Cleanse. Soap and water can't erase him. The soft wash rags the hotel supplies aren't anywhere near strong enough to peel back tainted flesh. Not like the ones at Winthorp Manor, anyway. Those long, hot showers could make me feel new again. Strong again. Afterward, I could always face Robert *again*.

But the longer I stay beneath the scalding spray, the more I'm sure of one chilling truth: I can't ever leave this room. I can't face Mischa. There won't be much left of me to clean if I do.

I think I hide for hours, searching for a state of mind I know I'll never find. My fingers feel bloated, the skin pruned to the point that I can't hold the cloth anymore. It lands at my feet, stuck to the bottom of the tub like something used that can only be scraped off. I'm not sure how long I can last when the door rattles on its hinges.

"Open."

This isn't fair. Even Robert let me escape him for at least a day or two at a time. He gave me that much.

Mischa has no mercy. No fucking soul. When I don't open the door myself, he slides it aside on his own. Dominating the doorway, he's a specter decipherable only in pieces snuck from behind the curtain of my wet hair.

He changed, swapping the suit for his usual fatigues. His hair hangs loose and wild around his shoulders and a sudden memory leaves me trembling: feeling that softness for myself as my fingers gripped his shoulders. Grabbing. Pulling. I stare down in horror at the hands in question, sticky with soap, forever unclean.

"Come," Mischa commands, his voice grated and low. "We need to move. Now."

His tone spurs me into action. I switch the water off and pull my new clothing on without bothering to towel off. He watches me, his gaze searing my bare shoulders while I drag the jeans up over my hips and shimmy into the shirt. They're both too big. I have to roll the pant legs up twice and tuck the shirt in to find some semblance of comfort. By the time I turn to the doorway, he's already entering the hallway.

I follow him and watch as he returns the keycard to the base of the potted plant. It's a quick, silent trip back out to the van, and we leave the hotel behind just as night falls.

Locked in the confines of the vehicle with him, I can't breathe. It's too close. Too quiet. Too dark. My face burns as I remember his cruelty...but my body remembers something different entirely. *Thick, heavy, hot, wet, raw.* Those adjectives trickle across my brain, explicit and vulgar. Robert was firm. Robert was familiar. He never made me say the wrong thing.

More.

My fingers fly up to my lips as if to capture whatever insane impulse made me utter that word. What did I want? More pain? More hate? *No.* The answer lingers in my mind, resisting all attempts to forget: hooded, terrifying eyes. A voice like thunder growled into my ear. More *him.* The living, breathing antidote to my husband. Someone more twisted, and broken, and fucked than Robert could ever be.

My only comfort is that any longer with Mischa and there won't be anything left of me for Robert to reclaim.

"Tell me something. You were more than just his wife." He hisses the words out and veers the van suddenly to the right. "Weren't you? Maybe you fucking planned it, huh? He let me take you? To get inside my fucking head. Is that it?" he demands.

"W-what?" I shake my head. God, the things he's saying. He sounds insane. "What are you talking about—"

"This!" He takes a hand off the wheel and jabs the fingers in my direction. "You're a whore. A snake. From the first fucking second I took you, I knew something was wrong. And now you say you remember me?" He laughs bitterly at the idea. "There's no way in hell he'd let you go. Not without a reason."

Fear renders me silent as the gauge on the dashboard slowly ticks up, up, up. The engine revs as if echoing the way its master speaks.

"Admit it," he snarls. "You aim to seduce me? You really think you can?"

Seduce? Shock overrides every survival instinct warning me to stay silent. "No—"

"No?"

The van comes to a violent stop, which flings me forward against the console. My ears ring. A door opens and slams. Footsteps crunch over gravel, circling over to my side. Cold air rushes in as my door is opened and I'm dragged out onto the side of the road.

"Tell me he sent you," Mischa demands, wrenching me around to face him. "Admit it."

I stumble for balance, forced to confront a terrifying reality. If Robert did plan anything, I'd have been the last to know.

"He didn't," I insist, more to myself than the man beside me. "I swear. He didn't."

Something ugly flashes in Mischa's gaze. He turns, dragging me along with him. *Wham!* Heavy hands slam me against the side of the van and pin me there without mercy. They tug at my jeans, wrenching them down. Then he shoves a fist between my legs, roughly spreading me open around the width of his thumb.

I groan, flinching in surprise.

He hisses. "Fuck. If this isn't a game, then why are you so fucking wet?"

Pressed against cold metal and glass, I say nothing.

Wet. That word means nothing to me. To him, it sounds like a curse, explaining how easily his fingers navigate my flesh without arousing the pain of Robert's groping.

He feels…different. Too raw. Too real. My legs spread without permission, allowing him more access as his snarled insult echoes in my mind. *Whore.*

"Jesus Christ, he *had* to send you," Mischa mutters, sounding crazed. His fingers curl against me, stroking the flesh still sore from his last assault. "But I won't fall for your fucking scheme. Be a good wife, now. Tell me to stop."

Stop. My lips flutter, struggling to form the words. "I…"

"Say it."

I sense him shift as a dangerous rasp echoes. His zipper? Yes. The second the hum trails off, his weight slams into me from behind. Then *he* slams into me, replacing his thumb.

My lips part around a single gasp. It's nearly impossible to describe the sensation of him—massive.

He's in too deep. Deeper than anyone has ever reached, scraping me hollow and shoving himself into crevices even Robert left untouched. My inner muscles clench, desperate to register the intrusion. In or out? Nerves ignite. Flesh tightens, clamping down, drawing him in. In. In. In.

All at once, my throat remembers how to make words. "Oh…*God*—"

"Fuck!" He throws his weight into me.

I see black. Can't feel. Can't breathe. Every sense turns inward, riveted by the sensation of his cock. Twitching inside me. Filling me. Breaking me.

Enraged, he roars. Thrusts. Brutalizes. "Tell me to fucking *stop.*"

"More…" It's not the word he wants to hear.

"No!" He grabs my throat from behind, grinding my face against the window, still thrusting. Grunts rip from him with each pass of his hips, each more unsteady than the last. Gritted. Grated. Gasping. "Tell me to stop."

My head is spinning. My body is on fire. Unbearable pressure gathers in my abdomen. Am I suffocating? *You're dying.*

"Fuck!" He bucks into me, twisting his fingers through my hair, grasping, pulling. He's afraid of something. I hear it in his voice. I feel it in how he trembles. His hand leaves my throat and plunges between my legs, pressing into the flesh that surrounds him as if he can stave off whatever I feel building there, gathering in intensity. "Don't you fucking dare."

Too late. The pressure builds and then spills over. It's like a dam breaking: unwelcome, consuming pleasure flooding every fucking pore, crashing through parts of me I kept safe from even Robert. Too much. Not enough. My head rears back against his shoulder as my eyes widen to a mocking view of the endless night sky. God, that's how he feels. *Endless.*

Pain rips through my shoulder: his teeth sinking deep, even as he spits words out against my skin. "You goddamn bitch."

He's furious, but I don't know why. *He's* not the one boneless and senseless, held up only by the weight of his body crushing me to the van. He's not the one with nerves so stimulated that it *hurts.* My nails scrape the window glass, desperate for leverage, but I find nothing. Just cold night air and the taste of a stranger's musk on my tongue.

Still thrusting, he commands me in a twisted language of curses and grunts. "Prove you're not his. Scream for *me*."

I do. Long and loud, without a damn given for who might hear me. I scream until the sound breaks off and air just wheezes from my lungs. Only now does he come, howling his release into my hair. Biting me. Digging in with his nails. The pain keeps me grounded. It makes it harder to ignore what's happening. Harder to forget. Harder to survive.

With one more jagged pass of his hips, he *kills* me. Ellen Winthorp is no more, and there's no one around to mourn her demise. Left behind is a hollow shell that falls to her knees in the dirt while her murderer looms above, wrestling his cock back into his pants.

Limp, I collapse against the cool earth, tears seeping from my eyes as my chest heaves. I'm sobbing in a way I haven't…ever. Not after my mother died. Not after Robert made me his. Not after a madman mistook me for the sister who betrayed me.

Nothing has shattered me like this: his seed seeping out of me and his scent on my skin. Curled into myself, I howl, and I cry, and I *bleed*.

"Get up." He nudges me with his foot when I don't move. "Get the fuck up!"

I don't. So he lifts me himself, hefting me by my shoulders with my legs dragging over the ground. He doesn't return me to my seat. Instead, he moves to the back of the van and opens the trunk. It's connected to the back seat, with a view from the rear windshield. Hiding or terrifying me isn't his goal by shoving me onto the ledge and slamming the lid over me.

This way, I'm out of his sight. Only my mewled, smothered cries give me away as he returns to the front seat and continues to drive.

The van comes to a sudden stop. It's too dark to get my bearings. I have no choice but to wait for the next phase of this ordeal in darkness.

My only coherent thought is to pull my pants up and refasten the zipper before the hood of the trunk raises and night air floods in. Blinking back moonlight, I can only make out a man's general shape looming above me, rigid and shrouded in shadow. Mischa.

He says nothing as I huddle beneath his scrutiny. Instead, he turns away, his footsteps heavy and grated over an uneven surface. Gravel, I see once I lift my head. It paves a makeshift driveway stretching toward a weathered, two-story farmhouse a few yards away. It isn't until I climb out of the van and approach the structure that I realize it's the safe house—and that Mischa never covered my eyes this time. Why? A part of me hesitantly ventures an answer.

Because he knows I won't be leaving. Alive, anyway.

Heavy with dread, I linger at the mouth of the doorway as my vision adjusts to the darkness. He's paces ahead of me, and when he disappears down the hallway, I choose to follow him, finding my way through feel. Disorientation isn't the only reason I cling to the wall for balance. I'm limping. Even Robert never left me so sore after one of his sessions. My legs shake, incapable of supporting my weight.

Breathe, Ellen.

Hushed voices drift from a nearby doorway, giving me some context as to where to go.

"I'm surprised he didn't demand that fucker's head on a platter," a man says. Vanya? "Either way, it was smart to appease him. You can't risk any more enemies. Not while we're out in the open like this."

"Even Nicolai wouldn't dare challenge me," a gruffer voice replies. "He knows who he owes his empire to."

All conversation ceases the moment I reach the doorway. As it turns out, Vanya was the owner of the first voice. I spot him crouched in a corner, cleaning the parts of his gun. One look at me and the color drains from his face while round pieces of metal clatter from his lap to the floor.

"What the hell?"

I should move. I try to, but my legs don't bend correctly. Before I hit the ground, someone grabs me, wrapping their arm around my waist. Vanya? No…

He's in front of me, gazing on with horror as I'm lowered to the ground. "Mischa… *Mal'chik,* what have you done?" The fear in his voice wasn't there before, not even when he warned me of what his leader was capable of. *He won't fuck you, but he will hit you.*

"I'm done lurking in the country like a fucking animal," Mischa says, continuing the thread of whatever conversation I interrupted. He sounds distant, as if he's walking away, leaving me on the floor. "Tomorrow, we come out of hiding. We're going home."

A door slams shut, rattling the floorboards, and I know without even having to look that he's gone. I can breathe again, noisily and labored.

"Fuck." Vanya crouches beside me, swiping my hair from my wounded cheek. Agony alights his gaze: a pain I've never witnessed on anyone before—I've only ever felt it. That horrible feeling that someone you love might have done the unthinkable. Betrayal. "Did he…did he hurt you?" he asks softly.

He's not referring to physically. Somehow, he's been able to rationalize that difference to himself. His Mischa may hit and abuse others, but violate them? That would cross a line even he can't fathom.

Slowly, I shake my head. It's the truth. Mischa hasn't hurt me. He's decimated me.

And you wanted him to…

Vanya clenches his jaw, biting back a question he can't voice. Instead, he rolls me onto my side and covers me with a jacket shrugged from his shoulders. "I'll bring you food," he tells me as I give in to exhaustion. "Get some sleep…"

For the second time in a row, I awake on my own. A hazy, dreamlike daze coats everything in a fog. As I blink up at a peeling ceiling, I almost don't remember. Where I am. What I've done.

I almost forget…

But then an undeniably masculine scent slams into me, ripping away the ignorance. I feel him, even before I see him towering above me.

"Get up."

I comply, maneuvering my sore limbs just enough to rise onto my knees. Vanya's jacket pools on the floor beside me, but I know better than to reach for it, even as my teeth chatter. I'm shocked to find a bottle of water and a sandwich on the floor as well, a few feet away. He kept his promise.

"Eat." Mischa jerks his chin toward the food.

I don't wait for a more explicit invitation. I cram the sandwich into my mouth and barely take a sip of water when he turns for the door.

"Come."

I stagger, an uncoordinated heap. After I nearly run into a wall, he snatches my arm and manually steers me into the hall and out of the house. Outside, a strip of orange accents an otherwise dark sky. Sunset.

Once again, I've slept for an entire day. During that time, Mischa and his men have been busy. There are four vans gathered out front. The men move freely between them, packing materials. In one, a familiar face watches mutely from behind the glass and my heart aches. Small. Round. The girl.

Mischa kept her alive—for now.

"Look at the ground," the man in question hisses.

I obey, allowing him to shove me toward one of the vans and inside it. I expect him to leave, but no. He climbs in after me, this time smothering any space that might separate us. His shoulder deliberately presses against mine, his thigh searing my hip.

As the door closes, his voice trickles down my spine, low and dangerous. "Did you think I'd let you stay near Vanya so that you could feed him more lies?" He rakes his fingers through my hair, unconcerned when they catch on tangles, making me wince. "What did you tell him?"

"N-nothing." I breathe the truth against the window nearest me. Beyond it lies a lonely landscape of naked trees swaying in the darkness. The moon shows full and round—like his thumb blazing a trail across my shoulder and down, igniting a path through the cotton of my shirt.

My chest tightens as the air thickens in my lungs. *Breathe, Ellen.* But I can't. He's in my head as much as he's beside me. Taunting. Teasing.

Destroying.

"Did you tell him that you threw yourself at me like a goddamn whore?" he snarls, his voice low for my benefit.

The driver doesn't react. Not even as his leader's hand creeps…

I stiffen as his thumb grazes the clasp of my jeans. A slow, ruthless tugging undoes my zipper, link by goddamn link. Without panties as a barrier, his nail grazes my curls, tugging so hard that I jerk in place.

"Did you tell him that I forced you? Huh?" Something in his voice tugs at my consciousness through the building heat. An emotion. What is it? "Or maybe you came clean to him? Perhaps *he's* the one encouraging you? I wouldn't put it past him. The old man thinks a woman might save me—" A hiss rips from my lips as he tightens his grip on my hair, forcing my attention back to him. "Is that it?"

I risk more pain to shake my head. "N-no—"

"Maybe you're right." There it is again. That subtle dip in his inflection. Guilt? Fear? Suddenly, the answer comes to me. *Shame.* He cares about what Vanya thinks of him. "Vanya isn't that selfish. He'd think you're too good for me. Too innocent. Damn, you have him fooled."

His thumb continues its deliberate descent, grazing me beneath the denim. I'm still sore from the night before. I haven't washed. Wet, tender skin is an easy target. When he shoves his hand down the front of my pants, my body turns against me; muscles and nerves take on a life of their own. My thighs jerk. Spread.

"Maybe this is all your doing? Your plan to stay alive?" Mischa demands. His fingers cup me fully even though his seed is still there, drying between my legs. Rather than cringe in disgust, his hand twitches at the realization, stroking… "Are you really that desperate?"

"Y-yes." The word comes unbidden as his fingers still. My hips jerk, seeking out his touch. I need it. Dark thoughts in my head battle for supremacy. But this…

As humiliating, and wrong, and terrible as it is. *This* keeps it all at bay like nothing else.

But I've angered him again. His thumb flicks against my needy flesh, nowhere near hard enough. Punishing me.

"Robert must like his whores cock-hungry," he hisses into my ear while his thumb laves a slow, cruel circle along my entrance.

Cock-hungry. My inner muscles clench at the word. The raspy, dangerous way that he says it. Cock. His cock. Inside me.

My eyes flutter shut at the thought. The air feels thicker. My teeth descend into my bottom lip without permission, maintaining what little pride I have left by locking away a moan.

"What the fuck are you?" Mischa asks, flexing his fingers, dipping them inside me. "Do you really think this changes anything?"

Of course I don't. Not even as my hands grip the seat on either side of me, my nails breaking off against the leather. That pressure begins to build again, sweltering in my stomach. Spreading. Tightening.

And then, just when I fear it might boil over...

He pulls his hand away.

Before I can regain my senses, something nudges my lower lip, ripe with the musky scent of me. It's like I know what he wants before he even grates out the vulgar request through clenched teeth.

"Suck it."

My tongue shoots out, tentatively brushing the rough pad of a finger. I taste myself. His sweat.

I swallow it down.

"Fuck." He shoves away from me.

I open my eyes and find him glaring toward the front of the van. My legs are still spread, my pants hanging open. Slowly, I draw my knees together, hissing at the pressure still mounting between them. My fingers shake as they redo my zipper, but the tight confines of the denim aggravate the reckless heat he already started.

Cock-hungry. Cock-hungry. That phrase circles the inside of my skull incessantly. I can't escape it. I can't escape *him*.

My only refuge is found when I close my eyes and focus on my shallow breathing. Only now do I dip into the one arsenal I have against Mischa. I think of Robert. His face. His mocking, lethal smile. His brown, soulless eyes.

I remember the words he told me nightly, smothered against my hair.

"You belong to me, Elle. You belong to me…"

CHAPTER 14

"Get up."

A car door slams in addition to the shout, snapping me awake. We're here. Wherever here is. A hotel? As I peel my eyes open, I make out a shape looming in the darkness. Tall. Grand. A house? It's nearly twice the size of Winthorp Manor, casting an impressive silhouette, even in the dark.

"I said get up," someone commands. Mischa.

I scramble in the direction of his voice, stepping out onto a paved courtyard. A grand array of stone steps lead to the front of the house. The lair of another criminal who deals in cocaine?

No… Mischa's posture is too relaxed for that, and his past words to Vanya spring to mind. *We're going home.*

There's an undeniable familiarity as he mounts the steps with me in his wake. Around us, the other vans park and the men disperse, carrying various materials in different directions on the property. I expect Mischa to shove me aside or direct me to Vanya.

But no.

I'm the sole possession he hauls with him to the front door of the mansion while his men clutch their guns and fall in beside us. I'm his *captive*, dragged across a grand entrance and up a winding staircase too quickly to even get my bearings or take in the finery.

His shoulders serve as my only scenery. Tense, solid muscle.

I'm not sure which direction he takes me in. I only know when he stops—at the mouth of a room with solid oak floors and a bed in the center.

It's his. I smell him on the air, faint, as if he hasn't been here in a while. The black sheets still contain some part of him, however. It's a far cry from the lumpy mattresses he's dominated before now.

"Take off your clothes." He issues the command while slamming the door behind us, twisting the lock.

It's a test. For some reason, he feels the need to try me in this arena. Like Robert, he's addicted to this violent game.

But Robert never broke the rules. Impatient, Mischa rushes me from behind and strips me himself.

There's no finesse in the way he yanks my jeans down my legs for the second time. There's no predatory care taken to heighten my fear with every touch. His erection pulses against the base of my spine. Thick. Heavy. Like a steel rod encased in denim.

"Get on the fucking bed." He shoves me forward.

I obey the command, mounting the mattress on my hands and knees. For a split second, I'm back with Robert, trapped inside his private suite while he runs his hand down my spine and watches me tremble.

"Beg," he'd prompt me, like always.

"Jesus Christ, you're perfect," Mischa growls, fury lacing every word. "*Too* perfect." He shoves his palm against my ass, making enough room for him to brace himself behind me. His fingers return between my legs, finding that same slickness from before. "Fucking hell." A sound rumbles from him I've never heard a human make. Deep. Throaty.

It rips through me, leaving me quaking in the aftermath.

"You…you're wet for me, Little One," he accuses in a tone that proclaims it's the worst possible offense I could have committed against him. "Say it."

My lips move of their own accord, breathing the words against the silken comforter in front of me. "I'm wet for you."

"Damn." He doesn't expect the candor, sucking in a breath. A grunt breaks loose when he exhales, his breath fanning the back of my neck. "Say it again."

My entire body shivers beneath the weight of such an insane command. I obey anyway. "I…I'm wet for you."

Hissing, he rears back, forcing his legs between mine so that I'm straddling him from behind. He hooks his knees against me and spreads his open, forcing mine to part even wider. I have to brace my hands against the mattress for balance while he slides his fingers beneath me, cupping my thigh.

"Then show me." His erection nuzzles that tender place between my thighs, impossibly hard.

Without thinking, I reach for it, blindly wrapping my hand around the base.

"Easy," he snaps, grasping my wrist and forcing my grip to loosen. "Slower," he explains. "Like this."

Numb to reality, I keep going. He hums low in his throat as I stroke him from end to tip and my mind reels. He feels terrifyingly big. How the hell did he ever fit inside me?

My grip falters as he grows slicker with sweat. I have to rely on him more to support my weight. My knees shake, threatening to pitch me over at any second. I'm too far gone to give a damn about anything but this. His teeth graze my throat without a shred of gentleness or mercy. Just naked, scorching lust. The slower my hand moves, the more his cock twitches impatiently, until finally he bucks out of my grip altogether.

"I see it now," he tells me. "Why he wants you back so fucking badly."

I whimper as his teeth seize a chunk of skin, grinding it between them. My eyelids flutter, my spine curling and driving my hips against him. Nothing describes how it feels when his crown grazes my entrance. Nothing.

I'm still gasping at the feeling when his hand finds mine, guiding me to the sliver of space between us. He forces my fingers to curl and places them along the ridge of his shaft. Then he arches his hips, wedging the tip of himself between my folds. "Put me inside you."

My eyes widen. Robert would never issue such an insane request. He'd never give me that kind of control. Over him. Over myself.

But it's not surrender Mischa offers as he allows me to steer him inside me inch by painful inch. It's possession in an entirely different way than domination. It's madness.

It's fucking unbearable.

I can't stifle my moan. It trickles out of me, high and tight as my head falls back against his shoulder. Once again, he sinks in easily. Too deep. Too real. Desperate, my nails scrape at his hips, hunting for stability. Just when I find a position that works, he lunges, shoving me onto my hands and knees.

The mattress trembles as he rears back and slips from my grasping channel. Before I can even catch my breath, he slides back in.

And then he fucks me.

I forget everything but how to breathe. I forget my own fucking name. The fact that he has no soul. His cruelty.

Each drive of his hips pushes a tiny bit of *my* soul out. Through my pores. My throat.

Robert made a boast once. *I'll fuck your brains out.*

He never came close.

Mischa drives my entire being out of my body, forcing himself into the empty spaces left behind. He's primal, inching our bodies closer to the headboard with every thrust. Closer. Close. My fingers are braced against the wood before I know it, and his hands tighten over my hips, pulling me into him with every brutal claiming.

I'm painfully aware of the fact that *he* is the one inside me. The one demolishing me. No one else. For once, my thoughts only contain a single name and it spills from my lips like a prayer. "Mischa—"

Blood rushes to my head as his fingers find my neck and squeeze. He shoves me down, pinning my face to the mattress. "Again," he grates out between pants. "Say…again."

I do and the final thrust undoes him. He comes with an intensity that catches me off guard. Molten energy spills into me without a valve to slow the overwhelming pace. The last spurt has barely entered me before he draws back, letting me collapse breathless against the twisted sheets.

I hear the hiss of a zipper being redone. Then footsteps retreat from the room. A door opens.

Slams.

And I'm alone.

I don't wait for shame to descend this time. In the aftermath of the chaos, I manage to scrape together what's left of my pride and gingerly stagger to my feet. The room is not only spacious, but grander than I first realized. The furniture is old but well maintained: polished oak. Just where are we?

The light fixtures are silver, made of delicate designs that resemble vines twisting from the paneled walls. It's a style that reminds me of Winthorp Manor's—at least before Briar convinced her father to "update" some of the interior rooms.

The smell here is the same. Old. Prestigious. Unwelcoming.

For all its grandeur, this room could be no less personal than the one in the hotel, but subtle clues lurk in plain sight. The black sheets are of the highest quality. A polished dresser contains a neat array of men's clothing. Not gray fatigues, but shirts and slacks. There's an en suite bathroom grander than the one attached to my room in Robert's suite. The floors are gleaming obsidian marble. There're a sunken tub and a separate enclosed shower. Granite countertops support a double sink, while the polished mirror above them displays a reflection that appears hideously out of place among the finery.

The shadow of Robert's wife stares back at me with hollow eyes. She seems so lost. So broken. Her healing wounds look even worse in the soft glow cast by the ornate light fixtures that illuminate the room.

Mischa's brand screams against my pale skin. My right eye is purple, partially shut beneath swelling. My neck is reddened, my body a collage of scars and bruises both new and old. It should be hard to discern what marks were left by Robert and those inflicted by Mischa. Hard, but not impossible. Robert is methodical in his madness. He placed his wounds strategically, with thought and care put into every scrape, scratch, and cut.

Mischa is reckless. My body isn't his canvas. It's his plaything.

Which is worse? To be used slowly and sparingly? Or to be chewed and swallowed alive?

My eyes water in my reflection and I turn away, unwilling to learn the answer.

Were I to play by Robert's rules, my next action would be to huddle on the middle of the bed and wait for his return. Only then could I bathe, and change the sheets, and finally rebuild my armor piece by piece. He'd break me down all over again, but that was the point. He liked me cleanly refreshed like a reset game board.

Now…

I run the bath, turning the water to scalding. Lying in the center of the tub, I wait until the water reaches my chin, bathing sore, battered limbs. I let time wash the pain away while my heartbeat settles into a gentle rhythm. In this sliver of peace, I try to forget both the man I was taken from and the man still inside me.

One dies quietly, his memories easily silenced.

The other…lingers. I smell him, even here. His flavor develops on the tip of my tongue, making it impossible to forget that I don't crave him how a woman should want a man. I don't want softness. No, I'm addicted to the sting of his poison. I like the way it feels when it's dribbled into my open wounds. The pain is different from what I'm used to. A distraction.

A drug.

My heartbeat flutters even before I sense that I'm no longer alone. I feel his breath first, ruffling my damp hair and basting my wet flesh. Alarmed, I fling my eyes open to his hardened expression. His narrow as they take in my half-submerged body. Is he surprised by my deviation from our usual script?

If so, he hides his shock well. The muscles in his arms ripple as he crosses them over his chest and cocks his head in an animalistic manner, like a wolf sizing up half-eaten prey. Does it deserve a killing blow yet? Or should it suffer a little longer?

"I want to know who you are," he says without revealing his final decision. "Not that bullshit you spewed before. Who you are *really*."

What a question. I draw my knees beneath my chin, wrapping my arms around them. Hot water continues to flood in, causing steam to waft from the surface. "I…I don't know what you mean—"

"Start with your parents," he suggests gruffly, "Who were they?"

"I never knew my father," I admit. "And my mother was a maid—"

"Don't." Suddenly, he's crouched beside the tub. The shadow he casts over the water reinforces his presence without him even having to touch me. "Don't lie to me, Little One," he warns. "You think I haven't shown my mercy when you have before? You thought I didn't notice?"

A shudder runs down my spine, making the water slosh against the sides of the tub. It's not fear of him that triggers the reaction, but of the words he wants to hear. The ones I've locked away for over twenty-three years.

Slowly, I draw in a ragged breath and brace the whole side of my face against my knee, eyeing the wall opposite him.

"My mother's name was Marnie Winthorp," I say haltingly. There's no point in holding anything back, so I don't. "*Yes*, that Marnie. *Yes*, Robert Sr.'s second wife. *Yes*, Briar's mother."

Our mother.

"But," I add haltingly. "I am not Robert Sr.'s daughter."

CHAPTER 15

"Marnie was your mother. How?"

I stiffen at how he voices that question. Cautious, not shocked. Intrigued, not disbelieving. It's almost as if he knew—or at least suspected the truth all along. Which is impossible. Unless Robert slipped in the handling of his most closely guarded secret.

The burning desire to know for sure gives me the strength to glance over my shoulder to decipher Mischa's expression for myself. He can't even hide the curiosity glinting in his eyes.

"I'm not sure," I admit. "All anyone ever told me was that she left the manor shortly after Briar was born—"

"Left?" He stresses the word, coating it in a warning.

"Yes," I say. "I don't know why. A year later, she returned, pregnant with me. Robert, out of mercy, let her keep me, as

181

long as she didn't claim I was his and kept her indiscretion quiet."

Though, ironically, he was the one who never let anyone forget it.

"And you know nothing about your father?" Mischa prods.

"No. She never mentioned who he was."

"And you're sure of that?"

Again, he sounds too careful. As if he knows a secret puzzle piece missing from the narrative that I've yet to see for myself. Something to explain the sadness that coated my mother's features like paint, perhaps? It's a dark thought I can't escape. In a futile attempt to, I risk facing him directly —and instantly regret the action.

He's cold again, eyeing me as if I'm something best viewed from a distance. A threat. An enemy to be conquered.

My body burns, remembering what it meant to be at his mercy, and I wrap my arms tighter around my knees—not that I can escape his scrutiny for very long.

"So you lived there, in that fucking manor."

I nod, almost grateful for the change in subject. "Yes. I grew up alongside Briar, but she was more my mistress than my sister. I played with her. I cleaned up after her. I…" *Loved her.* "I didn't know about the plan," I say instead. "That I was a decoy. I didn't… She asked me to join her at her wedding," I admit, not recognizing the hard note in my own voice. The memories of that day hurt twice as much to relive with him watching. How happy I was. How naïve. How foolish. "She bought me new clothes. She did my hair... I didn't know."

If he believes me, he says nothing and lets the silence linger between us while my own thoughts fester and feed on what little sanity I have left.

Finally, he asks, "And your husband?"

"Robert?" I inhale and exhale slowly, steeling myself for the next phase in my sordid tale. "He wasn't cruel to me, growing up," I admit. "His mother died when he was young and he rarely spent time at the manor. Though, when he did come home from school, he was never malicious. Some could say he protected me."

Or saved me for himself.

"When I turned nineteen, he expressed his interest. I accepted it, knowing full well what that would mean."

I suppose I learned that lesson as a child: he taught me who the real monster was all along.

"He never raped me." It feels important to say that. With rape, there was a victim. My body, however, had been sacrificed.

But did that make it any easier to bear?

My heart shies from the answer. *No.*

"I knew that he had f-fetishes," I add thickly. "I knew he could be violent. I knew that being with him would be an ordeal within itself. But he was better than—" A sudden tightness in my throat chokes off my voice. My wounded cheek burns as tiny ripples form in the water around my chin, created by falling tears. "I made my choice," I force myself to say. Hearing it out loud stings like nothing else. Not a million jagged cuts or bruises.

But Mischa isn't swayed by my emotions. He phrases an even crueler question as my tears continue to fall. "And me? You really think you remember me?"

"I remember a boy," I counter. "Someone who looked at me and showed me…"

What? An ounce of humanity?

"M-mercy," I decide, sucking in a breath. "He showed me mercy—"

"Don't pretend!"

I jump as his fingers slam against the rim of the tub, curling around the polished edge.

"You think I don't fucking know what game you're playing? That I can't smell it on you?" His nostrils flare as if to steal my scent. "*Cunning*. You feign your innocent act pretty well, but I've had more skilled women try to seduce me. Do you really think sex and false memories will make me pity you?" When I don't speak, he grabs my chin, grinding his fingers into my jawline. "Fucking say it. Admit why you let me…"

Fuck you.

Is there a reason? One springs to my lips of its own accord. "I-I deserve it." I don't know where the words came from. Why they hurt so much to say. Why a part of me feels like they were ripped from some vital part of my soul even Robert couldn't reach.

If being around him has taught me one thing, it's that all sinners receive their punishment eventually.

"Deserve?" Surprise flickers across Mischa's gaze for a split second before he lets me go and rises to his feet. "Trust a Winthorp to use sex as a punishment," he mutters, laughing coldly at the irony. Without warning, he whirls on his heel and slams his fist against the wall with a thud that resonates through my entire being.

Tense with anticipation, I wait for him to leave. To storm off.

Instead…

"Turn off the water."

My pulse surges as I lunge for the faucet and switch it off.

"We're not done," he says, turning the full brunt of his gaze on me once again. My mind plays a dangerous game of roulette as I try to guess where his next question might lead. "You said your husband made you keep numbers for him…"

"Y-yes."

"And you remember them? Don't waste your breath lying to me again."

I just nod, too exhausted to keep up the charade. Robert's secrets are my last to tell. "Every amount," I admit with a heavy sigh. "Every name."

It was the final act of our game in a poetic sense. Robert gave me enough to destroy him. Then he locked me up tight and dared me to leave him. Was it his father's idea to use me in his safety net for Briar? Had he let his son in on such a plan?

I'm not sure. The Winthorps have their own inner language of tricks and power grabs played between them, with a convoluted tally no outsider could fathom.

"You want me to give his accounts to you." It's not a question, and he doesn't bother denying it. "And if I do… will you still sell me?"

There's no playing coy with him. He frowns at my attempt, his eyes flashing midnight. "And why shouldn't I? I've experienced what you have to offer," he reminds me, making my cheeks flame. "Forget the five thousand Boris offered. I could easily charge double."

Somehow, I manage to ignore the ferocity of the threat— no, his promise. I run my tongue over my cracked lips, tasting dried blood. "Do you really think you can beat the numbers out of me?"

It's not a taunt as much as it is a genuine question. Can this man best Robert Winthorp at a game of his creation? Does he really have what it takes to rip the truth from my head?

Of course he does.

But does he have the time?

Precious minutes pass at his discretion, but the truth is clear: He doesn't.

"I'll give you all I know," I propose. "All I ask is that you don't sell me as a whore. I won't try to run. I won't resist. I won't fight when you…"

When you kill me.

"I swear," I continue. "All I ask is that you do with me what you want. I don't care. But don't barter my body."

It's a pathetic, simple request. Or so I believe, until I make the mistake of looking into his eyes and witness the darkness brewing there. The open hatred, so raw and consuming that it steals my breath away.

"You think that you can make demands of me?" His voice breaks into two bone-chilling notes. One low and hollow, the other guttural. Animalistic.

"N-no," I stammer before he can finish taking a step in my direction. "I only want…your mercy."

It's a word that I suspect would mean nothing to another man. A better man.

For him? It's a trigger. *Boom!* I've blown the lid off his rage without even trying.

"Mercy?" He's on his knees before I can blink, reaching into the tub for my throat, clenching the already sore flesh. "You think that you can demand *mercy* from me? Do you even know what that word fucking means?"

"N-not demand," I clarify, wheezing in my effort to get the words past his tightening grip. "Asking...for it."

Begging.

He tilts my head back while simultaneously leaning closer, heedless of the tremor that quakes through me in response. With that cold, piercing gaze as his weapon, he slices me open and searches beneath my skin, hunting down any hint of deceit. Finally, he draws back.

"I don't barter with *dead* women," he spits. "Or whores. Or the wives of my fucking enemies—"

"What about a human being?" I wonder softly, marveling at the fact that I've challenged him at all.

His fingers tighten in a silent threat, but I can still breathe. For now.

"Someone who has nothing left to lose?"

He chuckles at that and cocks his head to view me from a different angle. "And let's say I don't sell you. Am I supposed to care for two fucking 'human beings' out of the kindness of my soul, Little One? At least until I slit your throat?"

Two?

He laughs again as my brow furrows. "How quickly you fucking forget," he scolds. "The girl you protected. Nicolai's. I can't let her go. She already knows too much."

No. My veins run cold with ice. "You wouldn't…"

"I will. I can't keep her here out of charity. So, if I don't sell *you*, are you willing to have her be put in your place?"

No. I shake my head, feeling the ridge of his knuckles with every frantic movement. When he lets me go, I stare down at the water and fight to keep the fire building behind my eyes at bay. There's no use in admitting my defeat out loud.

Regardless, rare anger bubbles beneath my skin. Only the most subhuman of men use child pawns in their wicked games.

"There's something you want to say, Little One." Mischa runs his thumb along the bruised side of my face in a terrifying display of encouragement. "Go on. Say it."

My lips unlock painfully. "For someone who claims to hate Robert Sr. so much…you seem determined to emulate him."

I expect a blow as punishment. My shoulders tense in a futile effort to brace for its impact. Instead, Mischa laughs again. He growls. Aware of his shadow flickering over the floor, I infer that he moves to a corner of the bathroom and snatches something from the wall, which he then throws at me. It bounces off my head and lands partially in the water. A white towel.

"Get out," he tells me, his voice strained with that dangerous calm I've come to fear.

After releasing the stopper to allow the water to drain, I climb from the tub, draping the towel around my shoulders. Left with no choice, I follow Mischa into the main bedroom. Without a glance spared in my direction, he enters the hallway. Still wet, with only the towel to cover myself with, I'm forced to weigh embarrassment with obedience.

With Robert, my choice would have been clear.

Now? I turn my gaze to the wooden dresser and wrench a drawer open without giving myself the time to weigh the consequences. The first shirt my fingers fall over is black, finely tailored. Letting the towel drop to my feet, I scramble into the dress shirt, surprised to find that it reaches past my knees.

As my damp hair falls over my shoulders, I creep to the doorway and find Mischa waiting paces away. His eyes sweep over me once and then narrow.

"I suggest you remember those accounts, Little One," he warns before turning on his heel and marching down the corridor. "Come. It's time to prove just how valuable you are to your husband."

*W*e don't go far. A few closed doors down, he stops before another doorway and passes through it. There's a desk in the center of this room, with two leather chairs placed before it. A study? It's simpler in appearance, but it reminds me of the grand one where Robert Sr. holds court—a place I'm only ever allowed to venture in his son's presence.

In silence, Mischa approaches the solid oak desk and grabs something from its surface. A leather-bound book. He offers it to me, along with a silver pen. "Let's see how well your husband trained you, Little One," he taunts.

Slowly, I lower myself onto one of the chairs and I open the book to a blank page. Balancing it over my lap, I uncap the pen and place the nib down over the ivory parchment. Four names and four amounts—that's what I give him, fished at random from the recesses of my mind. It's nowhere near everything.

And he knows it. Still, he accepts the book when I hold it out to him and scans what I've written.

"This name," he says, pointing to the third entry down. "What do you know about it?"

"Barklow," I read aloud. I look down at my lap, turning my focus inward. "Tall man. Blond. Balding. He met with Robert at least once every few months." About what? I don't know.

Something tells me Mischa has a suspicion though. He nods to himself as if tucking that bit of knowledge away for later. "And what else?"

I stare at the floor, averting my gaze from his. "I...I can't remember."

"Oh?" He takes a step toward me, reaching out to run his fingers through my wet hair. Roughly. I flinch as they snag on a knotted tangle. "I wonder if I can refresh your memory?"

"You don't have to threaten me," I say, looking up to meet his gaze directly. "Even by giving you only four names, you know what that means…"

I've betrayed my husband. It's a reality that hasn't sunken in yet. I don't feel the fear I should. At least not yet.

"I'm tired," I insist, allowing my exhaustion to leak into my voice. "I haven't eaten in…" Hell, only he knows the exact answer to that. "There's no point in only committing half treason," I add weakly.

"And who says you'll last another day?" Mischa wonders. He lets the statement linger on the air between us, an unmistakable reminder of where we stand.

My life is extended only at his whim.

Not that I could ever forget.

"Starving me may be an enterprising way to conserve resources if you plan on killing me soon," I admit. "But it won't make me remember any faster."

"And how do I know if you have anything *worth* remembering?" he counters.

I lift my shoulder in a weak attempt at a shrug. "You wouldn't be asking if you knew that I didn't."

It's a dangerous game to mince words with him. I half-expect his anger to take hold once again. Instead, he surprises me by returning his attention to the book.

"You know more of your husband's accounts?" he muses openly.

Aware of him watching, I fold my hands together and rest them on my lap. Lying would be useless, so I say nothing. Finally, his fingers seize a chunk of my hair and he uses it as a leash to force me to meet his gaze directly.

"So, you are hungry, Little One?" he asks in a lethal murmur.

My stomach answers for me, grumbling loudly. Amused, Mischa tilts his head to the side, allowing his tongue to shoot out along his lower lip. Fire spreads through my stomach as my heart thumps unsteadily at the motion.

"Then ask me for food."

I don't hesitate. "Please."

"And you want to sleep?" He phrases the question in a way that reminds me of a hunter priming a trap.

"Y-yes."

"And you think that what you can offer me is *worth* those resources, Little One? The mere promise that you might have more to give? Your trust is truly worth that much?"

Is it? I honestly don't know. "Robert doesn't gamble," I tell him. "So…I don't know much about favorable odds."

"No?" The corner of his mouth quirks, but even that brief bit of emotion can't touch the coldness in his eyes. "You do seem to know a thing or two about Roulette, Little One," he suspects. "So we will play."

He turns to the doorway, beckoning me to follow with a nod of his chin. This time, he leads me back to the ornate entrance and I'm allowed to take more details of the interior in than before.

A crystal chandelier bathes the grand hall in a warm, orange glow, illuminating curved archways leading off into various corridors. When Mischa turns down one, I follow, keeping as much distance between us as I dare to.

"Here." He comes to a stop near an open doorway. Beyond it is a dining room with a long oak table and windows framed in cream curtains. "Sit," he commands.

I slip past him and take the seat farthest from his position. He laughs at the display, and I presume that he writes it off as an act of fear. But no. I can see him more clearly from here. How he stands. The tension in his posture. The way he hones his gaze on me as if it's the only way he can keep from looking at anything else. Then he leaves, and I know instinctively not to move.

I sit. I wait. His games aren't as predictable as Robert's. He leaves me guessing by the end of each round. He lets me sweat. Where my husband sought only to amuse himself with my pain, Mischa seeks to…

Ruin me. In any way he can. With brutality. With violent sex. With stingy mercy?

I tense as he reappears at the mouth of the room, holding a plate in his hand. The food on it is simple: a sandwich and scattered potato chips. My stomach pangs for it anyway, and I fight to keep utterly still as he carries the plate to me. When he stops beside my chair, I expect another display of dominance. *Beg. Ask.*

Instead, he unceremoniously slams the offering down, and I don't wait for his permission. I grab the sandwich, rip it in half, and shove as much as I can into my mouth at one time. In three gulping bites, I choke it down and start on the chips like a damn animal.

Ellen Winthorp dined with decorum. She ate her food from her husband's hand or devoured it slowly with whatever knife or fork the occasion called for.

That woman is dead. In Mischa's realm, there are no manners. Jus*t taking*—whatever I can before he rips it out of reach.

"And sleep," he says once I've cleared the plate, continuing our conversation as if never interrupted. "You wanted that as well…"

"Yes," I cautiously reply.

"Then come."

Grappling with a partially filled stomach, I trail him back up the stairs and into his room. The bed isn't meant for me. I know that even before he reaches down to tug his boots off and approach the mattress himself. "So sleep," he mockingly goads.

My eyes fall over the corner beside the dresser. I approach it, prepared to sink down and rest my head against the wall.

"No." He snaps his fingers, forcing my attention on him. He's seated, lying back against the headboard, his legs extended before him. "My floor is too good for you, Little One." He waves his hand, commanding me closer. It's only as he spreads his legs just enough to reveal a sliver of space between them that I realize just what he intends. "I said you could sleep, but I never said peacefully, did I? I will be waiting for you in your dreams." The malice in his voice robs my lungs of air. "You will smell me. Feel me. Taste me.

I won't let you escape, even for a second." He nods toward his chest. "Now, sleep."

I strip my face of emotion as I lower myself beside him onto the bed. Then I turn and brace a trembling hand against his shoulder, finding enough leverage to sink against him, trapped on either side by a massive thigh. His breath scalds the top of my head while his heartbeat thunders beneath me. He's right. I taste him. His scent floods my nostrils. A cold, sickening certainty fills me as I let my eyes drift shut with the bruised side of my face against his chest.

I'll dream of him.

I'll die of him.

Prisoners have no right to make demands. So I pray instead to whatever higher power will listen. For ruthless, vile destruction. *Amen.*

Torment is what I crave—at least when it comes to Mischa. Torment I can barely handle. Torture my body can only just withstand.

Pain, pain, pain.

It's the only way I can compare him to Robert, measuring their varying flavors of agony inflicted.

But there is no comparison to *this*. There is no chilling memory in my head to examine this scenario through. On the rare shred of untouched space on my psyche, Mischa carves a new terrifying ordeal to relive.

As promised, I dream of him.

And I wake up knowing what true hell is. It's not the measured cruelty Robert dished out. It's not fearful memories or repulsive scars. It's peace—being able to find it, even for a second, while in the arms of a monster.

What a terrible power to lord over someone.

The moment I regain my senses, my eyes fly open and I view the room from behind a cage composed of muscular, tattooed limbs. Regaining my bearings feels like assembling the pieces of a crudely made puzzle. It's morning. Gray daylight glimmers around the edges of the curtains. Beneath my ear, a steady heartbeat taps out a constant rhythm while thick fingers twist through my hair…

Not tugging for once. Just feeling, rubbing the strands together and testing their weight.

"You don't like to be held," Mischa declares as my body stiffens while his fingers brush my scalp. "You tremble in your sleep. You flinch."

He didn't sleep himself; I can hear it in his coarse tone. No, he studied. How to strip me bare and catch me off guard.

As if aware of my suspicions, he flattens his hand against my skull, applying slight pressure. "Your husband was lenient with you," he adds knowingly. "He kept you skittish."

Is that what he calls it?

"You know how they test when soldiers are ready for war? When they're broken enough?" He untangles one of his hands from my hair and snatches my wrist, displaying each finger. "They're ordered to stick their hands in an open flame, but it's not enough to just obey. Only a few can stand to watch their skin peel and burn until they're given the order to pull their hand away. *They* are ready. But those who flinch out of reach before the command is given…" He manually places my hand on his hip, watching how it quivers. "They are pathetic fools. Poorly trained."

Like young boys who leave little girls untouched?

I'm not brave enough to ask. When he releases me, I make the mistake of believing that he's made his point, ended the game. My heart races as I plan my escape. Cautiously, I brace one of my hands over the mattress and attempt to push myself upright.

One fierce tug on my scalp shoves me right back down. "Did I say you could move?"

But I need to. I can only ignore his nearness for so long. His thighs create a stifling prison, trapping me within a cage I'm not used to. He's right: Robert never wielded physical touch as a weapon. He slept beside me sparingly, only as his idea of a treat after a particularly brutal session. He never held me in his arms simply to prove a point.

But that highlights another difference between my husband and my captor: Robert wanted me somewhat whole.

Mischa wants me utterly broken, in pieces too small to ever resemble their original shape.

He extends his torture long enough to ensure I learn the rules. Only *he* can dictate how much I move my head and how much of him I feel against my aching, battered frame. But he can't control one aspect of his anatomy...

It slams against my stomach with every breath I take, dangerously hard. I cringe away from the contact as much as I can, and he chuckles, twisting his fingers more harshly through my hair.

"Don't act shy now." It's not a taunt, but a dare. "I'm sure your husband didn't let you rest for long—"

"I...I'm not on birth control." I don't know why I chose to admit that to him. Considering his threats to end my life, it doesn't really matter. Maybe I subconsciously needed to voice another comparison between him and Robert out loud.

While Robert hated the medicine behind hormone-manipulating drugs, he studied my cycle religiously, planning his "needs" around the days that would be most beneficial to him.

As expected, Mischa laughs, shrugging his shoulder. "Pregnancy is your last concern, Little One," he says, letting a lethal implication lurk in between the words. "But..." As he forms a fist and nudges my hip with the tops of his knuckles, I stiffen. "You've had a child before. I saw the scar."

Scar. Warily, my fingers creep to the mark in question, tracing it through the fabric of his shirt. It's one of the few I never observed in much detail. I can only recall its general shape: a curved, jagged line at the base of my abdomen. After a few brief seconds, I let my hand fall.

"Did your husband keep that a secret as well?" He nudges me more firmly when I don't answer.

But fear can't override every instinct, as it turns out. My teeth clamp down over an answer. My brain won't betray those memories. I'm forced to endure his curiosity for nearly a minute before he shifts his weight and knocks me off him without pressing the topic further.

"Get up."

I scramble onto my hands and knees and back away to the opposite end of the mattress. He watches me go with an unreadable expression before he stands and strips his shirt, tossing it onto the floor.

My brain short-circuits as I take him in. A collage of scars and varying tattoos mark his body like it's a vandalized canvas. Long, vicious marks. Snarling black skulls and swirling designs with undiscernible meanings. I'm not sure why my gaze settles over one brand in particular, sliced into his lower back. It's large enough to span nearly his entire torso, neatly integrated through several surrounding tattoos. A complex series of scars forms its construction: two vertical slashes beside a crudely etched V. Another Roman numeral? *Seven.*

The longer I stare, the more unsteady the world feels beneath me. With Robert, curiosity was a warning sign to back away from whatever sparked it. Nothing good ever came from learning his secrets.

With Mischa...

That same emotion is a drug, numbing me to the harsher reality. The promise of his secrets doesn't repulse me as much as it confuses me. Maybe because I can't escape the pathetic truth: I want to learn...everything.

I want to know what made him human once. Robert wasn't a monster so much as he was a beast. He was born that way. He'll die that way.

He doesn't use his body as a canvas to illustrate his descent into madness.

He has no Vanya mourning what he used to be.

Does the difference mean a damn thing?

Maybe...

"See something you like?" Mischa wonders, his cold tone snapping me back to reality.

I turn my focus to the wall beyond his head as he continues toward the dresser, swiping a clean shirt from one of the drawers. I hear a zipper come undone moments later, but when he finally reenters my line of sight, he's fully dressed in a pair of slacks and a lazily donned button-down. He fastened it up to his chest, leaving a sliver of defaced skin in view.

"Let's hope that sleep refreshed your memory," he warns before exiting the room altogether, leaving me to follow on shaking legs.

Morning casts an alarming pallor over the grand estate, and the daylight seeping in reveals secrets skillfully hidden by the dark. His men are a constant presence, lurking around doorways and wandering the ornate halls. There's a staleness to the wealth, like something long since abandoned.

Why?

The wooden floors and paneled walls reveal no answers by the time I'm led inside the barren office, forced to take a seat before the desk. Mischa hands me the leather book, which was still where he'd left it. I dutifully flip it open to a clean page and balance the pen between my fingers.

Memory is a dangerously unreliable thing. It's there, fighting to be known when you're desperate to suppress it. Yet it hides when you need it, obscuring details and blurring lines. Mischa watches, patiently impatient as I etch out another four names in painstaking fashion.

Upon snatching the book from me, he scans the page, his eyes narrowing over the entries. Then he rips it from the book and shoves it crumpled into his pocket. "More." He drops the book onto my lap and jerks his chin toward the pen. "Write them."

"I can't." My hand trembles, allowing the nib of the pen to broadcast my anxiety on the air. "It...it doesn't work like that—"

"Like what?" he presses, lethally soft. His hand cups my chin, wrenching it back so that my gaze meets his. "What doesn't work?"

I swallow hard, consumed by the vast emptiness that paints his irises. I always thought Robert was hard to interpret, but now, I know the truth. Robert hid nothing behind his darkness. There were no secrets to discern.

"I can't just turn it off and on," I admit. "M-maybe…if you told me what you were looking for—"

"Ha!" He lets me go and throws his head back for another chilling laugh. "Don't, Little One," he warns. "Don't attempt to manipulate me. I am not Ivan."

I don't know what he means. Looking down at my hands, I try again. "There are hundreds of names. Thousands of accounts—"

"Then give me the ones that you heard the most." His tone is less mocking this time. Something odd taints his expression and I struggle to name it. Actual interest? "Think." He comes up behind me to hiss the word directly into my ear. "Think hard, Little One. I suggest you hold my attention for as long as you have it."

My body resonates with the ominous suggestion, and I return the pen to the page. Three names spring to mind and I scribble them hastily, one after the other. When I hold them out to Mischa, I expect him to shove the book back in my face with a growled command. *More!*

But his eyes spark with interest as he fingers one name in particular. "Son of a bitch…" His gaze flicks up, burning through mine. "Him. How do you know him?"

I scan the letters partially obscured by his pointing thumb. *Kostas.* My stomach tightens ominously. *That* name. It's one of the few I can trace back to a clear memory. Several memories. He was one of the few men Robert made me pleasure for him. With my mouth. My hands. They tremble as the coarse images linger on my conscience.

Mischa says something else, snapping his fingers when I don't answer. Or at least it appears he does. I hear nothing. Just deep, masculine groans smothered on the air, paired with the burning humiliation of being used.

"Hey—"

I violently cringe from the hand that brushes my cheek. Beneath me, the chair slides against the wood, driven by the sudden shift in my weight. My eyes blink rapidly, but I'm not in Robert's room. And the man before me, he's…

Terrifying. I've never seen that kind of rage reflected on the face of a human being. It's raw. Animalistic.

It's…not directed at *me.*

"No," he snarls, gritting the word between his teeth. Deliberately, his hand comes for me again, cupping the side of my throat. "You don't flinch from me." Each finger tenses against my windpipe, but not to choke for once. To feel. To reinforce his presence. *You don't flinch.*

And I don't. Robert relished making me squirm. He chuckled whenever I jumped at the mercy of his fingertips. But I'd give anything to emulate that reaction now. Anything.

When Mischa captures my chin in his palm, I don't recoil. I shiver. It's a subtle difference that I feel down to the very nerves running beneath my skin. Fear is one thing. Anticipation is something different entirely. It's harder to stomach. Harder to reconcile with the rules I've lived by for so long.

"Tell me," he commands, urging me to face him. "What… Did he hurt you?"

He didn't mean to phrase the question so heatedly. His eyes narrow, directing that anger inward for a rare split second.

But he doesn't move, and his fingers never withdraw.

"He…he met with Robert regularly for a short time," I admit, barely recognizing the sound of my own voice.

Mischa blinks, cold and collected once again. "How regularly?"

"Weekly at some points," I admit. "Every few months at others. It changed."

"That son of a bitch." He turns away from me, and I'm ignored in favor of the man whose face I can still clearly recall.

Black eyes. Dark curls. Younger than most. He smelled like cigar smoke and thick cologne I'd still taste on my tongue for weeks. Before the worst of the memories can descend, however, movement catches the corner of my eye. Mischa, reaching into his pocket. For his knife? No, a cell phone, I realize as my heart creeps to my throat. He dials a number quickly and brings it to his ear.

"This is Stepanov," he says into the receiver. "I'm calling a fucking meeting. Pecavi. Midnight. Bring them all." He hangs up, turning his attention back to me. "You want to earn another concession from me, Little One?" he wonders. But there is no mistake: it's not a question, and he doesn't offer kindness. "Then I'm going to need you to put that memory of yours to good fucking use. Or," he adds, sweeping his gaze along my body, "I'll utilize your pretty head in another way. Understood?"

I can only nod.

CHAPTER 18

"You claimed your husband never mentioned the *Mafiya* around you," Mischa questions as we advance through the corridor.

My steps are hesitant in his wake. I know enough of him to suspect that he doesn't divulge information like this willingly. No, his sudden talkativeness hides a more nefarious purpose: the first round of a brand-new game.

Do I want to play?

It's not like I have a choice.

"No," I admit cautiously. "He didn't."

"Should I enlighten you?"

I swallow hard, weighing the implications of such a suggestion. Does the twisted reason for my fate really matter?

"Ten families," he explains, making the decision for me, "each one with more wealth and power than your fucking Winthorps. Together, we are united, under the guidance of one leader. In theory…"

A word springs to mind: *Pakhan.* Him?

"Twenty-four years ago, your husband's family started a war, Little One. I plan to end it, soon. Once and for all." His hands flex menacingly at his sides, the knuckles cracking in unison. "So do not make the mistake of assuming that, because you aren't dead now, I've changed my mind. In fact, I want you to tell me something."

"W-what?" I gather up the nerve to ask after seconds have passed, sensing that's what he wants: me to take the bait.

He continues past the door to his room and stops near the one beside it instead, heightening the foreboding tension building in my belly. "Think about how you want to die," Mischa commands as he opens the door.

I falter in the hall as my blood runs cold at the grim suggestion. He isn't joking.

Rather than demand an answer now, my murderer snatches my wrist and drags me over the threshold of the newer room. He switches a nearby light on, and with my thoughts stalled by terror, he pulls me in close, lowering his mouth near my ear. "So tell me, Ellen Winthorp. Strangulation? No…" He runs the fingers of his free hand along my tender throat and frowns. "You'd like that."

Would I? My lungs refuse to expand, and the sensation is anything but pleasurable. He could kill me like this easily: smothering my soul through nearness alone.

"What about a knife?" He sweeps his gaze along my chest as if hunting for the right place to strike. Eventually, his eyes settle over my rib cage and narrow thoughtfully. "I could make it slow, Little One."

His hand falls to his hip, and desperation makes my lips spring apart.

"G-gun," I rasp, naming Robert's preferred weapon. Whenever my husband eventually did tire of me, at least I knew for certain his method of choice. He'd dispose of me the same way he dispatched the animals he hunted: one bullet right between the eyes. Simple and clean, he'd say.

Mischa, however, frowns at the suggestion. "Shooting you." He shrugs as if considering it. Then he shakes his head and dips his fingers into his pocket, retrieving the hidden blade. "You aren't afraid of guns, Little One," he deduces musingly. "I've seen it. You aren't afraid of my hands, either. No…but the knife—" He raises the blade, brandishing it in the orange glow of the lamp. "This frightens you. Why?"

Hypnotized by the gleaming metal's edge, I can't answer him. Memories flash across my psyche too quickly to suppress: *pain, blood, so much blood.*

"You Winthorps and your knives." He brings the blade closer, positioning it toward my throat, and chuckles when I flinch. "This way." Nodding to himself, he steps back, returning the blade to his pocket. "Sit."

He gestures to the bed in the center of the room.

I sit on the edge of the mattress, and he stands over me without revealing a hint of what he has planned. I can't help the hesitant way my eyes trace the waistband of his pants. His hands remain open at his sides, but tension sizzles off him, prickling my skin.

"Are you afraid?" he wonders.

Am I? After a second's hesitation, I nod.

"You should be," he agrees, raking a hand along his scalp. "But...you *aren't*. Don't try to deny it. I've smelled fear on you before." His nostrils flare as if chasing that scent. Disappointed, he shrugs in disgust. "No. You are waiting. Watching. You still think you can survive."

"I don't." Once more, I question his assertions. The cunning woman he described sounds nothing like the Ellen Winthorp I know. "I-I—"

"I suppose I could threaten to kill you now, Little One." He pauses, letting the prospect linger while stoking my anxiety like flames. "But I might as well use you while I can. You said your husband never taught you how to gamble." His gaze roves over me, and with nothing to disguise my body's reaction, parts of me tighten. Stiffen. Heat. "I will make you a wager. Apart from your life, think of something you want from me."

"Huh?" I blink in confusion, unable to disguise the reaction before he notices. Something I want? *Mercy.*

As if aware of the desire, he chuckles again. "I know what I want from you. Fail me tonight and it's mine."

"And if I don't fail?" I'm not sure where the challenge came from. Why I even care. Men like him and Robert play their games with only one winner in mind.

Rather than reinforce that reality out loud, Mischa tilts his mouth in a wicked angle. "I'll humor you, Little One."

As he turns his back to me, I'm painfully aware that we're not in his room, but a new domain. This one is smaller, the furniture less ornate, the bed sheets a bloody shade of red. Rather than a dresser, there's a wardrobe tucked into the corner, which Mischa approaches. Beyond his shoulder, I only make out a swatch of colored fabric before he turns and tosses something onto the bed beside me.

"Put it on."

My fingers obediently clench the burgundy fabric. It's a dress. Thin. Small. Something sets it apart from the other skimpy items he gave me before though; it's finely tailored, comparable to what Briar would wear. This belonged to someone…

"Now," Mischa snaps.

Suppressing my questions, I draw the gown over my head, surprised by the modest length and plunging neckline.

"Forget Robert Winthorp," he warns. He runs his fingers through my hair, flicking the strands forward to cover most of my face. "Tonight, you are *mine*." He captures my chin in his grip and roughly runs his thumb over the healing wounds on my left cheek. Then he withdraws something from his pocket. Flat. Square. A bandage large enough to cover the worst of the cuts. Satisfied, he draws back, observing me from afar.

"Get some of that sleep you crave, Little One," he commands, heading for the door. "Tonight, you better be willing to place your bets."

*L*eft alone in the strange room, I notice nothing worth examining—at first. It's slightly smaller than his, with an adjacent bathroom composed of white marble instead of black. The bedsheets feel stiff, unslept in. There are few baubles or mementos on the nightstands and the lone vanity, just like in his room.

The wardrobe is another matter, however. The moment I open the doors, a scent rushes out to greet me. Sweet. Soft. Feminine. It lingers in every piece of clothing I find. Most are elegant gowns like the one Mischa picked for me, but tucked behind them, I find simpler garments. A blouse. A skirt. The style is older than the bright fashions Briar prefers, more modest. They're far from what Robert would choose for me, as well.

But Mischa? Was his woman this modest creature who preferred emerald silk and soft tweed?

I try to picture her, someone who could pique his interest in ways other than a hateful fuck. Only the haziest image comes to mind. Brown eyes, maybe? Someone taller, perhaps. The doomed Anna-Natalia?

Removing the clothing in question reveals no answers. I don't find her when I carefully shed my red dress in favor of one from the wardrobe. It fits me, which is the first surprise. The second is how lovingly it's been preserved. No one has worn them in a very long time, yet the fabric maintains its shape.

What are you doing, Ellen?

My subconscious haunts me as I approach the vanity. I almost don't recognize the person I find looking back. Her eyes aren't as empty as I'm used to. Something lurks there. Pain? Or a more dangerous, obscure emotion that would never take root in my husband's domain?

Curiosity.

Mischa's woman doesn't reveal herself, even in the drawers or the neat arrangement of items placed before the round mirror. Pink lipstick. A small vial of perfume. A silver brush. My fingers settle over each item individually, seeking any clue of their previous owner. I don't find a ghost. Just a strange, impulsive need to drag the brush through my tangled hair and swipe my lips with the lipstick. The perfume is the most dangerous item of all to disturb. I know that even before I spray a hint of it against my wrist, inhaling the feminine scent.

Who was this ghost who smelled of roses?

Trembling with apprehension, I shed the clothing and return it to the wardrobe. Then I redress myself in the red slip, climb onto the bed and wait. Sleep should be a tempting offer without Mischa there to haunt my every moment, but my eyes refuse to close. My heart refuses to still.

Instead, I breathe in shallowly and count the seconds as they pass. I wait, lingering in my monster's shadow. This room disguises his scent too well and I'm left inhaling a stranger—two of them. One is bloodied and broken, the wife of a distant villain. The other is an enigma, lingering in the home of an even worse creature.

And she didn't even bother to leave her secrets behind.

The moment my eyes finally begin to drift shut, Mischa comes for me. I startle to awareness and find him in the doorway, gesturing with a silent wave of his hand for me to follow.

Together, we return to the entryway of the manor, and I sense a drastic change in the atmosphere. Unease. It lingers as he marches through an archway opposite the one toward the dining room. Noises echo, betraying a flurry of unseen activity. Voices. Chaos. Suddenly, a man appears at the end of the hallway.

"There you are." Vanya approaches, wearing a black collared shirt and pants instead of the gray fatigues. He nods once when he sees me before turning his attention to Mischa. He eyes his leader warily, lowering his voice. "Are you sure about this? On such short notice?"

He's anxious, but if Mischa feels the same his posture reveals nothing. He's stoic, his jaw set in a grim line of determination.

"I am done playing the role of mediator," he says. "It's time we fucking fight for what we want. Those who refuse to fall in line can grapple with the consequences."

"You know most of them will follow you," Vanya agrees. "But Sergei—"

"I can handle him," Mischa interjects. "But can you? You made your choice to stay by my side, not his. Tell me now if you regret it?"

Vanya frowns, eyeing something far beyond this conversation only he can see. Finally, he shakes his head. "No."

"Good." Mischa squares his shoulders, continuing down the hall.

He wants to say more, I can tell. Something personal. Whatever it is, the words never leave his throat, and Vanya continues in the opposite direction.

"You're losing already, Little One," Mischa warns. He snatches my wrist, drawing me to his side. "You are mine, remember?"

It's one role I don't know how to emulate, ironically. Robert thought of me as his trophy. His wife. *His* prize. Mischa seems to expect a certain demeanor. Maybe the answer lurks in the heated way he uttered those words. *You are mine.*

But how does one display the ownership of a beast? It's a trick question. Monsters never possess their victims. They rip them apart. Devour. Destroy. Then they lord over the mangled pieces.

He already has me hanging together by a thread. I'm not prideful enough to deny it. I can sense my soul splintering around me with every passing second that his heat leeches into my skin.

There was a reason Robert never gambled. "Only fools with nothing worth having risk it all," he smugly claimed.

He was the son of a wealthy businessman with the world at his fingertips, after all. What use did he have for something as elusive as hope and luck?

I'm not even half as secure as he is, yet I still can't make the leap. So I eye the floor of the hallway and count the steps we take until Mischa finally pulls me to a stop. We're in a larger room I don't recognize. A polished floor stretches beneath a vaulted ceiling with scattered fixtures casting intermittent light. A meeting room?

There's a table in the center, like the makeshift one at the safe house where Boris haggled for me. More men fill this room, however. At least ten are seated around the table, with more lurking behind them, flooding nearly every available space. At a glance, the group appears homogenous, but on a second appraisal, it's easy to see the subtle divides that separate some groups from the others. Of the ten men seated, each one seems to command a section of the room wherein those gathered are facing him. Some are wearing suits. Others are wearing casual fatigues like Mischa. One man is even lounging in a simple tee shirt and jeans, smirking at those around him.

As Mischa approaches the remaining chair, a hush falls. Behind us, numerous footsteps echo in unison. His men, spearheaded by Vanya.

"So, Stepanov," one of the men says, seizing the attention as Mischa sits. He's older, his eyes piercing and narrowed. He glances Mischa over with barely concealed disgust, but there's respect in how he inclines his head toward him, even as he spits his words out. "You called us here. For what? To join in your insane fucking plan—"

"To talk," Mischa says, effortlessly cutting over him though he never raises his voice.

I find myself biting my lower lip in recognition of one tool I've only ever seen Winthorp men possess so freely: *power*.

It's in the way he holds his head. How his shoulders convey a fearless grace. He's not the oldest man here, or the biggest, or even the handsomest. But no one can keep their eyes off him for very long.

"To talk?" another man wonders, his accent thick and indiscernible. "Or to beg for help in your fucking war with Winthorp—"

"Show some respect," another man interjects, dark-haired and solidly built. His eyes hold an eerie sense of calm that negates the impatience of the other two men vying to speak above him. "Nikolaus. Yohan. You forget your place before your *Pakhan*."

That word has the effect of a whip. The two men stiffen in their seats. Their glares remain, but they hold their tongues.

"Now, Mischa," the calmer man says, meeting his gaze from across the table. "We're listening."

"It's time we head off the Winthorps at the fucking head," Mischa declares, his voice reverberating to the farthest reaches of the room. "And I don't speak out of some petty fucking feud," he adds. "This is about survival."

"Survival?" Nikolaus, the older man, scoffs. "You mean *greed*. There have been rumors, *Pakhan*. That you went after the man himself. Robert. His daughter. Considering the little bitch is on her honeymoon with one of the most powerful money lenders in the world, I presume that you miscalculated."

"I did lead an attack on her," Mischa admits without a shred of shame. "Robert was prepared. He used a decoy. Some disposable toy of his son's." He shrugs with a malicious jerk of his shoulder. "I gave her to my men and left her body for the bastard to find—"

"And found yourself a distraction, I see," Nikolaus snidely interjects, turning his attention to me. He sneers in disgust at what little of my face he can see through the curtain of my hair. "You're getting more blatant, Mischa—"

"Show some respect," another man cuts in, forcefully slamming his hand over the table.

"Enough." Mischa sits forward, his smile dismissive. "This bitch is more than a distraction." He grabs my wrist, tugging me closer to the table, until I have no choice but to sit on his lap.

The other men tense, warily watching the display. He's never brought a woman to their meetings before, I suspect. Not like this. His arm possessively encircles my waist from behind, but there's tension coiled into every strip of muscle. A warning, broadcasted solely to me. *Play your role, Little One.*

"She's more like a lucky charm. She's skilled at spotting liars, you see. *Traitors.*"

The way he stresses that word sends a ripple of unease throughout the room. Through one man in particular. My eyes go to him automatically, though I'm not sure why at first. He is standing just beyond the table, his face partially hidden by shadow. But his shape is familiar.

"Should I explain?" Mischa's fingers trail my cheek, turning my face toward him. The look in his eyes takes my breath away: hot, molten anger. For me? No… For once, his ire has a new target. "Show them, Little One," he goads. "You think there are any traitors in our midst?"

With his thumb pressing forcefully against my bottom lip, I sense what he doesn't say out loud once again: *Here's your chance. So, gamble.*

"Is this a game to you?" Nikolaus demands, his irritation visibly echoed by at least six of the other seated men. "Just who are you trying to accuse, *Pakhan*—"

"I don't know," Mischa says, his voice deceptively soft. "Just who among us would dare betray our families. Our blood. Our lives?"

With each word, his volume rises while a hush simultaneously falls over the assembled crowd. Out of shock. Disbelief.

"I suppose that you have more than some 'lucky' whore to bring charges against someone, *Pakhan,*" the calmer man wonders.

"What do you think?" Mischa tilts my chin down toward him. "Do you sense a fucking liar, Little One?"

Slowly, my gaze drifts across the room to the man in Nikolaus's section. He's moved deeper into the ranks, almost as if attempting to stay out of view. But I can smell him even from here; there is no escaping memory.

"Kostas!" Mischa declares warmly, zoning in on the same shadowed figure. "Come closer, brother."

"Mischa—" Nikolaus rises to his feet with both hands braced against the table. "You wouldn't dare accuse my son."

Several murmurs of concern rise, creating a chorus. *You're crossing a dangerous line.*

Mischa smiles, revealing nothing. "Let's hear it from the man himself," he declares, beckoning Kostas closer with a wave of his hand. "You wouldn't dare consort with an enemy, now would you, brother?"

Gradually, Kostas comes forward to stand behind his father, and I can't fight the instinctive tensing of my muscles. He hasn't changed much since his last meeting with Robert. Except for the fact that he's lost his mocking smile.

"You have a pretty little bitch," he mused once about me, his accent crisp and American. "She's almost as sexy as that sister of yours."

Robert, ever the businessman, laughed at the insult to me. Right before he formed a fist and punched the younger man's jaw for the insult to his sister. Blood was everything to a Winthorp. The blood they deemed worth protecting, anyway.

Mischa's words keep echoing through my thoughts. *You don't know a damn thing about your fucking Winthorp.*

"What is the reason for this, Mischa?" Kostas wonders, drawing me back to the present. His scowl betrays the same apparent lack of respect his father has. But, as his eyes flicker across me, they widen ever so slightly.

"Have you seen this whore before?" Mischa wonders, tilting my face in the other man's direction.

Kostas scoffs dismissively. "I don't remember every bitch I've fucked, *Pakhan*."

Mischa just chuckles. "This one remembers *you*." He casually flicks a strand of hair behind my ear, exposing more of my face. "She was a particular favorite of Robert Winthorp, the younger. Do you remember now?"

Chaos erupts.

Reddening with rage, Nikolaus nearly lunges across the table. "You've crossed a line, *Mal'chik*."

"Have I?" Mischa wonders.

This close to him, I feel the subtle changes in his body before they unfold across his face. The dangerous tensing. The faint flames of rage prickling against my skin.

"Then let me ask him directly. Kostas…have you been selling to Robert Winthorp?"

Redness blossoms over the younger man's cheeks. "You even have to ask?" But his eyes cut in my direction again, slower this time. In recognition. His throat bobs slightly as he swallows. "I'd never—"

"I assume you have your personal accountant on call," Mischa says over him, directing the question to his father. "Have him run these numbers through your accounts. See if any holes match." He fishes the crumpled notebook page out of his pocket and shoves it toward Nikolaus.

The older man sneers and then spits at the table. "How fucking dare you."

Mischa doesn't display any hint of regret. Instead, his smile turns feral around the edges, his eyes less mocking than before. "If you don't want your son's treason to reflect badly on you, Nikolaus, then I suggest you run the goddamn numbers."

For a tense few seconds, they eye each other with only the polished sliver of wood between them. Then Nikolaus snatches the page up and hands it off to one of the men behind him. "Do it," he commands. "And when my son is vindicated, I will demand more than blood in compensation for sullying my family's name."

Mischa nods as if to convey, *As you wish*, though he radiates tension like a furnace. Each wave of quiet, smoldering anger feels different from the rage he directs at me. It's colder. Harder. Terrifying. Being this close to him is like having the veil that usually shielded off my emotions ripped away. I feel it all. Fear. Uncertainty. Anger?

Survival.

Think, Ellen. My memories contain a different detail about Kostas, beyond something as intangible as money. Without giving myself the time to rethink the action, I lower my mouth to Mischa's ear. His jaw clenches at my nearness. The visible disgust is almost enough to make me flinch back in fear. Almost. Before I do, I whisper something so quickly that I fear for a second he misheard me.

He narrows his eyes further, processing the hurried words. Then…he throws his head back and laughs. "If your son won't come clean, Nikolaus, then perhaps we can settle another way?" He nods toward the younger man's waist. "The woman claims to remember something about your son. Something personal. Should I tell everyone just what that is?"

"I could have fucked that bitch from anywhere," Kostas snarls.

"Oh, but you couldn't have…" Mischa stands, jostling me from his lap and rising to his full height. Nikolaus may be taller, but it's clear who has the upper hand: Mischa isn't the one forced to bow in reverence.

"Do you want to know why?" Mischa pulls me closer. "Look at her face. Look closely. You couldn't have met this whore anywhere else because, as of four days ago, she belonged to Robert Winthorp."

"How can you know that?" the dark-haired man wonders, standing as well. His expression is more curious than hostile as he scans my face. He blinks. Frowns. Leans closer. There's a slight tilt to his mouth, betraying an emotion I struggle to name. Recognition? "The Winthorps wouldn't sell one of their women to you—"

"Because I'm the one who ripped her from his grip," Mischa says. "Isn't that right, Kostas?"

The younger man says nothing, his jaw clenched, his eyes blazing.

"And even if you don't believe me, can you tell me how she knows that you have a butterfly tattoo on your right hip?"

"I will not stand for this!" Nikolaus brandishes a fist, his voice booming. "How dare you—"

"Well, does he?" the dark-haired man interjects.

Nikolaus sputters. "S-Sergei?"

"Do you, boy?" Sergei presses, turning to Kostas.

"I… I…" The younger man can't even get a word out in his defense.

Not that Mischa seems to need one. "Run the numbers," he says. "If they are off by even a cent, I'll step down right fucking now. But if not…"

The murderous tone has the effect of casting a hush over the room again, thicker and heavier than any brief silence before it.

"If not, I demand retribution—"

"N-no," Nikolaus says, visibly deflating. His shoulders slump, his eyes widening with horror. "He is *my* son. *Pakhan*—"

"We put it to a vote," Sergei says, gesturing to the men around him. "If what the *Pakhan* says is true…then I second his suggestion. This would be beyond treason." His voice betrays an unsteady note: the only hint as to the rage lurking beneath his otherwise calm exterior. "The *Pakhan* should decide his punishment."

"No!" Nikolaus glances from man to man, searching for an ally among the sea of faces.

Two men nod solemnly in agreement, but they are vastly outnumbered by the quiet consensus. Before the decision can be reinforced out loud, however, one of the men behind Nikolaus taps his shoulder and hands him the slip of notebook paper. The look on his face is grim.

Without even waiting for the results to be read out loud, Mischa nods and two of his men circle the table for Kostas.

Before they can reach him, Nikolaus stands protectively before his son. "This…this is a setup," he snarls. "Revenge. How dare you—"

"Nikolaus," Sergei says sternly. "I suggest you use your head."

"Yes," Mischa says coldly. "I don't want to declare your entire family as my enemy. Step aside."

For several tense seconds, Nikolaus doesn't move as Mischa's men close in. Finally…he concedes, stepping back. Mischa's men, including Vanya, grab Kostas on either side and muscle him toward the back of the room.

Punishment. I shiver at Mischa's interpretation of the word.

"I suggest we end this meeting here, *Pakhan*," Sergei says, inclining his head respectfully. "This is more than enough excitement for one day." He eyes me once more before turning and marshaling the men loyal to him into action.

"Dismissed," Mischa says before exiting the room pulling me along after him.

My heart hammers a painful rhythm as he hauls me out into the hallway and through the rest of the house. He takes me directly to his room at the top of the stairs, closing the door behind us.

"You gambled big for your first time, Little One," he says, his voice low and grated. Here, the tension he wore like a cloak downstairs gradually reveals the exhaustion lurking underneath. His shoulders relax from their tense line, his jaw less hard.

The subtle changes aren't enough to humanize him though. Not even a little. But they keep my surging pulse at bay. I can breathe, at least.

"As promised, I'll uphold my end." He faces me, half in shadow. "Ask something of me, Little One. What do you want?"

It's a dare more than it is a legitimate question. He's curious. It's almost enough to counteract his earlier rage. Almost.

"I won't release you, of course," he adds. "But…tell me."

It should be impossible to settle on one thing. He won't uphold any request—I know that. Yet my mind hovers over a million different things I could ask. Tempting things. Irrelevant things. Before those thoughts can even take hold, reality shoves its way to the forefront.

"The girl," I say, picturing the waif from Nicolai's. "Don't sell her, regardless of what you do to me…"

I trail off as Mischa laughs. He throws his head back, choking out the vicious, hollow sound. It's still echoing on the air as he fixes the brunt of his gaze in my direction.

"You really thought I'd go so far as to sell a *child*, Little One?" Another laugh escapes him, sharper than the first. "The girl didn't ask for this. I have no reason to sell her. But you…" He approaches me, running his hand along my injured cheek once he's close enough. "*You* have a wealth of sins to atone for, Robert Winthorp's wife. Your fate is far beyond any mercy I could spare."

It's surprisingly easy to accept my death sentence when it's uttered so finally. Mischa doesn't draw out his torture in games and riddles. He murmurs the truth into my ear and watches me tremble.

"What else?" His thumb nudges my chin, tilting it upright. "Ask."

There's more than a mocking curiosity tainting his tone now. There's impatience. Desperation? He wants something to take his mind off of what happened below, I suspect.

Licking my lips, I spit out the first thing to come to mind. "Tell me. Was it really you? At Winthorp manor that night?"

"I won't humor a fantasy," Mischa warns. "Ask me something else."

"I…" I rack my brain and settle on a pathetic whim. "Can you call me by my name?" The plea sounds so breathless when voiced out loud. My name. Not bitch, or whore, or Little One, or Robert Winthorp's wife.

"Ellen?" Mischa wonders, drawing hard on the syllables. "What does your husband call you?"

I have to force the name off the tip of my tongue. "Elle."

"Elle," he echoes, tasting it. "Is that what you want *me* to call you?"

"No." I cringe at the thought. Robert's word, here. No. Even Mischa's brutality couldn't erase the dark memories clinging to it.

"Then what?" He's even closer, his breath scalding my tender cheek.

"I… My mother called me Rose." I didn't mean to tell him that. A part of me despairs at having let something so sacred slip. "B-but you don't have to—"

"Rose." His nostrils flare as if inhaling the name itself. "Is that what you want me to call you?"

No, a part of me whispers. Rose is beautiful. Rose is untouched. Rose is one of the few parts of me Robert never desecrated.

"Fine *Rose,*" Mischa says after nearly a minute goes by without a response. He lets his hand fall but doesn't back away. If anything, his heat soaks through the fabric of my dress, assaulting me just as brutally as his knife did. "Now, I want something from you."

My breath catches in my throat. "Y-yes?"

"Your husband. Do you love him?"

"Yes." My answer is more instinctive than anything. Loving Robert is akin to how I feel most people would categorize worshiping their God—at least the one the Winthorp's chosen priest described.

Robert was all knowing in my world. All powerful. He protected me when he felt the urge and punished me when he thought I deserved it. My life was ruled by his whims, and it was all I knew.

"Good." Mischa nods in approval. "It should make it easier to die for him."

"Does it?" Once again, words sprang from my lips without my soul's permission. "No one decides how they die."

Or anyone else's death, for that matter. Robert controlled my life. I'd always assumed he'd planned it down to the very end. And now?

There are blank pages hidden in the twisted book he wrote for me. While Mischa dictates the narrative, I have some control over what goes on every page. Some say in the final chapter of my story.

"The man, Kostas?" I ask, once again speaking without permission. "Will you kill him?"

Mischa's eyes lose what little patience they had, turning hard like flint. "I suggest you don't trouble yourself with Kostastantin Vorshev," he warns. "In fact, Rose…Vorshev should be the very least of your worries."

My heart races, pounding against my rib cage. Hearing him call me "Little One" is chilling enough. But *Rose?* His lethal cadence sharpens the name, transforming it into a weapon more than a moniker.

"Do you know what you've seen tonight?" he asks, his voice still dipping toward that alarmingly low octave. "Do you?"

I shake my head, even as my mind spits out what few adjectives describe it. Ten groups of men gathered together who, for the most part, deferred to him. What is that word he said before? *Mafiya.*

"Every last soul in that room wants your husband dead, Little One," he tells me, running his fingers through my hair without warning. "And not only that. They want his head on a pike, your family name ruined. You have no idea, do you?" He looks into my eyes and frowns at what he sees. "Even Vanya. He's not as innocent as he seems. Once, he was in my position so don't doubt for a second that he couldn't return to his old ways if given enough incentive. The Winthorps killed his daughter, after all."

He waits, watching as his words sink into my skull.

"You want to know what happened the night you think you saw me? A young fuck-up had been on a mission to claim the next victim in the feud. Thirteen. And he failed. But I haven't. You will pay the price for Anna's life," he declares. "She was the sole heir to the Vasilev name, niece of its head, Sergei. You haven't heard his name, either?" He chuckles, low in his throat as if amused by the absurdity of it all. "Oh, I'm sure your husband knows. He may seem collected now, but Sergei was a million times worse than I am, Little One. During his prime, he would have gutted you without hesitation, and so much worse. I can tell you for a fact that *he* wouldn't be fooled by your little stunts—" He breaks off, his eyes narrowing at his use of the phrase.

By accident?

"And neither am I." He shakes his head fiercely and grits his teeth together so hard that I hear them crack. "Sergei wreaked hell over the Winthorps. I will finish what he started." There's admiration in his tone. There's some disgust as well, lurking deep where I doubt he even realizes it. "You are nowhere near the prize Briar would have been. But your husband seems to want you back. The question is: How badly?"

Me? No, Robert wants his numbers back. His dutiful wife. His willing victim. So many titles are tied to me, personally. Yet here I am. Still captive. Still Mischa's.

Does that reality dishearten me? Or comfort me?

"Don't look so excited," Mischa warns. "I've been wondering why he let you go so fucking easily if he's willing to kill to have you back. Is he that confident I won't kill you? Or does he have that much trust in you?"

Heat prickles through my skin as he advances, backing my body into the wall with his sheer presence alone. I taste his flavor on my tongue, unwanted and unbidden. Salt. Musk. No Vodka, however. He wanted to be sharp tonight. For the meeting? Or to finally put an end to his game?

"T-trust?" I echo, playing along.

His nostrils flare in triumph and he nods. "Oh, yes," he murmurs. "You have Vanya wrapped around your finger—he begged me not to kill you. Did he tell you?"

I swallow hard. Is he lying? I want to assume so, but his eyes are too dark. Confused. "N-no," I croak. "He didn't."

"Your husband must have trained you well," Mischa admits. "I saw how Kostas looked at you, though I can tell that you didn't choose him for yourself. Did he make you, hmm? Your precious Robert?"

He pauses for an answer I don't bother to give. I can't.

"And yet, you *love* him," he reiterates, lowering his mouth near my throat as if to taste my pulse through my skin. "Describe it for me, Little Rose. How does a man like that earn your love?"

"W-what?" My thoughts run together and collide, thrown into turmoil by the question. "He is my husband—"

"That's not what I asked." He lunges, grinding his weight into me with more menace than any weapon could ever inflict.

I want to run. I want to shove him off and risk his anger. But I can't; my arms stay woodenly at my sides, paralyzed by his heat.

"When he touches you, what do you feel?"

He cups my breast through the silk of my gown. What do I feel? Fire.

"Does he make you scream, Little One? Do you come around his cock as easily as you do around mine?"

Too…dangerous. My mind shies from the mocking taunt, but there is no escape from him. No escape from the memories haunting me—not Robert. Just him. Wrecking, violent, unbearable *him*.

"If I were a good man, I would just kill you," he breathes out almost as if to himself more than to me. "But I'm not. Am I, Little Rose? I want your husband to suffer more than just your death." The words come in growled snippets. It's like he's thinking up the plan as he goes, embellishing his own twisted ending. "I'm going to break you…" He brings his massive hands to my skull, cupping both sides of my face. Bit by bit, he applies enough pressure to make me wince. "I'll exorcize him from your head, Little One. I'll rip him from you until there's nothing left."

It's a heated promise. A threat. And he means every word.

So why does a part of me sigh in relief?

CHAPTER 19

A world without Robert. Would I even survive such a reality?

The answer is simple: *no*. Which is the only damn reason why Mischa suddenly seems so eager to replace my husband.

Robert Winthorp *is* my identity. Without him, Ellen is a hollow shell with enough space for a new monster to infest.

"Killing you would be too easy," Mischa muses, lowering his head enough to pierce my shrinking bubble of personal space. "No…"

I jump as a fiery line of heat traces the edge of my windpipe: his *tongue* stealing away the gasp building in my throat.

"You deserve worse than that."

"W-why?" I instantly regret challenging him—a sharp, warning bite on my collar is his retribution.

Only *he* can do this to me: make me question despite the consequences. Make me disobey every instinct in my body urging me to do the opposite. Run. Scream. *Survive.*

"Because your sins are so much greater than that fucker's." He presses my skull tighter between his palms, breathing heavily into my skin. Lust mingles with the hate, a familiar, stomach-churning scent even he can't disguise. "You *love* him. You accept that evil, twisted fuck. Don't you?"

I can't escape the suspicion that he wants me to deny it. His eyes glint, illuminated by an emotion I'm unable to name. A part of me hazards a guess anyway and my stomach clenches in foreboding. *Jealousy?*

"You do," he deduces before I can answer. "Fine. Since you have no problem sharing your bed with a fucking monster, you should have no problem accepting me."

He grabs my arm and shoves me toward the bed. My back hits the mattress, leaving me looking up as he advances, his head bowed with predatory intent.

Fear shoots through my veins, stealing my breath away, even as my legs drift apart despite every instinct screaming at me to run. *You're afraid...*

"My Little Rose," Mischa murmurs, gritting the words out through clenched teeth. His gaze hungrily sweeps over my splayed limbs and the skewed dress. "Should I crush you all at once? Or rip you apart, petal by petal?"

The poetic language is a new weapon in his arsenal. It's devastating. I'm paralyzed as he uses his knee to nudge my legs farther apart, creating enough space for him to fit in between them.

With slow, deliberate motions, he tugs at his waistband but grunts in disapproval when I begin to stare. "Eyes up here. I want you to look at *me*. I want to see him die in your eyes."

Eyes. As commanded, I meet his gaze and hold it. I fracture beneath the strength of it. His deepen to a shade unlike any I've ever seen. Endless amber. Fathomless. *God*. Ripples of tension release all over my body, making me quake against the sheets. They still reek of our combined scents. Blood and sweat. Harsh and soft. The conflicting aromas flood my nostrils as the rasp of an unraveling zipper pierces the air.

"I want you to think of him." The request resonates down my spine as his silhouette flickers in the shadows, suddenly looming larger. Closer. "I want him in your head when I fuck you."

Think of him. That's impossible. For the first time in so long, Robert isn't here, and the silence left behind is deafening. A new man fills the abandoned space, his pupils pinprick as his body effortlessly mounts mine, his face coming within inches of my own.

Heavy hands palm my waist, wrenching the hem of my dress up, revealing me bare underneath.

"Look at me, Little Rose," Mischa hisses, his voice raspy, his gaze almost unbearable to meet head-on.

A heartbeat later I feel him: running his fingers between my legs before replacing them with something thicker. Harder. Pulsating.

Then…

One thrust takes him deep, jarring him closer, his nose brushing mine, his groan uttered against my parted lips. My eyes flutter shut as sensation floods my entire being. The world fades for a brief, cruel moment and I'm alone inside my body, even as he dominates it. God, the way he feels. It's. Unlike. Anything. Else.

My thoughts scatter. I can only piece them back together in snippets. Full. Need. More.

"Fuck, *look at me*." His eyes are heavy-lidded when I do. His teeth seize his bottom lip as he rears back on his knees, slipping his hands beneath me for enough leverage to control the depth of every thrust. Deep. Deeper. Deeply.

My head lolls—I'm a slave to every frantic motion.

"Should I tell your husband how fucking wet you feel, Little One?" he grunts out, yanking me closer. "How your eyes roll back into your fucking head when you come. The sounds you make…"

I can't. My eyes squeeze shut, blocking out his face, chiseled with concentration. He snarls in anger, and I feel his cock stiffen—thicker, harder.

"I told you to look at me." His nails pierce the flesh of my hips in a warning. "Look at me, Little Rose."

I hear the threat of punishment in his voice. Still, I shut my eyes tighter. It's an act I'd never perform with Robert. I'd *never* disobey him. I'd never tremble at the brutality as anger takes over his movements, driving him even deeper. Into my head. Into my goddamn soul.

I'd never relish the violation.

But Mischa makes me speak a new language composed of frantic, whispered words.

"Please…p-please—"

"What?" He pauses, still buried to the hilt, leaving little room to suck in enough air to speak. "Please what?"

What? Those words won't come. I have to show him. My trembling fingers poorly convey what I want—*need*. They brush my breast in a timid stroke.

"You want me to touch you?" Mischa wonders, barely intelligible. "Beg me to."

I just nod, smothering my moan into the sheets as his thick, callused fingers graze my skin beneath the plunging neckline of my dress. He doesn't touch me. He violates me, clenching flesh and squeezing to the point of bruising. It hurts, drawing a gasp from my lips. It…feels.

My nerves can't resist him the way years of abuse trained them against Robert. His warmth sinks into my skin, his callused flesh grating over mine and melting any hint of resistance. The pinpricks of pain meld with the friction of him still inside me, churning my insides to mush and melting every sane thought in my head.

Mischa grates out something that isn't English, capturing my nipple between his thumb and his forefinger, guiding it to a stiff point. Then even words cease to matter. Our language becomes a series of groans and gasps smothered into silk and skin. His fingers roam without care or reason, fanning over my rib cage, plunging through my hair, and grasping strands so hard that my eyes water.

"Look at me." His teeth find my earlobe, grinding it between them. "Fuck. *Look at me.*"

I do. And the sight of his face, hard with determination, steals my breath away.

He looks too powerful. Too real. Too raw, hungry for me.

He crushes me with his last thrust, refusing to shift his weight even as he empties himself into me. I'm trapped beneath him, forced to bear every lethal pound. It's almost as if he's trying to drive Robert out through his presence alone.

I try to hang on to that familiar monster. I try…

But, with every passing second, his evil is harder to grasp, like smoke chased away by a raging inferno.

And, without his protection, I'm devoured whole.

CHAPTER 20

I wake up twisted in black sheets that smell of musk and sweat. For a brief, dangerous moment, I forget. My eyes flutter open as I expect what I'll see: a view of my suite at Winthorp manor. Breakfast should be coming soon, Robert soon after. Resigned, I turn toward the door—but white walls don't greet me. Then the hum of a man's deep, unsteady breathing rips the fantasy away once and for all.

Not Robert.

He always let me recollect myself in peace. He never *watched* over me in my sleep, his gaze searing my skin.

"I know you're awake," Mischa says after nearly a full minute of silence, his voice gruff. "Get up."

I dutifully roll onto my side, taking in more of my surroundings. He left me slung over the edge of the bed with my feet against the floor. I still feel his release drying against my inner thigh, along with his taste on my tongue.

A flicker of motion from the corner of my eye reveals him standing near the opposite side of the bed, fully dressed.

"Here." He lets something fall beside me onto the bed and offers an object clenched in his hand: a glass of water. "Swallow it."

Swallow? Groaning, I muster my sore limbs enough to sit upright as my hand feels over the sheets. Something small and round strikes my fingers. White. A pill? "W-what is it?" I risk asking, my voice hoarse.

Could he have devised some new plan to use me against Robert? Drug me? Poison?

He doesn't provide an answer for so long that my muscles start to protest from the awkward position. Is it a test? Or maybe something so much worse, I realize, looking up. His eyes are narrowed, his jaw clenched against a response.

"My plan doesn't include sending you back to your husband pregnant," he says finally.

Oh. The pill in my hand takes on a less nefarious purpose. I swallow it diligently and sip from the glass he's shoved into my hand. This action raises a question I don't have the nerve to voice: Why now? Only days ago, he scoffed at the idea of contraception.

Has he decided to extend his timeline for my capture? When put into perspective with my inevitable death, I'm not sure what's more appealing: dying sooner or later?

"I think you played your role too well last night, Little Rose," Mischa adds, frowning. "You caught more notice than I expected." His hand brushes my bandaged cheek and I recoil. The touch almost felt genuine. Unconcerned, Mischa curls his fingers into a fist instead. "Someone offered to buy you. They offered me *a lot* to buy you."

"You still plan to sell me," I deduce, folding my hands together.

Suddenly, his previous action makes perfect sense. Am I surprised? Disappointed? At least he saw the value in ensuring he only has one life to take when he finally tires of me. How noble.

"Who said anything about selling you?" Mischa wonders, tilting my chin toward him. "Oh, no, Robert's wife. I am not finished with you yet."

But… I sense a big one, even as the seconds pass without him saying it.

He scans my face with renewed interest. Something is on his mind. Something pressing enough to supposedly make him overlook accepting money for me. At least for now.

"You said Marnie was your mother."

It's surprisingly difficult, hearing her name come out of his mouth. His accent distorts the two beautiful syllables I've only heard uttered inside my head for so long.

"Y-yes—"

"When were you born?"

"She died when I was seven," I admit, skirting the question directly. Why? I don't know. He's asking for too much. More than Robert ever has. More than anyone.

"Which makes you twenty-three," he says, deducing my age for himself. "You are younger than I thought, Little Rose." He genuinely seems surprised, and I can't resist attempting to gauge his age as well.

His skin is weathered by more than just scars. Hard, long years. Brutal years. If someone put a gun to my head, I'd peg him to be around his mid-thirties, the same age as Robert.

He never reveals the number himself, however. Instead, he cocks his head, observing me even more closely. "I suppose it makes sense now," he says, almost to himself. "You must look like her. Perhaps he wanted to finish the job."

"W-who?" I don't know where the courage to voice the question comes from. "Who wanted to buy me?"

"A dangerous man, Little Rose," he admits. "Whoever told you that story about your mother lied to you. Or you've been lying to *me*—"

"No," I say, risking his anger to cut him off. "I'd never lie about her."

"Well, she didn't 'leave' Winthorp Manor before you were born," he says. "She was taken—no, she was *marked*."

"You mean..." I reach up automatically, feeling my brand sting beneath a layer of gauze. "My mother?" A part of this feud? It seems too fanatical. Too convoluted, even for the Winthorps.

And yet…

For the first time, Mischa doesn't sport either his mocking smirk or his hostile glare. "It seems I have much to teach you, Little Rose," he says softly, drawing his hand away. "I am not your only enemy. Not by far. In fact"—he rubs his chin while an unreadable expression shapes his features—"I'll leave the choice up to you. I won't bind you or lock you away tonight. You may have full run of the property to stick your nose where it doesn't belong. And I hope you remember what lurks beyond my protection."

"P-protection?"

It's the first time he's phrased my captivity in that way: *protection*. Mangled by his accent, the word sounds more like doom than salvation.

"Perhaps." His lip quirks in a dangerous imitation of a smile —or a grimace. "I don't want to break you just yet. Your death should mean something, Little Rose. I want it to count. I want you to know full well when and why your blood is being spilled. All in good time."

He pulls away before I can see his expression. I have to discern what little clues I can from his stance. His shoulders harbor tension, his spine rigid. He's serious. He means it— and something warns me that he's thinking over my eventual death very carefully.

In a sick way, he almost reminds me of Briar as she planned her wedding, pouring her attention into every tiny detail to distract herself from the overall picture: that she was marrying a man her father had chosen and what dress she would wear or salad she selected didn't mean a damn thing in the grand scheme.

I don't know what's worse, really: being a slave to the whims of others or believing that, even for a second, you can somehow shape the narrative. That you have say. Maybe that's one small part of Robert I admire. Apart from sex, he never planned a damn thing. He took, and he fucked, and he let the cards lie where they may.

He never left me guessing.

"Has Ivan asked you about your mother?" Mischa asks.

I shake my head. "No."

"Lie to him if he does."

I can't stop myself from questioning, "Why?"

"Should I tell you?" He cocks his head, glancing at me over his shoulder. "No, I don't think I should," he decides. "But I suggest you trust me on this, Little Rose. Vanya is a good man"—he frowns as if annoyed by that fact—"but good men can have their own secrets."

With that, he heads for the door and shoulders it open, leaving my head spinning and more questions on my tongue. This time, I don't have the energy to voice them.

"I'll say this again: Have your run of the property," Mischa calls from the doorway. "Explore to your heart's content and remember how many monsters are hungry for you beyond these walls."

The door slams behind him, rattling the ornate frame surrounding it.

And I just sit here on my captor's bed, drowning in his scent.

xplore. The guttural taunt echoes in my thoughts as I take the hottest shower I can stand. Still wet, I creep into the bedroom and venture toward the dresser for a second time.

His clothing is exquisitely tailored, meaning only his shirts have any hope of fitting me. I settle on a white one and roll the sleeves up. The high collar disguises the worst of my neck, at least. My hair, however, is a hopeless cause that I tuck behind my ears, and my face can only be salvaged by wiping away the fresh blood and ignoring the bruising around my right eye.

It's only as I smooth the hem around my knees that I recognize the routine I've fallen into. Pretending. Perfecting.

Robert liked me properly dressed at all times outside of his room. He liked me to smile, and preen, and primp like the prettiest bird, happy in her cage. He'd hiss in disgust at the sight of me now: a bruised and broken plaything, bitten by another beast.

Here, there is no use pretending, and I let my hands fall with a sigh as I heed my captor's words.

I *explore*.

A part of me half expects to find the door to the room locked as I palm the handle. But, when I twist it slowly, it turns in my grip and I swallow hard. Beyond the door, I don't spy Mischa lurking in the hall.

In fact, it's empty, devoid of even his men. I don't cross a single soul as I creep toward the central corridor. Rather than savor my rare moment of freedom, I remember Mischa's command. *Have your run of the property.*

It's large, for one—overwhelmingly so. High, vaulted ceilings capture every sound made beneath them and throw them back ten times louder. I swear I can even hear my heartbeat mocking me in an unsteady echo. The air feels stale, untouched. As if no one has been here in ages, yet at the same time, everything has been meticulously maintained.

Does Mischa really live here?

I don't find any portraits on the walls to give me a clue. No photographs like the ones covering nearly every inch of the grand halls in Winthorp Manor, either. Robert Sr. took pains to ensure that anyone who entered his home knew just who had built it. Prestige and acknowledgment were everything. In the eyes of a Winthorp, being ignored was a fate worse than death, one saved for only the most worthless among them…

The feel of polished wood beneath my fingers draws my attention back to the present. Instinct must have guided me here without any input from my brain: I'm before a door. The one to Mischa's study.

Stick your nose where it doesn't belong.

With his taunt in my head, I hesitate for only a second before palming the handle and crossing the threshold. Everything looks untouched. Still, I circle the desk and wrench a drawer open for the hell of it. Do I expect to find anything of value? No.

But I can't ignore the thrill building in my stomach as I run my fingers through loose pens and scattered bits of blank paper. He's messy, forsaking the strict organization Robert prided himself on. My husband arranged his pens by nib color and size, preferring to have them lined up on the right-hand side of his desk, at the ready. He kept photos on the opposite end. Of me, of his father. He would look at either one depending on which mood he felt like embodying at that given moment: ruthless or vengeful? He could switch them out like hats.

Mischa keeps no such reminders, at least none I can discern. There are no trinkets, no keepsakes, no women—family or otherwise. Oh, but there have been. I picture the red room with renewed interest. Where would a heartless shell of a man keep reminders of his woman?

The answer is as intangible as it is obvious: *everywhere*. My perfume permeated Robert's suite. I may have been rarely seen and barely heard, but he was aware of my presence. *Always.* He relished in it: the captive bird whose chirping he could sense, no matter the room she was in.

Maybe the identity of Mischa's bird lurks in plain sight as well?

When I leave the study in search of another room, I find nothing in it. It's empty, decorated in muted grays, with no sign of life in sight. The room beside it reveals nothing, either. Neither do the rest in the entire wing. Retracing my steps back to Mischa's room feels like a halfhearted retreat to familiar ground—at least until I enter the room beside his.

My fingers tremble as I switch the light on and scan the interior for the second time. In the end, the perfume and the old clothes are my only finds. Mischa guards his secrets too well. He upholds his end of the bargain by letting me explore in peace, but I can sense him waiting deeper in the house for me to find.

I chase his essence down the grand staircase and then through an array of cavernous rooms. I suppose it's only fitting that I eventually spot his shadow in one of them, seated opposite an imposing man with dark hair. He's familiar, in fact, conjuring uneasy tension in my belly. *Sergei.*

"I came here alone, *Pakhan*," he says, conveying his chilling sense of calm. "I have no motive."

"With all due respect, I have to wonder why a man like you would want to waste good money on a Winthorp whore," Mischa replies.

Heart in my throat, I freeze, watching the exchange from the mouth of the hall.

"Waste? No." Sergei inclines his head dismissively. "Perhaps I want to *spare* the girl from whatever fate you have in store. After all, your hatred is toward the Winthorps themselves, is it not? I know the boy has contacted you about her—"

"Do you now?" Mischa counters, sounding unnerved in stark contrast to how I feel.

My blood runs cold. My heart stops. It takes me seconds to pick apart the cryptic riddle: the boy. *Robert?*

"I also know that you've refused him, despite what he offered. Why? Does revenge really mean so much to you? Or maybe there's some other reason you want to torment this woman—"

"Perhaps," Mischa admits. "Maybe I'm simply not finished with her yet."

"And when will you be? Finished?" Sergei counters. "Or have you lost yourself that much you can't even foresee an end to your brutality?"

"Careful, Sergei," Mischa says softly. "One might think you've forgotten the mission you yourself started. Have you forgotten Anna-Natalia already?"

"Never," the other man counters. "But I've lived long enough to learn that violence solves very little."

"And yet, you gave up your title as leader. Unless you've changed your mind?"

"No." Sergei leans forward, bracing his hands against the armrests of his chair. "Don't challenge me, Mischa. I meant no offense. But if you wish to keep the girl, it's your decision." He inclines his head respectfully before rising from the table. "You know how to reach me if you change your mind."

He turns for the door, spotting me there. His eyes scan my body slowly, honing in on my face with uncomfortable scrutiny.

"I can show myself out," he says to Mischa before advancing over the threshold.

I scurry back, pressing myself against the wall to clear enough space for him to pass. But he doesn't. He inclines his head instead, observing me more closely.

"What is your name?" He speaks softly enough that only I can hear.

I say nothing.

"Can you speak?" He frowns, gingerly swiping his thumb along my wounded cheek. "Your face... You look so much like—"

"Pardon me, Sergei," Mischa says, appearing in the doorway with his arms crossed. "I should keep better track of my toys."

"It is no trouble," Sergei replies, stepping back. "I was just curious if she had a name."

Mischa shrugs. "Not that I remember and not that it matters." He sounds casual enough, but his tone is harder than it should be. *Why?*

Perhaps for the same reason Sergei's eyes narrow ever so slightly, even as he maintains that calm smile. "Of course." He shifts his weight, appearing to turn. *Wham!* Something nudges my foot, throwing me off-balance, right into a wall of rigid muscle. Before I can attempt to regain my bearings, hot breath nudges my ear, carrying two grated syllables. "Elena?"

There's pain in that hollow tone.

And even more alarming…

There's recognition.

"Something wrong?" Mischa calls.

"My apologies," Sergei mutters as his hand settles over my shoulder.

"No. The apologies are *mine*." Another grip seizes my opposite forearm, decidedly harsher. "It appears she requires more training," Mischa says coldly, yanking me back before positioning himself in front of me. "I'll be sure to see to that."

Sergei says nothing. From my position, I can only hear his retreating footsteps, slow and hesitant. "Wait—" He speaks rapidly in a language I can't understand.

Whatever he says makes Mischa stiffen, his head tilted thoughtfully to the side. He's thinking, mulling something over. Then he shakes his head. "*Nyet*. She is not for sale."

Sergei laughs. "As you wish. My offer still stands if you change your mind."

He continues down the entire length of the hall. Before I can be sure that he's gone, I'm yanked off-balance and into a vacated room.

"What did he tell you?" Mischa demands.

My heart pounds out a frantic rhythm. Since my capture, I've never heard him sound like this. Guttural. Raw. On edge.

His eyes flash menacingly when I remain silent. "I won't ask you twice—"

"N-nothing," I insist.

"Oh?" His nostrils flare as if catching the stench of the lie in the air. "Then what did you say to *him*, Little Rose?"

I shake my head. "*Nothing.*"

"Then why did he just double his price for you?"

His price? Only now do I remember his earlier threat. *Someone offered to buy you…*

"Can you tell me why a man like Sergei Vasilev would offer two million for a Winthorp whore?"

My mind reels. Two million? Shocked, I have to force myself to reply, "I-I don't know—"

"If you fear me, then you should be terrified of Sergei. I've kept your soul intact." He tilts my chin, forcing me to meet his gaze, and nods. "It's still there. I've shown you far more mercy than you realize. But Sergei…"

There's a rare note of respect in his voice that triggers unease in my body. I picture the man from the night before, with his unrelenting calm and quiet power. Mischa not only respects him, he's *afraid* of him.

"Do you believe that men can change?" he wonders, pressing his thumb against my lower lip to demand an answer. "Do you?"

"N-no." If life with Robert taught me one thing, it was that men, of all creatures in this world, are the most set in their ways. The most stubborn. The most fearful of change. Poor Vanya seemed to be learning that the hard way, though I'm not stupid enough to mention that now. I simply nod against his palm. "They can't."

"Then you, my Little Rose, have a new monster to hide from. Sergei offered money for you, but that was just a formality. He can't demand you directly…" He stares beyond me, and I suspect he's speaking more to himself than anyone else. "But when he wants something, he gets it eventually—"

"Why would he want me?" An answer comes from the back of my mind before Misha can give me one. It's something Sergei himself said. *You look like her…*

"To fuck," Mischa suggests crudely. "To kill. Take your pick—"

"M-my mother." Pain constricts my chest. I can barely get my next words out. "Did…did he—"

"Rape her?" Mischa wonders. "Probably."

He makes the violent act sound so casual. And I look like her. Marnie. Sergei could have some sick fetish for reliving his abuse of her. Or…

"You're wondering if he could be your father?" Mischa asks, intruding upon my deepest thoughts without care or permission. "The timeline works, but from the rumors I've heard, your father could be any one of the men in the Vasilev employ."

Hot tears escape down my cheeks too quickly to attempt to hold back. Memories of my mother are like delicate shards of broken glass I've carefully preserved all these years. Beautiful to look at, painful to touch. I look like her, now more than ever, in a way Briar could only dream. Our scars are the same. Haunted, hollow, empty eyes.

"This hurts you," Mischa says.

I expect him to laugh, savoring my pain. Instead…his thumb catches a tear and smears it against the flesh of my cheek as if to ensure it was real.

"Knowing that your father could be one of them—"

"Stop."

"Didn't you ever question why she never told you?"

I did, only to conjure more pain whenever I felt heartless enough to mention it. "*Stop*—"

"If you had a child with me, and I let you run back to your precious husband. Would you ever tell her who I was?"

The question is as cruel as it is unbearable to contemplate. "No."

"Is that the same courtesy you extend to your child with Winthorp?"

Enough. I squeeze my eyes shut, slapping my hands over my ears. No. He can't pull this answer out of me. I won't let him—

"Look at me." His voice echoes inside my head, impossible to escape. "I won't tell you twice—"

"Just kill me." I utter the words while peeling my eyes open to gauge his expression. I find nothing. Not even hate. Just emptiness.

"This *is* killing you," he says. "Knowing that I can get inside your head. That I can take whatever the fuck I want—"

"Then take it!" I'm screaming though I don't know why. Or why more tears fall, coating my chin in wetness.

Robert is a parasite, feeding on whatever I have to give—but Mischa is a virus, invading every inch of me and turning my own body into a stranger's. Someone I hate.

"Or is torturing me how you ignore your own pain?" I wonder, knowing full well that it's already too late to turn back. "Number *seven*?"

I see black. Feel fire. Taste blood.

As I blink frantically, I realize I'm on the floor, staring up at the face of a monster. His fist is clenched, the knuckles dripping blood as my left cheek throbs in agony. His eyes are downcast, his mouth tight. In shock? Horror? His fingers flex, and for the first time, I see something I could describe as *human* in him.

Regret?

Regardless, I wait for my stomach to clench in fear and the cowering instincts I've lived by for so long to rear their head. Instead, my skin burns, set alight by shame and hate. *Hate.* I've never hated Robert. I loathe Mischa. The foreign emotion festers inside me, controlling my muscles and blotting out every intelligible thought.

With my head throbbing, I somehow make it onto my feet. Onto him, nails drawn, legs kicking, hands slapping, biting. Anything I can reach. I've played one game for so damn long that I have no patience for another.

If he wants to kill me, then he can kill me.

Now.

Another blow knocks me to the ground—his entire body. He pins me with his weight, using his hands to trap me beneath him. He's impervious to every blow I land. Kick after kick after kick. But he never retaliates.

He just shouts. Something my brain refuses to decipher. I don't want to hear him.

So I scream, aggravating my own eardrums. Like this, he can't reach me, not even when he wraps his hands around my throat and squeezes. Robbed of air, I choke. I wheeze.

And when he finally lets me go, I sob, shutting my eyes against his presence. He's still speaking. Still threatening. Still growling.

But I hear nothing. Just my own racing heartbeat and a jagged fragment of memory, repeating on a loop: *Elena. Elena. Happy birthday, Elena…*

Footsteps rattle the floor. Advancing? No, retreating.

He's gone—from the room at least. But, like any devastating illness, he lingers inside my head, and I'll go insane trying to keep him out.

The memory is a cruel one, beginning the way the worst ones always do. With her.

Soft fingertips parted my hair in a gentle caress, coaxing me awake. "Happy birthday." The sweet voice sounded warmer than the purest ray of sunshine. So very beautiful. God, I'd give anything to hear it again… "My sweet girl," she murmured. "Already so big."

I peeled my eyes open, always in awe of her quiet beauty. Scars haunted her blue eyes, but I was young enough then to mistake them as a natural part of what made my mother so delicate. Her pain was a beacon, broadcasting to anyone and everyone the purity of her soul. It was the only thing of value she had left.

And for that reason, everyone wanted it.

"I can't stay long," she warned before pressing a kiss to my cheek. "I just wanted to wish you a wonderful day. Seven, already."

It sounded like such a prestigious age when she uttered it. Seven years. Seven long, painful years that had taken their toll on her youthful features. Only through memory can I track how she'd withered away right before my eyes. Her smile was fainter that day than any before it, shielding a million secrets I'd never learn.

"I have to go now." Noise in the hallway drew her attention and she hurried to her feet, smoothing the skirt of her dress.

Her visits had become less frequent by then. Sometimes days would pass without one. I'd only catch glimpses of her on my way through the halls as I assisted Martha, one of the servants. Always with Briar, her face turned away from me as though I didn't exist.

"Wait." A whine tugged at my voice, making her frown. "Please...can you sing it to me again? Just one more time?"

Her lips twitched, but with a wary glance over her shoulder, she returned to my side, placing her mouth near my ear. "Happy birthday to you. Happy birthday to you." Her fingers returned to stroking my hair, and I curled into her side, relishing the few extra moments of her attention. "Happy birthday, dear Elena. Happy birthday to you, my precious Rose..."

"Eat." His voice shatters the memory. The remnants of it cut into me—all of those questions I never asked. Like why she called me *Elena* only then, once a year, hidden away in a song.

Or why a monster would ever think to call me by it years after she's been gone.

"I said *eat*."

Something clatters onto the floor by my side. A tray, I see once I peel my eyes open. It contains a sandwich and a bottle of water. I ignore them both by turning my face into the space between my raised knees.

As he has for what feels like an eternity, Mischa lingers for only a second before retreating from the room, slamming the door in his wake. I'm on a lower level. A basement, I think? Somewhere he dragged me after I attacked him. Newer memories meld with older ones, distorting the past few hours. Twenty…thirty?

Three days. I've been in this room for three days. It's starting to smell. *I'm* starting to smell. I'm starting to die.

My muscles ache, wasting away as my stomach protests days of hunger. My throat is so dry that each breath irritates my tender esophagus, but at least there's no moisture left in me to waste on tears. Without the fear of triggering any sobbing, I delve into those dark, deep memories I've left untouched for over sixteen years.

I chase my mother.

And she avoids me, even now, lurking in the depths of my psyche that hurt to reach.

I was her biggest secret, hidden away in a room at the very back of the servant's wing. I was her greatest treasure. Only now do I realize just what she left behind for me, as her legacy. The *real* reason why Robert Sr. reclaimed her, even after she'd been tainted by his enemy. Why Robert wanted me.

We look alike, after all. Our eyes were the same, well beyond any resemblance we shared with Briar. Our expressions were fragile, sporting tiny, hairline cracks. To monstrous men, those flaws glowed like tempting signs proclaiming, *I am weak. Break me. Destroy me.*

In the end, my mother destroyed herself in silence, with the aid of a razor blade and a running bath. By doing so, she passed her curse onto me. She revealed the only way out for someone like us: A doe can only survive at the mercy of a wolf for so long.

"Damn you. Eat!"

Another monstrous clang rouses me from my thoughts, but it's harder to leave my head for the real world. My eyes refuse to focus. It's bright. Someone turned a light on, illuminating my sparse surroundings and the concrete floor.

Four days. It's been four days since he brought me here when I refused to move from the pathetic puddle he'd left on the ground of the upstairs drawing room.

Four days since I stopped eating or drinking.

Four days since I first utilized the only gift my mother ever gave me: silence. She used it as a weapon, breaking it only on the rarest occasions, like my meager birthdays, honored once a year for just a few minutes at a time. Briar had parties. She had gifts beyond anything I could ever dream of receiving.

I had Marnie's love, the cruelest present of them all.

"Eat." Once again, Mischa's voice yanks me from the past. Or does he? Is he even here, or have I imagined him? My mother's face morphs into his, invading my one and only sanctuary. "Fuck—eat!"

Someone grabs my chin and pries my lips apart to shove a warm object between them. Something metal containing a liquid I let roll off my tongue, even as my stomach lurches in desperation. I taste nothing. Feel nothing.

Just…rage, so palpable that it stings like a physical blow.

"Damn you."

More wetness. Cold. When I don't swallow, a torrent of fluid drips down my nose and rolls down my chin.

Again, I'm left alone with Marnie. She doesn't acknowledge me, even now. She merely lurks around the edges of my consciousness, always out of reach. *Four days.*

The count remains the same when I'm disturbed by a soft hand brushing my cheek—not Mischa's. The fingers are too small. So is the face staring back at me as I force my eyes to focus.

No. Not her… Mischa is a cruel, unfeeling bastard. Hatred for him is the first tangible emotion I've felt in days. It burns through my sore, wasting limbs, too weak to direct itself toward anything in particular.

Nicolai's girl watches me with an unreadable expression. Her brown eyes stare blankly, even as she pats my chin and guides a utensil toward my lips with her free hand. A spoon.

The urge to refuse is nearly impossible to resist. I'm so close. Marnie feels nearer than ever. A few more days and I'd finally find her again. Touch her. Be near her with no one to come between us.

But guilt is a terrible, persistent thing. Marnie may have been immune to it at the end of her life, but I'm not. When the girl nudges my lips with the spoon, I part them and swallow the liquid gathered on it. My shriveled taste buds fail to discern a flavor. I just drink each mouthful woodenly, emptying the bowl. Upon setting it aside, the girl reaches for a bottle of water and silently urges me to finish it next.

Someone's cleaned her up and brushed her hair, having plaited it into two small braids. They dressed her as well, in a clean pink shirt and jeans. Vanya? Only he would be kind enough.

Has he sent her to me?

No. Most men aren't selfish enough to use a child to do his bidding—but a monster would be. Not even because he cared about my welfare.

He just wasn't finished with me yet.

When I gulp down the last drop of water, the girl gathers up the bowl and the bottle and exits the room, leaving the door open so that a sliver of light can penetrate my prison. It's a silent gesture that conveys an unmistakable request.

Four days of filth waft from my skin. What little waste I managed to expel is in a bucket in the corner of the room. Mischa never locked the door himself—my imprisonment had been self-imposed. Leaving now would be a harrowing defeat.

But if I don't, he'll send her again, forcing her to feed my emaciated frame.

Forcing her to watch me die.

With a groan, I unfurl my sore limbs. Weak with disuse, my legs refuse to fully support my weight. I have to cling to the wall with both hands just to rise to my feet, and leaving the room is a slow, painful ordeal.

Somehow, I make it up the stairs to the first floor. I pass no one, not even the girl. Not Mischa. I can't escape the feeling that he planned it, this silence that chases me through the halls and into the red room beside his.

I choose it solely for its familiarity. Nothing else.

After wrestling the door closed, I lock it. Then I stagger into the bathroom and lock that door as well. The sunken tub is a tempting escape. I draw the water scalding hot and collapse in the center of it, letting the warm wetness consume me.

How pathetic. I always thought I was above such an act: suicide. Marnie took her own life, but even after years of torment, I've never done the same. Not even when Robert showed me his worst. Not even when he made me wish for death.

I've never been desperate enough.

Or brave enough.

Am I now?

The answer eludes me as the water level rises. I lie here motionless, letting the moisture seep into my nostrils and lap at my parted lips. Just as my lungs start to burn, I tilt my head toward the ceiling and inhale the humid air.

Only now do I hear it. Thunder? No. *Pounding.*

In the end, I don't know how long it takes him to break the door down. He appears in the room amid a sound like thunder, his chest heaving, his eyes a flashing amber. He deflates when he sees me in the tub, still alive, his hands flexing in and out of fists.

Meeting his gaze, I force my dry, cracked lips to part and address him for the first time in days. "Mention my mother again and I'll kill myself." The falling water adds an ominous backdrop I couldn't have planned on my own to the threat. "You'll have to send my body back to Robert, still *his.* Always."

I'm dangling before him an object every monster covets: ownership. Does he want it?

His expression reveals nothing.

Robert would laugh at such an ultimatum. Then he'd drag me from the bath and show me just how many ways he fucking *owned* me.

Mischa? He meets my gaze and I shiver despite the steaming water basting my limbs. Four days have changed him almost as dramatically as they've affected me. Something cut his cheek, leaving three slender red lines slashed into the flesh. My fingers burn as if in guilt. Did I do that to him?

Darker stubble coats his jaw, contrasting with the sun-kissed gold of his hair. Dark shadows taint the skin beneath his eyes. From exhaustion? No… From brooding, smoldering rage. My punishment lurks behind those dangerous eyes. Soon, I'll feel it. Our dynamic of master and captive will be restored.

But for now?

He doesn't drag me from the tub. He doesn't say a damn word to me at all. He turns on his heel. He leaves, and he lets me have the one thing even my mother never gave me.

He lets me have one single round all to myself.

He lets me win.

I lurk inside the red room, in self-imposed exile, while clues as to the goings-on of the rest of the manor's occupants seep through the door. Mischa's been busy, it seems. Shouts ring out from below as footsteps rattle the walls. Apart from a stern-faced man coming to replace the doors to the bedroom and bathroom, I'm left alone. The chaos rages around me like a storm, but I'm too tired to stick my head beyond the doorway and gauge its intensity. Instead, I sleep, savoring the precious hours of peace.

I bide my time.

Winning matters to men almost as much as their money does. Rarely do they lose their precious little games—and only when a greater prize is worth the forfeit.

So what is his end goal?

It terrifies me to admit the obvious: I don't know, and I can't even begin to guess.

Mischa's punishment lords on my horizon like a cloud, inescapable and building in strength with every passing second. How will he deliver it? With physical blows? With sex? By selling me?

The logical part of my brain does its best to muster up fear of any one of those scenarios. But it's no use. What little food I've ingested since leaving the basement doesn't return my itch for survival. I'm far too reckless when it comes to imagining what I can endure now.

A beating.

A rape.

Being whored out to other men.

None of those prospects inspire the terror they used to.

I'm too damn tired. I just want him to get it over with, whatever his plan may be.

But he's too damn patient.

When a knock rattles the door, he isn't the one behind it. Instead, I find Vanya, his expression wary. Balanced on his hands is another tray, this one containing a bowl of soup, a sandwich, and more water.

"Is…is something wrong?" I croak, alarmed by his serious expression.

"We will talk when you're feeling better," he says, his voice strained. "For now… Eat."

I take the tray from him without complaint, but he doesn't leave. Instead, he watches while I bring the food to the bed and force a few bites down. On behalf of Mischa or himself?

I can't tell.

Satisfied, he faces me directly, folding his hands over his lap. "I suggest you stay out of sight today. Mischa is planning —" He breaks off and seems to rethink his words. "Just stay out of his way."

"Why?" I can't stop myself from questioning him despite the part of me clenching in foreboding. Judging from the look in Vanya's eyes, whatever Mischa is up to, I don't want to know. "Is he planning to sell me?"

"Sell you?"

I'm caught off guard by how Vanya laughs.

"Things would be so much easier if he were, believe it or not."

I stiffen, but he doesn't sound malicious. Just…alarmed? "What is that supposed to mean?"

He meets my gaze. In the dim lighting, he looks so much older. Wizened and worn. "It means that you need to be more careful around him," he warns. "I won't pretend to know what you've been through before now. But Mischa… He can be a terrifying enemy. Or he can be a ruthless ally. If he sees you as a threat, he will eliminate you quickly." He frowns, eyeing me as if seeing me for the first time. His hand drifts toward my cheek only for him to lower it without touching me. "But if he sees you as a tool worth having, he will never let you go."

My brain mulls his words over, pairing them with the way Mischa cornered me in the bath, constantly weighing my worth to Robert.

I'm his enemy still. I'm sure of it.

So then why does Vanya's silence unnerve me as he leaves, closing the door behind him? Alone, I devour the rest of the food without dwelling on the tempting impulse to throw it away. When I finish, I leave the tray outside the door and climb onto the bed.

With Mischa's use for me in question, it's ironic that I've been forced to wear the strange woman's clothing once again. I chose a simple white dress that might have been a nightgown, yet I feel her in every inch of satin. She mocks me, this faceless predecessor. She taunts me.

You'll never know him.

Whoever she was, Mischa cared enough about her to save these delicate items of clothing. That act alone contrasts with everything there is to hate about him. It brought up an even more dangerous emotion: curiosity.

And, deep down, I know I've already learned far too much about my new monster.

I know what he feels like aroused.

I've tasted his rage.

As for his revenge…

It's dark when heavy footsteps approach the newly repaired door and give me an inkling of what lies in store for me. Unsteadiness. Each footfall scrapes the floor, slow and reluctant. The figure they belong to casts a wide enough shadow to blot out all light emanating from the hall. I'm bathed in darkness for so long that my eyes begin to adjust as the knob finally turns, revealing the creature lurking over the threshold.

Any hesitation he might have felt is left at the door. He strides boldly into the bedroom, slamming the door in his wake. The lock clicks and I watch him approach from the bed.

My stomach lurches as I spot something dangling from his right hand. Long. Thin…

Before I can name it, his knee extends, nudging me onto my side. My stomach. With me blinded, he mounts me from behind, ruthlessly using his weight to pin me in place. One of his hands cinches mine, wrapping something around my wrist. Rope? It bites into my flesh as he secures the limb beyond my head. To the bed frame? I tug it only to meet resistance.

With my thoughts still spinning, he does the same to the other.

And only now do I feel something: fear.

At his mercy, there is no escape.

I tense in anticipation as his hand grazes the back of my thigh and draws the hem of my dress up. Cold air kisses the flesh as if in warning: *Brace yourself.* He feels between my legs next, sliding what I suspect is the pad of a thumb along my entrance. Far too softly, so unlike his usual roughness. As if to spite me, he lingers there, testing me, and I can almost picture the thought circling his mind: hard or slow?

My punishment comes without delay. He chooses *both*. Every inch of his length slams inside me with no preamble. Stretching. Taking. Claiming.

Facedown against the sheets, I smother my moan into the silk.

Breathe, Ellen. After four choked gasps, I realize it's impossible. From this angle, he's deeper than he's ever been. Harder. Thicker. *Harsher.* The second thrust throws me forward, straining my binds and ramming the top of my skull against the headboard. My eyes shut as another gasp escapes my lips to sink into the sheets. Another. Another.

On the fifth brutal slam of his hips, real panic starts to gnaw away at the numbness. I can handle his hate. Or his lust. Not *this*.

Not silence.

He isn't frenzied, grunting with each thrust. He's slow. Careful. Precise. Each strike brutalizes a particular spot deep inside me that aches at the stimulation. It throbs. Heats. Ignites. The building pressure spreads through my belly, swiftly gathering in intensity until I'm moaning with every pass of his hips.

Robert fucked me only for his pleasure, taking what he wanted. Never *giving* this deliberate, callous…feeling.

I thrash, shaking my head, and buck against him desperate to arouse his rage.

Fuck me.

Hate me.

Knowing damn well how to attack, he *touches* me, sliding his fingers along the ridge of my entrance, above where we're joined. Too close. Too hard. Not hard enough.

Then he groans, smothering the sound against my ear. Words, I think. My brain struggles to interpret them.

"*Bea..tiful.* Fuck, you're beautiful—" Sharp teeth scrape the back of my throat and then bite down hard, grinding the flesh between them. *Take it.*

There is no reprieve. He rocks his hips, grinding the blunted tip of his cock against my abused walls. My eyelids flutter as my nails clutch at the air for stability.

I can taste his madness on my tongue. It grows more potent with every unsteady lurch of the bed and jolt through my core. Bit by bit, he loses that careful rhythm and just…punishes.

Slick flesh and sinful heat churn my thoughts into a senseless mass. Then, all at once, the harsh friction reaches a boiling point and every nerve short-circuits. Pleasure is a neutron bomb going off inside my skin. Muscles clench and tense, pulling him deep, deep, deep. Right when he begins to pulse inside me…

He wrenches himself out.

Fiery spurts of liquid splash against the backs of my thighs, and then he's gone. The mattress bounces as his weight withdraws. A metallic hiss betrays the sound of metal slicing through my binds, releasing me to lie here boneless and panting for breath.

He leaves me like that, huddled and used.

And, as the door slams, I begin to understand what other weapons he has in his arsenal besides physical violence.

He brings *pleasure*.

And, for the sake of my soul, I should fear every fucking drop.

❧

Robert never played with fire. At least not the brand Mischa likes to set.

Sex with my husband was an ordeal I knew how to cope with. I'd studied how to bear it.

I never dreaded it.

Five hours after he left, I know that my new tormentor will return. Soon. He'll do this to me again.

Will I let him? A shudder ripples through me; I've never contemplated such a thing before. Choice. I've never had to weigh the consequences of one action against the pain of another. In twenty-three years, I've *never* feared reaching my breaking point—not like this. I've never had to look in the mirror and wonder, *How much more can you take?*

The woman staring back at me doesn't seem to know. Her blue eyes sport visible cracks, splintering her stoic façade. Something terrifying lurks underneath those delicate features. I feel it running through my skin, causing my fingers to tremble against the countertop. In a desperate bid to suppress whatever it is, I draw another bath and scrub myself clean of every ounce of Mischa. When I return to the bedroom wrapped in a towel, I find another tray waiting for me on the bed.

I dress first, raiding the mysterious wardrobe for a modest black frock. Then I sip from a bowl of soup and obediently empty the accompanying water bottle.

After leaving the tray outside my door, I retreat within the room and wait. It should be a familiar game—the preferable option to any other. I used to wait for Robert without fail, anticipating his various moods to better withstand them.

I try to predict Mischa. I let the darkest depths of my imagination play with inventing the multiple scenarios he could have lying in wait, ready to spring. He could sell me to Sergei or return me to Robert alive. Any one of those outcomes would be better than the horrors my brain starts to conjure.

Him, returning to this room late at night with more rope.

Me, unable to stop him.

Not *wanting* to…

Suddenly restless, I rise from the bed and stagger to the doorway. My heart flutters at the thought of leaving my refuge. Regardless, I twist the knob and step out into the hall.

This part of the floor seems empty, but muted noise betrays a commotion lurking farther within the house. On bare feet, I find myself tiptoeing toward it. Why? I *know* what happens to those caught underfoot in the world of men. I also know just who most likely awaits at the heart of the tension resonating through the walls.

Like a moth to a flame, I can't escape the invisible shackle drawing me forward, anyway. Curiosity.

It feeds on the pathetic part of my soul that flares to life the moment I reach the stairs and spot the monster lurking at the base of them. His gaze finds me instantly, narrowing over my hiding spot in the shadows. God, his face looks even worse from this angle. The triplet slashes gleam in the glow of the overhanging chandelier, conjuring another memory from the depths of my psyche. Hellcat. *That's* what Robert's men called a "feisty" woman. *The bitch was a hellcat, fucking scratched me all up.*

They usually punished those women for their resistance. In my experience, hellcats wound up in the place of their namesake: hell.

Perhaps this is *my* tailored version of it? Trapped in his house, at his mercy, with no escape in sight. The flames are invisible, but the real burn comes from the deep-seated knowledge that I haven't tried to escape.

Not yet.

"Let's go." Turning from me, Mischa inclines his head, and only now do I notice the other men gathered around him. They crowd before the door and they leave in single file, their jaws clenched in stern determination, weapons in hand.

Something is wrong, and I recall a snippet of the conversation I overheard with Sergei. Robert? Could he be here? Now? My heart races at the thought. From *relief*. That's what I tell myself as I pick my way back to the red room and close the door.

I *want* my husband to find me. To save me? Something in my soul takes issue with that phrasing. I have to sink down, with my back pressed against the door, and find a new term to use. Find? Reclaim? Purify? Yes, I want my husband to *purify* me before Mischa's taint can take over.

As the daylight wanes, I let myself imagine how a reunion with Robert might unfold. He'd never storm into Mischa's compound on his own. No, a group of his men would do that. They'd be the ones to find me and drag me to the safety of Winthorp manor. He'd never consent to see me like this, so I'd have to be bathed first, have my wounds cleansed and all traces of another man erased. Only after Mischa's bruises have healed would he touch me again.

He would never knock.

But neither would Mischa.

The sound intrudes on the heavy silence, startling me to my feet. "Come in," I call out, expecting Vanya.

Hunched over and cautious, the older man enters my room —but a second is all it takes for me to register the features that don't belong to my kind benefactor. This man is taller. Older, even, with gray speckling more of his longer, darker hair.

And his eyes…

Unnervingly sharp, they hone in on me and narrow. "Don't scream."

I don't realize I've been on the verge of doing so until he advances, his hand outstretched, and the air dissipates from my lungs.

"Please," Sergei murmurs just loud enough to prevent being overheard by anyone in the hall. "I won't hurt you—"

"W-what do you want?" Instinct drives me back against the wall. My heart pounds as I struggle to take in as much of the intruder as I can. He's dressed in a dark suit, conveying a polished aura so different from the harsh one Mischa projects.

He sighs when I stiffen, shaking his head. "I want to talk," he says. "Alone."

"About what?"

You know what. I can't escape the suspicion that that's what he wants to say. His gaze is more piercing than Mischa or even Robert's. It penetrates my soul, slicing through my pathetic attempts to protect myself—but there's a softness to him my other tormentors lack. Even now, I can't deny that.

"Your mother was Marnie Winthorp," he says softly. "Wasn't she?"

My chest burns, and I can't stop myself from scanning the corners, hunting for Mischa. Is this another one of his games? He may be forbidden from using my mother against me, so perhaps he enlisted someone to do it for him?

But no. Only now do my ears register how he said that name. Reverently.

It's too terrifying a thought to consider. So I don't. "You should leave—"

"I won't upset you," Sergei says. "And I won't insult your intelligence by pretending that you don't know who I am. All I wanted was to give you this…"

He reaches into his pocket and a silver glint catches the light. Whatever he's holding is small, slender. A necklace?

"Here." He offers the object to me, clasped between his fingers. "Take this. And I don't know what Mischa's done to you or said—" He pauses as if waiting for me to explain, but when I say nothing, he sighs. "But know this: Whenever you need an ally, you come to me. No questions asked. No price to pay. You say my name and invoke my protection and no one will harm you. *Then* we will talk."

"W-why?"

A noise sounds from the hallway and Sergei cocks his head, frowning. "Remember that. Always. You have an ally in me."

He grabs my hand, shoving the hidden item against my palm. Then he turns to the door and is gone before I can choke a question out.

"Wait!"

Only silence greets me, and for whatever reason, I can't make myself move to follow him. The item was a necklace, I realize. It sparkles against my fingers, a delicate silver chain.

Dangling from the center is a small charm that somehow feels familiar, though I'm sure I've never seen it before: a small metal rose.

S ergei carried a woman's necklace in his pocket.

A rose.

My husband never plied me with jewelry. He dressed me in pretty silks and housed me in luxury—but, as Mischa pointed out, he never gave me a ring, or a broach, or a necklace. Is that a good thing? I have nothing here to remind me of him. Nothing but memories and this instinctive need to compare him to the man holding my figurative chains now.

Robert would never leave me unguarded like this.

He would never scar me publicly so that the world knew his claim.

But for what reason?

Paranoia keeps me awake. I twist Sergei's necklace around my fingers until something makes me creep toward the vanity and place the chain against my throat. It settles there uncomfortably, like a missing piece I'd never realized was gone. My hands shake as I fasten the clasp and let the rose charm hang against my collar.

It's as if the charm is magic. My resemblance to Briar is all but gone. I look more like another person now than ever. Minus my scars, we could be the same haunted woman.

Marnie.

Trapped in Sergei's grasp, did she huddle in her prison and wait for the end of her nightmare? Of course she did.

But I can't. I won't.

For once, my mantra feels meaningless. *Breathe, Ellen.* But for what? To stay alive at Mischa's demand? To follow even further in Marnie's footsteps?

To die alone.

To live in a cage.

To remain a selfish, captive bird.

I can't.

So I *stop* breathing and hold my breath as I creep to the door and press my ear to the wood. It's silent, but something won't let me grasp the handle. Mischa isn't foolish. I'm sure he has his men watching the doors, just in case.

So I turn to the windows and shrug aside the heavy drapes shrouding them. I didn't notice before exactly where this room is positioned. Below stretches a wide field, and ivy creeps up a stone façade. The rusted latch squeals as I test one of the panes, but they open smoothly only to present a stark reality. Over a full story off the ground, I either have to jump or climb.

Shadows shroud the type of surface waiting down below. Stone? Earth? The more I contemplate my options, the more escape feels like a cruel whim than an attainable reality. Tears prickle behind my eyes. It's no use.

Or is it?

I find myself observing the ivy again and brush the tip of a plant with my fingers. It's rooted firmly to something I didn't notice before: an iron lattice strong enough to support my weight. Or at least I hope as much as I climb onto the sill and brace one of my feet in the gaps. Tentatively, I sink down and nearly sigh in relief as the support holds.

Without stopping to acknowledge the consequences, I guide myself lower, clinging to whatever part of the lattice I can reach. I'm slow. Too slow. Noises of the night echo, but it's impossible to decipher if they belong to woodland creatures or Mischa's men.

But there's no turning back now.

I keep going, forcing myself to climb until my bare foot brushes what feels like packed earth. Up above my window glows, a beacon in the darkness. How long until Mischa comes for me? Minutes? Seconds?

There isn't time to plan. I set my sights on a copse of trees in the distance and run. An icy wind nips at my skin and tears at my hair. It's like the earth itself is cackling at my futile attempts. *He'll find you, Ellen. He'll find you.*

Deep down, I think a part of me knows that. I keep running anyway, letting my surging pulse spur me on. Branches and dried leaves crunch underfoot. It's bitterly cold, and my breaths paint the air in tufts of white.

But I keep running.

Defying.

Breaking…

Sergei's necklace hammers my chest with every sprint, and I can't get his face out of my head. Hers. Did she resist him? Fight him? Hate him?

Was he the reason she was burdened with me?

Suddenly, the ground changes beneath my feet. My heel slips over a slick patch of mud and I trip, landing on my knees, tasting dirt. It's so silent here. Too silent. All I hear are my own frantic breaths and… Noise?

Faint. Rapid. *Footsteps*, heading right for me.

Gasping, I scramble to my feet, knowing in my soul that it's no use. He's too fast, crashing through the trees near my right. I can't get my bearings. The air changes. Shadows shift underfoot.

Wham!

I'm struck so hard that I go sprawling and there's nothing I can do but brace. Groaning, I rise to my knees, making a note of my surroundings. Faint moonlight illuminates a stark landscape of winding hills and looming trees.

Then nothing. Whether by the grace of God or accident, I tripped mere paces from a sharp drop. The earth gives way to a cliff that overlooks looming darkness.

And makes for the perfect trap.

Leaves rustle nearby, and I lurch to my feet, squaring my stance. To fight? God, I don't know. Maybe I will. At least this time I won't let him corner me like an animal. When footsteps near my position, I turn to face him, hunting his form in the darkness. Sure enough, I spot a breathless figure crouched nearby.

But their shape is wrong. Too small. Too slender. And their face…

Graced by a beam of moonlight, pale skin glows, delicate and pure. Wide, blue eyes gleam in a face so familiar that it's like looking into a mirror—an enchanted one that shows my reflection as it once was, free of scars and bruises. The shocked expression even matches mine, I'm sure.

But then my doppelganger's eyes narrow in recognition, and pink lips form a voice much more charming than mine. "Ellen?"

Numb with shock, all I can croak is, "Briar?"

She's still so beautiful. Is that what shocks me the most? Huddling under the threat of Mischa, it was easier to ignore the damage done to me then. Not now, with a perfect version of my features forming a stark contrast.

She's still wearing silk, her hair slicked back into a neat bun. So polished, in fact, that she could have come from a ball or gala.

Not a madman's backyard.

I've gone insane. That explains it. Still, I find myself talking to what must be a figment of my imagination. "What are you doing here?"

The mirage of Briar blinks, startled. Then…she throws her head back to display her pale throat and laughs. She's loud, no doubt catching notice for miles—but that's not what makes my stomach sink. It's the coldness reflected in her gaze as she meets mine directly.

"I fucking knew it," she hisses, her hands clenching into fists. "That bastard. I fucking knew it!"

"Knew what? How did you get here?" A sudden thought takes my breath away. "Did Mischa—"

"I should have known he'd do anything to have you back." She takes a step back, still laughing. Lost in amusement, she doesn't seem to realize just how close she is to the ledge. Her heeled feet kick up loose rocks that clatter into the abyss. "I was hoping you would just stay gone. Why couldn't you?"

Once again, I'm not sure if she's really here or a hallucination. A nightmare. In twenty-three years, I've never heard her sound so lost. Or so damn cold.

"What are you talking about?"

"Seriously?" She cocks her head. "You're *still* so fucking stupid." One of her hands drifts to her cheek, brushing the unblemished skin. "They really thought you were me…"

I copy her, flinching as my palm grazes my injured cheek.

"Why couldn't you just keep your mouth shut?" Briar wonders so softly that I barely hear her. "Did you really think he'd save you? No!" Her voice rises in pitch, alarmingly loud. "I won't let him use me as his fucking pawn—"

Above her shouting, I almost miss it: the earth crunching— warning of the approach of a larger creature. I smell him before I even see him, so potent that it chokes me. Raw strength. Unbridled rage.

Mischa.

Briar doesn't notice him until he's already stepped from the cover of a nearby tree. Her skin goes even paler, her legs trembling.

But she isn't the figure caught by the full force of his gaze. He doesn't say a word, but his posture reminds me every bit of a hunter's. Waiting for me to move. To run.

"Stay away from me!" Briar staggers wildly, her arms outstretched. Her foot catches a stray branch, sending her stumbling.

I race for her without realizing, grabbing her arm. "Stop—"

"Let go!" She flails and her hand connects with my chest, knocking me back.

I careen against a firm surface. *Mischa.* He grabs my waist to steady me but shoves me aside. I can only stare as he moves with predatory grace, lunging for Briar.

"No!" I strain for them, but the terrain is too uneven. I can't regain my balance and my fingers grasp at muddied earth. Then air.

What must take seconds feels like an eternity of falling… Eyes shut, I brace for the end that I'm sure is coming. *Wham!* I feel it: sharp, unrelenting pain searing through my shoulder. From above?

"Fuck! Give me your other hand."

Dazed, I look up. Thick fingers encircle my wrist, belonging to a figure hunched over the cliff, his eyes like fire.

Mischa.

"Give me your other fucking hand!"

I try, straining my fingers through the air. But his are too far away. My legs kick at nothing. His grip is slipping…

"Don't let me go." I don't even know why I beg. Because he will go after Briar. I can sense the hesitation in how his eyes cut to his right. He shifts his posture, adjusting his grip and my heart sinks. "Don't!"

Agony rips through my shoulder as I'm suddenly yanked higher. Wet earth scrapes along my flesh. Solid ground. Looking up, I see Mischa hunched over and panting. I barely register the look in his eyes. Relief?

It's only there for a second before his hand curls into a fist. I hear the sickening blow as white dots explode across my vision.

Then darkness.

Pain.

And silence.

✦

I'm home. Either that or dead. Only in heaven or hell could the air be so still and the world so quiet. Silk sheets chafe against my skin, and it's painfully easy to picture what will await my eyes when I dare open them.

White walls.

A canopy.

My old cage.

Already, my capture lurks nearby, tainting my reality with his scent. Male. Unbearable. My lips flutter to put a name to him. "R-Robert?"

But Robert never smelled like blood.

"No," my captor replies. The voice. The accent. They tether me in place more securely than physical binds ever could. "Guess again, Little Rose."

My eyes open, but the reality facing me isn't the one I pictured. These walls are red. Heavy drapes shield the windows, and a lone figure lurks in the corner. His hair is unbound, partially shrouding his face. The only hints of his expression I can make out are a stern, clenched jaw and hollow eyes.

"W-what happened?" I croak, though the question is merely a formality. It's like we're following a script, he and I. I feign ignorance while he smothers with rage, ready and willing to exert his authority.

"You tried to run away, Little Rose," he says, crossing his arms over his chest. Mud and leaves cling to his fatigues and I remember.

Running. Falling. Briar…

My heart is throbbing. I cradle it in both hands, desperate to make sense of my thoughts. Sergei came to visit me. Like a fool, I escaped. I ran. But, of all people, I ran into my sister?

"You hit your head pretty hard," Mischa warns. "Hopefully there is no permanent damage—"

"You went after me," I whisper, ignoring every instinct in my body warning me to stay silent. "Not Briar. Why?"

"Hmm?" He cocks his head. "I don't know what you're talking about, Rose. There was no one else. Just you. This property stretches for miles. Tell me, what would Briar Winthorp be doing so close?"

My heart beats frantically in my chest, picking up on the suspicion lacing his tone. Is he being serious? Or merely trying to confuse me?

Groaning, I dig my thumbs at my temples. "My head hurts—"

"Drink." He nods his chin toward the nightstand.

I spot a tray waiting there, complete with a glass of water. Sitting upright, I grab the drink and drain it, never taking my eyes off him for a second.

Laughing, he basks in the attention. I jump when he starts to advance. Only now do I notice the vibrant, red substance painting the flesh from his nose down to his jaw.

"You're bleeding."

He frowns at the sound of my voice, weak and hoarse. Almost like I really give a damn.

But I don't.

More memories return in painful snippets, demanding my attention. "Briar. Where is she—"

"Tell me. What did we decide on, Little Rose?" Mischa wonders as one of his hands feels along his thigh. With predatory grace, he slides his fingers into the pocket of his fatigues and withdraws something long. Gleaming. "That's right. You want to be sliced into pieces." He feigns ignorance as he hefts the blade for inspection. "Think. If I were to give you the choice right now between a permanent divorce or severing that pretty head from your body, which would you choose?"

He seems to think it's a serious question, one that requires ample thought and consideration. But it doesn't.

"I'd want you to kill me."

"Oh?" He laughs, spitting more blood down the front of his shirt. "Are you sure about that, Little Rose? No. I think you want to live. Badly enough you'd *beg* for it."

My eyes go to the knife. His fingers twitch over the handle, tightening, relaxing…tightening, relaxing. Clenching. For a second, I'm back in the woods, dangling by a thread. *Don't let me go!*

"Are you just going to watch, Little One?" he asks, drawing my attention back to his face. He watches me coldly and jerks his chin toward the door to the bathroom.

I recognize the silent command. Not from Robert this time. Briar used to issue the same order whenever I found her hidden away in a room with a knife to her wrist. She never cut deeper than the surface layer of skin. Just enough to bleed. Her blue eyes would meet mine without a shred of concern and she'd always nod, merely once, when found. *Clean me up.*

Silently, I climb from the bed and smooth out the skirt of my borrowed dress. As my bare feet brush the tiled marble of the bathroom floor, I realize I'm limping.

"Your legs aren't broken," Mischa remarks as if in afterthought, but I catch him watching me, hunting my every step. "But you'll bruise."

Bruises deep enough to ache with every step I take. Even so, I make it into the bathroom alone. After spotting a shelf of linen, I grab a washcloth and wet it beneath warm water from the sink.

When I return to Mischa, he cocks his head back, directing with his gaze where I should clean first. His *chest*, not his face. Someone hit him there, drawing a stream of blood from his nose and splitting the upper lip. He'll heal with a bruise, but nothing more.

Below his collar, however, someone struck him with a knife. From a layer of rent cotton, I can tell that it's deep. He'll have another scar to add to his collection.

"What happened—"

"Your husband," he says, gritting his teeth against the pain. "Did you ever see him wear a ring? You don't."

I glance down at my naked fingers and swallow my instinctive answer back. My husband didn't need a ring to own me. "Yes," I say instead, picturing the silver ornament my husband was rarely without. "He wears the Winthorp insignia on his right hand." It was an ironic signature for such an infamous family. Beautiful, even: a dove carrying a delicate blade between its talons.

"So you'd recognize it," Mischa says, almost to himself. The movement must irritate his wound, because he sucks in a breath and snaps his fingers.

Obediently, my free hand drifts to the hem of his shirt, aiming to help him remove it, but he shakes his head, clenching his jaw. So I press the cloth against the wound over the fabric and hold it there. He hisses but then grinds his teeth to suppress even that much sound. After a few seconds, he bats my hand away and grabs the cloth himself.

"I don't dole out second chances, Little One," he says, ignoring how fresh blood begins to taint the white fabric between his fingers. "But ignorance is bliss. So, this time, I'll let you make an educated decision."

I flinch as he lifts the knife only to return it to his pocket. Before I can deflate in relief, he takes something else from his pocket. Something small. Bloody. It leaves a smeared trail of burgundy as it lands on the sheets before me.

"Do you want to die as Ellen Winthorp or become someone new? Either way…" He stands and approaches the door while I observe the small object he left behind, attempting to identify it. It's round. Shiny. Metal?

"Your husband is dead," Mischa tells me at the exact moment I recognize the item as a ring. One I only ever saw on one man's finger. "I suggest you plan your future as a widow carefully."

A thud echoes as the door slams in his wake.

Or does it?

Perhaps the thunderous sound is just my heart stopping? I'm on my knees, clutching fistfuls of the sheets in search of stability I'll never find.

There is no mistaking that ring.

There is no ignoring the blood.

There's no escaping Mischa.

Your husband is dead.

And so am I.

CHAPTER 23

Robert Winthorp is my identity, and he never needed a shiny diamond trinket to prove it. He adorned me with blood instead. With wounds, and scars, and terrifying marks on my psyche that could never be symbolized by something as frivolous as a ring. So how ironic is it now that one of his is all I have left of *him*?

I can't touch it. I can't take my eyes off it, either. It speaks to me. I hear it hissing a vow to my very soul: *I fucking own you, Elle.*

A shadow falls over me, darkening the scarlet sheets clenched beneath my fingers.

"H-how?" I don't even have to turn to know just who I'm speaking to. Mischa couldn't leave me alone for long.

No, he couldn't resist. He had to watch. Whether he saw Robert's demise with his own eyes or not, it wasn't enough. After all, he warned me himself: This…this is how he wants to see my husband die.

In my eyes.

"How did you kill him?" I rasp, repeating the question when he hasn't given me an answer. I can't look at his face. The ring has my sole attention. Even now, Robert commands obedience. "Tell me how—"

"Do you really want to know the answer?"

I flinch at something I find in his tone—mainly what I don't: there's no mocking in it. He's tired. He's on edge. *He's not lying.*

"All you need to know is that the fucker's dead, and you're running out of time to decide whether or not you want to join him."

My heart falters, but not out of fear. Burning tears well from my eyes, spilling down my cheeks as hot as blood. Are they for Robert? Maybe. Maybe not. Perhaps they're more selfish than anything else. Ellen Winthorp dies in an instant and it hurts. There's no one there to mourn her. Just a monster who watches her agonizing end without a shred of mercy to spare.

"Why?"

For once, I've given him a question he doesn't know how to answer. "You know why—"

"No." I shake my head, still transfixed by the tiny sliver of metal resting on the bed. "Not that. I want to know *why.* Why you hate the Winthorps. Why you—"

"You have a lot of demands for a dead woman." There's nothing to temper the threat in his voice. His tone falls flat as the usual fire is extinguished from that piercing gaze. Left behind is a hollow mask, and for the first time, I'm faced with the *real* Mischa: a creature without a shred of humanity to hide behind. His accent takes over. Was he even speaking English in the first place, or had I conjured up some semblance of intelligible words in the grated series of growled syllables? "I guess you've made your fucking choice."

He advances a dangerous step, but I don't cringe back. Not even when I focus my blurred vision in his direction and meet his gaze fully.

"Tell! Me! Why!" I hardly recognize the shouting woman who utilizes my body to speak. I've only heard her once before, the same night he went too far and slandered my mother's name. "What did they do to you?"

"You want to know?" He snatches the bloodied cloth from his chest and throws it at me. Rage disrupts its aim and it smacks off the wall, inches from my head. Gritting his teeth against any pain, he wrenches his shirt over his head and turns, revealing the mangled flesh of his back. "You really want to know? Twenty-four years ago, your precious Robert and his fucking father had a plan to end the feud, you see. They meant to take my father but changed their target at the last minute. They took me and my mother instead. They locked us in a cage and placed bets on which death would matter more."

His vile words paint the scene for me. I see it. I see him. He had to be young. Twenty-four years.

"Robert would have been a child—"

"A child?" He sneers at the word, meeting my gaze from over his shoulder. "I don't think you've ever met a fucking child, Ellen Winthorp. They lined my mother and me against the wall of their fucking dungeon and told me to choose. Your child of a husband gave me my options, barely as old as I was."

Eight, to be exact. Robert would have been eight. The Winthorps rarely displayed pictures of themselves as children, but I have no trouble imagining him: a beautiful boy with golden curls and soulless, brown eyes.

"He told me to choose who would die. Me or my mother?" Mischa's voice deepens, straddling the rasping edge of a growl. "They wanted me to pick but she…she made the choice for them. She begged for my life. So—" He breaks off, staring through the walls of the manor and into the past. "They made her watch them carve their mark into my back." He extends his arm behind him, tracing the rough tip of the scar along his spine. "They made her watch them beat me within an inch of my life. And then they gave her a gun and told her I would only live if she made *me* pull the trigger—"

I can't hear this. My hands claw at my ears, but he's there to wrench them away, ensuring I hear every word he has to say.

"Her fingers shook, but I was too weak to pull away. She died with her brains in my lap, you little cunt. And then I had to watch the rest of my fucking family, picked off one by one. You ask why I hated your husband?" He shoves me back so hard that I fall to my knees. "That is why. But *you* disgust me more than that piece of shit. He knew what he was. You're just a pathetic bitch, clinging to his shadow. So I'll ask you now. Who do you want to be?" He drops something down in front of me. The knife, its edge mocking and bright. "Ellen Winthorp? Or the bitch *he* never let you become?"

He kicks the blade closer to me when I don't reach for it. Then he sinks down, caging my body against the floor with his own. Thick, wet fingers fist through my hair, using it as a tether to force me to face him.

I'm sobbing, gasping and moaning through waves of tears. For Robert? For me? There's no end to the grief, yet it has no true purpose. It just consumes, like fire.

"Decide," he snarls.

What?

Terror rips through me as he captures my hand against his palm, forcing my grasping fingers to scrape the carpet, grabbing something solid. It's hard, conforming to my grip. I identify what it is without even having to look down: the knife. It's almost too big for me to handle with one hand. Too heavy. It takes two tries before I can lift it and eye the beautiful, lethal edge.

"You think you can kill me, Little One?"

I've pointed the blade at him without realizing.

Laughing, he tightens his grip and lowers the tip toward another target. "I'll give you the same choice your husband gave my mother," he explains. "Decide who you want to kill. The part of you that belongs to him?" He applies enough leverage to force the sharpened tip to kiss the flesh of my forearm. "Or the small, pathetic piece of you he never managed to touch?"

Oh. My free hand trembles against the floor. Reaching around me, he seizes my wrist and tilts it, exposing where the veins lie. Instinctively, my naked ring finger flexes, sensing the imminent danger.

"Do it," Mischa commands. "Make your choice. Or are you so fucking weak you'll die completely for him?"

He lets me go, leaving my trembling hand to hold the knife alone. It twitches in the air, wavering toward various directions.

Him. Me. The floor.

Back again.

"Do it," Mischa goads, his mouth near the nape of my neck. There's no fear that I might turn on him again. The enemy he's presented is far more formidable than he will ever be: myself. "Do it!"

The blade falls, cutting side down, and pain explodes through my entire being. White. Endless…

Through a haze of tears, I see red. Red floors. Red walls. Red, painted skin.

My heartbeat surges, forcing hammering blood through my veins. With the scent of salt tainting the air, Mischa's grating voice is my only anchor to sanity.

"Keep going," he says thickly. "Do it. Do it!"

But I don't even know where exactly the knife continues to strike.

Or, in the end, which part of me is cut away.

Rose? Ellen?

Regardless, one woman dies in the fiery torrent of blood and agony.

And she doesn't even scream.

VII: (SEVEN)

ACKNOWLEDGMENTS

Mickey, thank you so very much for taking the time to help me perfect this draft. As always, your feedback and expertise have been invaluable. Thank you, Charity for applying the final touches on this draft.

Thanks so much to everyone who supported this draft along the way, including the many beta readers who provided encouragement along the way! Please keep in mind that this story includes dark, graphic and explicit content matter that is not suitable for readers under the age of 18—or for readers who are uncomfortable with the following subject matter: explicit sex, mentions of sexual abuse, and graphic depictions of violence.

PREFACE

Shakespeare once posed the infamous question, *What is in a name?*

Everything, of course. Your soul. Your identity. Your fate.

It's why Robert feared his. That fancy, official moniker was a constant reminder of what his title as a Winthorp truly meant in the grand scheme: that he was nothing more than a pawn shoved across the game board by his own father.

Deep down, my husband thrived on the only aspect he ever had control over: terror. Like an artist, he cultivated it in other people and despised it in himself. He died of it.

In a suitable irony, so did his wife.

How fitting is it that the old Ellen Winthorp meets her grisly end in a madman's lair, surrounded by scarlet? In a mocking array, the color paints the walls, accents, and every bit of furnishing. Red is all I see—like fire, consuming the remnants of my soul.

Curled on the floor, clutching my hand to my chest, I choke back a scream as the weight of my injury registers throughout my body. *Fire, pinching, aching, throbbing…* But, of all the emotions to feel…relief shouldn't be one of them.

"Ellen?"

A calloused palm grazes my cheek, jarring me from my thoughts. I blink, surprised to find my eyes are overflowing. The moisture blurs my vision, obscuring the figure crouched before me. Vanya.

"Let me see it," he commands. "Give me your hand!"

I can't silence a groan when he pries my arm from my side. Even the slightest touch triggers an avalanche of throbbing pain. Instinct warns me not to look down at the source: my left hand. Snippets of memory sneak into my thoughts anyway like a mocking slideshow. Blood. Bone. A sawing blade…

What the hell have I done?

"Jesus Christ!" Vanya recoils from me, his face pale. "Don't move!" He scrambles to his feet and returns a moment later, juggling an armful of supplies. Standing over me, he bites his lip, eyeing the puddle of blood spreading across the carpet. "Mischa… He didn't—"

"No." I shake my head. I'm not trying to spare Mischa further judgment, either. I need to hear it said out loud. "I… I did it to myself."

"Why? What the hell were you thinking?" He grits his teeth, but a relieved sigh robs his voice of any true anger. "Never mind. It doesn't matter. I need to stop the bleeding."

He sinks to his knees and presses a wad of cloth against my hand. I'm only vaguely aware of what he's really doing: staunching the bleeding from the grotesque stump where my ring finger used to reside.

A strangled laugh rips from me before I can help it. What a shame that Robert never gave me a ring—severing all ties to him would be a lot less dramatic in that case.

"Stay with me," Vanya warns, his voice gruff with concern. After a few seconds of pressure, he withdraws the bloodied cloth and wets it with liquid from a brown bottle. "I'll have to stitch it shut or it will continue to bleed. This will hurt like a son of a bitch."

I wince as he reapplies the cloth, but the physical pain is nothing compared to the chaos raging in my psyche. Twenty-three years of my soul have been sliced away without a second thought, and I don't know who's left behind—or what she wants.

Pain?

Torment?

Or, dare I even think…*Mischa*?

"Keep this covered," Vanya warns.

I glance down and find that he's wrapped my entire hand in gauze. Regardless, scarlet seeps through in vain.

"Damn it!" He fumbles to grab a small vial from his scattered supplies. "Here, hold on—" After priming a needle with the clear liquid from the vial, he injects it into my arm. The brief sting barely registers as a wave of dizziness washes over me, smothering the pain. "Now, stay here." Almost in afterthought, he mutters, "I need to find Mischa."

With that, he gathers his supplies and leaves.

Despite his warning, vanity wins out over exhaustion. I need to see…

Biting back a cry, I stand, holding my left arm awkwardly at my side. My knees feel like jelly and the room spins as I stagger to find my balance. In the end, I have to cling to the wall and make my way step by step into the bathroom. There, in the mirror, I find a stranger.

Her blue eyes are familiar. Briar? Ellen? Marnie? But no. Her cold, empty expression is the handiwork of only one creature. Mischa. He's claimed this new, untouched part of me. He's even given her a name.

Little Rose.

He doesn't let me sleep. The moment I drag my battered body to the mattress and attempt to lower my head, the door flies open and my tormentor invades. I open my eyes to track his predatory advance across the room. He's dressed in black now, a color-choice which just so happens to disguise any blood.

But at least he's whole. Both of his hands are intact, gesturing sharply as he speaks to someone behind him.

"…I went to him," he growls. "The asshole wouldn't dare attack me directly—"

"Oh?" another man interjects. Vanya? "Before last night, I would have believed so. Before I learned that you baited him. Toyed with him. And her? You let her think you killed—"

"Enough."

"Fine," Vanya concedes. He's changed his clothing and wiped the blood from his hands, but his haggard face betrays only exhaustion. "Play your game. But is *this* necessary?"

"*You're* the one who suggested I make her useful," Mischa snaps. Cocking his head toward Vanya, he adds, "So here's a chance for you *both* to prove your loyalty. Do the job without word of it getting back to Sergei."

"And her?"

"Get up," Mischa hisses, this time directing the words at me.

I flinch as his arm lashes out in my direction. Rather than a blow, something lands inches from my face. Square. Small. Plastic. My brain scrambles to identify it. A credit card?

"I have a job for you," he declares.

"J-Job?" I roll onto my side, biting back a groan. "What are you—"

"You're no longer my captive," he snaps, crossing his arms. "And with your husband dead, you're no use to the Winthorps either. So I suggest you choose your next steps wisely. Work with me or take your chances out there."

His words batter my exhausted brain. Deciphering them is like putting together a puzzle with jagged, razor-sharp pieces.

"So…then what am I?" I ask, my voice hoarse. "Why keep me?"

"Maybe you should ask how?" He raises an eyebrow. "How can you make yourself useful? Do what I fucking ask. Unless you think you can go crawling back to your precious Winthorps. With the son dead, maybe you can marry the father?"

I flinch. "So what do you want?"

"Go with Vanya," he says, jerking his chin in the other man's direction. "Buy a wardrobe fit to mourn your husband in. I'm tired of watching you sully my mother's clothes." He leaves, storming into the hallway.

"Don't worry about him." Sighing, Vanya comes to my side and hooks his hand beneath my shoulder, helping me to my feet. "Just move," he urges, guiding me forward. "I've got you."

The halls of the manor pass in a distorted blur. It's almost as if I blink and we're outside where the blazing sun reflects off a black van waiting at the foot of the steps. After fastening me inside the back seat, Vanya climbs in beside me.

"We've got at least an hour's drive," he says, casting a wary look at the manor behind us. "Get some sleep. Don't ask questions. You don't realize how lucky you are…"

But maybe I do. At least an hour, free from Mischa.

I couldn't have prayed for that much…but it's not a reprieve.

Time is just another weapon in his arsenal. Now I have longer to ponder what use he has for me now.

Because, without Robert, I'm useless to him.

And we both know it.

"We're here."

Vanya shakes me awake, but it takes several slow blinks before my eyes focus well enough for me to regain my bearings. Narrow space. Enclosed. We're still in the van. Beyond the window, I make out a row of buildings. Their black awnings and brick façades stand out—seemingly not one of the hotels or mysterious venues I'm used to being smuggled into.

"Just take it easy," Vanya warns as he maneuvers my arm around his shoulder to ease me from the van. "We'll make this quick, and then you can sleep on the way back."

Quick. My stomach lurches at the word. Was that twisted code for a more nefarious game?

After a few short paces, we enter the nearest building. Inside, clothing hangs from black velvet walls while a hostess mans a desk at the center of an elegant lobby. Beyond her is a waiting area with leather chaises. A store of some kind? It reminds me of the exclusive boutiques Briar frequents.

The people here must be used to patrons a bit more haggard than the polished circles my sister surrounds herself with, however. The girl who greets us doesn't bat an eyelash at my battered, bruised frame.

"We made an *appointment*," Vanya says.

"Of course." She nods and beckons us forward with a wave of her hand. "This way. Your men can bring the delivery around back."

Delivery. Her careful tone strikes a nerve. So Mischa planned this trip to mean more than a shopping spree. Of course he did.

I crane my neck and spot one of his men carrying something from the van out front. Before I can decipher what it is, Vanya tugs on my arm.

"Come." He guides me to one of the chaises at the center of the waiting area before he takes up a position near the mouth of the showroom. "Quick," he mouths.

But when the sales girl returns, I doubt speed is what she has in mind. Behind her, another woman pushes a rack filled with various items of clothing.

"We were told to select some items for you," the girl explains. Her name tag reads Jenny, and her smile is genuine enough. "However, we still like to get a feel for the style of our clients. Perhaps you'd prefer to select them yourself?"

Select. Style. Myself.

I don't think I've ever had clothing of my own. Always Briar's old things or hand-me-downs from the servants.

I don't even think I have a favorite fabric, or cut, or style.

Mischa had counted on that. Apparently, he had them just give me clothing "at random" without any thought put into what I might like. A part of me is exhausted enough to feed into the narrative of his prisoner and refuse to supply any input. It's what Vanya expects, and he eyes me with more concern than I'd like.

To be fair, I don't even know which of the garments hanging on the frames calls to me the most.

"You can show me," I hear myself croak. "I'd like to see what you have."

An hour later, Vanya finally intercedes, cutting the shopping trip short. With swift efficiency, he has the items I already selected brought out to the van before he comes for me himself and helps me to my feet.

I barely have enough time to choke out a parting thanks before we're back on the road and whatever drug he injected me with earlier takes its full effect. My tongue feels too heavy to control, and questions spill from it unbidden.

"Did I just help him commit another crime?" It's funny. I can't even come up with a solid tally of the criminal acts I've done for Mischa so far.

"Don't worry about it," Vanya replies. "You did nothing."

"He sold something," I decide, using what little logic I can muster as pain gnaws at my consciousness. "What?"

"Nothing. At least… *You* won't be the one forced to answer for it." He looks away, his jaw tight. "Just try to get some rest."

But I don't sleep on the way back. I die, am reborn, and awaken as something else. Someone else.

Someone whole despite her broken body. Her clothing and her life have been bought on a monster's dime—but she's more reckless than the old Ellen Winthorp ever was. Or maybe she's just that damn tired.

"Easy does it." Vanya's breath bastes my cheek, drawing me awake.

The world sways around me, but it's seconds before I realize why: I'm in his arms.

Gingerly, he carries me into the red room and sets me down on the bed. "Sleep."

Already numbed by the drug and pain, I don't resist unconsciousness as my identity continues to morph around me.

CHAPTER 3

"Get up."

I groan as awareness returns in agonizing snatches. Whatever drug Vanya gave me was of dangerous quality—the type of all-consuming drug the old Ellen Winthorp might have chased to numb the pain of her existence. For the first time in days, I didn't dream of a damn thing, and yet I awaken to an unfolding nightmare.

"I said get the hell up."

I blink my eyes open and find a demon with golden hair standing above me. He's still wearing black and his hair hangs loosely around his shoulders. "Get up!"

When I don't comply with his commands, something hard nudges my side. His boot?

A mattress conforms beneath me, but when I turn my head, the carpet is closer than it should be. Am I in another dungeon, or did he move me to a different room while I was asleep? But no…

The red walls are the same, as are the sheets. But the bed frame is gone, and so is the vanity, and the wardrobe, and any other sense of furnishing.

Like magic, he's turned the tables once more.

"From now on, if you want a fucking thing, you buy it your damn self," Mischa snarls, proving my suspicion correct: Somehow, he stripped the room bare. "Get dressed." He kicks the mattress, spurring me into a sitting position. "I have a job for you."

Unease coils in my belly. "A job." After swallowing hard, I add, "Being a mule for you to smuggle something into a boutique?"

His eyes widen. He didn't think I noticed?

"Or," I continue, "as a whore?"

With Robert gone, those are the only two uses he could have for me.

But his expression reveals nothing. Just bitter impatience that bristles as our gazes meet.

"Do not test me, Robert's—" He breaks off, scowling, but I can guess what word he held back. *Wife.* "Get. Dressed."

He didn't remove my new clothing, at least. The items are still packaged in boxes and bags piled behind him in one corner of the room. Cautiously, I stand and take a step, but my buckling legs nearly pitch me over.

"Easy," Mischa hisses. He grabs my arm, steadying me—but, surprisingly, I don't feel any pain. The drug must still be in my system.

"I'm fine." Taking care with my bandaged hand, I stagger toward the clothing and fish out the first outfit I can reach: a white dress.

I shed my filthy clothes and pull on the new dress over my head one-handed. When I try to smooth the hem, a drop of fresh blood seeps into the fabric. Spreads.

"I…I need to wash," I croak as my thumb rubs at the spot in vain.

He says nothing, but he doesn't stop me, either, when I turn toward the bathroom and limp over the threshold. Spotting my reflection in the mirror, I freeze, fixated by the mound of bandages around my left hand. It looks worse than I've imagined. A vibrant scarlet taints sections of the white gauze. Within seconds, it's dripping red, red, red.

Vanya left some supplies for me. I spot them arranged neatly on the counter, and perhaps it's delirium from blood loss that makes me sway, rather than gratitude. With my intact hand braced against the counter for leverage, I use my teeth to snag a piece of gauze from the bandage and unravel it layer by layer. There's no point in being brave. Not here. I moan and gasp at every tendril of burning pain that roils through my arm as more of the injury is exposed.

Reddened, inflamed flesh. A bloodied, gaping socket.

Oh God. I turn away, choking back bile as the gravity of what I've done sinks in. I've never hurt myself before. I never held a knife against my own flesh and contemplated the damage I could do.

But I remember it all now. Holding the blade, pressing down, tasting salt on the air… It took me three agonizing attempts to cut through the bone on my own. Then I vomited and dropped the knife. So someone else had to sever the last bit of muscle and tendon.

The same man who snatches my wrist now, preventing me from dripping more blood onto the floor. "Look at me," he growls. "Don't you dare pass out—*look at me!*"

Too exhausted to turn my head, I settle for watching him in the mirror's reflection. My blurred vision creates a twin for him, equally as cold as the original. Both hiss in disgust as my head lolls, too heavy to lift.

"Sit on the counter." He clears a space with a swipe of his hand, sending medicinal bottles and tools crashing to the floor. "*Sit on the fucking counter*—come here. No! Hold on to me, damn it!" Grunting, he grips my thigh and lifts me onto the counter's ledge himself.

"I…I'm going to faint," I admit against his shoulder. My head feels hot. I have to suck the air down into my lungs and hold it there before exhaling. In. Out. Slow. Slower.

Mischa says nothing. He muscles in closer, forcing my legs wider to make space for his bulk. Like a wall, his body pins me against the mirror. To keep me from falling, I realize. At the same time, he douses my hand in searing liquid and reapplies more gauze with much less tact and expertise than Vanya.

"You won't die," he mutters as if annoyed by that fact. "But it shouldn't keep bleeding with the stitches…" He steps back while I cling to the faucet with my good hand. "Don't move." In a ruthless motion, his gaze sweeps over me.

I copy him and choke on a gasp. So much for the new Ellen; my pretty white dress is ruined, painted red.

As I stare, Mischa snags the front of my dress in his fists and yanks, ripping the expensive material right down the middle. Before I can protest, he tosses the remains into a nearby trash can.

"You have five minutes to get changed, then meet me downstairs," he declares before storming from the room.

Five minutes. I waste three of them trying to remember how to stand on my own before I give up and crawl back to my stack of clothing. This time, I select a black dress. It's longer, made of wool, with long sleeves. With less than two minutes to spare, I stagger to the top of the stairs and find Mischa glaring up at me from the bottom of them.

I take my time, inching down each step, but he never moves to rush me along. Just as my foot hits the ground floor, he snatches my wrist and pulls me through the front door. The moon hangs above, adding a silvery glow to the harsh darkness that obscures most of our surroundings. I faintly make out three of his men lurking beyond the threshold. They follow us into a waiting van.

In a way that's beginning to feel routine, Mischa sandwiches me between himself and the door, all but daring me to test the lock on my own. Two of his men take the front and passenger's seats while the third lingers behind, openly sporting his weapon.

The driver must already know where to go. He takes off without any input from Mischa and the trip commences in tense, unbearable silence. Only a few hours ago, I would have maintained that silence.

Now, a question springs from my lips. I blame the drug. "Have you gone back on your threat? Will you kill me now? Or will you whore me—"

"Oh, but I *did* kill you," Mischa says. He doesn't bother to lower his voice in the presence of his men. His poisonous tone drips into their ears, infecting us all. "I killed the pathetic little bitch you used to be. And as I told you, whoever you are now…you work for me. Or can you not survive without that fucking mask you called Robert Winthorp?"

"Why?" I'm not talking about the violence or the money. "Why does it even matter what I do? Without Robert, I'm worth nothing to you—"

"Oh." He chuckles darkly, eyeing his scarred knuckles. "He wouldn't try to barter for you if you were worth *nothing*."

My mind goes blank. "R-Robert tried…to barter for me?"

He didn't mean to tell me. Irritation flickers across his expression like a ripple in a pond's otherwise calm surface.

"What did he offer?" I ask.

Rather than answer, he turns to gaze out his window. Everything down to his posture warns me to shut up. Back down. But as he said himself, the woman I once was is gone.

"Money?" I ask. "Land?"

His mouth grows tighter with every guess. I'm shooting in the dark.

"Tell me what he offered!"

"More than a million," he spits, grating the words through clenched teeth. "And don't you fucking think for a second that I won't still slit your goddamn throat—"

"What?" I jerk back against the stiff cushions of the seat. "You're lying."

Mischa raises an eyebrow. "Am I?"

My head hurts. I cradle it in my good hand, digging my fingertips into my aching temple. The harder I press, the more confused I feel.

"Then why not trade me? Or send my body to him?" A million. That amount sends a shiver down my spine. Robert was frivolous with money, but never like that. "Why—"

"This was never about *you*. You were always a worthless fucking token that fell onto the game board. And now?" He gives me a cold, soulless appraisal while stroking his chin. "I just want to see how long it takes me to break the little toy I stole."

The threat is almost convincing. Almost. But he's forgotten one thing: I grew up in this world as well and I am well-versed in the language of men and money.

"That doesn't make sense—"

"I suggest you shut your fucking mouth and carefully consider your remaining options," he warns. "I don't have much patience for either widows *or* wives—"

"Enough! You are not my husband."

He blinks. So do I. The grit in my tone shocks even me. "You…you are not Robert," I add. "I don't owe you a damn thing. If you want to kill me, kill me. I'll even do it myself…" I eye my mangled hand, horrified by my own boast. How easy would it be to cut a little lower and a lot deeper? "I'm not *your* captive anymore. So if you want me to work for you, then you earn my respect. My trust... This toy is not afraid of being broken."

I'm panting with the effort it took to get the words out. *Stupid.* Shutting my eyes, I press my skull back into the headrest. Do I regret what I've said? The answer terrifies me more than any rage Mischa could ignite.

No. I don't.

Not even as his breath scalds the tender flesh of my throat.

"And there she is," he growls. Is the grudging respect I hear a result of delirium? "The bitch without her mask. Can she back up the bullshit spewing from that pretty mouth?" He presses something against my palm and my brain shies from identifying it. Hard. Leather? "She better be able to."

He pulls away, and when I open my eyes, I find my hand wrapped around something thick. Long. Partly metal.

A knife.

A thrill runs through me as I tighten my grip on the handle. Am I its intended target—and he's just toying with me—or is the weapon meant to serve a more nefarious purpose?

Maybe as a reminder: *you've already sliced away part of yourself...*

Are you willing to sacrifice more?

You better be.

"Hide it," Mischa commands, nodding to the blade. "Now."

It's too long to smuggle beneath the dress. Thinking fast, I lean forward and slip it handle-first into one of my new boots. Luckily, the blade is slim enough to avoid slicing into my skin, but the added weight is a chilling burden.

Sitting upright, I stare out the window and avidly study our surroundings. We're in the country, just beyond civilization, judging from the power lines that span the distance—but near a Winthorp stronghold if Robert was willing to trade for me. That detail should narrow down the potential areas, but in reality, I could be anywhere. The Winthorps owned property all over the world.

It was one of the many reasons I could never dream of leaving Robert.

He would always find me.

"We're here," the driver announces.

Here is…nowhere. We're parked on a dirt road that extends beside a thicket of trees. Only the glow from the headlights casts enough illumination to see by. From what I can tell, there isn't a building in sight.

In fact, it's the perfect place to bury a body.

I jump as Mischa muscles open the door on his end and takes my arm. "Come on."

He shoves me forward, toward a narrow expanse of naked field. An ominous shiver racks my spine as paranoid suspicions fester on my unease. Is this how he'll do it? Shoot me from behind?

"Hurry up!"

My hesitant, wooden steps are too slow. He gains on me in no time, drawing even with my shoulder.

From the corner of my eye, I see him manipulate an object held between his hands. A gun.

With deft motions, he removes the safety and cocks it. "You're afraid," he murmurs when I jump at the sharp noise. "Even better. You may not like to gamble, Little One, but you've been playing the wrong game. This is your biggest risk yet. You fuck up and we're both dead." His gaze warily sweeps the landscape, searching for anything that might raise alarm.

"Why trust me?" My nerves hum, awakened by his unease. I flex my fingers impatiently. Should I reach for the knife now? "In fact, isn't your war over now that Robert is—"

"Who said anything about trust?" Mischa wonders before I can decide on an answer to my dilemma. "No, this is about survival. Do you want to die as a worthless pawn, *Ellen*, or do you want to live?" He tucks the gun into the back pocket of his jeans and comes to a stop a few paces ahead of me. "Make your choice now."

He lifts his foot and slams the heel over a seemingly random spot in the ground. A spot that *moves*, breaking away from the rest of the earth to reveal a roughly dug hole. A wooden hatch covered it, blending in with the dirt in the dark. Beneath it, a man peers out, a pistol raised. My heart falters as the barrel drifts in my direction before settling squarely over Mischa.

"State your business."

"I have an appointment," Mischa retorts without a shred of concern given to the weapon. "Your boss is expecting me, and I'm short on time, so I suggest you take us to him before I give him advice on how to better train his dogs."

The vicious taunt goes unchallenged by the man. He merely nods toward the ground. "Leave your weapons here."

With a sigh, Mischa withdraws his gun and places it at his feet.

Unsatisfied, the man in the hatch turns to me. "Weapons."

"She's unarmed," Mischa says. His smug scoff portrays indignation I doubt even Robert could pull off: *As if I'd ever arm a bitch.* "She's my accountant. I already cleared her with your boss. Besides, if she *were* packing, the men you have lurking in the woods would have alerted you."

Mischa cuts his gaze to the swath of trees behind us. Only then do I make out flickering shadows among the underbrush. So we were being watched the entire time. If he knew, then why the blatant show of cocking his own weapon? Looking at him, I can't tell. His expression reveals nothing.

Sighing, the man in the hatch lowers himself deeper into the hole. "Come in."

Mischa starts forward, and I creep in his wake. Between his feet, a ladder descends into the hole. At the bottom of what appears to be at least a ten-foot drop, a faint glow betrays a larger space below. Turning to face me, Mischa descends the ladder first. When his head disappears below the earth, I follow, using my uninjured hand to feel for each rung.

"Watch it." Someone palms my waist when my heel strikes the bottom level: packed earth. Mischa.

I look at him, blinking as my eyes adjust to the surprisingly bright lights strung along a wire hanging along the top of a short tunnel. A few paces ahead, it opens onto a cavernous space cut right into the belly of the Earth. Wooden stakes reinforce the square structure, and near each corner stands a man hefting a large, semi-automatic weapon, like the ones carried by Mischa's men.

Seated on a metal folding chair is a balding man who's watching us approach, his arms crossed over his ample stomach. Surrounding him are several wooden crates. Only one has its lid removed, revealing the cargo it contains: black weapons packed into straw.

"Mischa," the man greets, his voice cold. "I have to admit that this is a surprise. I never thought I'd see the day when the pampered fucking prince would dare come crawling to me for lead. Who did you piss off this time? More Winthorps? Though I heard that the old man is gone. How's that for fucking irony? Done in by his own—"

"Anders," Mischa says over him, his tone equally cutting. "One would think that *you* weren't begging to sell your shit to *me*. Is this it?" He nods curtly toward the open box.

"It's pretty pricey for shit," Anders remarks. He cuts his gaze over to me before returning his attention to the man by my side. His disinterest makes one thing certain, and my sigh nearly barrels me over: I'm not one of the items for sale. "But you need the guns, or you wouldn't come to me. And," he adds with a hollow laugh. "You must have pissed off Sergei, or you would get your goods from him. Unless…" He rubs his dirt-covered fingers along his chin. "Unless you're trying to hide what you need the guns for. Ah, but concealing something from one of the ten heads. That would be against your fucking rules, wouldn't it?"

"Enough." Mischa's voice rings out through the room, ripe with authority. "The girl has the money. Name your price, and I'll take what you have now."

"My price?" Anders laughs darkly. "My *price*, Mischa, is way more than what you could offer for a few fucking guns."

"Oh?"

I taste the danger in Mischa's tone, even before his body jars mine, conveying a silent command. *Get ready.*

"And what would that be?"

"Your head," Anders says simply. The foreboding click of five guns cocking in unison bolsters the words. "It seems that the Winthorps have put a mighty big bounty on your head. From what I can tell, two have become one, and the remaining piece of shit wants you very, very badly, Prince."

Robert Sr.? It's almost funny how only now does it sink in, just what Robert's death means. His father will be on the warpath, and he will most certainly not want to rescue me. Mischa's lost his bargaining chip. Any benefit he might have gained from keeping me alive is surely good and gone now. So maybe he means it. A madman's curiosity is the only reason why I'm still breathing.

"So place your bets, Little Rose…"

My toes flex in my boots, dislodging the blade and coaxing it closer to the rim.

"Is that so?" Mischa says with a casual shrug. "By attacking me directly, I suppose you know what this means? You've just forsaken the protection of the *mafiya*."

"Now, tell me: What the hell do I need protection from a dead man for?" Anders chuckles, rising from his chair.

Slowly, he fishes a pistol from the waistband of his pants, but he doesn't bother to aim it. "All bets are off now. You wanted a war, Prince? You just bought yourself one—"

"You're right," Mischa says. "I have."

Boom!

Gunshots ring out as the world lurches, plunging everything into chaos. Dust flies. Darkness. Light. I'm choking on the thickened air, feeling for anything solid to cling to. I find it in the form of a muscular arm that flexes in recognition.

"Move!"

A chorus of pained groans almost drowns out the shout. More gunshots echo, but they sound too far away. Up above?

"Go!"

A hand rams against my back, shoving me forward. Up. Out.

Fresh air trickles into my lungs as someone manually hauls me out of the shaft and onto the field. Mischa. There's no time to get my bearings as he lunges forward, tugging me by my arm. I just run, giving in to his guidance. Eventually, we reach the trees where shouts echo, too chaotic to make sense of. Dirt and brambles nip at the bared skin of my legs and dislodge my boots. I'm clinging to Mischa more than I'd like—*clinging*, rather than letting him drag me along.

Suddenly, he comes to a stop, pushing me against a harsh surface. My heart stammers as my senses fight to identify it. Dry. Cold. Bark. A tree?

"Climb," he hisses.

I twist around to witness him peel his shirt off and tear it down the middle.

Cold, his gaze slices through mine. "Fucking climb!"

I reach for a low-hanging branch and attempt to use it for leverage to get off the ground. With only one functional hand, it's a pathetic attempt.

Behind me, Mischa scoffs. "Stay still." He seizes my waist and lifts, all but throwing me onto a narrow fork between two splayed branches.

Bark scrapes my palm as I scramble for purchase. "I'm slipping," I croak to him, fighting to keep my voice down. "I'm—"

"Don't panic," he warns from down below. "Wait for me."

With uncanny dexterity, he vaults into the space beside me and tugs my arm, righting my balance. His shoulders ripple as he manipulates the remains of his shirt. Twisting the fabric like a makeshift rope, he secures it around a higher branch and draws both ends taut. It holds just enough to help him climb to a higher ledge, and then another. He reaches down for me each way.

We're maybe twenty feet off the ground when he finally settles into a crook between two sturdy branches and pulls me up into the space beside him. It's precariously narrow. I straddle the thicker end of the branch, facing him, while he ties one end of his shirt around a higher branch and then twists the rest around his shoulder, securing himself to the tree.

"You'll fall from that end," he warns, flicking his gaze over my awkwardly splayed limbs. "Come here."

I make a show of scanning the ledge for a safer spot—but there's nowhere else to run. Below, footsteps crash through the forest and more shouts rise up. Something tells me they don't all belong to Mischa's men.

Yet, apart from panting with exertion, he doesn't seem too alarmed by our predicament.

"Unless you've slept in a tree before, I suggest you listen," he says as casually as if he were referring to the weather. "Come. Here."

Left with no other choice, I brace my hands along the branch for balance and inch my way toward him. I freeze when I'm close enough to sense the heat wafting from him like a furnace.

"Do you really think you can support yourself all night?" he asks.

A part of me wants to refuse and take my chances. But there's a dare lurking behind those dark eyes. One I know better than to ignore. *How far will you go for survival, Little Rose?*

"You went there unarmed?" I pose the question as I peel my good hand from the branch and brace it over his waist instead. A shiver runs through me at the contact. Gritting my teeth, I fight to disguise any reaction he could interpret as weakness and shift an inch closer. "Do you enjoy tempting fate?"

"Maybe I enjoy tempting *you*," he counters.

Up this close, there's no escape from his scent. It floods my head in dizzying waves: sweat, fresh air, blood. Most maddening of all, his pulse is racing beneath the calm exterior. Without being able to touch him, I might have been fooled. Rather than alarmed by the danger, he's *excited.*

"How?" I rasp, raising my voice as loud as I dare. "By nearly getting me killed—"

"I took a gamble," he explains, shifting to fully face me.

I look away, staring beyond his shoulder. From this angle, I have a direct view of the ground looming below. Fear is what makes my stomach clench—nothing else. Especially not him.

"Anders was a greedy little prick," Mischa continues near my ear. "One of the many men who underestimated me. Like your husband, he acted exactly how I predicted he would. And now…when the dust settles, I'll have his guns and no one will be able to do a damn thing about it."

A gamble?

"You knew he'd attack you," I deduce. "And yet you went there anyway."

"I knew that the benefits vastly outweighed the risks, Little One," he says. "That's your first lesson. Never risk what you aren't willing to lose."

Like his life? And mine.

"What about Sergei?" I ask. Anders mentioned him. Is this why Mischa did something so insane as meeting an arms dealer who wanted him dead? All to keep something from Sergei?

"Sergei…" Mischa sighs thoughtfully, his chest rising and lowering beneath my chin. "Sergei has his own goals in mind. They tend not to overlap with mine." His finger strokes my throat and I'm painfully aware of the necklace hanging from it. I can't stop myself from brushing the lump where the charm lurks beneath my collar. "But you wouldn't know anything about that. Would you?"

I grit my teeth. It's nearly impossible to tell if he's joking or if he knows.

And he's just toying with me.

"Don't think too much of yourself, Little Rose," he scolds, letting his hand fall. "Look at it this way: You are just a little pawn I'm not done playing with. But at least I'm honest in my intentions. In case you forget that, I suggest you remember that Sergei wants you only as a trophy—"

"Don't." I close my eyes as if to fend off the dark direction he seems determined to lead me down. Not again. "You've made your point."

"Have I?" Mischa wonders. He takes his unsecured hand from the bark of the tree and captures my chin with it, forcing me to meet his eyes directly. "You think I'm a monster," he says as if reading the word etched into my gaze. "I *am*. But I have always given you one thing that not even Sergei or your fucking husband ever would."

"Oh?" I somehow manage to copy his rasping tone, surprising myself with the ferocity. "And what is that?"

"A *choice*," he says. "Between being locked in a fucking cage or glimpsing what waits beyond it."

What a vicious, cruel lie. And he believes it. Though maybe it's true.

He gave me a choice between dying as Robert's wife or living as someone else—which puts him in possession of a dangerous weapon Robert Winthorp never utilized: power.

"So, what happens now?" I wonder, feeding off my latest dose of his hateful drug.

"We wait," he says, shrugging. "Vanya knows what to do. In the morning, my plan should come to fruition. When the dust settles, we return to Pecavi—"

"Pecavi?" I echo. I've heard that name before. "Is that the name of your house?"

Rather than supply an answer, he deliberately lets my question hang on the air. It seems I've found his own Sergei: the house is off-limits.

I let him draw his boundary and leave it be. But I don't sleep. I cling to my tormentor and listen to his heart beat as the forest sways around us.

And I never let my guard down.

CHAPTER 5

Mischa finally guides me from the tree as a sliver of light begins to paint the horizon.

Disoriented and sore, I don't question him during the long trek through the woods. Finally, we return to that expanse of dirt road and find a van waiting with keys already in the ignition.

"Keep alert," Mischa tells me as he climbs behind the wheel. "Don't forget you have that knife."

After claiming the passenger's seat, I take his advice and scan our surroundings. Apart from scurrying creatures, I find nothing worth notice. Eventually, the motion of the van and the silence work to lull my brain into a false sense of monotony. The kind of dull idleness where dangerous thoughts take root.

My husband is dead. I feel a sudden urge to say it out loud, just once.

"He's dead." The words ring hollow, solidifying a thought that hurts to admit. I'd have to see it for myself. To truly know…

Robert owns me in a way that surpasses any other emotion I've lived by. I feel him in my bones. In my head. Death won't separate him from me so easily.

"How can I believe you?" I ask Mischa. Something he said keeps circling my skull. "How do you know it was really *Robert* who died? What about his father—"

"Tell me," Mischa says without taking his eyes off the road. "What reason would I have for lying about the *only* worth you had to me?"

He has a point.

"So, why keep me alive?"

This has to be the third time I've asked him as much in so many words. Why. Why. Why?

He has yet to give me a convincing answer.

"Should I kill you?" he wonders, turning the wheel to avoid a dip in the road.

For the first time, the landscape draws my attention. We aren't on our way back to his manor—unless he's taking a different route. We don't pass any of the landmarks I noted on our way here, and the fields grow more mountainous with every mile.

"Killing me would make sense," I reply, phrasing my answer carefully.

"Sense." He scoffs. "I don't deal in sense, Little Rose. I deal in what I can taste. Feel. Blood. Killing. Fucking. *You* can play with sense."

"So, fucking." My brow furrows as I parrot the coarse word. "Is that why?"

He looks at me sharply, forsaking the road. "Your cunt is nowhere near that good."

The vulgar terms set my cheeks on fire. "So, then—"

"Why?" he finishes for me. "How about I tell you *how*. How you can enjoy this gift of choice, Little One: You shut your goddamn mouth and you enjoy the ride."

"But why not let me go?" Testing him is a game I can't stop myself from playing. A gamble with brutal, unattainable dividends. I'll bankrupt my soul trying to win, but the few, rare lucky hands I've already won sate my nerve to try again.

"I may not be your husband, as you so kindly reminded me before," he says, "but make no mistake: I own you. You've seen too much. You can try to run if you want, but I will *find* you."

I swallow hard, sensing the threat resonate somewhere deep down in my belly. It's a promise.

"Though is dying with me any different from dying in Winthorp Manor?"

"Is it?" With Robert, I knew my place. I had a role and I performed it the best I knew how.

Here…

There are no rules, which upends my comfortable, if tiring, routine. Three days into my marriage with Robert and I had him pegged down to the minute as to how a typical encounter would begin and end. Twice as many days with Mischa and I still can't predict him from one second to the next.

As if to feed that narrative, he takes one of his hands off the wheel and swipes it along my cheek. "Since you seem so fond of ultimatums… Mention your husband again and I'll remember more stories about your mother and Sergei Vasilev." He presses his thumb over my lip, sealing the promise. "He's dead. From now on, you say only *one* man's name."

He doesn't identify just who that man is, but I have a sinking suspicion regardless.

"Do you understand, Little Rose?"

"Fair enough." I breathe the words against the window glass and watch them burst into puffs of fog. Just as quickly, they fade into nothing.

"Fair? I don't do fair. I calculate risk and I weigh my benefits."

And the benefits of keeping me alive? He doesn't reveal them, and maybe I prefer it that way. Few things could entice a man like Mischa. As a matter of fact, he's already named them: *"I deal in what I can taste. Feel. Blood. Killing. Fucking."*

One item can already be checked off that list, leaving just two…

Blood and killing.

CHAPTER 6

Despite what feels like hours on the road, the only semblance of civilization we come across is a small gas station consisting of two pumps and a tiny storefront. Faded advertisements obscure the windows, and there are no other patrons—or anyone, in fact—for what seems like miles.

Just empty, barren land.

Surprisingly, Mischa pulls into the lot and circles around to the building's rear end. There, my suspicion is proven false: A lone man is waiting, guarding a battered door. Dangling from his hip, in plain sight, is a gun. Alarmed, I look over at Mischa, but a faint smile shapes his lips and I bite back my warning.

"Stay here." He climbs out of the van, taking the keys with him. Together, he and the man enter the building and exit it moments later with something slung between them—a wooden crate.

In their wake follows a third man, hefting another intimidating weapon. They pack the crate into the van, and then Mischa forces me into the back seat. His two men occupy the front, and the driver takes off without a word of direction.

Ignored, I endure the silence as the daylight progressively fades. Eventually, the sound of a door opening jostles me back to awareness.

"We're here."

I blink my eyes open and find Mischa waiting for me outside the van. Behind him looms that impenetrable manor bathed in shadow.

I follow him silently, keeping as much distance as I dare. Inside, Vanya is standing near the foot of the stairs, his arms crossed.

"What did I say?" Mischa says to him. "There is *always* another method."

He must be alluding to a past argument, because Vanya sighs in exasperation and nods. "Yes, yes. But sometimes it's better to use caution—"

"Caution? Such as letting your brother continue to pull my strings?" When Vanya says nothing in response, Mischa chuckles. "It was a joke, Ivan. Did you handle things on your end?"

"Of course." Vanya shifts to reveal something I didn't notice in his hand: the handle of a gray duffle. He lets it fall to the floor and kicks it open to reveal the contents.

I can't stop my eyes from widening at the sight.

Money. Stacks of it.

"Good." Mischa crouches to rifle through the bills. He grabs a rubber-banded stack at random and then shoves the amount toward me. "Your cut," he explains as I gape at the offering. "Welcome to your new family, Ellen Winthorp."

When I don't reach for the money, he grabs my wrist and presses the bills against my palm until I have no choice but to accept them.

"We don't give a shit about blood here. This"—he nods to my hand—"is the only life we value."

With that, he snatches up the handle of the duffle and carries it across the hall. This time, I know better than to follow him.

"Be careful." Vanya's watching me, his expression thoughtful. After a tense second, he nods to the stairs behind him. "Go get some sleep."

"Goodnight."

I slip past him, entering the room beside Mischa's a few minutes later. It's still bare, devoid of anything but a mattress. Ignoring the sight, I switch on the light and rip the rubber band off the stack of dollars.

Sinking to my knees, I count them, peeling the bills apart with my good hand. Slowly. Precisely.

My price for joining Mischa's "family" is a hefty one, in the end. More money than I could ever dream of owning. More than Robert ever let me handle at one time. More than any man should ever give a "worthless whore."

Unless, of course…

He placed an even bigger bet on her life.

I'm still running my fingers through the loose bills when the door opens and Vanya enters. Facing me, he braces his back against the wall and nods to the money.

"Keep it safe," he warns. "The men won't dare steal from Mischa, but you…are not him."

"Thank you," I croak, my voice thick.

"Don't." He shrugs the gratitude off, squaring his jaw. "I'll get you something to put it in. Keep it on you always—"

"Why are you so nice to me?" I don't mean to come off as rude. Perhaps desperate? Mischa, as brutal as he is, speaks a language I can understand. But kindness? That is a foreign commodity in my world, and if Robert taught me one thing, it was that nothing came for free.

"Why?" Vanya looks beyond me, his mouth twisted thoughtfully. Finally, he sighs. "I would hope that, in her final days, someone would have shown some kindness to my daughter."

I cringe at the barely concealed pain in his voice.

A good woman wouldn't probe it.

"I saw her," I admit. Like a coward, I stare at the floor rather than meet his gaze. "At Winthorp Manor when she was held captive. Did Mischa tell you?"

"Yes."

I lift my head and meet his gaze, but he stares back unflinchingly, hiding nothing.

"He told me. And in her name, I want you to know that you have nothing to fear from me. However, I do have something I want to ask you, if that is all right."

"Anything." I can't help how eager I sound. "Please ask."

"You grew up there? In that place?"

I force myself to nod. "Yes."

"And your parents?"

Alarm dances down my spine. "Dead."

"And…your mother?"

My lips part just as Mischa's words come back to haunt me: *"If Vanya asks about her. Lie. Trust me on this."* The concept should be laughable. Trusting Mischa over the only man to show me kindness here.

But…

My new tormentor may be many things, but I'm not sure if a liar is one of them.

"Her name was…Martha," I lie. "She was a maid on the Winthorp estate."

"A maid?" He raises an eyebrow. "It's just that you remind me of someone."

"Oh?" My heart lurches in my chest. "W-who?"

"Someone," he repeats, staring past me. His mouth sags into a wry frown, but not even a second later, he shakes his head, banishing the expression. "Get some sleep. I'll get you something for the money in the morning."

He's gone a heartbeat later, closing the door behind him.

When heavy footsteps near the room, I assume it's him, returning for one last word. But no. Another man throws the door open, looming in the doorway.

"I gave you your payment," Mischa tells me, his voice rough. He found a new shirt from somewhere, though he wears the same filthy pants. "That is how it will be from now on. A transaction. You prove your worth—"

"Like by being a mule for whatever illegal things you sell?"

"Ah." He raises an eyebrow, his mouth quirked. "I gave you your cut, didn't I?"

I eye the money, flexing my fingers. "As if that makes it any better—"

"Don't lie." He advances a step closer. "You fucking like having it—payment. But since I've given you yours… I'm here to take mine."

I glance at him sharply. "And what is that?"

"Hmm…" He strokes his thumb along the bottom of his chin.

My heart races with every second he stalls. Anger is unnerving in him, but so is this: calculated thought.

"An answer," he finally says. "Was it really you?" When he glances at my bandaged hand, I know what he means. Was I the one controlling the knife? "Or will you play the victim? Claim you had no choice—"

"*I did it,*" I hiss, drawing my bandaged hand to my chest. "Does that make you happy? The fact that I mutilated myself?"

His eyes narrow. I've caught him off guard. "Not mutilated," he insists softly. "I'm after your honesty, Little Rose. The one thing I fucking know for a fact he didn't teach you."

"And now he's dead." Spit flies from my lips, laced with vitriol. "So you can stop comparing yourself to him. Robert—"

"No." Anger resonates in his voice like a slap. "Have you forgotten so soon? Take a good look."

He sheds his gray shirt, tossing it into a ball on the floor. His arms flex in its absence, displaying every muscle rippling with tension. "I told you that you are only allowed to utter one man's name. Shall I teach you how to say it?"

The coldness in his gaze is such a stark contrast to the beautiful collage of scars and tattoos unfolding across his ribcage. My breath catches as my nerves spark, aware of his nearness.

"Mischa Mikhailovich Stepanov." He takes another deliberate step as I watch. Then another. When he's close enough, he cradles my chin against his fingertips, grazing my skin with the tips of his nails. "Now…I want to hear how it sounds when you scream it."

He shoves me back and works on the waistband of his pants with slow, deliberate motions. Anticipation ricochets through my veins, rendering me paralyzed as my heart picks up speed.

"I-I…I'm not your captive anymore," I gasp out. Though am I speaking to him? Or myself? "I—"

"I don't really give a damn what you are," Mischa says. He sinks to his knees over the end of the mattress, grasping my thighs in each hand. Then he waits as if he's expecting me to run. When I don't, he parts them slowly, watching my face with every inch of space revealed. "All I want is what I'm owed."

"Get off of me—"

Stealing my breath, his fingers slip beneath my dress and find me quivering—even as I try to bat his hand away. I'm slick. Ready. It's impossible to hide the truth from his touch. With him inside me, there is no escape.

"I knew it." His eyes flash as he swipes his thumb along my entrance and my body quakes in response. It's like each nerve short-circuits, rewired by every brutal caress. "*This* is how a woman speaks to the man she needs. You can't lie to me like this. You can't pretend…so don't. You've never ached like this for him."

I gasp out, squeezing my eyes shut against his heated expression: clenched jaw, heavy-lidded eyes. My inner muscles spasm, grasping greedily at his fingers. He's right. We speak our own language, and he's drowning me in nonsense.

"So, what will it be, Little One?" he wonders as he rocks his erection against my entrance, teasing me with the unbearable fullness. "Hard or slow?"

I writhe against the bed. Avoiding him…drawn to him. A pathetic whimper bubbles in my throat.

"Both?" Mischa murmurs into my ear. "As you wish. But first…" His fingers sink into my hair again, tugging. "I demand my payment in full."

He gives me no warning before he stretches me open with one thrust, pushing the air from my lungs and every thought from my head. My hips arch, driving him deeper even as I turn my face into the sheets, desperate to shut him out.

But he won't be erased so easily. His teeth nip at my earlobe, insistent and unforgiving. "Look at me. *Fuck*—look at me."

I open my eyes and cry out at the monster I find staring back. His eyes are aglow with unholy fire, his lips drawn back to bare his teeth. He grunts as he fucks me. Takes me. Breaks me.

There are no rules. Just chaos and the violent tempest that drives him in and out. Harder. Deeper. *Too much.*

"Give it to me, Little One," he demands, clawing at my hips for enough leverage to change the angle of his thrusts. It's like his aim is to bore through me. Into my soul. Into my head. "Give it to me."

My lips flutter and then fly apart as broken noise tears from my throat. "M-Mischa."

My cheeks heat with shame. I've lost this game. Or have I?

The sound of his name makes him rear up on his knees, his head thrown back, a groan building in his throat. Like a growl. Like thunder. Hungrily, his fingers bite into my flesh, claiming, grasping. "Say it again."

It's not the triumphant command of a conquer. It's...a plea?

"Shit... Say it again." Corded muscles strain against his flesh, distorting his outline. He's more beast than man, howling for release. "Fuck, say it—"

"Mischa."

His name holds its own power. Too fucking much for my head to contain. He bucks at the sound of it, hunching forward to sink his teeth into my shoulder so hard that I see white.

My lips part, but rather than a cry, something else slips from them, broken and bleating. "Mischa…"

The word ends on a moan as he flips me over, pressing my face into the sheets. With my body prone, he enters me from behind. His hips slam into me, and I take him as deep as I can—then even further than that. I taste him. I'm consumed by him. He beats his ownership into my battered flesh and rakes his name into my skin with his teeth.

I lose track of how long it lasts. How brutal he becomes. Bruising. Punishing.

Thoughtless.

Reckless.

Boneless.

I'm a mass of exposed nerves when he finally groans into my ear, flooding me with his release, but he never moves. I'm crushed beneath his weight, too exhausted to resist the unbearable pressure. A part of me considers lying there, letting his bulk drive every ounce of air from my lungs until there's nothing left. I could die like this.

"Hey." As he finally rolls onto his side, stars dance across my vision. "Look at me."

He's frowning when I do. With one hand, he reaches out to flick the sweat-soaked hair from my face. Whatever he finds makes him scoff in disgust.

"Still there," he declares, rolling onto his back. "Tell me, Little Rose. What would it take to drive him out of your skull for good?"

Robert? It's a comical question, though he doesn't seem to see it that way. His voice is gruff. Stern. Serious.

"Twenty-three years," I reply, alarmed by how dead I sound. How tired.

"What a shame," Mischa muses. "I don't have that kind of time." He shifts, turning his back to me.

I wait, but he doesn't stand yet. His heat prickles my skin, a foreign sensation. Robert never extended his presence beyond this point. Only now can I entertain the small possibility that it might have been some shred of mercy on his part.

After all, he never wanted to ruin me, break me, destroy me…

He just wanted to own me. I still wear his shackles, and I'm at a loss as to how to find the key—or if one even exists. What would it take to drive him out of my skull for good?

"He kept me blind."

Mischa stiffens at the sound of my voice, but I'm more shocked than he should be. I'm not used to speaking like this. Freely. Unease mingles with the breathless aftermath of the sex, churning my thoughts into a senseless mass that makes it hard to discern what's smart and what is…not.

"He never told me anything," I add. "And he used my ignorance as a cage."

There's so much I don't know about the Winthorps, or my mother, or the *Mafiya*. So much I'm not sure I ever want to learn.

"If you want to erase him, then…" The words linger on the tip of my tongue, too stupid to utter out loud. Too reckless. I'm tempted to swallow them down.

But no. I've already piqued the monster's interest. One taste of my bleeding soul and he wants more.

"What?" He's harsh, impatient. Curious?

I raise my gaze, hunting for his body through the dark. He's faced me again without my realizing it, meeting my probing stare with a brutal scowl of his own.

"Name your price, Little Rose."

Perhaps he's not far off. Maybe my cage never required a key. Just a price some mercenary would pay to buy his way in.

"Open my eyes," I say simply. "Let me learn this world for myself and tell me everything. Everything he never did."

I don't dream...

But I know I'm in one before the cruel curtain is ripped away. I'm too happy. Too content. The warm body in my arms conforms to mine like no one ever has. So perfect...

I blink to make the scene clearer—to see his face just one last time.

I call for him...

But *then* reality returns and I wake up to a cruel world that looks the same as it always has: distorted snippets seen through the bars of the cage. It seems my current captor needs more convincing to release his pet bird from her prison. He wants me to ask him twice.

He wants me to beg.

One wouldn't know just from looking at him, however. He's still sprawled on his side of the bed, facing away from me as light streaks his back. But it's surprisingly easy to sense which directions his thoughts take in this moment.

Wherever a sane man's mind would venture, his travels the opposite path. Almost as if he likes to spite that tiny bit of humanity inside himself that only Vanya seems to think still exists.

"Little Rose…" He inhales deeply, as if sensing my attention, causing the muscles along his spine to ripple. "Did I say you could move?" He sounds half asleep.

But I'm not fooled. This creature, man or monster he may be, doesn't sleep. He watches me during the night. He studies me.

He still is.

Aware of his scrutiny, I lie back down, staring up at the ceiling. Whatever drug Vanya gave me all those hours ago has finally worn off.

It. Hurts.

Everything.

My hand is just another agony adding to the symphony of it blaring beneath my skin. My head aches. Back aches. My soul…

It's the most battered by Mischa's violent whims. He manhandles it even now as he makes me listen to every lazy breath he takes while I wait for his command to rise.

Seconds pass. Minutes. My reprieve never comes.

"You don't like being touched." He makes that claim while a shadow creeps toward my side of the bed, cast by his hand. A heartbeat later, he boldly strokes my hip. "Oh, I don't mean in *this* way."

As I shudder beneath his touch, his breath bastes the base of my throat, igniting sweat gathering there. In an instant, I'm ablaze.

"You don't mind the fucking. You tolerate it. It's the nearness you don't like. Contact." His hand stills as he comes to a sudden realization. "He never slept in your bed."

I say nothing, distracted by the sensation of his callused palm. Too heavy. Too warm. Too real.

"I will not show you the same mercy, Little Rose."

He tugs on my hip, yanking my body onto his torso. I'm now facing him directly, our bare flesh meeting with a wet slap. His eyes are heavy-lidded but stern, contradicting the slow, lazy smile shaping his lips.

"You will *breathe* me." His coarse tone transforms the words into the most dangerous threat: a shackle of promises. "There will be no escape. No reprieve. Whether you are awake, or asleep, or in my bed, you will never know any reality that doesn't include me."

His promise festers like poison in my stomach, eating through what little resolve I have left. I survived Robert, a badge I wear with pride. And yet…

Mischa is a whole new creature. One who's adapted to hone every weapon my husband never bothered to use. As if to feed that fear, his hands caress my shoulders, raising goosebumps with every bit of flesh they claim.

"Don't look so alarmed, Little Rose." He brushes his mouth against my cheek. "I think I've changed my mind. I *will* do this slowly. I might have twenty-three years to break you after all. In the meantime…"

He shoves me off and rolls effortlessly into a sitting position. With his back to me, the scars there stand out in stark contrast, catching the light.

"You want to be enlightened?" He stands and fishes his clothing from the floor. Once dressed, he looks at me from over his shoulder. "Then come and open your fucking eyes."

I rise obediently and stagger toward my pile of clothing. At first, I intend to grab whatever I can reach. He beats me to them, kicking a bag over so that its contents spill out for his inspection. One by one, he nudges the expensive fabrics with his bare toes.

"The black," he grunts finally. "Wear that."

I eye his selection and bite my lip: a thin dress with spaghetti straps.

"Why?"

"Why?" The smirk he's wearing alarms me more than his raw anger. "You're not with him anymore. So don't fucking dress like it."

"What do you mean?" Exasperation taints my tone. So many rules. *Don't do this. Don't think that. Don't wear those.*

My entire being must remind him of Robert. But how much of my identity is my husband and how much is just me? I'm terrified to realize that I don't know the answer.

"Why can't I wear this?" I point to a shirt in a delicate shade of pink.

He scoffs and snatches the garment from the floor. Then he rips it in half and tosses the torn pieces at my feet. "Because you aren't a fucking Winthorp doll in their pretty glass house."

He moves quickly, drawing a gasp from my lips before I even process why: He gripped my chin with one massive hand, tilting it roughly so that he can view me from a different angle. I'm not sure what he sees from his vantage point. Fear? Submission?

Or a challenge?

"Unfold your arms."

Alarm jolts through me, locking the limbs to my sides. "W-why?"

"Your arms." He snatches my wrists himself and wrenches them apart. His eyes rake over my exposed torso without mercy, but I don't miss how his tongue flicks along his lower lip with every inch gained. "I want you to think," he demands. "You listen to your body. Tell me how it wants to be dressed—not with fucking pink. Not like Briar.

Like…" Chuckling low in his throat, he leans in closer, and I assume he's relishing the involuntary swallow racking my throat. "You. How does little Rose want to be dressed?"

"Not like your doll." My fingers shake slightly as I test his grip, and I'm surprised when he lets me go. Slipping past him, I snatch another shirt from my pile on the floor. It's a light shade of blue.

Mischa says nothing as I pull it on and then shimmy into a pair of jeans. When I gather the nerve to face him, he's already near the door.

"Come." He jerks his chin and enters the hall. Daylight streams in from a nearby row of windows, ghosting over the ornate wall fixtures and painting a stark contrast to my barren room. Enlighten me, he said?

Perhaps he'll start with this.

"Do you own this place?"

Another raspy laugh rumbles from his chest—but this time, it lacks any humor. He sounds more guarded than anything. When we reach the staircase without him responding, I assume he won't play this game after all.

"Tell me," he says as he descends the first few steps, proving me wrong. "If I did, would that impress you?"

His back is to me, meaning he can't see how my mouth twists in genuine contemplation. Would it? The answer comes quickly. No. Robert possessed wealth in spades. Yet, underneath, he was a simple man who craved simple, base things.

"Of course not," Mischa assumes, answering for me. "You grew up in fucking Winthorp Manor. I'm sure your husband bathed you in diamonds."

Ironically, he's not far off. Though none of Robert's many gifts were truly mine. I had nice dresses that he kept locked in a closet, allowed to be worn only at his discretion. I had trinkets and baubles that were his taste, not mine. Even my own servants deferred to him always.

"You don't give a fuck if I own this," Mischa declares, gesturing to our surroundings with a wave of his hand. We've reached the lower level, and he leads me past the main entrance and down a hallway. "A better question is how. Go on. Ask it. I know you want to."

"Robert made his money through investments," I say, parroting a term I've heard flung around my entire life to explain away the wealth of the Winthorps. Investments. With money. Into something. The details were never explained.

"You know that's a fucking lie." Mischa doesn't waste putting any effort into the assertion. "The Winthorps trade in *flesh*, Little One. Women. Girls. They hide their business well, using a shipping company as a front, but it is slavery nonetheless."

"Y-you're lying," I rasp automatically. Robert was a lot of things, but a sex trafficker?

"Don't sound so surprised." Mischa shoots me a glance over his shoulder. For once, his smug grin is absent. "I'm sure you've suspected as much. What other 'investment' could amass a man enough money to buy the whole fucking world?"

"Maybe I was that naïve," I croak. So many things take on a darker connotation now. The foreign maids who staffed the manor. The secrecy around Robert's accounts. My heart pangs as I consider the unthinkable: Could I have played a role in it all unknowingly?

"So you didn't know." He sounds doubtful, even as the words leave his mouth.

"And you?" I wonder, eyeing his back. I've seen the scars that mark his body, but what horrors might lurk on his soul? "Do you trade in 'flesh' as well?"

The way he stiffens makes me second-guess that suspicion. His shoulders tense, almost as if he doesn't even recognize his own disgust.

"My family has always been less complex than your elegant Winthorps," he calls from paces ahead, continuing to walk without me. "We trade in simpler things: drugs, and guns, and money."

I force myself to keep moving, chasing him down a narrow corridor and into the dining room. When he takes a seat at the head of the grand table, I maintain the distance between us, staying near the wall.

"No slaves?" I don't mean to sound mocking.

"Oh, don't tell me, Little Rose." Mischa cocks an eyebrow. "You're *still* not impressed. Maybe I've pegged you wrong? You more than knew of his business. Maybe you got off on the thrill of it? Being the one woman he chose to keep?"

"The one?" I echo, my brow furrowing. "What makes you think I was his only woman?"

I expect him to sneer at the statement. Not frown.

"You *were*," he insists. "He may have fucked his whores on the side. I don't doubt that. But *you* were the one. The one he claimed. The one he needed."

It's almost too twisted to consider. "Needed?"

He laughs. Then he scowls. "To keep him sane."

A chill runs down my spine. God, it's like I'm hearing Robert again, hissing his insanity into my ear. *I need you, Elle.*

"Did he tell you that?" I rasp hoarsely. "Did you talk to him? Before—"

"No." Mischa shakes his head. "He didn't have to tell me a damn thing, Little Rose. I just know how pathetic men like him operate. How they crave a woman's devotion. Especially someone like you, pathetic and weak. If such a creature could still see the good in them, they can justify their fucking madness. *You* helped him sleep at night—"

"Don't blame me for what he was." I don't realize I've spoken out loud until he chuckles, eyeing me with amusement.

"Why not? You said it yourself: He never forced you. You chose to marry him. You chose to fuck him every night. You *chose* to give him your devotion. Don't lie to me and say you don't believe for a second that having you in his bed made it easier for him to do the twisted shit you know in your soul he's capable of?"

Maybe it did.

"But what about you?" I say, turning the tables the only way I know how: comparing them. "If your logic holds, then where is your woman? Your excuse?"

"She's dead." His mocking smile falls flat. "And I don't need anyone to fucking justify my actions." He shoves back from the table and advances on me too quickly to outrun. When he's paces away, he cradles my cheek with alarming gentleness, contrasting the anger smoldering in his expression. "You can try your little tricks on me, Little Rose," he taunts, stroking my jaw. "But I don't believe salvation can be found in your cunt."

"S-stop it!" My cheeks flame. "You have a strange idea of love."

His concept of the emotion is much more potent than mine. To me, love is duty. Sacrifice. But he makes it sound alluring. Dangerous. Capable of shaping men, and even more fantastical: changing them.

"And you don't?" Frowning, he draws his hand away. I think I've confused him. "Don't tell me… You never believed your fucking Winthorp was a white knight, capable of saving your soul?"

"Of course not." I force a laugh for good measure. He's mocking me. He has to be.

"You're serious." A shadow falls over his face. "That poor fuck. He thought you were. His wife. His love. He would have fucking begged for you—"

"But now he's dead," I interject, my throat tight. "And you? Did you beg for your love?" I don't know where the question came from—or why I'm so curious as to the answer.

Alarm runs down my spine as his eyes narrow.

"I didn't," he says in a soft, lethal tone. "Because I was a stupid fucking fool. I traded her life for another's. And you want to know something, Little Rose?" His fingers come to trace the hollow of my throat, catching me off guard. "That person wasn't fucking worthy."

I recoil and race to the other end of the room, desperate to put distance between us. Anna-Natalia, Vanya's daughter. He's talking about her. Traded her life, he said? I have a sinking suspicion whose life he traded it for.

Mine.

"Don't blame me for what you are, either," I hiss at the wall —but it's more of a plea than a rebuttal. Robert's already tainted my soul. I can't take any more.

More guilt.

More pain

More envy?

"Oh no you don't." Laughing, Mischa moves to stand opposite me, refusing to be ignored. "Look at me."

A sliver of blond hair obscures his gaze. Only the stern set of his mouth gives me a clue as to what he's feeling.

"You want me to enlighten you?" he asks. "Teach you what he never did? Let's start with the truth: All I want from you is the one thing you never gave him." He waits, ensuring he has my full attention. Then he smiles, displaying a terrifying array of white teeth. "I want your honesty, Little Rose. Can you give me that?"

He doesn't seem to really want an answer. Not now anyway.

"Let's start with your first lesson," he says, abruptly changing the subject. "Sit." He nods to the chair nearest him.

Heart in my throat, I approach it. This close, I'm aware of his scrutiny, how he eyes my quivering throat and heaving chest.

"Twenty-four years ago, the Winthorps started a war." He leans back against the wall, crossing his arms over his chest. Apparently, this story will be a long one. "Can you tell me why?"

I grit my teeth. My ignorance is a toy he constantly loves to play with. "You know I don't—"

"But you should." His tone softens, unnervingly quiet. "Because your mother was at the start of it."

I blink, unsure if he's joking—but there is no mocking smile to temper the impact of his words.

"Oh, don't look so shocked." He leans in and drags his thumb along my cheek as if savoring how my eyes widen. As I gape, he brings the digit to his mouth and flicks his tongue over it. Then he says, "I think you've suspected it all along, haven't you? That she was the very first. Marnie Winthorp. She was fated to be number one."

CHAPTER 8

I clutch the surface of the table if only to keep from reaching for the necklace hidden beneath my shirt. I know he can see it: the desperation to know more that I can't even begin to suppress. I picture her. Marnie, beautiful Marnie. Not only was she a victim in the feud, but a cause of it? "How?"

"It's not what you're thinking," Mischa scolds. "It wasn't some petty, romantic squabble. Your mother was meant to pay a price, Little One. A life for a life."

"Then how was she the first?"

I expect him to elaborate, but he doesn't. Instead, he extends the silence, reminding me of Robert when he hunted, patiently anticipating the moment his chosen prey would take his bait.

So I bite. "Tell me!"

"Fine. Your Winthorps weren't always so high and mighty," Mischa counters. "Years ago, they had an arrangement with the *mafiya*. They ran our accounts, and we protected their interests."

His subtle inflection betrays what he really means: that his people were the muscle for Robert Sr.

"But your husband's father got greedy. He thought he could betray us, his allies. Your mother was meant to be his punishment. When she was taken, I'm sure they thought she was dead. So they retaliated."

With him and his mother? I don't dare ask. Instead, I remember something else he told me once. Anna-Natalia was number twelve. Was Briar meant to be thirteen?

"You said you traded one life for another," I say cautiously. From his expression, I can't anticipate his reaction. I have no choice but to forge on. "Mine? Briar's? For Anna—"

"*You* were never a damn factor in any of this," he says, reminding me of my fate: a decoy. How ironic that in both my encounters with him, I was always standing in for someone else. "It was always about Briar."

But he's lying.

"So then why didn't you go after her? In the woods," I say. "Don't lie to me by claiming it never happened. I know what I saw."

It wasn't a vivid dream after all. Briar was in those woods— and once again, he saved *me*.

Something flits across his gaze too quickly to name. "I miscalculated," he says finally and I flinch, caught off guard by the truth. "I thought that you might mean more to him."

"Either way, you killed him."

"But if I didn't?"

My stomach drops as Mischa turns from me, his voice a thoughtful murmur.

"If he lived. Would that make you turn against him, your precious husband? Knowing that he would have let you die as a sacrifice?"

"No." I'm as surprised by the admission as he seems to be. He whips around, eyeing me with predatory focus. "If Robert chose his sister over me…it would have been him being selfless."

Briar didn't carry his secrets. She couldn't warm his bed.

She never carried his seed.

"Selfless?" Mischa's thumb grazes my cheek and I jump. He's frowning again. Confused? "To let you die for him?"

"No." I shrug him off. "Because he would have finally let me go—"

"Mischa?"

We both turn to the doorway and find Vanya standing there.

Warily, his gaze darts between the two of us. "Your...input is needed," he says, wording the phrase carefully.

To hide something, I suspect.

From me.

"You can speak freely, Ivan," Mischa says. He passes me and enters the hall with his mentor on his heels. "It's not like Little Rose has a family to run to, should she escape."

I grit my teeth against a reply. Instead, I stand and pad after him, straining my ears for more. Maybe there's a reason Robert never enlightened me more than he needed to. Knowledge is addicting. It's power. Already, I'm seeing slight nuances in a different light.

Everything seems clearer, and maybe, deep down, I'm... relieved? Briar thought Robert would trade her for me. Is that why she used me as her own decoy? In the end, he proved her wrong.

And she finally won the only game that mattered.

"There was a complication," Vanya says, drawing my attention back to him. He and Mischa are paces ahead, navigating a section of the house I don't recognize. It's darker, the walls plainer and less ornate. Somewhere I suspect they utilize for business over leisure. "Nikolaus hasn't let your treatment of his son go uncontested. He's been spreading rumors to other members of the syndicate, the fucking worm."

"Rumors?" Mischa questions, but I can't help feeling that he sounds disinterested. Distracted. I'm not the only one haunted by our last conversation, it seems. "Rumors like his son being a fucking traitor who deserved to be gutted?"

"No." Vanya looks back as if remembering my presence. "Rumors that you…"

"I told you, Vanya," Mischa scolds. "You can speak freely around her."

He sounds so damn smug. Whatever the topic of this conversation is, I suspect that it revolves around me.

"Fine. That prick has been saying that you're too busy fucking Robert Winthorp's leftovers to properly lead. It's gotten the others talking. Some are grumbling that Sergei might be more level-headed—"

"Is that so?" Mischa laughs, stroking his chin. "Maybe it's time to pay Nikolaus a visit? Perhaps later. But for now…"

We round a corner, coming to a narrow room that must be at the very back of the house. Blinds shroud the windows, choking off most natural light. I can only make out the shrouded shapes of various objects. Boxes? Furniture?

"I want to show Little Rose what her life is worth," Mischa declares. He flicks a light switch, flooding the room with the glow from a single lightbulb dangling overhead.

This space might have been a study once, like the one he has upstairs. Now, it's a storeroom containing the mysterious cardboard boxes I spotted in the very first place he kept me after my capture. After approaching one, he pries the lid open and grasps one of the items within.

"Look," he commands, holding it out to me. "Your husband dealt in flesh. But this is what I deal in."

Butterflies squirm to life in my stomach. I don't know what to expect. Cocaine like the awful packets Nicolai possessed? Bloodied coins?

Anything but a long, black object. Its infamous shape leaves no question as to what it is.

"Guns?" I whisper.

According to him, my husband made his fortune on the literal backs of others. How fitting that Mischa trades in violence.

"So unimpressed," he muses as he returns the gun to the box and closes the lid. Is he disappointed? When he captures my chin in his grip, I can't tell. He merely observes me, hunting for secrets within my skin. "The way you act when I say his fucking name…" He chuckles, but there's a harshness to the sound that steals my breath away. "It's like he had you in a fucking cage. But I don't believe that." His nostrils flare as he leans in close. "He kept you so fucking pampered a handful of diamonds wouldn't faze you."

The sound of a throat being cleared makes me jump, and Mischa turns away from me as if realizing Vanya is even there.

"I'm going to track down Nikolaus," Vanya says, his tone gruff. "Before that bastard can spread more lies. In fact, I think you let him off too easy the last time. If his son traded with Winthorp's, who's to say the father didn't, too?"

Mischa's eyes narrow into lethal slits. "Who's to say."

"Then let me handle this." Vanya turns and exits the room.

I make the mistake of thinking we're through and start after him, desperate to retreat to quiet again. Robert, bathe me in gold? Maybe. Gold chains. Golden cuffs. Golden bars over every window.

"Oh no you don't."

I stifle a gasp as Mischa grabs my other arm before I can slip past him.

"I want to know," he snarls against the back of my throat. "I want to know *more*."

About Robert.

"Why?" My voice comes out pained. Afraid? "He's dead—"

"So you keep saying. But he's alive and well in here, Little Rose. Isn't he?" He grips my skull between his hands, applying just a taste of the brute strength he's capable of. "He didn't give you a fucking ring and yet he was willing to kill for you. He hid you. He beat you. Scarred you. Raped you. And yet, every time I'm fucking inside you, I know he's there."

"And if he is?" I spit, exasperated. When he doesn't answer, I can't help scoffing. "What do you want from me?"

His grip tightens, and the room blurs as he drags me into a corner and shoves me against the wall. He gives me no time to regain my bearings. Hot fingers slide around to my front, wrenching at the fastenings of my jeans. Too hard. The clasp breaks, opening me up to a ruthless assault. Then he palms me completely, groaning at the feel.

His hand is too rough. Raw. My breath catches, chest heaving, as individual fingers writhe against my flesh, wringing sounds I don't even recognize from my throat.

"Ride me," Mischa grates into the nape of my neck. "Fuck. Do it."

His index finger parts my folds, flicking in a sinful downward motion. It's like my spine is on a puppet string, controlled by that single, callous touch. Again. Harder. Deeper.

My hips start to rock in time with each motion and he grunts in approval.

But it's still not enough.

Suddenly, his hand withdraws only to tug on my arm, wrenching me around to face him. Shadows exaggerate the amber gaze I've come to fear. A million hidden emotions lurk within it. Demanding things from me. Craving.

But he never says what out loud. He strips me bare instead, shoving his hands beneath my jeans, opening me up to the cock he's palming with trembling fingers. When I start to look down, he grabs my chin, forcing it up. Forcing me to watch him. How his eyes narrow when he sinks into me. The way his nostrils flare with my scent. How he groans at the sinful fit.

His eyelids flutter as he begins to move, thrusting deep. Hard.

Too deep.

"Don't," he warns when my gaze starts to drift. "Look at me. You fucking—" A harsh buck of his hips makes me whine, which almost drowns him out. "Look. At. Me."

Our gazes reconnect and it's like he's in my head more than my body. Boring in too roughly to stop. Showing no mercy. No sanity.

Just taking more. More. More.

My teeth clench around a hollow moan. My knees are jelly, leaving my arms no choice but to grab him for stability. My face aims for his shoulder. I need to hide my gasps. My searing cheeks inflamed with shame for how my body grips him. I need to smother the things I shouldn't feel.

"No." He tilts his head, jarring our noses together. Our mouths. Nipping teeth capture my bottom lip, holding me captive. His eyes are hollow, devouring mine. Something flashes across each fiery iris, gone in an instant. "You've never been this wet for him," he insists between harsh, laving strokes of his tongue. "This loud. Fuck, you're whining for *me*." His eyes close as he savors the high-pitched cries rolling off my tongue.

God, he's moving faster. Harder. I can't breathe.

"You've never needed him like this. Have you?" A brutal thrust makes my vision blur.

Need?

"You were made for this," he tells me. "For *me*." He bucks forward, twitching, straining, spilling.

My thoughts fade. The world spins and spins, and for a split second, my body is the center of the universe. The orgasm slams into me so hard that I can feel the Earth fucking move.

I regain clarity on my hands and knees, gasping on dusty, still air and masculine musk. He's behind me, hunched over my shuddering frame.

"Even now, he's still there," Mischa accuses, nipping at my collar with punishing jabs of his teeth. "Still inside you. Still owning you. I could fuck you for hours and I still couldn't drive him out."

He stands, staggering to find his balance. In seconds, he's redressed, heading for the door.

To leave.

To brood.

Alone.

But something holds him back, making him pause over the threshold.

"Tell me something," he demands, sounding ragged. Empty. Soulless. "If I offered you your freedom. Money. Your fucking soul. Would you ever, for a second, feel for me what you felt for him?"

What I felt for Robert? My blood runs cold, erasing the aftermath of my climax. I shiver at the thought of it, and nothing could disguise the horror that racks my voice. "N-no."

He laughs, even as his eyes darken, sending a chill down my spine. "Why am I not surprised?" He leaves, slamming the door after him.

Angry?

If I felt for him what I felt for Robert…

It would be easier to bear him, certainly.

Because I'd feel nothing.

Mischa is a fickle captor. One moment, he's seemingly merciful, offering my heart's desire. The next, he's content to let me rot.

I'm too tired to put up much of a fight. Instead, I return to my room and curl up on the lone mattress.

My body hums in the aftermath of his violence, like an instrument played to the breaking point—but one used how it's meant to. Ruthlessly thorough. His hands stroke parts of me to exhaustion, making them sing a painful tune.

But it's not music. It's twisted, ugly noise.

In contrast, Robert used me like a tool. His lust was a sledgehammer against a glass nail. Two items well-suited in theory—but in reality, the latter was destined to break. I can't recall the way he felt inside me. I don't want to. Thoughts of him are the remnants of a terrible storm. The details are hazy, but the aftermath is a stark nightmare I'll always relive.

And Mischa wants to be him.

In a funny, terrifying way, it should be easy to swap them out. Pain for pain. Lust for lust. Brutality for brutality.

It should be easy...

But Mischa brings a different kind of agony, so unique that I lack the vocabulary needed to describe it. If Robert had my love, Mischa claims something else. Some hateful part of me I loathe almost as much as I desperately want to feel it. I'm not a numb bird in a cage when he touches me.

I'm a hellcat, aching to scratch him as viciously as he brutalizes me.

In his bed, I'm angry, and vengeful, and *alive*.

Even scarred and brutalized, I can endure every second of his torment.

Maybe the constant game is better than the surrender I'm accustomed to.

At least I'll go insane faster.

What a pathetic creature he's turned me into.

I find snatches of sleep in his absence. When I finally crawl from the mattress, it's dark. Shadows paint the corners of my room and I have to feel my way into the bathroom.

I shower quickly, scrubbing my tormentor away. Naked, I retreat to my bedroom and fish a new outfit from my piles of clothing. My fingers settle rebelliously over one garment in particular: a simple pink dress nearly shapeless in design with a modest neckline.

He accused me of still dressing like I belong to Robert—but when I remember my reasoning for choosing this dress, my husband isn't who comes to mind. Robert liked me swathed in layers and festooned with pretty, frilly things. Lace. Ribbons.

He liked me bundled up like a package only he could tear apart.

This dress? I could smuggle cocaine underneath it in the place of a child if I had to. It would provide sufficient cover if I were locked in an animal's cage, and I could also climb trees in it.

More importantly, a madman could easily slide his fingers beneath it.

And every time I look down at the soft, delicate color, I would remember who I am. *Ellen,* who likes pink. Not because of Briar or Mischa—but in spite of them both.

My fingers shake as I wrench the dress over my head just as sounds drift from the hall. Footsteps. Mischa? Only God knows what new horror he has in store.

I wait, my spine rigid, as the figure advances toward my door and the doorknob rattles. Strange. Vanya knocks, whereas Mischa would just barge in. The second I think as much, the door opens.

A man stands there. He's too thin to be Mischa, his face obscured by shadow.

"I'm supposed to take you to him," he says.

"Who? Mischa?" I take a step forward, so conditioned to follow orders. But then something tugs at the back of my mind and I stop short.

As much as he loathes Robert, Mischa has performed similarly in how he lords his ownership over me. He comes to me himself. Alone. Never before has he sent anyone but Vanya in his place.

I scan the new man more intently, hunting for anything worth noting. Though he's wearing the same gray fatigues as Mischa and his men, I don't recognize his face.

"Where is he?" I ask, not moving another inch.

"He's—" The man cocks his head and suddenly steps farther into the hall. Something about the way he moves makes me creep to the threshold to watch him. He's stiff, marching past another man who rounds the corner. This figure passes me with no interest.

I clench my teeth, uneasy. Is Mischa up to yet another mind game? If he is, I should just retreat to my room. Wait. Hide.

My heart pounds in horror as I enter the hall instead. The unfamiliar man is already halfway to the grand staircase. I presume he'll be descending the steps, but I don't find him in the main entryway. I continue down the hall anyway, toward the dining room. Paces away from the doorway, I hear Mischa.

"Come here."

His irritated tone spurs me closer, but I pause just before entering the room.

"I thought I told you to stay out of here? Don't give me that look," he scolds in a tone so sharp that I flinch. "You're going to hurt yourself if you keep playing with those. Huh? You want to learn to use one?"

I strain my ears, but I don't hear anyone respond.

"I don't think you're ready," Mischa replies to silence.

Is the man truly insane? I inch closer and make out his shape hunched over a glass table in the center of a wide room. In one of his hands is a large knife, which he wields effortlessly.

He tosses it by the handle and catches it, avoiding the blade. "These aren't toys."

Beside him, barely coming to his waist, stands a tiny figure with wild, blond hair spilling over her shoulders. The girl Nicolai wanted used as a drug mule. She watches Mischa intently, and when he catches the knife again, she points to his hand.

"What?" He hefts the blade for her to see more clearly. "You want to try holding it? I don't know... Can I trust you not to cut your damn fingers off?" He laughs and I'm left reeling. Deep and booming, it sounds real.

Insistent, the girl points again.

With a sigh Mischa crouches down to her level and snatches one of her hands. "All right. Hold it like this. Not too tight, but not too loose, either. You drop this and you won't just lose a toe or two, but your whole foot. Understood?"

The girl nods as Mischa adjusts her grip on the blade.

"Now, move your feet. Always brace. Don't think that if you stab something the knife will just go through like paper. You always need force." He makes her sharply jab the tip of the blade into the air and his lips quirk into a satisfied grin. "Like that. Not that you're ready for something like this any time soon."

He stands and takes the knife, returning it to what I realize isn't a table, but a glass case.

"Someone your size needs something smaller," he explains. "I'll see if I can find something later. For now, stay out of this room, got it?" There's no mistaking the authority in his tone, but it's so much softer than I'm used to. He ruffles the girl's hair and she playfully swats him off. "You took the braids out again, I see," he scolds. "As much as you play in the fucking dirt, you keep it clean. If you catch lice, I'll make you sleep with the rest of the stray dogs. Got it?"

The girl's expression conveys something that makes him laugh again.

"Fine. Come here." He sits on an armchair in the corner of the room, and the girl sits on the floor in front of him. Sighing, Mischa smooths back her tangled hair and braids it into a single plait. There's an ease to his movements; he's done this before. "There." He shoos her off with a wave of his hand. "Don't mess it up again. Same goes with the clothes. They belonged to someone special, so don't even think about getting them muddy again."

He bares his teeth, but I marvel at the lack of true anger in his voice. Were he any other man, I'd describe his tone as *playful* even. The girl just grins, scurrying in my direction. Suddenly, her mouth falls flat as she spots my hiding place. She glances back at Mischa but continues down the opposite end of the hall without alerting him.

Alone, I stare, watching him.

He has his face in his hands. In the dim light of the room, his hair gleams, ghosting his shoulders. Like this, it's almost too easy to forget who he is. What he is capable of.

But then he shifts, raising his head and fixating those piercing eyes toward the doorway.

"I gave you permission to scurry around once," he murmurs to the silence. "But I don't remember doing so twice."

Caught, I shuffle forward, entering the room fully. "You called for me," I point out, hating how breathless I sound. Air sticks stubbornly in my lungs, making it a struggle to even form words at all.

"Did I?" He beckons me with a crooked finger and stands. As I near, he grabs my forearm, pulling me even closer. "Now why would I do that?"

His gaze is narrowed. Thoughtful. Alarming. He eyes me the way Robert used to inspect his shooting targets. He'd load his gun, lazily deciding where to aim first.

"To sell me again, maybe?" I gauge his reaction with every word, but he's careful to reveal nothing behind his mocking smile. "To Robert Sr.?"

"And what would the old man want with you?" he asks in a dangerous whisper. "Don't tell me you shared his bed as well?"

He frowns in a way that makes my cheeks flame. He's serious.

"Of course not!"

"Because you were *his*." He nods to himself, as if a suspicion of his has been proven once and for all. "He would have never used you as a decoy, not even for his sister."

"Why does it matter?" I try to wrench my arm back, but his grip tightens and I wind up stumbling into him.

"Because him, I understand, Little Rose," Mischa utters near my ear, his voice cold. "I know your husband. I know how his brain works. But you…" His fingers sink into my hair, grasping strands at random. "You are a mystery that makes no fucking sense."

He lets me go so suddenly that I stagger into the table, forced to brace my hands against it to stay upright. His footsteps advance on me and I sense him standing there, inhaling my scent, breathing out hate.

"You say you love him," he accuses, "but he's hurt you. You jump when I say his name." His touch nudges my spine as if to point out the reaction I wasn't even aware of. "But you call for that fucker in your sleep. You moan for him. Did you know that?"

I didn't. Heat sears behind my eyes as my body stiffens. He's lying. Though maybe he isn't. I haven't remembered a nightmare in years. There's no point. I wake up and purge my soul of anything I might have dreamt of.

Until now.

"I want to know," Mischa demands.

I gasp as his fingers slip beneath my dress, brushing the back of my thigh. Instantly, I regret wearing it. Though, ironically, isn't this one of the many reasons I had in mind for choosing it in the first place?

There's less hassle when his mind switches to sex—which it seems to do so often around me. But as if reading my mind, he grates out a harsh scoff and his nails dig in, making me flinch.

"You play your innocent act. You walk around here, batting your fucking eyelashes, getting Vanya to do your bidding. Was he easier to seduce than I was, Little Rose? Has he tasted you already—"

"Stop!" I push against the table, attempting to flee.

Laughing, he presses harder, grinding my stomach into the wood. "You are very skilled," he insists. "Sometimes, you even have me fooled. Convinced that it's *my* cock getting you off. Making you come. But it's not me, is it?" He grabs the hem of my dress again, lifting it.

"What are you doing?" I try batting his hands away, but he pushes me aside and yanks the dress up further.

"I could understand if he was a normal, pathetic, bleeding-heart motherfucker," Mischa says over me. Our eyes meet and the look in his sends my pulse hammering. "I would understand it. If he never hurt you, I would understand."

Still holding my dress, he brings his free hand to my cheek, nudging my healing wound. "But he did. *This* is me," he says, stroking the outermost edge of the wounds he inflicted. *XV.* Next, he traces the outline of my sore right eye. "So is this. And this…" He moves down to my neck and then my shoulder, aggravating old injuries I'd nearly forgotten. "But *these* are him." His gaze cuts a brazen path down my front, raking over the various scars. "This is him," he snarls, fingering a healed cut along my rib cage. "And this." He turns his attention to my stomach, stroking the length of a raised, silvery scar. "He's hurt you way more than I have."

But Robert had years to inflict his damage. Looking back, only now can I admit that—despite my insistence to the contrary—his true abuse started when I was seven years old and he made me ogle a captive woman for sport.

"And what about you?" I croak, shivering as he meets my gaze directly. "You don't talk about…her. Anna."

The woman who he inferred was his love. I picture her, those wide, brown eyes. With Mischa? It doesn't fit. Not until I envision the boy who crept into a room that he thought was Briar's, intent on using her as a tool in their war. *That* boy would belong with a girl like Anna.

"You say Robert is in my head," I point out when he says nothing. "But you don't mention her. You have no pictures of her—"

"Who says I don't?" His tone sets my nerves on high alert. Dark. Grated. Ragged. "Who says that I don't talk about her? Think about her? Because her memory doesn't rule my life the way your fucking Robert does?"

Danger! I've gone too far. Mischa fists a handful of my dress in both hands, and tearing cotton is my only warning to brace as he tugs. Tears. Strips me bare.

"You think I don't think of her every fucking second of the day?" He doesn't even seem to realize what he's done. What's he's doing: invading my space, crushing me against the table, all while bringing his face within inches of mine. "You think I don't miss her?"

I shove against his shoulders, but he doesn't budge. "N-no."

"No?" He laughs, tossing the remains of my dress to the floor. "She was better than you. Better than you will ever be." He roughly tilts my chin, probing my gaze from a different angle. "She was good, and innocent, and sweet. And your husband destroyed that innocence."

I gasp as he grasps the back of my scalp and wrenches my head back. Eyes streaming, I stare up at the ceiling while his breath fans my exposed throat. Panic renders me motionless—but deep down I know that he could truly hurt me if he wants to.

But he isn't.

"He killed her," Mischa hisses. "And I should have killed you. All this time, I thought it was him. That *he* was a sick, twisted piece of shit who got off on causing pain. But why wouldn't he?"

He tugs harder, turning my face so that my brand is visible. "He had *you.* Fucking him. Moaning in his goddamn ear. Making him feel… Making him feel fucking human."

The way he growls that word in particular resonates in my bones. *Human.*

"You talk about Anna, but you want to know what makes her different from you? She wasn't a cunning little bitch." He pulls harder. Too hard. I claw at his fingers, desperate for relief, but he's impervious to my attempts. "If she were here now, she'd want nothing to do with me. She wouldn't even let me touch her. She'd run. She wouldn't moan for me. She wouldn't compare me to her fucking husband. She wouldn't *look* at me—" He breaks off, inhaling raggedly. He has me pinned against the table's surface, breathing heavily against my throat. "With those fucking eyes. Like you're daring me to just do it already. Wrap my hands around your fucking throat. Squeeze. Put you out of your goddamn misery. You're teasing me, aren't you,

you little bitch?" He sounds crazed. Manic. Laughing, he spits out, "You're taunting me. I'll never fucking have you."

He lets me go, backing away while his fingers fist the air. "Run away, Little Rose," he commands, eyeing me with an unfathomable expression. "*Now*. Get the fuck out!"

I crouch for my dress, only to stare abjectly at the torn pieces of fabric.

"Here!"

I glance up as Mischa shrugs his own shirt over his head and throws it in my direction. Sweat-soaked fabric lands over my knees as he storms past me. "Maybe I'll reconsider selling you after all," he suggests, laughing. "I won't let you play your mind games with me."

The walls tremble with every thunderous step he takes as he retreats down the hall. Numb, I sit here, listening to him travel deeper into the house, trying desperately to anticipate his next move. I can still feel his touch, rough and scraping. Searching.

For what? As I crouch on my knees, shock gradually replaces the hold fear has over my lungs. I start laughing too, cringing at the unstable, high-pitched sound. *Ha ha ha.* Robert could be impulsive when he wanted to be—but even then, I could always predict him. Anticipate him. He liked me meek and pliable, like putty in his hands. Sometimes, he liked it when I put up a fight every now and again.

He never wanted more. He never punished me for not fearing him enough. Fucking him enough. Craving him enough.

Is that what Mischa wants? My blood runs cold as my laughter trails off. I'm shaking, my teeth chattering. Naked, I have no choice but to put his shirt on and hunch beneath the heavy cotton.

He smells so strange: a milieu of nuanced flavors that repulse me and intrigue at the same damn time. When inhaled, they're too complex to describe. This must be what rage smells like. Raw, incredible anger. Twisted musk. Spiteful sweat.

As twisted as he was, I always knew what Robert wanted from me. How to predict him. How to stay alive, even when he became his most unhinged.

But Mischa? There's no fucking point in even trying. He's a storm, changing intensity at his own fucking discretion.

I jump as my own fingers brush my throat, tracing my rapid pulse. He bit me there and the mark stings. Throbs. It's a warning.

Robert brutally scarred my body, but I was still Ellen in the end. Still me.

Mischa is changing me, and I don't know who I'll become when he's through. Someone twisted enough to want…

More.

Enough. I close my eyes, inhaling as much of the stale air as I can until my lungs fully expand. Then I slowly release the breath and reenter the hallway warily, praying that I don't run into Vanya. What would he say if he saw me like this?

Do not fear him. He wasn't always this way...

A flickering shadow draws my notice as I turn into the entryway. Mischa?

The figure lunges before I can be sure. Air whistles past my head, and then... *Pain.* Darkness rushes me, swallowing my vision. A faraway thud echoes as my vision goes white. It's like my senses scatter in a million directions. I feel air. Hardness. Coldness.

Then nothing.

"Wake up!"

Agony rips through my chest, drawing a gasp from my throat. Cool, damp air settles on my face—I must be lying on my back. My head throbs, and my hip is on fire.

"I said wake up," someone snarls. "You little bitch! Look at me!"

My eyelids flutter as I struggle to piece together my surroundings.

Wherever I am, it's dark. Faint light glosses over the hazy outlines of various shapes. One mass in particular looms over me. Tall. Bulky. A man.

But his voice…

It's not Mischa's.

"I said look at me!" Harsh fingers seize my chin, wrenching my gaze toward the figure. His face is familiar. Older. Stern. Dark hair.

A name flickers on the outskirts of my consciousness as a memory of him replays in my head. Him, sitting across from Mischa in a crowded room, while his son, Kostas, was declared a traitor.

"Nikolaus," another man scolds, though I don't recognize his gruffer tone. "If you're going to kill her, do it already. We need to dump her body before Mischa realizes she's gone. Dima said he kept her close. Too fucking close—"

"Kill her?" Nikolaus echoes, his teeth bared. "I'm going to make this little bitch suffer!"

"Use your head," the other man interjects. "I get you want your revenge. But do you really want to fuck with Mischa? That motherfucker will have your head on a spike. Kill her quickly and he won't be able to tie it to you."

"Revenge?" Nikolaus shakes his head. "No!" Grunting, he kicks my hip, knocking me onto my side.

From this angle, I can only watch the muddied tips of his boots move in tandem. Every step echoes, and the air smells damp. Dank. A basement?

I strain my eyes to make out any defining details—and I barely see Nikolaus's foot shoot out to kick me again. Hard. I choke back the scream surging up my throat, but a moan trickles out regardless. Breathing is the only way to regain my composure. *In and out...*

"This little bitch got my son turned into a fucking cripple," Nikolaus rants between heavy pants. "I'm going to rip her apart and drench that whelp Mischa in her fucking blood."

Crippled? Just what did Mischa do to him? Nausea roils through my stomach at the grisly possibilities—I don't want to know.

"Do you know who this bitch is? Who she is really?" Nikolaus laughs, nudging my hip with the tip of his boot. "She was closer to the younger Winthorp than your precious Pakhan let on. Much closer. I know for a fact the bastard wants her back. Rumor is he even offered to trade his sister to Mischa. For this little cunt!"

Another blow draws a groan from my lips, which drowns out whatever he says next. A deafening surge of blood rushes against my eardrums. Bright colors paint my vision. Reds. Greens. Silvers.

Your ribs are broken, a small voice inside me whispers. That's why each breath burns, taking ten times the usual effort.

"I'm not going to kill her," Nikolaus says, his voice drifting back into focus. "I'm going to teach that bastard Mischa why he should never turn on his own fucking kind."

Movement catches the corner of my eye. His boot. As if from miles away, I hear the stomach-churning crack of it connecting with something. Crunching.

Heat runs down my spine like a lance. *Fire.* My vision swims and tunnels; then all senses fade. The terrifying beauty of it is that I feel nothing—even though I'm painfully aware that one of my legs is dragging behind me as I try in vain to crawl away from the source of the assault. The scream that rips from me is more involuntary than anything—my body knows that something is horribly wrong.

"Run, you little bitch," Nikolaus goads as I scrape at the concrete floor in a desperate bid for leverage.

My senses blur and memories meld into the present. I'm with Robert again. He went too far. Again. He's toying with me—*again.*

Running from him will only buy me seconds. I need to plead. Beg. Lie at his mercy and pray to God that he'll stop. Please stop! My lips are already moving to form the words.

"That fucking Mischa thinks he can treat my family like a whipped dog?"

Crunch. Crunch! The veil that shielded my nerves from pain gives way and I feel everything. *Fire, burning agony…*

My thoughts threaten to scatter the second I attempt to focus on it. So I don't. Mischa. His name is like a trigger to all the emotions forbidden to Robert's precious Elle. Hate. Rage. Survival. Above my thudding heartbeat, I can sense that Nikolaus is close, pacing once again.

I try to stand but my limbs refuse to obey the commands my brain issues.

So I crawl, dragging my limp form into a corner. We must be in a basement. The walls are gray gunmetal. Rectangular windows are set high above, revealing pitch-black darkness. In addition to Nikolaus, another man lurks near a shadowed doorway. I vaguely recognize him as well, but I can't place him to a name. Another man from the *mafiya* gathering, maybe?

"Enough," he hisses out when Nikolaus makes his third trip around the room. "Kill her now. You've made your point, and you can laugh yourself to sleep at night when you relive getting one over on Mischa. But do it now—"

"I'm fucking thinking!" Nikolaus tears his fingers through his hair, a wild smile shaping his lips. "Kill her? I could use the little bitch as proof. Mischa's gone insane. This fucking feud. He'll kill us all!"

"He'll kill you," the other man interjects calmly. "If you don't smarten up and take your chance. Who cares if she's important to the Winthorp boy—"

"He might pay for her," Nikolaus muses, stroking his chin. "They say he killed his own father with his bare hands just to get her back. Nearly killed Mischa from what I hear—the bastard refused to give her up."

No. Confusion strikes like a freight train at full force. *Killed his own father…*

The room spins. I can't breathe. An image of a bloodied ring replaces the horrific reality before me, but in some ways, it's so much worse.

"We could sell her to that punk. Make a deal. Teach that bastard Mischa a lesson—"

"He'll kill you," I hear myself croak. God, my voice is a rough, dry whisper. It takes everything I have to make it rise even an octave higher. "He'll make you a deal. Then kill you anyway."

Both men turn their attention to me.

"Shut your fucking mouth!" Nikolaus crosses the room in seconds. His hand lashes out and the world goes black.

I taste blood. When my vision returns, I'm staring at the floor, clutching my jaw. I try to speak but every word comes out garbled.

"Maybe the little bitch is right," the other man says, oblivious to my attempts. "Either way, I say you kill her now. Get it over with."

"I'll do what I fucking want!" Nikolaus shudders, wavering unsteadily on his feet. His eyes reconnect with mine and in them I find nothing. Just hollow emptiness. "I should fuck her," he declares, his tone soft. "Mischa's a jealous little prick. I'll send her back to him. Say she came begging for it—"

"Do you hear yourself, Nikolaus?" the other man asks, but he sounds more impatient than horrified.

Instantly, I know he's no protector. He'll watch. He'll wait.

But I won't be violated again. Not like this.

"You couldn't," I rasp, barely intelligible. But Nikolaus cocks his head, laughing as he tries to decipher my words. "You're...not...man enough."

My brain skips ahead, devising a plan utilizing the only weapon I have left: pride. There was one thing that could make Robert more furious than anything else. One name when mentioned that could make him more skittish and doubtful than a teenage boy during his first encounter.

I suspect that Nikolaus is no different. But where Robert feared his father's presence, this man is terrified of another.

"Mischa is twice the man you are." The pathetic, broken creature speaking doesn't even sound like me—she's bolder than I ever was.

"What did you say?" Nikolaus advances, his fingers curling.

"I said you couldn't even come close to him—"

"Shut up!"

Lightning. I see it. Taste it—coppery, wet warmth dripping off my tongue.

"Look at me, you little cunt! You think you've handled a real fucking man?"

My heart stutters as fabric tears nearby. Cold air assaults my body a second later.

I've failed. Failed. He's already crouching over me, spreading my legs apart.

Breathe, a part of me whispers, clinging to my old mantra. *You can survive this, Ellen. Just breathe...*

Or I can fight.

My eyes stream as I crane my neck, repulsed by what I see. His pants are down, his palm clenching his cock. I override every instinct urging me to scream and I...

Laugh. Loudly. Hard. I cackle mercilessly even as I lose feeling in my toes. Fingers. Arms. An invisible vise is tightening around my chest with every second. Blood floods my mouth.

You're dying, that honest voice in my soul hisses.

When Nikolaus curses, I know I've succeeded in one aspect so far. Men like him can't bear being taunted. They feed off fear and cowering.

So I force my tongue to move and mock him instead. "I... was...wrong. You aren't even a fraction of the man Mischa is."

How ironic that thinking of him anchors me when my thoughts fight to fade and my limbs grow heavier. Mischa, my tormentor. He'll chase me into the grave.

God, it's like I fucking hear him. Shouting. Roaring...

Pounding?

A man groans amid a crunching thud of bone. Suddenly, Nikolaus is gone and someone new takes his place, crouched over me.

"Look at me, Little Rose," he demands, haloed by a wreath of wild, golden hair.

My eyelids flutter. I'm dreaming.

"Look at me. You fucking hear me? You can sink into the black. Think you can run from me… But you'll die when I say you can, Ellen Winthorp. And I'm not done playing with your fucking soul just yet."

Numb limbs weigh me down in a sea of endless black. I feel nothing. Hear nothing...

At least at first.

Eventually, snippets of sound and scattered phrases puncture the silence.

Broken ribs.

Shattered femur.

Broken ankle.

Dying.

Dying.

"Open your eyes, Little Rose," the devil growls.

How fitting that my soul would be claimed by him.

"Open your fucking eyes. I know you're still in there. I'm waiting. So open your fucking eyes…"

But even he can't keep me grounded for long. My soul is tissue paper, caught between two unreachable worlds. One is bright and soft. It calls to me in delicate whispers.

Come home.

The other is dark, and painful, and loud. So damn loud. It snarls into my ear, increasingly incessant.

"Look at me, Little Rose. Open your fucking eyes…"

I long to sink into the warm light and forget the madness, and the torment, and the pain. So much fucking pain.

Death is so quiet…

But a world containing Mischa is impossible to ignore. He drags me back, bit by bit until sensation returns in agonizing snatches. I can't move. I'm lying on my back, aware that I'm on a mattress. Light and shadow flicker behind my eyelids as people move nearby. Talking.

"I thought I told you not to come in here?" a man scolds, but his tone is gentle. And familiar, though I've never heard it so hoarse. "You wanted to braid her hair again?"

He pauses, but no one responds.

"Fine," the man says, sighing. "But you're going to make her bald."

Me? My head throbs, but through the pain, I sense a gentle touch moving through my hair, gathering up various strands and carefully arranging them.

"Don't give me that look," the man says, and I can finally put a name to that husky rasp. Mischa? "For a girl, you have an odd idea of what looks pretty. And you're lucky I'm even letting you stay after what you did with the crayons—" He breaks off as if interrupted. Then he laughs. "Keep it up and I'm going to sell you right back to Nicolai."

Sell? I try lifting my eyelids. Moving. Speaking. Even breathing is a struggle. Mischa must have devised a new form of torture: sitting on my chest.

"Don't stay in here too long," he warns amid the thud of heavy footsteps. "And no more fucking coloring."

He's gone, but I'm not alone. Someone continues to stroke my hair, styling it with all the care that I used to take with Briar's. Vanya?

Again, I try opening my eyes. At first, I can only make out snippets of detail. White walls bathed in daylight. Crisp ivory sheets. A bulky, round shape that I think is my leg propped on a pillow.

Straining with the effort, I manage to hold my eyes open long enough to acknowledge that I'm in a small room, on a bed positioned near a row of wide windows overlooking a swath of green. There's a doorway up ahead, leading into shadow. Someone's perched beside me on the mattress, partially visible: tiny legs sheathed in oversized pants and slender arms that go still the moment the figure must realize I'm awake.

I'm jostled as the slender person in question leaps from the bed. In a blur, they race from the room. Pale. Blonde. The little girl from Nicolai's.

I try to sit up only to wheeze, my eyes watering as the pressure in my chest tightens. Mischa isn't sitting on me after all. Vaguely, I remember being struck. Beaten. By Nikolaus.

He broke my ribs, I think.

And my leg. Both of them, it seems. One is encased in a bulky cast, propped upright, while a neat array of bandages covers the other. My blankets have been pulled back to reveal both, including the strange purple markings marring my cast. I scan them all, increasingly confused. One drawing consists of a lopsided smiley face. Another is of a crudely etched tree. And finally, a man with long, squiggly hair and exaggerated magenta eyes glares at me from the space near my ankle.

I stiffen as someone approaches, traipsing down what I assume is a hallway. Two footsteps, one light and swift, the other heavy and slow.

"What is it?" Mischa grumbles. "If you drew on the goddamn cast again, I swear I'll—" He breaks off the second he rounds the corner, spotting me awake.

By his side, leading him by the sleeve of his shirt is the girl from Nicolai's.

"I see." Mischa's expression falls into the stern mask I know so well. "Leave." He wrenches his arm from the girl.

Despite the authority lacing his tone, she lingers, watching me with wide, owl-like eyes.

"Go," he snarls more harshly, and she finally scurries off.

Alone, my captor watches me with an unreadable gaze, and paranoia eats at my pain. How often has he lorded over me like this? Waiting for me to die. Daring me to.

Silently, he advances. Outstretched fingers reach for my cheek, but I turn away, gritting my teeth. My jaw is so sore that a moan escapes when I don't mean to do it.

Mischa draws his hand back anyway, his eyes narrowing. Then he turns and leaves without a word.

I must fall asleep. When I come to again, someone is spooning warm liquid against my lips, encouraging me to swallow.

"Nice and easy," they urge. Vanya.

I fight through a layer of exhaustion to open my eyes, meeting his startled expression.

"That's it," he praises as I sip from the spoon. "Now, just rest."

It's so easy to surrender to his care, letting myself drift off once again.

When I open my eyes a second time, something is different. The pain has lessened, for one, and I can haul myself upright, bracing my trembling hands on either side of my body for balance. I'm alone as well. What I first mistook for a hospital room must be just another part of Mischa's manor. I recognize the dreary lawn from the windows, and the furniture has the same stifling, ornate air to it.

However, I'm on an unfamiliar bed from my usual mattress. Someone changed the sheets while I was out, exchanging the white ones for a softer gray. They changed me as well.

Once… Years ago, Robert hit me harder than he meant to. I wound up in bed for weeks, forced to endure a painful recovery. Out of duty, or maybe guilt, Robert had an army of servants provide me with round-the-clock care.

But none of them bathed my skin with scented soap. Or washed my hair so that it smelled faintly of fresh flowers. Or kept me so clean that I didn't feel like an invalid.

But I was. I am. A metal tray stands a few paces from the bed, complete with a steaming meal someone must have been in the process of feeding me. Memories return as cloudy, intangible snippets: soups and broths carefully poured down my throat while I was barely conscious.

By Vanya? Only he would have the patience. The care.

Only he would be so kind.

Gratitude unlike anything I've ever felt swells in my chest, making it even harder to breathe. Nikolaus inflicted his damage well. I wonder if the bastard is in hell.

Because he most certainly isn't still alive. I'm sure of it, just as I'm sure that Mischa is watching me. I can't see him yet, but I smell him. Lurking near the doorway maybe?

After swiping my tongue along my dry lips, I croak, "I know you're there."

God, I sound horrible. So pathetically weak. Pity must be what makes him drop his ruse and finally round the edge of the doorway.

My eyes widen at his appearance. It has to have been days since I last saw him. The stubble growing in along his jaw is thicker. Scraggly. Unkempt. His hair is a messy, unwashed tangle, his clothing a pair of faded fatigues.

"So," he begins in a low, gruff tone, "Little Rose has finally decided to grace us with her miraculous return."

Finally. The emphasis he placed on that word draws my attention. "How..." I wheeze as my chest constricts and take my time forming my next words. "How long was I out?"

"A month," he says, shrugging. "Maybe more than that. Your injuries were stabilized within a few days, but you..." He grunts a sound that could be mistaken for a laugh had it come from any other man. "The stubborn, spiteful Little Rose wouldn't let a mere doctor dictate her recovery."

He enters the room and his scent descends at full force. Sweat and animalistic musk. How long has he been there, watching me? Long enough, a part of me suspects. Long enough to immediately go to the food and wrestle the tray closer.

My stomach grumbles, embarrassingly loud, but when he shoves a spoonful of broth beneath my nose, I shake my head, choosing to speak instead.

"You...lied."

He drops the spoon into the bowl, spraying broth across the tray's surface. "Did I now?"

But it's a reality that haunted me, even as my soul drifted for days at a time.

"Robert," I rasp. "He's alive. You lied to me. He's *alive*."

Fire ignites in my jaw and I gingerly reach up, brushing my fingers along the sore tissue. Even that slight motion takes more energy than I have in me. Groaning, I slump back against a wall of pillows, forced to view Mischa from a newer angle.

He's chuckling, his gaze averted away from me. Down at his hands. The nails are ragged, with a dark substance caught beneath them. Dirt? Or Blood?

"Does his life matter to you that much?"

I frown, caught off guard by the venom in his tone. "*You* told me he was dead."

"And as concerned as you are for your husband's welfare, you should be more concerned for yours."

Concerned? I open my mouth to reply, but he moves, wrenching the blankets back.

"Look," he commands.

Startled, I stare down at my pale limbs stretched out beneath a white nightgown. My legs aren't the only parts of me bandaged: my nightgown has been folded down to my waist, but my chest isn't bare. Tan bandages constrict it—part of the unbearable pressure I feel.

"You were intubated for three days," Mischa announces. "Your lung was punctured. It's barely healed. So I suggest you save the sobbing for your husband's soul for another week at least—"

"What happened to Nikolaus?"

"What he deserved," he says. "And you have another surgical scar to join the one from your C-section, Little Rose."

I cringe at the reference, but the painful memories are easier to ignore in favor of deciphering him. His voice is colder than it was only a few minutes ago. Irritated.

Scowling, he tugs my blankets back into place, covering me again. "If you won't eat, I can assure you that you'll be here for another fucking month. Though, hell, that might make it easier for your precious Robert to come for you?"

I'm too tired to feel the full brunt of the terror that threat should inspire. I just let my eyes drift shut and focus on breathing. In. Out. Slower. When I feel confident enough to speak, I don't even waste any real effort on sounding insulted. "Where is Vanya?"

It's like my words are his cue. Another figure approaches from the hall, his steps uneven.

"You're awake," he calls as I open my eyes again. His wary smile is a godsend. Even Mischa's brooding presence can't erase my relief.

"Thank you," I tell him as he draws up to the other side of my bed. "For caring for me."

Even now, the gentleness with which he must have done so takes my breath away. A month in bed could have gone so much worse. That I know from experience.

Vanya blinks. "I…" His gaze cuts to Mischa, who abruptly storms from the room. "I'm glad you're all right," Vanya says, turning his attention back to me. "You had us worried."

Us? I don't question the word choice out loud. Instead, I watch him circle around to the tray of soup. He carefully ladles a bit of broth to my lips and I swallow. When I've consumed half the bowl, I gather up the nerve to finally ask, "Did Mischa kill him?"

Nikolaus.

"Yes," Vanya says as he maneuvers another spoonful to my mouth. His gaze turns inward, alarmingly stern. "The bastard had it coming. I still don't know how he infiltrated the manor. He wasn't that smart—"

"Someone else was there," I rasp. "Another man. He talked about…" I rack my brain for the specifics. "He talked like he knew some details firsthand."

"So a spy," Vanya deduces, his gaze cold. "I'll alert Mischa. But you shouldn't have to worry about this." A sigh rips from his mouth as he sets the bowl aside. "You get your rest. I'll come check on you in the morning."

He gathers up the empty bowl and leaves, avoiding any further questions. Alone, I can only anticipate Mischa's next actions.

I've angered him, and a sick part of me wonders if I should be relieved.

At least I'll no longer be his focus.

CHAPTER 13

"Get up."

I know instantly that Vanya isn't the figure I awaken to find standing above me.

Mischa's clean shaven, his face pale in the dim glow of dawn. Somehow, he looks more unstable this way. Dark circles paint the flesh beneath his eyes, and a muscle in his jaw twitches once he catches me staring.

"The man you say you saw. Did you get a name?"

"What?" My eyebrows furrow. "I…"

"I guess not." He scoffs, radiating suspicion. "Maybe you'll remember when that cunning brain of yours decides it's in your best interest? No matter. It's time for *Vanya* to give you your bath. You stink."

I do. Like sweat, from tossing uncomfortably all night. I smell like fear of what might lurk beneath my scars. I smell like Robert's wife again.

"Where is he?" I anxiously scan the room for Vanya, but Mischa yanks the blankets from me instead.

He nudges the pillow from under my casted leg and slides a hand beneath both.

I suck in a startled breath. "What are you doing?"

Without warning, he pulls me into his arms.

"S-stop!" I cling to his shoulders—but he isn't being rough. Not even as he swiftly carries me into a hallway.

We don't go far. A few doors down from the bedroom, he turns into one bathed in shades of black. His.

He takes me into the bathroom, where running water is filling a sunken tub. A plastic bench is positioned beside it, and an array of tools are within reach. But the man who sets me down and tears at my thin nightgown isn't the patient, calm Vanya.

Tension stiffens his posture as he snatches up a rag and wets it.

"Lift your arms," he grates.

I want to refuse, but curiosity is a strange thing.

He starts to wash me without waiting for me to comply, dragging the rag over my exposed thigh. His teeth are gritted, his eyes downcast. But even so…he's careful. Clinical.

And now I know just who cared for me all these weeks.

The thought of it weighs me down with an unexplainable emotion. Shock? Perhaps. Or maybe resignation to one simple fact I'm too tired to resist: I'll never fully understand him.

And I'm not sure if it's a good thing.

Or horrifying.

"Lift your arms," he commands through gritted teeth.

I obey, alarmed to find that I can only raise the limbs to the height of my shoulder without triggering pain. As Mischa peels down my nightgown and starts to unravel the bandages, I see why. Beneath carefully placed gauze is a half-moon-shaped ridge of reddened flesh.

Punctured lung, he said. The kind of injury that I doubt could be safely treated in a mobster's safe house.

"Was I in a hospital?"

Mischa continues to tug my nightgown off, lifting me with one hand to pull the fabric free.

"I have power everywhere, Little Rose," he says. Power, meaning control. Spies. A presence, should I ever think of running away again.

Warm water spilling across my lap alerts me to the fact that he's still washing me, guiding the cloth against the bruised flesh of my hip. I suck in a breath and he pauses, letting liquid drip from the rag onto the floor.

"I killed him," he says, so low that I barely hear him. "With my bare fucking hands."

I close my eyes against the imagery, but it's no use. I see Mischa, his hands drenched in blood, his teeth bared, his eyes flashing with crazed menace. And his voice… Something in the cold, satisfied tone he used makes my lips spring apart, rebelling against my common sense warning me to stay silent.

"Is that supposed to impress me?"

"It doesn't," he says, sounding unsurprised.

The rag returns to my hip and I jump, anticipating roughness. His pressure, however, never changes, even as his eyes darken.

"One man's death would never impress the innocent Little Rose—"

"No one's death would impress me."

"Oh?" He laughs. "You're wrong. For all your games, I won't let you deny it now: All along, deep in your fragile, little soul, you knew he wasn't dead. You tried resisting it." He nods to my severed finger. "But you knew. And though you won't say it out loud, you're glad he's still alive. Why?" he asks when I say nothing. "Because for all your fucking insistence to the contrary, you want to see him choke out his last fucking breath for yourself. You won't believe it until you do. And you don't want it any other way. Your precious Robert dies when you say he can. Isn't that right, Little Rose?"

Rather than humor him with an answer, I close my eyes and cling to my one and only escape. *Breathe.* My nostrils flood with the steam from the running bath and the musk of his sweat, tainted with something sweeter. He scented the water with something. Oil? Soap? It smells like lavender, whatever it is. I can't ignore it.

That stench makes all of this feel so fucking real. A nightmare wouldn't be perfumed with flowers. Mischa's touch wouldn't be gentle over my bruised, broken limbs.

My heart wouldn't be swollen with conflicting emotions, and tears wouldn't be forming behind my eyes, desperate to fall.

I try to breathe, but in the end, all I can do is voice a plea that comes out as a whisper. "I don't need your help."

"Fine."

My eyelids jolt upright as water splashes nearby. He threw the rag into the tub. Without looking back, he stands and marches to the door. Then he wrenches it open and slams it shut behind him. Beneath the pulse of rushing water, I hear myself wheeze as I try to catch my breath. Air is a fickle, elusive thing, rebelliously escaping my lungs.

Maybe I'm afraid. I want to be. Terror is much more preferable to guilt. Shame. Regret.

I attempt to bend for the rag, but it's too far. I can't reach the faucet, either—not that I'm left floundering for long. Mischa is like a dog. He'll run away when spooked, only to circle back snarling, twice as aggressive as before.

"Sit up," he commands, storming back into the room. He switches off the running water and snatches a new rag from a stack placed just beyond reach of the bench.

As I struggle to haul myself upright, he sinks to his knees and returns to washing me. He's never too rough or intentionally causes pain. But his shoulders are rigid, his eyes downcast and stormy.

Consoling him feels more like a necessary survival tactic than any form of pity.

"Thank you," I rasp as he stands and circles the bench. Warm water grazes my back next, soothing aches I didn't even know I had. "For washing me—"

"For filling in for *Vanya*, you mean?" His nasty tone betrays an emotion I don't even think he's aware of. Could it be wounded pride? "Let's agree on something, Little Rose."

He throws the rag down beside me and crouches low again, this time right near my side so that every word strikes my throat in a burst of heat.

"I know you want to be the helpless victim, and I am more than willing to indulge you." He drags his thumb across my cheek, but there is no clinical care this time. He makes me flinch and smiles when I do. Despite the quirk of his lips, nothing reaches his eyes. They're endless, fiery pits. "You willingly played the part of your husband's dutiful doll… and now, you're mine. I'll make you dance and scream how I want to. I'll keep you close, Ellen. So fucking close…" He's nearer, murmuring each word in my ear. "I'll make you choke on me. You'll fucking hate me—but not because of him. Because you'll need me more. You can't fucking breathe without me."

He rises to his feet and approaches the tub. After testing the water with his fingers, he cuts his gaze in my direction. Then he takes his shirt off before tossing it into a corner of the room.

My heart races with every step he advances toward me in no apparent rush. When he grabs me, I tense in anticipation of a pain that never comes.

He's done this before. I'm sure of that one fact as he places me on the floor beside the tub and begins to encase my cast in something. Plastic. He secures it tightly over the entire plaster. Then he starts to unravel the bandages on my other leg. It must not be as injured as the other, just badly bruised. Sprained, I suspect when I wiggle the toes and wince as lightning-sharp heat surges through the muscle.

I'm resigned to the crippling senses of immobility when he lunges, plunging into the bath despite still wearing his slacks. The next second, I'm in his arms again.

My stomach lurches up my throat as my lower half descends into the warm liquid. I flail, my arms splashing uselessly as my head goes under. Water floods my nostrils, overwhelming my weak lungs—for a second. The next, I'm held tight against a firm, searing surface. Mischa. I'm clinging to him, my nails scraping against his forearms for leverage. Gasping, I find that he's holding me at an angle, placing more of my upper body into the water while leaving my leg exposed and supported by the edge of the tub.

And now I understand what he means.

His doll.

At his mercy.

At his whims.

He keeps me in the tub just long enough to douse me thoroughly in the places his rag won't reach. My hair. Between my legs. My once-bandaged leg. Water stings as it sweeps against my injuries, but when my eyes start to water, he carries me from the tub and returns me to the bench.

He towels me off in silence, and I'm forced to bear his resentment. It's only when he leaves the room and returns with a garment dangling between his fingers that I lose my resolve. I sigh.

"Lift your arms," he tells me, bringing the nightgown close.

A creation formed of light-pink silk, it looks like something Briar would wear—as a joke. Something too frilly even for Robert's taste. A mocking caricature of what a living doll might be adorned with: white lace and pink ribbons.

Once I'm dressed, Mischa returns me to the large, white room. The sheets on the bed have been changed, the air scented. Every seemingly kind gesture only unnerves me more. Especially one small detail that catches my eye as I'm lowered to the mattress: He leaves space beside me. The bed is large enough for him to do so, with room to spare, but an extra set of pillows have been placed beside mine. The tray that I assume is for my meals has been moved from its position near the wall toward the opposite end of the room, closer to me.

Leaving the remaining half as the dominion of one person.

He doesn't say it out loud, not yet. He yanks the covers over me and exits the room without hinting at his true motives.

But Mischa Stepanov is quickly becoming as familiar to me as a damaged, twisted book I have no choice but to study. He'll be back.

Sooner or later, he'll be back.

CHAPTER 14

He lets me luxuriate in the uncomfortable reality of being his doll. For the most part, it's rather boring, no different from my life with Robert. In short, I'm left alone to rot in a room I can't explore, utterly at his mercy.

Are physical limitations so different from mental ones?

I'm not brave enough to decide on an answer, and approaching footsteps draw my attention, giving me a small reprieve.

Vanya enters the room, carrying a tray between his hands. Another bowl of soup and a thin slice of bread. After perching himself on the end of my side of the bed, he feeds me slowly. All without a word.

Even though there's something he wants to say.

I can practically see the words straining in his throat, fighting to lurch off the end of his tongue. In the end, he pats the blankets covering me and leaves.

As he fades into the shadow beyond the doorway, I know exactly what he left unsaid. He wanted to warn me.

Of all of his whispered insights into Mischa, one rings the loudest in my memory. *"If he thinks you're worth having, he will never let you go."*

If only it were me he really wants. I'm an expert at selling myself. Molding myself. Suppressing myself. I've done it for years under the watchful possession of Robert. Hell, if my life was reversed, I might do it all over again. It's easy to sacrifice that which you've never really had in the first place.

From the day I was born, I was always a burden, forced to hide. Pretend. Submit.

But Mischa… He wants something else. Something more than anyone has ever demanded of me before. Something raw and unguarded, found in the sleep he wrings from me. Something I can't change, or morph, or control.

I think he wants my soul.

Not to keep, but to break—right between the rough, callused fingertips that graze my forehead, rousing me from a fitful sleep.

It's darker in the room now. Not quite night, but close. My stomach rumbles, though not from hunger. Just an uneasy apprehension of the unknown.

He switches a light on. With his back to me, he starts to pace. Then he lifts his shirt over his head and tosses it onto the floor. I hear the zipper of his jeans come undone next.

And I'm breathless, gulping at the thinning air. It never ceases to amaze me just how beautiful he is—or what some might call him anyway. How rugged. He is scarred over and broken in so many places, I wonder if he remembers what the original flesh and bone look like. The marks of his brand gleam silver in the orange glow of a lamp. VII. They ripple with his every movement, proclaiming his place in the feud as he removes his pants one leg at a time and stands there only in a pair of gray boxers.

He waits as if to torment me, stretching out the seconds, ensuring I'm riveted for every torturous one. Eventually, he cocks his head, finding my position. It's unfair how quickly he moves, denying me the chance to gather my senses or play my part by cowering. He's lying beside me before I even remember to cringe beyond his reach. One of his hands grasps mine, forcing it to his chest.

At first, I think it's a perverted mind game designed to test my reaction. But no. He wants me to feel. Ropey, jagged skin dips and curves beneath my fingertips. His wound from the day he delivered "Robert's" ring.

"Your husband fought for you, Little Rose," he tells me, his voice thicker than I've heard it. "He fought like hell for you. Enough to dirty his pretty little hands." He grips mine roughly, unfolding every digit for his inspection. "Shall I tell you all of it? He offered to trade you for Briar—to give me better leverage with his father, you see. I didn't think he was serious, but she was there…" He laughs brokenly, shaking his head. "But I refused. And he tried to kill me. We've met before, you know. I've baited him before. Taunted him before…" He trails off, lost in a thought I can't stomach to consider.

Regardless, his words fester and stew within me. Robert fight for me? Never.

"He did," Mischa challenges as if reading my mind. "That fucker was willing to die for his precious little wife. But I won, didn't I, Little Rose? Even if I left his fucking life intact. I have you…"

My heart clenches before I even feel a telltale brush of warmth against my throat: his mouth, murmuring words there in a dangerous whisper. "I have you, don't I? All of you. Even if you don't want it." He shifts, sliding one of his hands beneath my blankets, aiming for my inner thighs.

Weighed down by my cast, I can't even move. I just stiffen as he finds me beneath my nightgown, inching higher with every strained breath I take.

"Even if you can't admit it. I have you. I can keep you. Or I can kill you."

Air wheezes from my lungs as he slides the ridge of his finger against me. Inside me. My heart churns uselessly as my chest tightens. The sensation of his touch works like an invisible vise, tightening. Smothering. Suffocating.

I pant. "M-Mischa—"

"He killed his father for you. Do you know that?"

My thoughts swim. My head feels heavy. Air becomes a scarcer commodity. Frantic, my fingers scrape at the blankets beside me. "Please—"

"The bastard never dared to stand against the old man before." His voice is my only anchor as his touch grows bolder and my vision narrows. A gray haze shrouds everything but his face, half obscured against my breast, laughing at the dark irony. "I told him I strangled you," he admits, sounding miles away.

Everything is white. Then gray. Then quiet…

Finally, air! I gulp noisily for every breath as his hand withdraws.

"He hasn't come for me yet," Mischa grumbles, more to himself than me. "But he will."

He watches me collapse against the pillows as I strain my lungs as much as my sore chest allows. Finally, he moves, but not to retreat. Oh, no. He tilts my head toward him as he settles further on the mattress beside me.

"Shall I tell you a story, Little Rose?" he murmurs, only to force my head to nod in agreement. "Fine, then. You ask me how I can care for you so well? I was number seven, but there was an eight... Her name was Aljona and she was better than you in every way. Sweeter. Kinder. She deserved mercy where your precious Winthorps deserve none." He waits, allowing every word to sink in. Every insinuation. He lets my mind race to put the pieces together: the real woman who haunts him. Not Anna. Not even his mother.

"She was my half," he rasps brokenly as heat springs beneath my eyes. "We shared a womb. A soul. Your Winthorps left her for dead when they forced the car my mother was driving into a ditch. They left her twisted and broken in the wreckage when they took my mother and me, but she survived, Little Rose. She clung to life…until it became too fucking much."

He's on his feet, halfway across the room before I can even register the vicious steps that take him there.

"When she died, *I* died, Little Rose." His back is to me, his posture rigid. "So don't for a second make the mistake of believing that anything I've done is for you. You're merely meant to serve a fucking point: Even now, I'm not like them. I won't let you compare me to him." He laughs and braces a hand against the wall. For balance, I realize. He's shaking, trembling from head to toe.

It's terrifying. Like witnessing the worst dredges of a storm unfold with no hope of shelter within reach. Emotion from him is a drug: a terrifying injection of toxins and hallucinogens. I see things I shouldn't. Experience sensations that aren't real.

Mischa…moaning in pain isn't real.

I blink and he's upright, his bloodshot eyes finding me from over his shoulder.

"You want to stay a shell? I'll make you a fucking proxy. You can die here for all I care."

And he means it. Every word rings true as he dresses himself and leaves.

He didn't save my life out of any ounce of human pity.

He did it as a test.

And he failed.

CHAPTER 15

Vanya greets me in the morning, and he's the one who helps me bathe with as much dignity as I can muster. There's a notable difference though.

Vanya is clinical.

Mischa was…methodical. Damn near obsessive, even—like my body was a tool he'd studied every inch of. A collector, polishing his favorite toy.

I'm sweating beneath the sheets. The air in this room has little circulation, and a part of me longs for the warmth of bathwater. A change of scenery.

Anything.

Vanya does his best to linger, entertaining me with small talk, but he can't stay long.

And I'm alone again.

It's the loneliness that feels so different from my time with Robert. I used to crave it. Cherish it. Only in silence could I gather up the broken pieces of my soul and try to reassemble them. I was Ellen, always Ellen. Sweet, dutiful, doormat Ellen.

It's only hours after Vanya delivered my second meal for the day that I sense someone else there, lingering on the outskirts of my room, recognizable only by smell.

He waits like any predator, anticipating the moment I tense with an awareness of him. Maybe he can hear my pulse surging in a pathetic patter of noise. When the symphony of heartbeats reaches a crescendo, he steps forward.

From my position, I can only make out his profile. Long and unkempt, his hair shrouds most of his face, leaving the rest of it cast in shadow. The stubble has returned already to coat his chin, which flexes as he prepares to issue a command or another insult.

Hoarse and weak, my pathetic tone beats him to the punch. "I can't live like this."

He jerks in place as if he'd been about to lunge. Pounce. Attack. Now? He stands there, his head cocked.

"I can't," I admit, hating the fear so plainly evident in my voice. Leaving any part of myself bare to him disturbs me like nothing else. But it's better than the alternative: this fucking endless silence. "I refuse to live like this—"

He turns for the door and I can't stop myself from leaning forward, clutching fistfuls of the sheets for balance.

"Please…"

He stops and I break.

"*Please* don't let me live like this. I'm sorry if I hurt you—if I *insulted* you," I add when he flinches. "But I'm so damn tired of begging you for mercy."

He stays just long enough to give me hope that my words managed to reach him before he slips over the threshold and escapes the room.

For the rest of the day, I'm left here, alone, trapped in bed, forced to listen to the ongoings of the manor seeping through the walls. Murmured snippets of conversation provide no context. No reprieve.

Eventually, I tune the noise out altogether and turn my focus toward gingerly stretching and flexing each limb, desperate to move. A funny thought makes me snicker as the daylight grows dimmer and Vanya appears with my evening meal.

Of all the various forms of torture Robert employed to break me, this might do the trick.

Sheer, utter boredom.

I'm startled awake by the sound of footsteps nearing my bed. Heavy and slow, they aren't Vanya's. Neither is the hand that snatches my blankets from me, leaving me shivering in the pale glow of dawn. The rest of the house can't be up this early.

Though I suspect that the figure before me hasn't slept at all.

He's silent as he slides a hand beneath my legs and lifts me from the bed. I settle awkwardly in his arms, aware of just how stiff he is against me. Still angry. Still fuming.

Still gentle.

A part of me marvels at that. Robert didn't have an ounce of the same control. Which made him easier to handle in a way. I could talk him down with a few groveling words at a time and all would be well—until the next time.

But Mischa broods. In some ways, he reminds me of a child, preferring to stew in his temper—because the alternative requires swallowing his pride and assessing his own actions.

So, instead, he ignores them stubbornly and I'm the one to suffer.

I stiffen as he carries me down the hall and into yet another bathroom. The bench has been moved here, with all the supplies neatly placed within reach, but the tub is bigger. Deeper. Already half-filled with water, it triggers my alarm like nothing else.

He could drown me.

Ironically, Mischa seems oblivious to the dark scenarios my mind conjures. He sets me down and wets a rag. Silently, he tugs my nightgown off and laves my skin with quick, efficient strokes. Watching him, I notice every nuance in him that I otherwise wouldn't. How tightly he grips the rag, for one—so hard that his knuckles whiten. How his shoulders ripple, distorted by bulging, tensing muscle.

He doesn't notice the moment I touch him, laying my fingers along his wrist. Not at first. He's that intent on ignoring me. Beneath my fingertips, I feel him suddenly jerk and he wrenches the arm away. Flashing, his eyes cut up to mine as his lips spring apart.

But I speak first. "How long until I can walk?"

He frowns, but just as quickly, his mouth quirks into a disarming smirk. "Who says I'll let you?"

He's joking. He has to be… The second I start to suspect the opposite, he lets the expression fall and returns his focus to the rag.

"The doctor will be here to see you again in a week, Little Rose. Work your charms on him and I'm sure he'll try to steal you away. You'll have your freedom in no time—"

"I don't like it when you mock me." I'm surprised by how strongly my voice comes out.

"Mocking?" He scoffs and observes me, his head tilted. "Oh no, Little Rose. I'm *predicting*. It seems that you have a knack for winning powerful men to your side."

There it is again. That prickling note of jealousy that seems so out of place in his gruff baritone.

"I don't want to play this game with you—"

"Game?" Mischa laughs. "Oh no, this isn't a game to you. This is life. Vanya pities you, but I *know* you. I know how you could survive a man like Robert Winthorp all these fucking years. You crawled inside his head like a parasite—"

"Robert is who he is without me," I counter. "I didn't make him do a damn thing."

"Oh really? Then you don't know the bastard as well as you claim to. And I'm starting to think he never knew you, either. His precious wife, a snake—"

"And you're a murderer."

"A murderer…" His eyes widen, and then he nods, chuckling. "Yes. Most recently for you. Isn't that right?" He fingers a strand of my hair, twisting it around his finger. Leaning close, he murmurs near my ear, "I killed Nikolaus for *you*."

"And again, I ask: Is that supposed to impress me?"

"It doesn't," he admits, his mouth tilted in amusement. "But you are used to grander displays of affection, aren't you? Men who parade you before their fucking captives for sport."

"Stop!" My heart races as my throat resonates with the force of the shout. Mischa has the rag against my thigh and I shove his fingers away. "Don't touch me."

"You really want to go through this again?" He drops the rag into the water and stands. "Be my fucking guest."

But he doesn't leave. He's there near the door, watching. To mock me. To gloat.

"You want to know the real difference between you and Robert?" I croak, knowing he can hear me. Goading him is a dangerous, foolish act—but I can't stop myself. My eyes burn as I shift my weight as much as I dare. My bandaged foot might be able to bear weight. Gingerly, I lower it to the floor, guiding my thigh between my hands. I tentatively bear down and the knee buckles. "He is selfish," I say, gritting my teeth in frustration. My body is too weak to stand.

So I'll crawl.

I don't think about the pain or the potential consequences of injuring myself further. Clenching my jaw, I throw my weight to one side of the bench and brace myself with my hands. Sure enough, the bench topples beneath me and a monstrous crash echoes throughout the room. Pain sears along my side, but I can still move.

"He is selfish," I repeat, dragging myself forward with the friction caught beneath my fingertips. "But you? You are childish. I knew what Robert thought of me. What he felt. What he feared. He could admit it out loud." Even in the form of a mindless, enraged rant. "But he didn't lash out and brood like a child—"

"Enough," Mischa growls as I reach for the rim of the tub. "Stop this. You've made your point."

He advances and shuts the water off. Then he grabs my waist and positions me upright by the water's edge.

"I understand now. You have the bastard whipped." He fishes the rag from the tub, but when he brings it to my skin, I slap his hand away. When he tries a second time, I swipe at his arm, knocking the rag from his grip. A low, ragged inhale is my warning of his annoyance.

But pain is the only antidote to fear.

"I said don't touch me."

"Then wash your fucking self!" He snatches the rag and throws it at me.

I flinch as it slaps against my hip, but then I grab it and dip it into the water myself.

"While you're at it, get yourself back into fucking bed as well."

"I will." Crawling to my room seems impossible—at least until I look him in the eye. I'll do it. Even if I have to use my fucking teeth for leverage. "I'd rather break every damn bone in my body than rely on you for anything."

His mouth quirks again and my stomach clenches in response. "Do it," he goads. "I'll even bring you a fucking hammer. Then you'll just remain my captive forever."

"Captive?" A nasty, broken sound rips from me and I barely recognize it. A laugh? I try smothering it beneath my palm, but it's too late. I force my trembling fingers to my side and meet his gaze head-on. "I thought you said I wasn't? Or is liar a term I should add to the list of differences between you and Robert?"

When he says nothing, I gamble my little bit of pride on two snarled words: "Get out!"

He shouldn't leave so easily. Not without putting up a fight or biting out one final insult. Regardless, the door slams behind him and I'm alone.

Which would be a welcome fact in any other context but this. Mischa fits the dog comparison well; he only retreats in order to plan an even more vicious assault.

Still, I swallow hard and pick up the rag, washing myself as best as I can. He left clean bandages for my chest, which I don't have a hope of tightening, as well as a fresh, plain cotton nightgown. After cleaning myself as much as possible, I pull the nightgown on.

And now what?

I eye the door and brace my trembling fingers over the marble flooring. I'll crawl. I will. Determined, I start to shift my weight, pushing off with my palms, moving toward the door inch by inch.

It flies open when I've barely made it a foot away from the tub.

"Here." Mischa shoves something into the room that clatters over the floor.

I cringe as it comes close, only to blink as my brain struggles to register the bulky shape. It's black and small, rolling with its own weight. A wheelchair?

"So you say you don't want to be a captive?" Mischa echoes. He grabs me by my waist and hauls me into the wheelchair. "Then come. And earn your fucking right to call yourself anything else."

My heart pounds as I watch him leave for the umpteenth time. I want to ignore him. Ram myself into him. Scream. Shout.

Anything but follow. As a compromise, I delay the inevitable by sinking back into the chair. With both hands, I ease my casted foot into the closer leg rest and gingerly maneuver the other the same way. My fingers drift to the wheels on either side, testing them. With moderate effort, I maneuver myself from the bathroom and into the hall.

Mischa's there waiting. Without a glance in my direction, he starts down the hall. To his office. I recognize the wide study beyond the doorway.

"You want to talk business, Robert's wife?" He's behind me in an instant and quickly wheeling me toward the desk.

Alarmed, I throw my hands out to brace myself against the wood, but he pulls me to a stop at a safe distance.

It feels so strange to be out of bed. Despite knowing that he has yet another game in store, I can't smother a sigh of relief. His office is a new dungeon at least. A new battlefield.

"So talk to me, partner," Mischa says mockingly. "Tell me something amusing. Maybe…" He taps his chin as if he's thinking, but there's something on his mind. The reason behind his hostility maybe?

I'm caught off guard by how desperately a part of me wants that to be the case. At least we can finally get it out into the goddamn open.

Then he says, "Maybe you can tell me why Sergei Vasilev stopped asking for you?"

"What?" It takes everything I have to school my face into a blank mask. "What are you talking about?" At least the confusion in my voice sounds genuine. The last time I saw the wizened rival to my captor, he gave me a necklace. One still around my throat now, though I don't dare reach for it.

"Don't play dumb." Mischa circles to the opposite end of the desk and leans against it, bracing his palms flat over the surface. "The old man is planning something and you are in the center of it, I bet. I noticed his sudden change of heart *before* your little accident."

Yet he said nothing. Why? He turns away, denying me the chance to discern anything from his expression. His posture is just as inscrutable.

"Did you speak to him?" he wonders. "Or maybe you made a deal? He'd treat you to a nicer cage if you traded yourself in return. Was he the one who served you up to Nikolaus—"

"Why are you so concerned about me and other men?" I find myself blurting. "Even my husband wasn't that possessive."

It's a lie, but Mischa chuckles nonetheless. "Possessive? Oh, no, Little Rose. I'm on my guard."

The look in his eye chills me to the core.

Licking my lips, I risk asking, "What could I possibly do to you?"

The answer is obvious without him having to say it: nothing.

Right now, I couldn't even slap him if I wanted. Already, I'm doubting that I'll have the strength necessary to return to my room without his help.

Lost in self-pity, I almost miss his genuine chuckle.

"What could you do?" His eyes narrow and focus inward at something only he can see. Finally, he grits his teeth. "A woman like you can do more damage alone than a thousand Robert Winthorps. Do you want to know how?" He pauses for a second before answering himself. "Because you can sneak into someone's fucking head and twist it. You play them like little puppets. Don't you?"

Denying him would only set him off. I can see it, the anger lying in wait, anticipating the second I'll light the fuse. With Robert, I'd know exactly what role to play and what words to say.

With Mischa? I can only act on instinct and hope for the best.

"I want to ask you something," I tell him. "And if you answer me honestly, I'll forget how you've insulted me. I won't mention Robert again and I swear that I'll respect whatever boundaries you set—"

"And there you go," Mischa growls. "Trying to get inside my fucking head!"

"A question," I say calmly in the wake of his shouts. "Just one. What did I do to make you so goddamn angry? Do you even know?"

His nostrils flare as he pushes back from the desk. Deliberately, his hands flex in and out of fists, and I tense in anticipation of his next move. To hit me?

"Why? *You*," he finally admits. He approaches me and flicks his finger along my jaw once he's close enough. "You made me so goddamn angry—"

"Tell me why." I bite back another phrase. *Use your big words.* It's what Mother would sternly encourage Briar during the worst of her tantrums. *Speak. Explain.* "Just say it!"

"Fine." He frowns, still stroking alongside my chin. "Did you mean it?" There's no anger in his voice. Just cold curiosity.

"Mean what?"

"Those things you said to Nikolaus. About me."

"W-what?" I rack my brain, fighting to remember. "Oh," I rasp as my own boasts come back to haunt me: *You are half the man Mischa is.* Fire floods my cheeks as I recall the other things I said—to save my life. Did I mean them? "I…"

"And there you go." He sinks down into a crouch and grips my chin, forcing me to face him directly. "Playing your mind games again."

"And what if I did?" I say. "What if I meant them?"

His mocking sneer falls flat, and he stands, withdrawing his hand. "Then I'd know you really were a goddamn liar."

"And you?" Consequences aside, I reach out, grasping his forearm. To my surprise, he doesn't wrench away. Yet. "For all your talk of hating me and how fucking awful I am, why do you even care? Are you jealous of him? Of Robert?"

He laughs. "Oh, Little Rose. I wouldn't get any cute ideas. I would be wary of you even if you weren't his wife." His tone is too smug.

Experience warns me not to challenge him. The words are already out of my mouth regardless. "Why then?"

"Why?" He brings his face close to mine, inhaling my scent. "Because of who your mother is, Little Rose. I've heard the stories… But I'm not allowed to mention her, am I?"

I can't disguise the pain constricting my face. Satisfied, he turns away, another battle won.

"Wait." Fighting back tears, I fix my gaze on him as he stops paces from the door. "I can't make it back to my room alone," I admit. "And you can hold your grudge if you want and insult me if that soothes whatever pride of yours you think I damaged—"

His lips spring apart, but I keep talking.

"Just know that I'm too tired to hate you. In fact, I don't hate you. And I refuse to be your punching bag."

He grinds his teeth, smothering whatever words are fighting to escape his throat. Or perhaps he's chewing on them, ensuring each one is loaded with lethal, biting candor.

"You don't hate me, huh? So then why do you flinch every fucking time I touch you? In the bath," he adds as my eyebrows furrow. Then he puffs up confidently, ready to challenge a lie or excuse.

I recall my shock at how he maneuvered the rag, and the confession spills from me before I can censor it. "I...I didn't expect you to be gentle."

Faced with the truth, he deflates, frowning. I don't know how long we stay like that, watching each other in silence.

Mischa senses someone approaching first. He's already standing by the desk, his arms crossed, when one of his men enters the room.

"Pakhan, I..." The man trails off, spotting me.

"You can speak," Mischa commands. "What is it?"

The man casts me another furtive glance but then sighs before clearing his throat. "You wanted to know if anyone might oppose you at the next gathering after what happened with Nikolaus?"

Mischa tilts his head at full attention. "And?"

"Your position seems solid. Nearly everyone responded to our inquiries with full support—"

"Good," Mischa says, nodding.

"But…" The man rocks back and forth on his heels. "Gabriel Medvedev and Sergei Vasilev haven't responded. Yet."

"Oh?" Something icy flits across Mischa's gaze. "Now I know why Vanya sent you in his place."

"Pakhan—"

"Enough," Mischa snaps. "Inquire again, and this time, you come to *me* directly with their answers. Especially Sergei's."

The man nods and races off.

"And you…" Mischa addresses me, his eyes downcast. He rubs his chin, thinking. "You really want to prove your worth to me?"

"And I haven't already?"

He seems to mull it over. Then he shakes his head. Apparently, I haven't.

"What do you want?" I demand.

"You," he says simply. The candor in his tone makes my body deflate of anger. "I want your loyalty, Little Rose. Are you willing to stand beside me if I ask you to?"

He's deliberately vague—not that it makes a difference. In his world, I have few options but him.

Or Sergei.

I fight to school my expression as I consider the possibility for even a second. Would I dare trust a man I don't know? A man whose only tie to me is through a woman who I'm beginning to realize I never understood at all?

It takes me just seconds to settle on an answer.

"I don't have a choice."

Mischa cocks an eyebrow, but for once, I sense that he's more intrigued than angered. "Oh, but you do, Little Rose. You know you do. But I don't want your answer now. In fact, I don't think I want you to say a damn thing. I want you to show me."

"How?"

Movement from the corner of my eye reveals that he's circling around to my end. His breath strikes the nape of my neck as my wheelchair jolts forward. Moments later, we're back in the room with my designated sick bed.

I eye the sheets as Mischa brings me up to the mattress. He pulls them down and a familiar scent irritates my nostrils. Lavender. When he starts to slide his hand beneath my waist, I stop him, gripping his forearm.

"I'm not tired," I croak. It's a more dignified way of saying what I can't out loud: *Don't make me stay here again.*

"Suit yourself." He releases the wheelchair and heads for the door. "Have your run of the house, Little Rose. *Walk* the grounds to your heart's content. I have nothing to hide."

The boast would sound more convincing if it weren't for the harshness in his voice.

A man like him *lives* to hide and obfuscate.

After all, what is a monster without his secrets?

CHAPTER 16

"$\mathcal{H}$*ave your run of the house."*

What I first interpreted as a cruel joke turns out to be far more nuanced once I inch my way into the hall, alternating arms to wheel myself along. Things I never noticed before take on a newer context. Like how, despite the obvious age of the manor, the rooms sport newer doors, slightly wider than most. Or at least I assume so given how easy I can maneuver my chair through them.

Aljona. Perhaps, after all this time, I've finally learned the real name of the woman haunting Mischa. Not Anna-Natalia, but his sister. A twin.

They left her there, twisted in the wreckage.

Was this chair hers once upon a time?

I wander aimlessly, creeping down the hall at a snail's pace, hunting for clues from a new perspective. I wonder if her room was the red one. Perhaps those clothes were hers. The perfume. The red bed with its heavy canopy.

No. Mischa would hide her memory somewhere more sacred than that. Perhaps down this hall I can't remember venturing in before? The soft carpet cushions the wheels of the chair and I only have to use half the effort. At random, I stop beside a door and open it.

I don't find a bedroom at the other end—or a figurative crypt. Instead, a section of the floor pitches gradually into shadow. Almost like a stairwell, but devoid of steps. Without thinking, I run my hand along the nearest wall, finding a light switch.

Orange light illuminates what could be a wooden slide that curves toward the interior of the house.

My throat goes dry as I ease myself along the curving path. It's no longer than the servant's staircase at Winthorp Manor. Within seconds, I'm on the lower level of the house. Back near the dining room, I suspect.

So Mischa wasn't lying about having a sister.

The reality of that fact stuns me, leaving me motionless in a shadowed section of the hall. All the things he said take on a new context. The pain in his voice. More than that: the skill and care with which he cleaned me. Cared for me.

And maybe now I know the real reason as to why he was so angry with me. Ironically enough, I doubt even he knows the answer. At its core, it's the same reason why Robert Sr. hated me.

I'm not his sister. If anything, I'm just a stark, painful reminder that she's gone.

And what he's become.

A monster.

A murderer.

My tormentor.

Lost in thought, I maneuver myself backward and escape up the ramp. Minutes later, I'm back inside the white room, and I risk injuring myself again just to crawl onto the mattress. It isn't long before Vanya delivers another meal.

When he's gone, I wait, somehow knowing what's in store before I even hear the heavy footsteps thud against the floor. When he appears in the doorway, he looks more ragged than he did earlier. His hair has been scraped into a messy knot on the top of his head, his jaw lined in a five-o'clock shadow. With little fanfare, he strips his shirt in the darkness but leaves his jeans on as he advances on the bed.

"I know you're awake, Little Rose," he calls to me. "I can smell you there, fucking festering in your haughty little pride. You got pretty far, even hobbled. Maybe I'll take the chair? Make you crawl? I'd love to see you always on your knees…"

I stiffen beneath the sheets. Did he sense me there in the hallway after all? But no. He sounds more callous than vengeful. Aggravated. Once again, something has him itching for a fight.

And a part of me feels exhausted enough to give him one. Let him play his silly game.

"Tell me about your sister," I demand, lunging for the one topic that I suspect affects him the most. "What was she like?"

He stops in his tracks, impossible to read in the shadow. "My sister?" he echoes thickly. "She was better than *you*."

"You never mentioned her before," I point out, ignoring his insult. "Why? You talked about your mother. Anna. Never her."

My skin prickles, and I can imagine his expression: eyes narrowed, spitting fire.

"Maybe you aren't worthy enough to hear her fucking name?" he challenges.

But there's more to it than that. It's in the pain lurking in his voice. The gritted, grated undertone to every word.

"How did she die?"

"Oh, Little Rose…" He laughs that cruel, callous laugh and my stomach sinks. I've gone too far. "Do you think you can handle the gory details? Are you that hungry to hear tales of your husband's crimes?"

Of Robert? No. My tongue flits across my lower lip in a futile bid for silence. I want to say nothing. "You said she had your soul," I blurt out instead.

"Oh?" The mattress jolts as Mischa lowers himself onto it, sitting with his back toward me. His shape flickers, followed by a heavy thud. He's taking off his boots. "Do you think I'll cry if I relay her pain to you? You want to feel sympathy for me, the monster of your precious fucking fairytale with Robert Winthorp?"

"I want to understand you." My cheeks flame at the confession, but it's too late to take it back. Sighing, I continue. "Vanya said that you used to be different—no. I *know* you used to be different."

Sixteen years ago, he saved my life. Even if he didn't realize just who I was at the time. For the first time in ages, I let myself picture him as he must have been then. His face was softer. His posture was lighter. His sister was still alive, I suspect.

"She died, Little Rose," Mischa says, his tone cold and final. "It doesn't matter how. All that matters is the why: Your family took her away from me—"

"You're not the only one who lost someone to the Winthorps."

Oh, God no. My fingers fly to my lips as if to seal the confession away. But it's too late.

Like a shark sensing fresh blood, Mischa cocks his head. His arm sweeps out and the fingers aim for my stomach. "You mean *this*," he says without elaborating. It's like the bastard is in my head, sensing the thoughts I've locked away, even from myself. "Tell me."

"No."

His hand presses more firmly, as if he can crush the answers from me. "Why?"

"Because…" I close my eyes as the truth escapes me once again. "Because I don't trust you. I don't trust you not to use it against me—and I will *die* if you use this against me."

"Die," he scoffs. Then the bed shifts as he lies back, stretching his legs out before him, but he says nothing as he thinks. "You think I care about what upsets you?"

I'm prepared for his mocking, but his voice lacks the hostility I'm used to. Instantly, my guard rises. "I think you care about very few things."

"You're wrong."

I jump as my hair is disturbed. He's taken a lock of it, twisting it around his fingers.

"I don't care about a damn thing."

"That's a sad way to live," I say, my voice rasping.

"Is it?" His voice is louder, murmured near my ear. "And what about you, Robert's wife? What do you care about in that tiny, shriveled heart of yours? Him?"

I sigh, suddenly exhausted. Years of suffering Robert's games have never drained me like a few minutes with Mischa does.

"I want to know why you are the way you are," I tell him. "I want to know what makes you tick. I want to know why a man like you is so afraid of seeming like anything less than a heartless monster. Even for a second."

"And I want to know why a woman like you would sell your soul to Robert Winthorp." He grips my chin, wrenching my head in his direction.

In the dark, he looks more demonic than human. All I can make out are his eyes. Flashing, fiery embers.

"I want to know why that same woman would give herself to me. Why sometimes she looks at me like I'm her fucking dog and she owns my leash." He yanks me closer and his breath on my neck burns me. Consumes me. "I want to know why she moans my name when I'm inside her and whispers *his* in her sleep. I want to know why she's in my head. Inside my fucking skin."

He slithers over me, bracing his weight on either side of my head while his torso hovers above mine. His mouth is a furnace, scorching the skin of my neck, each word like a flame. "I want to know why she plays her games with me. Toys with me. Am I that much of a fucking animal to her?" Then he lifts a hand from the bed to grasp my chin, forcing me to meet his gaze when I try to turn away. "That much of a fucking fool…"

He lowers his face to my neck. Sharp pinching pain makes me gasp and flinch into the sheets. He bit me.

"I want her to answer me," he growls into my skin. "I want her to fucking admit it. Come clean. You want to seduce me. None of it is fucking real—"

All I have to cling to are his own words. "It's just sex."

"*No.*" He rears back, hunched like a predator ready to pounce. "It stopped being sex when you said those fucking words to Nikolaus. It stopped being sex that night in the fucking hotel. From the moment I first touched you, it stopped being sex." His hand slips between my legs, plunging beneath my thin nightgown.

I cringe, my cheeks flaming. I should feel disgust. Weak and at his mercy, I should feel helpless.

Not senseless.

One touch and I forget. This room. This place. His fucking twisted insanity. One touch and he's inside me, and he feels so different from Robert...

"You fucking see?" he hisses, snapping my attention back to him. "This is what you do. You pretend and you trick, and —" He breaks off, his teeth clanging as he shoves a finger inside me. I barely hear him above the moan that rips from me. "And you make me fucking think for a second that I could have you."

He sounds crazed. Obsessed. Insane. His voice deepens in ways I've never heard, not even at the heights of his rage.

"You're praying to go back to him, aren't you?" he wonders, still stroking me from the inside out. "Not that it fucking matters. I'm inside you, Ellen Winthorp. I'll always be inside you..."

There are no words to describe what he does to me. It's a torturous style of fucking I've never been subjected to, not even at Robert's most sadistic. Fingers, rubbing… everywhere. Igniting me. My hips writhe, desperate to stifle the flame he ignites. Chase. Evade. Anything to feel more. Feel less.

He's ruthless, wringing something from me I never thought was possible before him. A high and a fall so mind-blowing that all I can do is wheeze, and pant, and suffer.

His hand is still between my legs when I come back down, punishing me with slow, deliberate flicks of his thumb.

"Tell me what your game is," he murmurs, but there's no anger in his voice. Just a naked, terrifying plea. "Tell me. Just fucking admit it. Say it. Tell me!"

His teeth snag my lip—hard. I choke a cry against his tongue, and his lips move harshly, capturing the sound. His tongue does to my mouth what his fingers did to my body. Capture. Control. Claim. But unlike with Robert, he doesn't want to smother me. Each ruthless, hungry pass strokes something in me, like blowing on a smoking bit of wood. Within seconds, it's blazing with no end in sight.

"You want to drive me insane," he suspects against my quivering lips. "You want to. Like him. But I'll take you down with me, *Elle*." He nips again, drawing blood. I swear he does. At the same time, he smooths over the wound with a laving stroke and all pain dissipates. "I'll make you crave me just as fucking much. I'll burn you down to the ground and there won't be anything left for him to steal back."

We're fused, mouth to mouth. Soul to soul—and it's so easy to let him swallow me whole. His fingers return between my legs, stroking and teasing, but never hard enough. Fast enough. He's always an echo of what I know he can be.

"Not tonight," he whispers, finally drawing back. "Not tomorrow. Not the day after, but soon. When I've decided to put you out of your fucking misery. When I've had enough of playing your game—because don't you forget for a second: I've always been playing your game."

He stands, but he doesn't leave. Not right away. He stalks to the other side of the room instead. I see him there, a shadow flung against the wall, slinking and blending into the darkness. He moves into a corner and takes up a post there, watching me well into the night.

CHAPTER 17

I shouldn't have been able to sleep. Nonetheless, I come to on my side, blinking in the harsh light of dawn. At first glance, I assume Mischa's gone: I don't see him nearby.

Then I feel it. Warm breath on the nape of my neck. At the same moment, I sense the slight pressure over my waist, just enough to avoid jostling my injured ribs.

He isn't awake. I realize that the second I flinch and he doesn't issue a mocking taunt. He groans instead and the mattress shifts as he withdraws his arm—only to fully turn toward me, releasing a heavy sigh.

He smells strange like this. There's no vodka. No musk of hate. Just the heady scent of his breath tainting the air. Watching him, I subconsciously tally up all the differences between him and the figure I know him as most often, stricken with rage. The lines of his face are softer now. He looks younger.

He looks…tired. Like someone who's lived a long, hard life and deserves every ounce of sleep to be found. But the second I let myself think as much, his eyes fly open and he's transformed. So much of his appearance hinges on his mouth. Flattened in the peacefulness of sleep, he's almost beautiful. Hardened and cautious, he's an enigma, impossible to decipher.

Especially in silence.

Without a word, he stands and redresses in the clothes he left on the floor overnight. Then he turns to me and rips the sheets from my body. I'm in his arms with no warning, forced to cling to him during the trek into the bathroom.

After he sets me on the bench, I watch him run the water and gather his supplies with clinical precision. His focus makes it harder to reconcile the harsher, violent pieces with a man capable of unfurling a roll of bandages and lining up a row of soft rags to clean me with.

Perhaps talking to him is the only way to shatter the awkward thoughts going to war in my head. "The little girl Nicolai gave you…" I cringe at my own word choice, though I'm not sure how else to phrase it. "Does she have a name?"

Mischa stiffens, still crouched, his head bowed. "Why the fuck would I know or give a shit about something like that?"

I swallow hard at the grit in his tone. He's not bluffing—or so I would believe if I hadn't seen for myself the different side of him. A man who can braid a child's hair and teach her how to hold a knife. In some alternate universe, I assume the act would be equivalent to showing someone how to ride a bike. Parental.

"Because I saw you with her," I admit.

Predictably, he stiffens, his gaze shooting up to mine. His eyes narrow and I can see the word aching to leave his tongue: *snake.*

"You were good with her. Do you have children?"

Given his lack of protection with me—the wife of his sworn enemy—I have no doubt that a child must have come into play at some point. His quick smile, however, is too feral. Only now do I realize that I've opened myself up to his new favorite line of attack.

"Do you?"

I turn away, blinking rapidly. "Why you and not Vanya?" I ask, changing the subject to one even more lethal. He simply can't resist the bait: the mentioning of another man. "Why did you care for me?"

"You'd like that, wouldn't you, Little Rose?" His hand captures my chin, forcing me to face him. He observes me closely, nodding as if finding the answer to a puzzling question in my expression. "You would. You're a tough woman to crack, I will give you that." His fingers curl, stroking along my jaw, raising goosebumps. "But you are easy to read too. Too easy. I just have to know where to look. And it's this…" His finger creeps down to my collar, brushing my throat with a teasing swipe. "I've decided that this is how I'll break you."

"How?" I rasp as air sticks to the inside of my lungs. A complication from my injuries? No. It's him, poisoning every breath I take, invading my bloodstream in place of oxygen.

"With warmth. With that gentleness you fucking crave so much." He stands and cinches the hem of my nightgown in his fist. Then he raises it, forcing me to lift my arms or get caught in the motion.

My cheeks flame as I watch the fabric hit the floor. His scrutiny is a razor, slicing through my thin resistance.

Maybe he's right. I don't know how to protect against him when he's like this. But I'm quickly learning how exactly to fight back.

"How many women have you had?" I wonder, my voice rasping. Licking my lips, I try again, willing my tone to be stronger. "A wife? A mistress? Someone like you..." I trail off pointedly, surprised by just how wild my imagination runs. I can see them all. Tall women. Thin women. Empty, moldable, breakable women. "I'm sure you have a harem somewhere."

"A harem." He seems to taste the word and then grunts, dissatisfied. "Weak men surround themselves with scores of easy whores," he says. "Just as weaker men surround themselves with one—"

"So a wife, then," I assume, curious despite myself. A wife, with a mistress or two on the side. "Where is she?"

"Who says I have one?"

He sounds so smug. Damn it. I've misread him again. Going off his voice alone is too risky—I have no choice but to chance observing him directly. He's standing before the tub, his expression confident. But something in his eyes draws my attention. A hostile, defensive gleam.

"You don't have a wife," I say. "You don't keep a woman at all."

It's a strange way to put it, downright misogynistic. A man keeping a woman—but that's how Robert saw it. In a way, maybe that's all love really is. Beautiful, polished ownership.

But it's a role Mischa hasn't undertaken. Why?

Women flock to him, I'm sure of it. Women like the desperate maids of Winthorp Manor who hunted Robert's men—or, in some cases, my husband himself. They liked the thrill of playing with dangerous, damaged men. Some of them entertained fantasies of fixing them.

Most quickly learned the folly of that hope.

"You don't share your bed with anyone," I add, furthering my suspicions. Yet he has no qualms with doing so—he's certainty haunted mine. Could he simply be a lonely man, unable to attract the opposite sex? No. There's more to it. Hell, it might be the most obvious explanation of all. "You don't trust anyone. Not to say you trust me," I add in a rush, "but I'm under your control. I can't leave. There is no real risk in using me."

"If only that were the case," he says quietly. "But there is more to you than meets the eye, isn't there, *Ellen?*"

"Maybe there is." The words are out before I can take them back. Perhaps there is no point in resisting him. He frowns at my change in tactic, wary. "I give up. You're right. Everything I do is a ploy to seduce you."

Even admitting as much, apparently.

He cocks his head to the side, suspicious. "Do you really think you can?"

I remember that I'm naked as his gaze rakes over me. Suddenly, he stoops to lift a rag from the floor. Then he switches the water on, making it hot enough that steam forms as it pours into the tub. In silence, we wait as the water level rises. From the corner of my eye, I catch the moment he finally comes for me, rag in hand.

He lifts me sideways, sliding one arm around behind my waist and the other beneath my legs. My arms automatically go around his shoulders, tightening as he steps down into the tub, still fully clothed. He sets me on the floor and wraps my cast in plastic. Then he turns me to face him, muscling into the space between my legs.

"You're shivering, Little Rose," he scolds as he wets the rag with one hand and glides it along my shoulders. "One might think you're afraid."

"I'm not." I sound so tired. So…bored. A man who's tormented me for weeks is bathing my limbs with all the care of a nursemaid and I don't care. But I do. There's something unsettling about him when he's up this close—in a way more than just fear.

I think I can see it now, what Vanya does. Mischa isn't evil. He just smothers whatever strives to do good inside him. It's obvious in how his fingers twitch as he washes my arms and then my torso. It takes effort on his part to resist the urge and gingerly cleanse my every bruise and scrape without rousing pain. He *wants* to rub and scrape and hurt—I can see that.

Humanity is a battle for him, one he has to fight tooth and nail.

I'm not sure how much time passes before he finishes. Hours? Minutes? When he finally lets the water drain out, he dresses me in a plain nightgown and returns me to the wheelchair.

"I want to know something," I blurt as I watch him pick up his supplies. "You said you're the leader of your *mafiya*—"

"*The mafiya*," he corrects.

"How?"

He isn't terribly young, but he's definitely not the oldest of the men I saw at his last gathering, either. Vanya alone possesses his own quiet strength and wisdom that would make him a suitable leader in his own right. And Sergei. For whatever reason, the other man stood aside for Mischa.

Why?

"You certainly ask a lot of questions."

"You promised to enlighten me," I point out. "I want to know."

More than that. I want to know why a man like him can amass seemingly so much power and yet have so little. Robert pined and scraped in the shadow of his father for years, but one might think he ruled the whole world because his arrogance was so unmatched.

"Should I tell you a story, Little Rose?" he wonders as he tosses the soiled rags into a hamper. "About how a stupid, young prick worked his ass off to earn the right to be a fucking king? In your world, power is handed to those who are born with it stamped on their asses by virtue of whose dick they sprang from. But in mine…" He runs a hand over his arm, drawing back a sleeve to reveal a hint of the patchwork of tattoos adorning it. "In mine, it is paid for in blood and politics. I am where I am because I bled for it and clawed for every piece of it."

"So tell me how," I hear myself rasp. I sound genuinely curious despite myself. Maybe a little desperate as well. I could keep comparing him to Robert—but there's no point. Every tool of survival I honed until now is rendered useless in this realm and against this monster. I have to relinquish all of my old, pathetic habits. I need to study this man from the ground up.

Starting with anything he'll give me.

"I… I'm listening."

He frowns, cocking his head. "Are you now?"

I stiffen as he advances, only to watch on in confusion when he brushes past me and enters the hall. He lingers near the doorway, a silent command for me to follow. My heart races as I trail him down the hall and toward his infamous study. Once we're both inside it, he closes the door and I hear him lock it.

Purely to intimidate.

"Come here." He approaches his desk and snatches something from an open drawer. A notebook, the one he wrote my recollection of Robert's accounts in. Beside it, he places a pen, and then he looks up, finding me still near the door. "I suggest you take notes."

He leans back with his hips braced against the desk and addresses me from over his shoulder. "Where should I start? Oh, I know. You women are so drawn to sentimental bullshit. My father was Sergei Vasilev's right-hand man, and from the moment I was born, he informed me that I would never succeed him. I was too weak, you see. And, like a fool, I thought that was a *good* thing."

My fingers graze the wheels of my chair, inching me closer despite the tension in my gut warning me to flee.

"I thought he was ruthless. Brutal. That he would rather fight than fucking listen. I used to think that made *him* weak. But now I know…" His eyes flicker toward me, meeting my gaze. "He knew what it takes to survive, Little

Rose. Your husband's father killed him personally. Put a bullet right between his eyes." He taps his temple. "But even then, I could ignore their petty war. What is that saying? You live by the sword, you die by the sword. But my mother? My sister? No. They lived by flowers, and ponies and goddamn sunshine. They didn't deserve to die like animals, but it didn't make a difference in the end, did it? Life isn't fair, Little Rose. Men like your husband get to die peacefully in their beds, surrounded by their fucking spawn, while those they torment and terrorize suffer. So why shouldn't they also suffer?" Suddenly, he tilts his head back, facing me again. "I thought I told you to take notes."

I reach for the pen, forcing the nib against the notebook's page.

"There are ten families," Mischa explains. "Though each member isn't necessarily related by blood. They designate loyalties. Each leader is responsible for running a different aspect of the syndicate. We are not like your husband's family, who uses virtual slave labor and money to sway politics to their favor. We put in the hard work to run our empire."

"Your father was one of the leaders?" I ask.

"One. He managed the business aspect but wasn't strong enough to lead. He deferred to Sergei."

Again, his voice holds the same mixture of fear and respect that taints it whenever he refers to the former leader.

"Sergei led the *mafiya* from the time he was twenty," he continues. "He was fearless and branched out into new territory. He was the one who stood against the Winthorps when they became too bold. He used their own ruthless tactics against them—"

"And," I add, my voice shaking, "he took my mother."

Mischa nods. "That was just the beginning."

"So why did he step down?"

Misha shrugs again. "I don't know." He sounds annoyed by that fact. "One day, he just did. The only way someone can be named the Pakhan is with a majority vote by the other leaders. When I bid for the right, Sergei put his weight behind me."

"But you don't trust him?"

"I trust *Ivan*," he says. "His support is all I need. But should I lose it…" He turns, bracing his hands flat over the desk. Hunched forward, he looks like a wolf readying to pounce on its chosen prey. "He's drawn to you," he admits. "I'd be damned if I knew why. But know this: I won't let you poison him against me."

He's not joking. He really believes I could. Is his paranoia that great? Or is he that worried about what he's become? Or not. Maybe he simply knows that, at some point, Vanya simply won't follow him anymore.

He starts to say something else, but a knock on the door draws his attention. "What is it?" he demands.

One of his men enters the room—I guess the door wasn't locked after all.

"Sir, you wanted me to tell you when Sergei responded?"

Mischa nods. "And?"

"Well, he requested a meeting. Tonight."

Mischa frowns, his brow furrowed. "A meeting? With who?"

"You," the man replies. "And…" His gaze cuts nervously in my direction. "Her. He mentioned her by name."

"Did he now?" Mischa's eyes narrow into slits. "Tell him I'll accept, but on my terms. Go."

The man leaves, taking most of the air in the room with him.

Without even looking in his direction, I can sense the vicious verbal tirade brewing under Mischa's skin. The hate. The jealousy. I could wait and brace for the tempest.

Or I can sigh and head him off with a dare of my own. "You said you wanted my trust?"

He says nothing. Because he's brooding, I find when I look up. A wild mop of golden hair obscures his eyes as if he raked his fingers through it.

"Take me to the meeting," I propose. "Let me talk to Sergei on my own, and then you tell me why I shouldn't trust him. Let me decide on my own who to believe."

"And why should I?" There's no coldness in his tone, for once.

"You told me I should stop acting like a doll," I remind him. "So don't treat me like one. I can think for myself—"

"Fine." He rises to his full height and moves to the door. Wrenching it open, he addresses me without looking back. "I'll let you gamble, Little Rose. Let's see just what you're willing to bet."

He's gone in seconds, and alone, I listen to the thud of his retreating footsteps. My heart races, tracking the time with every frantic beat. What the hell was I thinking?

The answer is simple. Nothing. For once, I wasn't thinking —I was surviving the only way that seems possible where Mischa is concerned. Pure, volatile instinct.

He finds me in my room when night falls. Dangling from one of his hands is a black dress, which he has to help me into. Then, still without word, he seizes my chair from behind and wheels me into the hall.

We don't take the ramp. He brings me to the top of the staircase instead and then lifts me from the chair entirely. Startled, I cling to him as he brusquely carries me down the stairs and through a corridor I recognize as the one leading to the large meeting room he held his last gathering in.

This time, a table has replaced the circular arrangement of chairs, and only one man is seated.

Sergei's aged at least ten years since I saw him last. More gray streaks his hair, and lines surround his mouth, etched into the skin. When he sees me, he stands abruptly, his expression constricted. "I heard about the…incident with

Nikolaus," he states as Mischa approaches. His side of the table contains two chairs, one of which Mischa shoves me onto.

But he doesn't rush to claim the one beside me. Instead, he extends his hand, his gaze guarded. "Sergei."

"Mischa." The other man clasps his hand in return, shaking it. "I thought it was about time we talked."

"So talk," Misha commands. He's being rude.

I'm not well versed in their hierarchy, but I can suspect from Sergei's raised eyebrow that he's caught off guard. Still, he disguises his alarm well.

"I want you to reconsider your options," he says. "By now, you know what the boy is capable of. He'll retaliate. The girl will be safer with me."

"So this is what this is about…" Mischa laughs, shaking his head. Then his hand moves so fast that I almost miss it. In a flash, he yanks a knife from his pocket and has the blade against my throat.

"Stop!" Sergei nearly lunges across the table as the metal grazes my skin. "What are you doing?"

"Something I should have done a long time ago," Misha replies. He presses the knife harder, drawing a gasp from my throat. It's not for show. Sharp, pinching pain alludes to the fact that he's already sliced through skin. "What is she to you? Enough fucking games. Just come out and say it."

"Let her go." Sergei's eyes move from my captor to me, flashing with uncertainty. "Mischa—"

"Fucking say it!" The knife withdraws as he slams the blade onto the table so hard that the legs shudder. "Now. So she can hear you. Is she yours? Is that it?" When the other man doesn't answer, he points the knife at me again. "I fucking swear to god—"

"Remember who you are talking to."

I jump at the authority ringing in Sergei's tone. He's transformed in an instant, and now, I see that Mischa was right to be wary of him. "You show me respect, boy."

"And you show respect to me!" As Mischa grabs me from behind, his hand forming a collar around my throat, a gasp rips from me. "Tell me who the fuck she is. Tell me now."

Sergei's gaze flickers beyond us to the doorway. "Mischa…"

"I said tell me! Is she your fucking bastard—"

"I think she's *Ivan's* bastard!"

Silence descends so abruptly that every breath I take echoes tenfold, deafeningly loud. Mischa's gone from my side, standing paces away. "How?" he demands.

"How else?" Sergei shrugs. "Her mother was Marnie Winthorp, wasn't she?" When he doesn't receive an answer, he nods anyway. "She was. Ivan may seem grizzled now, but don't be fooled. He's younger than I am, always too damn soft for his own good. And to be honest…" He trails off, eyeing his hands. "I thought I'd erased any threat that woman could pose to him years ago. In fact, I'm surprised my brother hasn't already deduced her identity for himself—"

"He hasn't because she's not," Mischa snarls. I turn to face him, standing paces away, his eyes fiery. "Her mother was a fucking Winthorp whore. She's no more Vasilev than the dirt on the bottom of my fucking shoe."

"And if you were lying to me, you know that alone would give me enough of a claim to challenge you." Though he and Mischa are the same height, Sergei suddenly seems larger, exuding a confidence he lacked before. "Because if she is of my blood, you know what that means."

"Do I?" Mischa counters.

"It means my bloodline would have life in it, Mischa," he replies, his tone deadly soft. "It means I'd have an heir to my name. And it means that perhaps I wouldn't be so content to sit back and watch the next time your carelessness puts my people in danger."

He eyes me pointedly, as if demanding I come clean now. Admit it.

"Do not get me wrong," the man adds, returning his attention to Mischa. "I do not want to challenge you. But if I feel that you may have insulted and battered my family? If I feel that my bloodline is in play once more? *If* I sense that you are more of a threat than a true leader..." He lets the unspoken threat hang in the air. "For now, continue your war with Winthorp if you have to. You still have my support. But think carefully about where you lead from here. And let me know if she happens to remember anything that may clear up her paternity."

He leaves, carrying himself with that dangerously subtle aura.

And Mischa waits, reminding me of a child ensuring that the adults are out of earshot before resuming his bullying of those weaker. "Don't tell me you believe him? He's a feeble-minded old fool—"

"You knew." My voice clashes with his, a weak whisper against a shout. Surprisingly, mine wins out. "All this time…and you *knew*."

His face blurs as my eyes well over and tears spill down with no hope of suppressing them. Everything he said flashes through my mind. His jealousy. His paranoia.

And Vanya…

His kindness. His gentleness. Did *he* know? The answer sits like a stone in the pit of my stomach. No. He didn't.

"Did you get a sick kick out of it?" I snarl, surprised when he flinches. "Watching him care for me? Holding my life over his head? Did you love teasing me about my mother when all along you knew!"

"And that is why," Mischa says softly. "Why you shouldn't believe everything you fucking hear. Don't entertain your childish little fantasies because the reality isn't what you want it to be—trust me on that."

He could be mocking me again. I wish to God he were, but for a rare, stark moment, he's being honest. I can see it in his face, the hints of pain that only slipped out when he talked about his sister.

"Vanya treats you kindly now, but that's because you're a nameless victim. An innocent. But if he knew the truth? Not only would he hate you, but the pity. The disgust. Bitch at me all you want, but trust that I know what it is like to be shunned by your own father. It's a pain I wouldn't wish on anyone."

"And I'm supposed to believe you?" I croak. "You don't give a damn about me. If I'm his niece, Sergei has a reason to want his throne back, doesn't he?"

His jaw clenches over an answer, but he doesn't have to say a damn thing out loud.

"You're a selfish bastard. God, I hate you—no, I pity you. Now I see why Vanya sticks around. It's not because he knows you can change—he doesn't. He's just waiting for the moment he'll have to put you down like the mad dog you are!"

I blush at my own vitriol. I've never spoken like this to anyone. Not Robert. Not Briar. In a sick, twisted way, it feels so damn good. At the same time…

Mischa's face reveals nothing but a careful, blank mask— and I'd prefer any other reaction.

Without a word, he turns, leaving the room, his posture relaxed.

But hatred is like a boomerang. I feel the aftereffects strike me long after he's gone, lancing across my chest in an unexpected manifestation.

Guilt.

I don't return to my room. Instead, I crawl into a corner and sleep in a chair, tucked away in some distant corner of the house. Maybe I do it out of spite, shunning what few items of comfort he's provided.

Maybe it's shame.

In some ways, it helped to believe that my father was some faceless, nameless monster. Even when I thought he was Sergei. Those possibilities were men I didn't know, whose kindness and mercy I couldn't recall. Had my parentage been more sinister, it would hurt but I could handle it.

I can't handle this.

The lies, and the intrigue, and the secrets. Vanya wasn't always the man he is now, Mischa warned me once. If Sergei really is right, could I reconcile that horrible monster with the man who treated me with more kindness than a majority of the people in my life?

And Mischa…

I hate him. At the same time, I know it's pointless too. You can't blame a dog for biting and howling when it's all he knows. You can't expect a monster to feel an ounce of goddamn mercy.

So I don't. Gritting my teeth, I focus on the only person I have control over in the situation. The only fool I can blame. Myself.

Alone in the silence of a forgotten hall, I contemplate every fucking mistake I've made up until this point—trusting Mischa even for a second is one of them. My fingers absently trace the fresh scratch he left over my throat. Did he goad Sergei intentionally?

Or did he mean in every word of his threat to kill me?

I should believe so. I should fester over it—another reason to hate him. Loathe him. Despise him. He's a childish bastard with no fucking soul, but that's the catch.

Children are never malicious without reason. They're defensive, like Briar all the many times she made me submit to her. At his core, Mischa is an insecure, immature bastard. But there's a reason behind his madness, and I can't shake the sinking suspicion that he lied to me, and to Vanya, for a reason.

What exactly that may be?

I don't care.

I *can't.*

If I stay hidden, I can almost pretend I'm back at Winthorp Manor, a realm I know well. Robert would give me a day or so of peace, just long enough to recharge my soul and lick my wounds. He'd never have to hunt for me because I'd instinctively know when to return to my cage and wait for him. I was a well-trained bird.

I'd never listen to heavy, thudding footsteps I knew to be his pacing the hallway nearby. My new captor never calls for me out loud. He can smell that I'm close. Sense that I'm near.

Overall, he has too much damn pride to surrender.

So we play our silent game for hours. His footsteps retreat. Return. Retreat again. I think it's hours before a door finally opens, revealing the creature standing behind it. He's dressed in black from head to toe, his hair a stark contrast over his pale skin. Shrouded by a wild fringe, his eyes glow —intense, but not angry. Beside him is the wheelchair.

For what feels like an eternity, we eye each other until he finally moves, turning his back to me. His hand shoots out, shoving the wheelchair further into the room. "The doctor is here," he growls, his voice hoarse.

I watch him go. Only long after his final steps trail off do I move. Mischa isn't waiting for me in the hallway or by the main stairs. Alone, I find the ramp and maneuver myself to the second floor. Inside the white room, I find a strange man wearing a white coat.

An hour later, my cast is in pieces and the doctor props a pair of crutches against the bed.

"Practice bearing weight gradually," he warns. "I'm going to recommend that Mischa allow a physical therapist to come."

With that, he leaves, and I attempt to stand only to cling to the bed frame with white-knuckled hands. The crutches are harder to maneuver with than the wheelchair and I can only move a few feet at a time. Sweat dribbles down my neck by the time someone enters the room to witness my struggle.

"Careful!" Vanya races to set down a tray of food. His arm goes around my shoulders, providing enough stability to keep me from pitching over. Then he steers me to the bed, murmuring the whole time. "Do you want to fall and break another bone?"

It's too much. His voice, the soft, gentle cadence. His touch. My head is spinning and I clutch it beneath my fingers as if stroking my temples can unravel the tangled thoughts. "I'm fine. Just please… I-I need to be alone."

"Are you all right?" His fingers still over my shoulder, but I don't look up to see his reaction.

"I…I'm just tired," I force myself to reply. "I just need sleep."

"Get some rest. I'll leave the food here for you." He pats me gently and then leaves, and the dam of emotion I didn't even know I was holding back breaks loose.

I manage to smother the first sobs beneath my palm. Eventually, that isn't enough. A handful of bedsheets. A pillow. Only by biting down over my palm can I stay silent in the end.

My eyes stream as my body heaves. There's no comparison for this pain. I just have to suffer through it, experiencing every emotion I've ever felt tenfold. Agony. Guilt. Relief. Gratitude.

It doesn't last long. The second I hear someone approach, I choke my sobs down and fight to compose myself. Not Mischa. I'm aware that my newcomer isn't him even before I face them from over my shoulder. This figure is smaller. Thinner. Her blond hair is a wild, matted tangle, clashing with the blue, feminine dress someone gave her to wear.

She eyes me from partially behind the doorway.

"Can I help you?" I rasp when she doesn't move.

She shakes her head. Then she points to the tray near my bed and mimes eating with her hands.

"Mischa," I snarl. Once again, the bastard proves that he isn't above sending a child to do his dirty work.

"I'm not hungry," I reply politely, hoping my irritation doesn't seep into my voice. "I'll eat later…"

I trail off as she pads closer and lifts a bowl from the tray. Holding it out to me, she nods to the broth within. Apparently, I have no choice.

It's a thin, simple soup but still delicious. I drain it quickly under the girl's watchful eye. Satisfied, she starts to leave the moment I swallow the last drop.

"Wait," I call out, and she pauses near the doorway, impatiently fidgeting with the skirt of her dress. "What's your name?"

Her wide eyes meet mine and she shrugs.

"You can't talk?"

She shrugs again and then scurries away before I can ask her something else. This time, however, I follow her. It takes me ages using the crutches—or so it feels like. By the time I enter the hallway, I only have the sound of her quick steps rounding the corner to guide me. It isn't long before I can get a sense of where she's headed. Sure enough, not far from Mischa's office, his voice greets me.

"Did you do it?" he demands gruffly. "She ate all of it?"

The girl must nod or whisper something to him, because he grunts, satisfied.

"Fine. Here's your share."

I come close enough to make out the smaller shape of the girl standing before the desk. Mischa must place something onto her hand, because she draws it back, observing the contents intently. Then she extends the same hand toward him again.

"Good," the man praises, slapping something else onto her palm. More money, I suspect. "Never trust anyone not to cheat you. Always count your shit. You catch on quick—" Suddenly, he cocks his head and a frown distorts his mouth. "But next time, I will teach you how to ensure that you aren't followed."

The girl whirls around, spotting me.

"Go," Mischa tells her.

She whizzes past me, and I attempt to follow her.

"Wait."

I don't want to. Every cell in my body is screaming at me to keep moving. Ignore him. Resist. I manipulate one of the crutches forward and take a step.

"I said to fucking wait."

Old Ellen Winthorp would have obeyed the twisted baritone. She would have cowered and let him inside her head again. New Ellen, however, is too fucking tired. I keep inching along as my neck prickles with an awareness of the man glaring after me.

He doesn't follow me though. I reach my room alone and collapse, panting, onto the bed. Here, I curl up and try once again to process everything swirling around my head without going insane. When I hear the soft steps of someone approaching, I don't try to be polite.

"I'm sorry, Vanya, but I'm not hungry—"

"Look at me."

I guessed wrong. My body stiffens at the sound of Mischa's voice.

I lift my head just enough to spit out, "I'm not in the mood to be used as a fucking pawn in your goddamn war, either."

He stands there so long that I'm sure he'll attack. Lash out. Insult. I'd like to think I'm ready for him, but I'm not. I'm so tired of his game.

Closing my eyes, I lie here with my face buried in the sheets. I'm not sure exactly when he leaves. The only thing I'm aware of is that darkness falls gradually, confining me like a cocoon.

And that he's gone.

He doesn't come for me in the morning—or if he does, I don't give him the chance to. I hobble to the bathroom myself and bathe behind a locked door. For clothing, I settle on one of the items I picked out for myself what feels like an eternity ago: a dark sweater and a loose pair of jeans.

A part of me wants to stay in here forever. Hide from the monsters in my life. Pretend I have any say in doing so. Lie to myself. Is that how my mother survived her days? The more I think of her, the less clearly I can recall her memory. Not the sweet, smiling woman who tucked me into bed some nights, but a haunted shadow. Someone with more secrets than answers, and even now, I'm not sure I want to learn them all.

Eventually, the heat of the bath water fades and I have no choice but to escape into the hall, using my crutches for balance. Out here, I realize that Mischa might be the least of my worries. Something in the air is different: a sense, a feeling. It permeates the narrow hallway, seeping through my skin. Unease? Just a few paces from the bathroom, my ears catch the distant sounds of men talking. Furiously.

"What do you mean?" a man demands. Mischa. "You think they're here? Would the bastard really be so fucking bold?"

"What is your gut telling you?" someone replies gruffly. Vanya. "Something isn't right—"

"It's Winthorp," Mischa hisses. "He's planning something. Or maybe Sergei… Fuck these goddamn games!"

"Well then what are you going to do about it?"

I hear them both move farther into the house, splintering off in different directions. Vanya's slow, uneven gait heads away from me, while the other set…

I watch him ascend the stairs dressed in gray fatigues, his hair wild and untamed. His eyes find mine, dark with an unreadable emotion. Without a word, he cocks his head, beckoning me to follow him into a nearby room. His office.

My heart beats unsteadily, and I start to turn away.

"We need to talk." The grit in his voice draws my attention despite everything. He's wary about something. Me?

He's seated behind the desk when I finally enter the room, his hands braced flat over the surface.

"You're coming with me tonight." He looks up, seeking out my gaze. "I'm meeting someone with information on your husband. You say you're truly free of him? Prove it to me—"

"Why should I?" I counter, my voice soft. "Why should I believe anything you say?"

"You don't." He pushes back from the desk and stands. "But use your brain, Little Rose. You want information on your husband? Your mother?"

He lets the question hang in the air like a tempting piece of bait.

"Then be ready tonight." He wants to say something else, I suspect. His lips twitch and then twist into that stubborn frown. Without another word, he leaves, retreating down the hall.

My heart clenches with an emotion I can't name. More confusion? The man delivers it in spades, like a poison meant to affect me when all of his other attempts have failed. All I can do to survive the effects of it is…

Breathe.

I inhale raggedly between every step I take. At first, I head for my room, but something makes me pass it and turn the corner to that forgotten wing. I test the doors one by one, surprised to find most of them locked. The few that aren't open onto dark, dusty closets that contain nothing of real interest.

Mischa guards his secrets well, it seems. Well enough that I'm exhausted by the time I return to my designated sick room—not that I can enjoy the peaceful quiet for long.

He comes at the time when Vanya would usually bring my evening meal, his steps hesitant near the threshold. With the door already opened, I can make out the sliver of his shadow outstretched over the floor. He says nothing, and I have to rise from the bed and approach him to convey my intent.

His eyes narrow, and then he turns, leading the way to the lower level. To my surprise, he takes me to the stairs, forcing me to hobble down and balance my crutches while clinging to the banister. Dripping sweat, I watch him, trying to decipher his motive. To punish me?

No. His arms twitch at his sides as if he's stopping himself from offering assistance. Maybe because he knows I'll rebuff his attempts—regardless, he stays close. Close enough to catch me should I fall…

His eyes, however, reveal nothing as they track my descent, and the moment I'm close enough, he marches for the door, leaving me to follow. Two of his men wait outside near an idling van. One takes the driver's seat, while the other climbs into the farthest row at the back of the van, which leaves me and Mischa to claim the middle.

Mischa makes me get in first and snatches the crutches once I'm seated. To my alarm, he leaves them there on the driveway before climbing in himself and slamming the door after us.

"What are you doing?" I croak.

"You won't need them." He stares from the window on his end, his posture tense.

Alarm dances down my spine in deadly anticipation. Very few things make Mischa pensive—none of them good for me.

Are we headed toward another meeting? Another dark, sordid trade? Perhaps, even now, he still plans to sell me, a task made much easier if I don't have full use of my legs.

The twisted scenarios form unabated in my head. My breath is baited by the time the vehicle finally slows to a stop. When I look out the window, all I feel is…

Confusion. "Where are we?" The question slips out before I can remind myself who I'm with.

We're near a secluded building. A home maybe? It's not as grand as Nicolai, the drug supplier's, but it's not small, either. It's perhaps the size of the guest house at Winthorp Manor. In the darkness, I can make out two men standing guard on a short set of stone steps leading to a door. Orange light illuminates square windows, but I can't make out any hint of what might lurk within.

"Get out." Mischa shoulders the door open on his end and renders his command moot when he reaches for me. Before I can protest, I'm in his arms. "Don't worry, Little Rose," he grunts as he heads for the front of the building. "I'll release you soon enough."

The reassurance rings more like a threat as we near the two men who eye me warily before nodding in deference to Mischa.

One of them opens the door, allowing us inside. A narrow foyer decorated in shades of black and gold greets us, a much chicer interior than I would have expected. Mischa enters boldly and turns through a nearby archway, entering a wide, simple sitting room. A man dominates a leather couch in one corner of the room. I stiffen the second his eyes connect with mine.

I don't even register grabbing Mischa's forearm until he shrugs, testing my grip. "What—"

"He was there with Nikolaus," I say. "The night he attacked me."

"Pakhan," the man greets, his tone soft. "How kind of you to join me."

"It seems you've been busy, Gabriel," Mischa replies. He sets me down on an armchair positioned slightly beyond the circle of couches. Turning his back to me, he claims a seat directly opposite the other man. At a glance, I can't tell if he believed me or not, but then—as if he read my mind—his hand goes to the bulging pocket of his fatigues. "Care to explain yourself?"

"Can you blame me for assisting an old friend?"

"Maybe… *If* you have the information you promised," Mischa counters, "I suggest you make it good."

"Yes…" The man shifts, unfurling his long limbs. He places his hands on either knee, and a ring on his left hand draws my eye. Thick. Silver. It looks similar to a Winthorp insignia ring, but different. Older. "You've been busy yourself, Mischa," the man says. "But Robert Winthorp? Well, he's been busier."

"Cut to the chase, Gabriel," Mischa scoffs, crossing his arms. Then his eyes cut in my direction before flicking away. "I'm listening."

"He's consolidating," Gabriel declares. "Everything that bastard could inherit from his father, he's already pried from the man's cold, dead hands. The docks. The ports. All of it."

My skin runs cold at the mention of Robert. Still alive. Still fighting back. Without his father, I can only imagine how far the depths of his greed might extend.

"I'm not worried about the Winthorps and their toys," Mischa says.

"Ha!" Gabriel throws back his head for a guttural laugh. When he meets Mischa's gaze again, he isn't smiling. "You should be. With the power at his control, he could crush you in a matter of weeks. With or without the *mafiya*. And if he's bold enough to come after you directly, all it would be is catching you off guard. Not to mention your little rift with Sergei…"

"A matter of weeks, you say?" Mischa strokes his chin, seemingly unconcerned—but I can see through the act. His eyes are molten, swirling with dark conspiracies.

"He's been busy, Pakhan. Making alliances. Scurrying in your shadow. You think you have a good grip on your men. Maybe you do—but don't doubt for a second that Winthorp isn't in the background, sniffing around for any hint of weakness. If I could plant a man among your ranks, just imagine what he could do?"

Interest crosses Mischa's expression. "So what do you suggest?"

Gabriel eyes me again, a slight smile shaping his lips. "Well, if you had some *insight* into who his allies are, that might help."

"That's what you're for, if you haven't forgotten," Mischa says coldly. "Unless I need to find another man whose palms require grease. Preferably one who won't scurry around with my fucking enemies—"

"Relax, Pakhan. Nikolaus was a cousin of mine, you understand." His gaze turns distant for a brief second. Then he shakes his head. "Rumor has it that Winthorp's moves are a bit too bold. He's more confident than he's ever been, but why? Or maybe it's self-preservation. His father had several businessmen who might think they have a claim to what the old man left behind. Robert's consolidating power quickly. They might be willing to whisper to any man who could guarantee their safety."

"And I assume you have someone in mind?" Mischa wonders.

"That I do. I'll pass on his information to you, but there's more."

"Oh?"

Gabriel nods, suddenly serious. "There are more rumors, a bit more outlandish, but I think you might want to consider them nonetheless. One is regarding Winthorp's sister. Her wedding's been mysteriously called off. The whereabouts of her fiancé are unknown—"

I must have made a noise, because the man breaks off, turning his attention to me.

"Some say it's coincidence," the man continues, "but I say that the bastard is getting rid of any threats to his power, even his own blood."

Mischa shrugs, disinterested "What else?"

"Another rumor. This one is…more gossip than anything, but it might serve your purpose if it pans out. There is talk that Winthorp wouldn't cut off his own sister and attack his father without securing his own bloodline. His father was a madman, you realize? Had it specified in his will the exact stipulations of any inheritance."

I remember them. Archaic nonsense Robert used to scoff at. He could only marry someone his father approved of and produce a male heir. One of the many reasons our relationship wasn't valid in the eyes of his father.

Briar's wedding, in terms of succession, put her one step closer to securing the elder Winthorp's favor.

"You know how some of those old-fashioned fucks loyal to that family are," Gabriel sneers. "They've all supported him, but they wouldn't without proof that he's established himself as the head of the Winthorp name. Dogs need their rewards, you see."

"Proof?" Mischa sits forward, an eyebrow raised. "What kind of proof?"

Gabriel shrugs. "The kind that would make a man bold enough to imprison his sister—allegedly—and kill his father. There's talk that he had a pet he kept close." Once again, his dark eyes dart in my direction.

This time, Mischa copies him and my heart stalls at the intensity of his gaze.

"And?" my tormentor prompts.

Gabriel's lips quirk into yet another quick smile. "*And* there's talk that he may have cemented his bloodline, if you know what I mean."

I stop listening. My stomach churns ominously, even though I know it's a lie. I *know*. But the knowledge swirls in my blood like poison, making it harder and harder to breathe...

"I need fresh air."

Both men turn in my direction as I rise from my chair, using the arms for balance.

"Wait." Mischa advances on my position before I can even make it to my feet. Within seconds, I'm in his arms, being carried from the room. "We'll continue this later," he calls to Gabriel.

The other man merely laughs. "Of course."

Tension radiates from Mischa, seeping through my skin as we enter the cold night air. He all but shoves me into the van, climbing in after me.

"Drive," he snaps to the driver. "And get Vanya on the phone as soon as you can. The fucker's up to something. I can sense it. And you…" His eyes cut to me. Before he even opens his mouth, I beat him to the punch.

"It's not what you're thinking." Even now, I can't even force myself to say it out loud—the scenario that I know is on his mind. "It's not."

"Oh?" He laughs. "And I'm supposed to believe that because you fucking say so?"

"Yes." The simplicity of my answer makes him grunt in shock. "I wouldn't lie about this—"

"About what?" Mischa demands as his man dutifully puts the van into motion. "About your fucking spawn with Winthorp? Let me guess. *Now* is the time you beg me to spare them both—"

"There is no child." My fingers fly to my lips, suppressing the confession. It's not the whole truth. Inhaling raggedly, I try again. "They… He died."

Mischa says nothing, even as my body deflates with the admission. Hunched over, I focus my attention on breathing. In and out. Ironically, he's the one who taught me this mantra—how to survive when it feels like the world is caving in and nothing could possibly slow the onslaught.

So I breathe.

When I finally let myself refocus on my surroundings, the van has stopped. Muted noises echo as if I'm hearing them from underwater. Shouting. Mischa. We aren't near his manor, I realize, but parked along a country road. Shadows obscure any defining features and I can't even begin to guess our location.

Mischa stands outside the van, with the door on his end wide open. Carried by a harsh wind, his voice drifts to me, tense and low.

"What the fuck do you mean?" Suddenly, he breaks off, his eyes wide. "Shit!" The next second, he's lunging into the van, shouting in the driver's ear. "Drive! Fucking drive!"

The van explodes into motion, kicking up mud as it peels down the road. Soon enough, Mischa's manor appears on the horizon like a smudge of brown over an inky sky. A smudge is quickly enhanced by strokes of orange and yellow.

"No! Fuck, no!" Mischa slams his fist into the back of the seat before him as the driver swerves off the road, cutting through a field to reach the house sooner. Yards away, Mischa flings the door open and jumps out with the driver hot on his heels. "Safe house," Mischa shouts.

Gritting his teeth, the driver turns back to the road, and the sudden increase in speed jolts me forward—but he's not fast enough. A dark shadow swerves from a curve in the road up ahead. A quickly approaching van—but it's not one of Mischa's.

I only have a second to make out the blurred faces beyond the tinted glass before everything explodes into noise. I'm spinning. Falling…

Crashing.

Pain licks lazily at my throbbing limbs as I feel out with my hands, desperate to get my bearings. It's dark, barring a faint glow of moonlight that illuminates nothing in particular. But I can get my bearings, at least. I'm lying on my side, caught between the front and middle seats of the van.

"Hello?" I call out, but the driver doesn't answer. Groaning, I manage to climb to my knees only to find the man slumped over the steering wheel. I don't think he's breathing.

And then I hear them: footsteps crunching over grass and dirt, racing toward me.

The van must have stalled rather than crashed. It's still upright, and someone grunts as they wrench the door open. Blinking, I struggle to take them in. A pressed suit and gleaming headset affixed to his ear confirm the worst: He's not Mischa's.

Frowning, the man observes me. "It's her," he grunts into his headset. "I've found her. She's alive." He tucks his gun into the pocket of his coat and extends his hand. "Come with me, miss. You're safe."

Safe. Safe. Safe. That word echoes hauntingly as my ears ring and broken glass crunches under my fingertips, a painful reminder. This man will take me to Robert.

"We need to hurry!" The man stoops to my level and reaches for my arm.

Robotically, I reach out in return, letting him guide me to the door.

A hiss escapes him as he observes my legs. "She's injured," he barks into his headset. "Our location is—"

"Help me up!" I command over him.

He frowns but assists me to my feet. In the distance, Mischa's home glows, engulfed in flames, and shock renders me speechless. All those secrets I'll never uncover. The memories Mischa obviously holds dear. And the people…

Vanya. The little girl.

Mischa.

"We need to move, miss." The man beside me loops an arm around my shoulders, steering me toward the sleek, black vehicle idling paces away. He must have driven it himself. There's no one else inside as he sets me on the passenger's seat.

Faintly, I can hear shouting in the distance. Screaming.

"What's happening?" My voice comes out a dry croak.

The man shoots me an odd look and once again fidgets with his headset. "Have medical standing by," he mutters. "She's injured—"

"What's happening?" My heart races as the man takes the steering wheel. Rather than head toward the house, he turns down the road. Toward Robert.

"You're safe now, miss," he explains, his voice terse. "Mr. Winthorp decided to put an end to this little game once and for all."

That damn word—*safe.* From who? Mischa? With Robert?

"Stop the car."

"What?"

"Now!" It's like another woman is speaking, not me. One who sounds so damn cold. Determined. She sounds like Mischa. "Now!"

"Miss?" The man narrows his gaze and the van seems to move faster. We're nearing a bend in the road. One that will take us beyond Mischa's property and into the unknown. "We'll be there soon enough—"

"I said stop the car!"

I lose my mind; that's the only way to describe it. It's like my consciousness detaches from my body. I can see myself lunging for the wheel, batting the man's hands away. I can sense the vehicle swerve dangerously. Then a violent jolt as everything comes to a sudden stop.

But it isn't until I'm blinking up at an impassive night sky that I register the pain flooding my body. I taste blood. My ears ring so loudly that I can barely hear the telltale crunch of footsteps racing toward me. Something is still in my hand. Sharp. Jagged. Broken glass. Dazed and broken, I somehow manage to lift it, brushing the tip against my collar.

Do I really have what it takes? Maybe I do. Anything to avoid returning to Robert…

"Easy!" someone shouts, sounding nearby. "Easy…"

I inhale sharply at the familiar accent and try to focus my vision in the speaker's direction. "Vanya?"

"Don't speak." Darkness descends as he drapes something over me. A coat? It smells like him: musk and smoke. "Just hold on to me. Hold on to me."

"Don't get up too fast."

The warning comes as my eyes flutter open to an unfamiliar room. Tension laces my limbs, making them spring into action before I even fully regain consciousness. To run?

Maybe not.

Instead of a cell, I'm on a leather couch in a dimly lit room. Only a faint orange glow illuminates the weathered face of the man crouched beside me. Vanya. A cut on his forehead bleeds freely, and his left eye is partially shut and swelling fast.

Shock erases my panic. "What happened?" I hear myself rasp. But hazy images are already flickering across my mind. Fire. Shouting. Robert's men.

"It was an ambush," Vanya says gruffly. He rises to his feet, wincing, and starts to pace. "All I know is the goddamn house was on fire and we were being shot at like fish in a fucking barrel. I swear to god, if that bastard Medvedev—" He breaks off as if remembering I'm here.

"Where's Mischa?" A part of me steels myself for the obvious. He's dead.

"Mischa?" Vanya runs his hand across his face. "He's—"

The sound of squealing tires cuts him off, and Vanya lurches across the room to a window. I crane my neck to follow his gaze, catching the approach of a white van that skids to a stop near a rickety porch. The vehicle door flies open and Mischa jumps out, shouting.

"Ivan! Come help! Now!" His blond hair casts a shadow over his features that makes him appear years older than he is. Blood streaks his jaw, and he looks more predatory than ever. Inhuman. I barely recognize him as he turns and lifts something from the floor of the van.

Make that *someone*: a body, small and pale. The little girl.

"Mother of God." Vanya lumbers through the doorway as Mischa races toward the house. Somewhere beyond this room, a door opens, slamming against a firm surface. The floorboards shake as a stampede of men enters the room, led by a frantic Mischa.

"Move!" He lunges toward the couch, placing a small body down beside me, forcing me to my feet.

The girl. All I see is red. In her hair. On her face. Her chest.

My mouth falls open in horror. "What happened?"

"Don't just fucking stand there!" Mischa cuts his gaze to me, and the ferocity in it takes my breath away. "Help me!"

Instinct guides my motions. I sink to my knees, gritting my teeth against the pain, and reach for the nearest item I can find—a small throw pillow. Wadding it in both fists, I press it to the largest splotch of blood as my mind tries to process the culprit of such a wound.

A knife?

Gun?

I must have asked the question out loud, because Mischa shoves my hands aside, his voice like thunder.

"She was shot. Move!"

His hands tear at the girl's chest, ripping her shirt away to reveal the true extent of the wound: a gaping hole on her left shoulder, gushing blood. She's still alive. My eyes track the fluttering motion of the pulse in her throat to ensure that much. But her eyes are closed, her breathing rapid and labored.

"Help me," Mischa snaps, raking his bloodied hands through his hair. "Fuck…"

There's no time to think. Plan. Something inside me takes hold and drives me closer to his side, submitting myself to his silent command: apply pressure with a wad of cloth he fished from seemingly nowhere. The girl moans when I press down, her eyelids fluttering.

Gritting his teeth, Mischa barks an order over his shoulder to Vanya. Only after my brain tries to decipher it do I realize he spoke in another language. Russian? Whatever he said makes the older man move in between Mischa and me, forcing me farther from the chaos.

Eventually, I find myself shoved beyond the room entirely, into a hall that opens onto a narrow room containing a bed and little else.

Here, I listen to the noise seeping through the walls. More shouting. Hushed voices. A lone, plaintive, childish cry.

Then nothing. The silence stretches on for what feels like an eternity, broken only by the eerie creaking of the old wood of the house. The stench of dust and musk irritates my nostrils, betraying the fact that this dwelling hasn't been inhabited in a long time. Another safe house?

I don't find any clues giving a definitive purpose. Just darkness and empty spaces. Eventually, the sounds of footsteps retreat down the hall and my heart kicks into overdrive. Hesitant, I linger near the door, unsure if I should exit the room myself in search of answers. In the end, the choice is made for me when the door opens from the outside.

A shiver runs down my spine as Mischa advances a step, his head cocked to seek me out, his gaze piercing.

"I suppose you're happy now," he says. "Your husband wants you back so badly, he's willing to kill a child just to do it—"

"Is she okay?" I can't seem to breathe again until he finally nods.

"For now," he says, advancing another step. "Does that disappoint you?"

I flinch, gritting my teeth against an impulsive reply. It's what he wants, I realize. To fight. He wants anger and rage. He wants to feed off it. Exhausted and sore, I find that all I can do is sigh, noticing the reality of his exhaustion even his bravado can't hide.

"You're covered in blood," I croak.

It paints him. The dark splotches almost seem like a part of his skin when seen through the darkness. I can smell it: salty musk that conjures unbearable memories. My fingers twitch, grasping at the air, and I approach the bed and snatch a ratty bit of cotton from one of the pillows. Balled in my fist, the fabric serves as a makeshift cloth.

Mischa stares blankly as I approach him with the cloth held before me. Days ago, the look in his eye would have made me fall back. Maybe it's the pain that drives me forward? I'm limping, inhaling sharply every time my foot connects with the floor.

Even so, he looks worse.

"Here…" My hands shake as I swipe at his chin with the edge of my makeshift rag. Stiff with disuse, the fabric barely soaks up any of the reddish liquid. I have to scrub, and scrub, and…

"Enough!" Mischa wrenches from my grip, slapping my hand away.

"Sit down." My voice is a shallow whisper in the shadow of his, but he stiffens regardless.

"Why?" he counters. "So you can have better access to my throat, Robert's wife?"

"No." I swallow hard, clearing my throat. By some miracle, I'm still holding the cloth. "So that I can help clean the blood off of you before she wakes up and sees."

Something flashes across his gaze too quickly to identify. Shock, maybe? Like I've struck him. Perhaps I should. The boiling tension from the last few weeks feels like it's building to a fever pitch beneath my skin, tainting every bit of muscle and bone. Violence is a tempting outlet.

For me and for him.

I gasp as he grips my wrist, which forces me to take a step closer. At the last second, he turns and winds up dragging me toward the rickety mattress in the corner. It expels a cloud of dust as he sits, flooding the already still air.

"Before she wakes up," he parrots, tugging me even closer. "But will she? Not if your husband has any say in that—"

"I would never want to see the death of a child," I snap, tugging my arm away.

"Is that so?" His voice. He sounds too damn smug.

Here and now, I can't overlook yet another childish jab at my past. Not again. "You want to know?" Exasperated, I pose the question without thinking it through, and my heart pounds as if in protest. *No, no, no.* "Fine," I rasp, despite myself. "I did have a baby. But he—"

It's like rocks lodge in my throat, formed from years of suppression. I don't revisit these memories. Not even as every other vivid horror echoes on an endless loop. Never this. Maybe it's the one way I've followed completely in Marnie's footsteps: Some things are easier to ignore.

Closing my eyes, I inhale deeply, fighting for the strength. I can't think. Only speak. "Robert wanted the baby, at first."

It feels strange to say so out loud. Despite his overbearing possession and meticulous planning of our life together, the one-time reality shattered his façade, he welcomed it.

"I think he thought it was a benefit to him." The cold, detached woman speaking sounds like me. At the same time, I feel as much a listener as Mischa: spellbound by a story that sounds so foreign. Like it happened to someone else. "I didn't—I was… I didn't want him. Not right away."

I had nightmares, in fact. Of a tiny female or male Robert with soulless eyes. Horrible, terrible nightmares.

"But then… I started to feel him." My hand flutters to my stomach, chasing that phantom sensation. It's so real to me, even now. A strong, insistent pressure, like reassurance. There was a chance that whatever was growing inside me could turn out to be just like Robert. But it was a chance. He deserved that chance.

"My feelings changed. I think that's when he started to resent it."

I recall the slow, deliberate increases in Robert's coldness to me. The searching looks he'd cast my way. The narrowed, suspicious glances whenever he noticed me standing as I am now, with my fingers ghosting my belly.

"It's crazy… But I noticed that my meals would decrease in size. He took more maids—practically paraded them in front of me. He made—" I break off, brushing my fingers along my lips. Why? It could be the silence lingering in the wake of my confession. I don't think he's ever let me talk like this before—uninhibited, without a single cruel interruption.

"What happened next?" he prods, but his voice lacks the venom I'm used to.

"Robert got angry. I had an…*accident*, and he was stillborn," I croak. "They took him away before I could even hold him. See him. I never got the chance…"

I shake my head and lock the images away before they can descend.

"I've never spoken about it before."

Mischa is silent for so long that I think he's satisfied. Finally, he makes a low sound in his throat as if he just solved a tricky puzzle.

"Robert. It was *his* name you call out in your sleep," he deduces. "Not—"

"Yes." A dry swallow pushes the rest of the memories back. Turning to Mischa, I find him watching me, his expression more unreadable than ever. "Call me a bitch, or a whore, or Robert's fucking wife—that's fine. But don't you dare for a second insinuate that I don't know what pain feels like."

Fire sears across my vision. I'm blinking too rapidly to see. Just blurred smears of light and shadow. Swiping at my eyes with the back of my hand, I start toward where I guess the door to be.

"Wait."

Shock lances through me as he snatches my arm and tugs me backward. Why? So he can rub my nose in more agony?

"Here," he grunts, and I jump as he presses something rough against my palm.

My trembling fingers struggle to identify it: coarse, gritty, bloodstained fabric, I realize looking down. While I'm caught by his grip, he forces me to unfurl the rag and lift it to his jaw.

Up this close, there's no telling just who the blood belongs to. The girl? Him? Another? There's just so damn much of it. I can taste the salt on my tongue, cloying there like so many spilled secrets and dark memories.

Grunting, Mischa presses my hand to his cheek, issuing a silent command. *Clean me up.*

I watch my hand contort and move seemingly on its own, rubbing ineffectively at the drying substance. He'll need water and soap if he wants to make a real difference. Still, he makes me rub and scrub until he's only symbolically clean.

To him, maybe that's enough.

$\mathcal{I}$ don't know how I fall asleep. Or where, exactly…

Blinking, I let my exhausted brain piece together various clues like a faulty jigsaw puzzle. A looming ceiling. Dark, wooden floors. A dust-covered blanket shrouding my sore, aching limbs. I force my fingers to curl, grasping the edge of the stiff cotton. Vanya did it, his kindness striking once again.

Telling myself that is the only way to keep my heartbeat steady enough for me to deduce the rest of my surroundings. I'm sitting directly on the hardwood floor. In a corner? A quick glance around reveals shadow broken by strips of yellow sunlight streaming in through boarded-up windows. The safe house. I recall that much.

Among other things.

Like the man looming above me, standing so tall that he nearly blots out everything else.

"Get up." He sounds rough, but I can't tell if it's due to exhaustion or rage. He changed during the few hours I slept, exchanging his fatigues for a pair of dark pants and a gray shirt. His arms are bared beneath quartered sleeves, and in the dim lighting, his tattoos resemble tendrils of darkness attempting to swallow him whole.

Cautiously, I rise to my feet, clinging to the wall for balance. I slept in the same room he cornered me in, tucked into a space across from the bed. Through the doorway, I can make out the couch in the other room. Did they move the girl during the night?

"Look at me." Mischa stops short of actually touching me, though his hand parts the air between us, ghosting the length of my jaw.

"Is the girl okay?" I ask, ignoring the part of me aching to flinch. Cower. Run.

"For now." He cuts his eyes to the doorway. "She's alive. But you and I need to talk about something else, Little Rose." Two heavy steps bring him closer to the door, allowing him to easily slam it shut. Turning to face me, he rakes his gaze along my body, his eyes narrowing over what he finds. "You really want me to believe that little sob story you told?"

I blink, more shocked than angry. Deep down, I'm not really surprised. Expect a monster to reason? Only a fool would be so naïve.

"Of course not," I spit back. "That might require some human compassion—"

Rugged fingers capture the back of my hand and the rest of my insult dies on my tongue.

"Compassion?" he wonders, tracing the line of a vein up my wrist.

Paralyzed by disgust, I can only watch, hating the feel of his skin on mine. "Let me go."

"Let's not play any more games." Something in his voice draws my interest. It's deeper than before. Tired. As if he stayed up all night, mulling this potential conversation over in his head. "No more lies. No more pretty word games. You give me what I want, and I will give you what you want."

My throat goes dry. Tentatively, I flick my tongue along my lips. "And what do I want?"

He cocks his head back, and of all things to shape his mouth, this new expression is the most alarming yet. A dangerous, half-moon shaped smirk that conveys more than the malice I'm used to. It's resigned. As if he's confident that whatever he's about to ask me to do, I'll refuse. And he's counting on it.

"You want revenge, Little Rose," he tells me. "Though I doubt you even realize—no." He shakes his head, suddenly stern. "Don't argue just yet. You want revenge on your husband, and I can give you that and more."

"But what do you want?" I demand, overlooking his assertion—for now. "You have his accounts. His secrets. I've told you everything I know—"

"And that's the problem." The intensity in his voice makes my heartbeat stutter to nothing more than a thready pulse.

He's closer, leaning in to bring his mouth near my ear. His stench assaults me, heavy and ripe. I don't think he's bathed since last night and it shows: blood and musk.

"I've drained your little skull dry, but it's not *your* head I'm after." Two of his fingers stab at my tangled hair, working their way through the matted strands. "It's his. I want to know what makes him tick, Rose. I want to know the little secrets and fucking fears even you aren't privy to. He thinks he can take me on? Well, I'm going to destroy that motherfucker from the *inside* out."

The stress he puts on *inside*…

My cheeks flame and I step back, wrenching out of his reach. "So you think the key to 'knowing' Robert is sleeping with me?"

"No." He frowns as if insulted and advances a step, heedless of how it blocks me in—though maybe that's his real motive in the end. His fingers return to my hair, parting the strands and testing the weight of a lock against his palm.

My chest tightens as I watch him. I half expect him to smell it, some primal action that would make more sense than what he actually does. He twists the stringy locks. Pets them.

"You are the key to that motherfucker," he declares after a moment. "Inside you. That's how I'll destroy him."

"You're insane." I croak, attempting to turn away.

"No." He tugs on my hair, forcing me to face him again. "I'm impatient, Little Rose. As I said before, give me what I want and I'll let you have a little taste of the one thing you've convinced yourself all along that you didn't crave."

"And what is that?"

His teeth flash. "Power."

"Really?" A mocking laugh sticks in my throat. "*You* crave power."

"Bullshit," Mischa counters. "You want it, all right. You just don't know how to fucking reach out and take it. But I can show you—"

"Oh?" I fail at bravado; my voice is a dry rasp. "And how will you do that?"

He smirks, and this time, the expression unnerves me even more. "I'll put some right in the palm of your greedy, fucking hands."

He eyes the hands in question, still grinning. Then, all at once, his mouth falls flat as footsteps approach and the door opens from the other side.

"Mischa," Vanya calls, his expression wary. "You were right. Winthorp has his men staked out for at least ten miles in either direction. He's blocking us in."

"Good." Mischa shrugs and passes him to enter the adjoining room, where a tiny body lies bundled on the couch.

The girl. I don't think I breathe until I notice her chest rise and fall with labored breaths. She's alive.

"He's planning another attack—but he'll try to isolate her first. So let him think he's won," Mischa suggests to Vanya. "In fact…" He turns to me, a mocking half smile on his lips. "I'll even let him get a taste of his prize."

"How?" Vanya wonders.

"Wait ten minutes and then lead the men west," Mischa says. Then he grabs my arm and drags me through a door that opens onto a narrow porch. One of the vans is parked nearby and he shoves me toward it before returning inside the house.

Seconds later, a low cry draws my attention to the doorway. Bundled in Mischa's arms is the girl, so pale that she practically glows in the faint sunlight.

"What are you doing?" I've stepped toward him without realizing it, my hands outstretched as if I mean to grab the girl from him.

Raising an eyebrow, Mischa descends the steps, barreling past me. "I'd concern yourself with what *you* are doing, Robert's wife," he grunts as he shoulders open the door to the back of the van and gingerly sets the girl on the farthest back seat. Crouching beside her, he looks at me and jerks his chin to the driver's seat. "She needs a doctor, and *you* are going to get her safely to one. Drive."

Icy shock paralyzes me. "You're insane," I croak.

"Yeah." He nods. "That's how I've fucking survived this long, Little Rose. Now, get in the fucking van—"

"No." I'm already backing away, shaking my head. "I can't drive."

Something crosses his face too quickly to track. Shock?

"Well, today, you're going to learn."

My heart stops as he lunges from the van and I'm reminded of just how big he really is: a towering hulk of sinew and muscle. He grabs my shoulder and steers me to the driver's seat only to shove me onto it.

"Gas," he grunts, pointing to a metal knob jutting above the floor. "Brake." He points to another knob beside the first. "Just keep us on the fucking road."

He slams the door after me only to climb into the seat directly behind mine.

"Now, drive." His breath bastes the back of my neck like a furnace, impossible to ignore. "And," he adds, "if you think of stopping to pay your husband a little visit, think again."

A hard surface nudges the back of my skull, a warning.

"Now, go."

"H-how?" My shaking fingers can barely grip the steering wheel.

"Turn it on," Mischa prompts, his tone oddly patient for once. "Like this." Reaching over me, he twists a key already in the ignition and the van roars to life.

From there, I manage to pull onto a narrow country road just beyond the driveway without prompting. If he's surprised, he says nothing.

But that distracting pressure is never withdrawn. I'm forced to contend with the silent threat it conveys while struggling to make sense of our surroundings—desolate, empty wilderness and a lone gravel road. Just where are we?

And where exactly is he taking us now?

"Why me?" I ask without taking my eyes off the road. We're traveling at a snail's pace, and Mischa nudges my shoulder in another silent command: go faster. Warily, I press the gas only to slam on the brake a second later as the van jerks forward. "Why aren't you driving?" I rasp, hunched over the wheel, my heart racing.

"Why?" He sighs like he's thinking over his answer. Then he scoffs. "Use that brain of yours, Little Rose." Again, he taps my skull with that threatening, heavy object. "Take a guess. Who do you think is watching you right now?"

"Robert?" I risk taking my eyes from the road long enough to scan the desolate fields and copse of trees beyond us. A second's appraisal reveals nothing. No long-lost husband lurking in the bushes. None of Robert's men, either.

"Don't be so naïve," Mischa hisses into my ear as if reading my mind. "He's not hiding in a tree, Little Rose. But he is watching. Yes." He inhales as if sensing the fear wafting from my skin. "And you know it—"

"I could have left the other night, you know..." I swallow hard as his eyes cut in my direction. I'm not sure why I'm confessing this now. "One of his men found me. I could have left."

"So why didn't you?"

"I don't know." I try to look at him directly, but that pressure on my skull grows.

"Look at the road," he snaps as I swerve to stay on the thin strip of gravel. "Let's just hope your husband keeps his distance now. Go faster."

Again, I hit the gas too hard and the car jolts forward. This time when I hit the brake, a small moan comes from the back seat.

"Easy!" Mischa snaps. Suddenly, a shadow flickers from the corner of my eye and a wall of heat maneuvers into the seat beside me. "Look forward," he commands as a heavy touch lands over my thigh, guiding how much pressure I apply. "Keep going straight until I say so."

He's crouched low, trying to hide as much of his bulk as he can—which is very little. His head is near my shoulder, his gaze intent. I feel it burning through my thin clothing to scorch the flesh and bone underneath.

"Faster," he warns before applying more pressure to my thigh, sending the speed gauge even higher.

At this speed, my fingers struggle to keep the vehicle straight. It's like I'm controlling my heartbeat more than four wheels and a metal carriage—with every touch, it strains against the bounds of my control.

Though maybe Mischa isn't even the cause. For the first time, I glance at the rearview mirror and Mischa has to grab the wheel in my stead, shouting as the car careens off course.

"What the fuck is wrong with you?" he hisses.

All I can say in response is, "We're being followed."

The sight of a black van in the distance isn't what triggers the panic building in my chest. It's a feeling. A deep-seated knowledge in my bones.

With every inch the approaching van gains, a part of me squirms in grim acknowledgment.

Robert didn't send just his men this time.

"Fucking focus!" Mischa grips my chin hard enough to reinforce his presence. "When I say so, you take your hands off the wheel and slam on the gas. Don't fucking let up. You got it?"

A hard swallow robs me of speech. All I can do is nod.

"Good."

I wait, but he doesn't increase the pressure on my leg, not even as the black van drifts closer and closer…

"Not yet," he scolds when my foot twitches against the gas unprompted.

The van is still too far away to make out the figure in the driver's seat—not that I need to. Robert never drove himself; he was always surrounded by his retinue of bodyguards. But he's here. I feel it. I can taste it—the fear that chokes me whenever he's near.

Like blood and ash. I'm suffocating on both.

"Now!"

My foot extends at the exact moment I'm shoved aside, crushed against the door by Mischa's bulk. At the same time, he snatches the steering wheel, twisting it hard to the left.

Vomit crawls up my throat as the world twists and turns. Tires squeal. Another cry comes from the back seat, and above it all, a deep voice reiterates the same statement.

"It's all right. It's all right."

The reassurance isn't directed at me, but it acts as an anchor anyway. I'm grounded by the unsettling baritone as my body is flung toward an unseen destination. Whether it's a comforting presence remains to be seen.

"It's all right. It's all-fucking-right."

I don't know how long he makes me stay like that, pinned beneath him, my foot on the gas. For hours, it seems like. When he finally grunts out a command to let up, my leg is cramping.

"Switch places."

The van drifts aimlessly as he shifts his weight to shove me into the passenger's seat while he claims my place with envious dexterity. The man moves like a dancer in some ways. In others, he's like a battering ram.

Looking out the window, I can't even begin to place our surroundings. Trees loom in every direction, rendering the landscape more desolate than before. There's nothing around for miles.

Including Robert's van.

"Where are we?" I warily ask.

"Far away from your husband." Mischa's disarming half-smile returns and my stomach dips in response. "Don't look so disappointed." He frowns, turning his attention to the back seat. The next second, the van skids to a stop and he's leaping from the vehicle and climbing into the back. Craning my neck, I see what caught his attention: the girl utterly still on her back.

She isn't moving.

"Fuck!" Mischa's beside her in seconds, tugging her small body into his arms. "Don't," he snarls. His eyes are wide—crazed. I've never seen him like this. "Don't you fucking dare, Aljona. Don't you fucking dare…" He lowers his head, eyeing her chest intently. Whatever he senses makes him sigh and he sets her down. "She's alright—"

"And you care." I don't mean to sound so cold. Judgmental, even.

"Don't sound so hopeful, Little Rose," Mischa scolds as he backs out of the van. "There's still some shrapnel in her shoulder that needs to be removed. How else can I sell her without keeping her alive?"

I try not to flinch. He's baiting me, and this time, I refuse to bite.

"You called her Aljona," I point out, my throat dry. "Is that her name?"

I know it isn't.

"What?" Mischa flinches and looks away. Annoyed? "She'll live," he says instead, slamming the door to the back seat. As he returns to the driver's seat, I hear him grunt, "For now."

"And you *do* care about her." Maybe I'm needling him. Maybe I need to see his face as it hardens against that assumption. He grits his teeth, glowering at the road.

But he doesn't deny it out loud.

Not once.

A monster could be concerned for the welfare of a child— but in my world, that shouldn't be the case. Robert taught me well, after all.

Or perhaps only now can I reconcile the fact that he only ever told me lies.

CHAPTER 23

"Wake up."

Someone shakes me roughly by the shoulders until I peel my eyes open. Mischa. He stares down on me, his face partially bathed in shadow.

"Come," he grunts, jerking his chin toward the open door of the van. "We need to move."

He reaches past me and gingerly grabs the girl, drawing her into his arms. Hunched over her pale body, he slips out of the van and into the night. I follow him warily, waving my hand to feel through the dark as my eyes adjust.

We've reached another deserted house, but this one isn't quite as desolate as the previous shack. Made of stone, it towers above, its silhouette illuminated by a row of windows on the bottom floor, ablaze with orange light.

We don't walk far before Mischa ushers me through a wooden door and slams it behind us.

"Vanya!" he shouts, barging past me, down a narrow hall that opens onto a wide entryway dominated by a circular staircase. "Vanya! Where the fuck are you—"

"Here!" The steps rattle as Vanya descends them. Then he stops halfway. "The doctor is ready. Bring her up."

They dash to the upper level and I'm alone. Literally. None of Mischa's men are lurking in the visible corners. I doubt there's anyone guarding the door we just entered from. If I wanted…

No. I shake my head, inhaling sharply. I *should* want to—leave. Run. Escape Mischa, and forget Robert. I'd try to make it on my own, far from the whims of spiteful men and their petty wars. I'd be free—

A high-pitched whine cuts the air and my body goes rigid. A scream? Before I even register moving, I'm halfway up the stairs, clinging to a rickety banister for balance.

This home is more spacious than the last. A long hallway stretches in a half-circle with numerous doors branching off of it. The door to one has been left open, revealing the chaotic scene within.

Mischa and Vanya have the blond girl pinned to a wide bed, one at each of her shoulders, while another figure hovers above her, a metal instrument glinting in his grasp. My heart lurches to my throat, and I start forward, unsure of whether to help or do nothing.

Her chest is bare and a circular gash in her shoulder stands out in stark contrast to her frail, pale skin.

"Keep her still," Mischa barks as the man I assume to be the doctor lowers a blade to the girl's wound. "Keep her—fuck! You!" His eyes lock onto me and narrow. "Don't just stand there. Do something!"

I jolt forward and grasp the only part of the girl within my reach. Her hand. I squeeze it as I sink to my knees beside the mattress and focus on her face. Sweat glistens on her forehead, and her eyes dart aimlessly around the room, the lids fluttering.

"It's all right," I tell her as the men continue to shout and clamor around us. "You'll be okay. It's all right."

Her eyes meet mine, wide and watering. She doesn't speak —not a single word—but I keep talking for the both of us, long after her eyes finally close.

"It's all right…"

Hours later, the doctor leaves and Mischa lifts the girl from the bloodied sheets. A square bandage on her shoulder is the only clue as to the wound lurking beneath, freshly cleaned of any shrapnel. She's unconscious, but her breathing is easier and Mischa takes care with her limp limbs, ensuring that her head is supported with every step he takes.

In the end, he doesn't go far, carrying her to the next room over. This one is smaller, containing a narrow bed with clean sheets. Drawing them back with one hand, he sets her down and covers her gently. Too gently.

Aware of me watching, he stiffens as he returns to his full height. "Have you grown tired of hiding your role as a spy for your husband?" he wonders coldly. "Good. Your boldness will make it easier to hunt you down when you finally go crawling back—"

"I told you before. I could have left." I sound so tired. The statement hanging in the air could refer to the weather for all the emotion it contains. Still, I sigh and give him a half-hearted performance of the show he seems to crave. "But if you want to lash out, I'll give you a reason. Why are you so afraid to let me see that you care about her?" I nod to the girl.

"My investment, you mean?" he counters, gesturing to her body with a wave of his hand. "I'm sure she'll fetch a good price on the black mark—"

"Enough!" I reach up, raking my fingers through my hair as if to arrange my thoughts before he can knock them off track—which seems to be his only goal.

Unnerving me.

Inhaling deeply, I meet his gaze and suppress a shiver that racks my spine. "So the monster has a soft spot for children," I say, my voice devoid of any mocking innuendo. "Why are you so against letting me see that?"

"See what?" He steps in close. His chest jars mine, knocking me off balance. When I step back, he advances, herding me into the hall. "Don't let your naïve little hopes deceive you, Rose—"

"You're right." I turn away from him. We're alone and the fact strikes me as odd. No Vanya. None of his men. Why? At least there are no witnesses. "I'm done being naïve," I continue, wringing my fingers together. "So I'll take you up on your offer. I'll give you my body—"

"Don't play." His sharp intake of breath catches me off guard.

Blinking, I scan his face, hunting through those dark eyes for any hint of the lust conveyed in that violent sound.

"Go on," he snaps, baring his teeth. "Or are mind games another trick you learned from your husband?"

"No," I admit truthfully. "He never taught me how to gamble. But he did teach me the power of bartering."

Sex for safety.

Brutality for security.

Ignorance for a lie.

"So I'm making you an offer. I'll give you my body—"

"And?" Mischa interjects. He's regained his composure already, and I force a hard swallow. "Name your fucking price."

"Fine… I want you," I tell him with a sigh. "You can 'learn' Robert through my body, but in return, you give me *you*.

You let me inside your head. You give me whatever I want to know—"

"Prove it." He encroaches on my personal space a second time, towering above, his breath on my forehead—but I don't back away.

Meeting his gaze, I swipe my tongue across my lower lip to find enough traction to voice, "How?"

He rakes his gaze down my front and jerks his head toward the end of the hall. When he moves, I'm forced to catch up, trailing in his wake like a lamb being led to slaughter.

Will I cower before his blade?

Or bare my neck for the lethal kiss?

"Strip," he commands as he shoulders yet another door open, revealing a larger room and a small bed. The mattress greets me mockingly, draped in a single crisp sheet. "Then get on the bed."

My fingers obediently fly to the fastenings of my jeans. "But first…" I scan the room, desperate to come up with my own test. In the end, I blurt out the first question to cross my mind. "The girl. What's her name?"

He hesitates. A sound catches in his throat—a cruel insult, I think. His first instinct is always to resist me. Bite. Roar. Anything to disguise the hint of weakness.

"I told you my price," I remind him. Slowly, I let my hands fall to my sides. "Unless you don't want—"

"She doesn't speak." As his breath fans the back of my throat, I jump. "So I don't know what it really is. I call her Mouse. She answers to it well enough."

"Mouse," I echo. Not bitch. Or whore. Or a mocking twist on a flower.

"Now, your turn," Mischa prompts, radiating impatience.

I picture him standing there behind me, his hands inches from my skin, ready to rip and tear into it. Then I let my eyes drift shut as I find the front of my pants and peel them open. It's surprisingly easy to tug them down my thighs and kick them off. My shirt takes more time to wind up. Maybe I'm testing him. Teasing him.

His breaths seem to grow hotter the more my skin is bared. Another low growl catches in his throat when I finally stand naked.

"Don't think you can just lie there like some sacrifice," he warns, drawing a single finger down my hip. "I need—want you to move. You moan. Don't you dare pretend like you're some martyr."

"I won't." I turn to face him, surprised by how true my voice rings out. "I don't mind having sex with you."

My cheeks sting to hear it said out loud.

"But that is all you will get from me without upholding your end of the bargain. A body. If you can't be honest with me—"

"But can you be honest with me?" He chuckles smugly, as if already aware of the answer. "It doesn't matter. You tout your body like it's a prize, but do you even know how to wield it?"

His hands fan out boldly over my hips, drawing me into him. Warm lips nudge my earlobe and I shudder. He's turned the tables already.

"You want power, Little Rose? I'll show you where it lies…"

The pad of his thumb traces a path down my belly, ghosting the flesh of my inner thigh before drifting even lower. Too low. Finger by finger, he cups me fully, forcing my legs apart. A low groan betrays his satisfaction as I resist my body's natural inclination to flinch.

"What men have killed for," he grates through clenched teeth. "Died for. And you don't even fucking know…"

All at once, he shoves me toward the bed. I throw my hands out in front of me, bracing myself over the lumpy mattress. Before I can regain my bearings, he's behind me, grasping my waist and flipping me over.

"I won't feed you the same lies he has," he tells me, sinking to his knees like a man before an altar. The altar of a despised deity he serves unwillingly.

Dark eyes flit over my naked skin, settling on my scars. My barely healed injuries. My eyes. He meets them directly, boring through me like a missile through paper.

"What lies?" I rasp when he hasn't elaborated.

He scoffs and my knees tremble as his breath scorches the flesh between them. One of his hands settles on my thigh, using it as an anchor to drag me close.

"The lies he used to keep you, Little Rose," he taunts, but the mocking smile shaping his lips falls flat. "You are beautiful. More than most women—even despite this." He gestures to my scarred limbs. "But that is not why he hunts you. Why he obsesses over you. Why, even now, the bastard is thinking of you. Dreaming of you…" A devious smile contorts his lips; he relishes that fact.

At the same time, it irritates him.

He slides his hand beneath my knee and tugs, opening me up to him further. "Ask me why," he murmurs as his gaze tracks a tortuous path down my neck, over my chest and lower… "Ask me."

Air wheezes in and out of my throat in pathetic bursts. I have to inhale deeply to find the strength to obey. "Why?"

"Because of your heart, Little Rose," he replies, sounding bitter.

Callused fingers inch along my skin, creating a numbing rhythm of sensation and friction. Up, up to my waist. Across. Down.

"Your eyes. You look at a man without the foolish hopes and dreams most women do. Or the greed." He sighs: a harsh sound between a growl and a laugh. "You look at a man…and you tempt him, Rose. You're naked and open, and you show him what he is back. Like a mirror. And some stupid men, like your husband… They believe that they can change that reflection. All they have to do is make you moan."

Wet heat explodes through my core, paralyzing me. Only vaguely do I realize what he's done as I watch his head move, crowned by wild, blond hair: use his tongue. *There.* Slowly and unhurriedly, without a goddamn care for the foreign sensations crashing through my body.

"If he can make you cry, Rose. Scream his name. Whimper." He speaks each word into me and my eyes flutter, threatening to roll. "Then he can…shape that reflection… He won't be a monster. Not anymore."

A cry chokes from my throat, drowning him out. All I can do is feel and writhe and reach for him. Push him away—I want to push him away. But my fingers disobey me, clenching through his hair, dragging him closer. Deeper. More. More more.

I'm on the brink, so close to going over the edge. One more flick of his tongue will get me there—I know it. So does he, because he draws back just as the sparks ignite and it's like dumping water onto a newborn fire.

"Like that," he tells me, his lips glistening, his eyes dark and unfocused. "You trick your men like that."

He makes it sound so evil. I tempt him. I torture him. *I'm* the one with the power, not him.

"Now…" He shoves his hands beneath me, cupping my ass, his nails drawn. "I'm going to—"

"No." I prop myself upright on my elbows and shove him off. Every movement takes twice the usual effort. It's like I'm drunk. His promise of power echoes in my head, drowning out all logic.

"Taking back your offer already?" he snarls.

"I want to taste you." Where did the words come from? I don't know. Unbidden and dirty—something I've never spoken before.

Taste. Only he makes it sound anything but degrading. It's a weapon. To learn and incapacitate your victim. To understand.

And I want to taste *him.*

His eyes narrow at the request. "I thought *your* body was the bargain?"

I can't think—so I don't. He doesn't expect me to buck free of his grip. His shock buys me seconds to slip from the mattress and grasp the front of his jeans. He stiffens like stone and it's nearly impossible to maneuver my fingers enough to undo the zipper.

"You bite me and I'll kill you," he hisses, betraying the source of his apprehension: He thinks I'll hurt him.

But when my tongue cradles the tip of him, I'm not sure what I want. Or what I'm hoping to find in his gaze as I part my lips around him. My heart pangs when he goes rigid. This is stupid. Demeaning.

But then his jaw goes slack around a hoarse gasp. His eyes widen. His head falls back, his lips parted. "Fuck..."

He breathes out with every stroke of my tongue and fists his hand through my hair.

And I feel it. Power.

His flavor explodes on my tongue, ripe and raw. His essence seeps through my skin, feeding me the secrets he won't say out loud.

Heat unexpectedly shoots through me, gathering between my legs. I'm rocking back and forth, grinding my thighs together to relieve the ache, even as he swells in my mouth, pulsing and thick.

"You think you're in charge, Rose?" He snaps his fingers to draw my attention, but I've never taken my eyes off him. "You are..." He reaches out, encircling my throat in his grasp. Then he squeezes just tight enough to tease the promise of danger. "This is what I can give you that he can't. *Control.*"

He tugs, forcing me to release him. Like a doll, he manipulates me to straddle his hips, his cock between my legs, throbbing on the brink of release.

"I can let you on top," he says with a groan as he lowers me onto him, inch by impossible inch. His mouth finds my ear as he swears, "I can let you set the pace. Take me as deep as you fucking can. I'm not afraid of you, Little Rose—not like him. I don't want a caged fucking bird." He grunts, bucking his hips as I settle against him, chest to chest, pelvis to pelvis. Our foreheads meet painfully, and his lips nudge mine, forcing them apart. "I want a woman," he says, snarling each word, forcing me to choke them down. "A woman who knows what she wants. Who knows which man can make her scream…"

My vision blurs as he rocks into me. Hard at first. Then unbearably slow. The greater the friction, the more weightless I feel.

Endless.

I don't even sense my climax until it barrels into me like a freight train. He grips me tighter, riding out his own release.

Spent, he shoves me off of him and throws his arm over my waist. This close, I feel his heart hammering madly in his chest. We're conjoined through sweat-slicked limbs and damp hair. Mine sticks to him, tugged with every move he makes.

He tenses, even before I break the silence.

"Tell me about your family." I'm testing him again.

He hisses at the challenge, his arm flexing over my hips. "I—"

"No," I say before he can reply. "Tell me… Tell me about your sister."

He turns to stone against me, painfully rigid. His arm is a steel beam, weighing me down and the heat from him cools as if snuffed out. "She died," he says, but there's more to it.

More than I know better than to ask for. The strength of his lust is the deciding factor here: Does he really want me so badly?

"And with her, so did my family. My father all but surrendered to the Winthorps after. I would have too, if it weren't for Vanya."

I stiffen. Vanya, who he loves like a father, and a man who may be mine as well.

"Does that bother you?" Mischa wonders. "That you could be his bastard?" He draws me closer, his lips finding my throat.

The intimacy of the embrace sends a shock through me—he knows that. Hell, he taunted me before, throwing my discomfort back in my face: *"You don't like to be touched."*

So he touches me, sliding his hands to the front of my belly.

"T-tell me about your father," I counter.

"He went mad when my mother died. And Aljona's death destroyed him." There's no emotion in his voice. He almost sounds too distant. Too detached—a stranger retelling some story he heard once upon a time. "But he grew bitter before the end. He started to resent the *mafiya*. Resent its leaders —Sergei most of all."

"And you?" For a second, I assume he didn't hear me. I'm not even sure where the question came from. Maybe it's something he said before: *"I know what it is like to be shunned by your own father."*

"He made his choice," Mischa says—but I cut too deep. His hands readjust in retaliation, sliding down my inner thigh. "And I made mine."

"And…" A grunt rips from me as he traces my outer lips in a series of featherlight touches. I pant, fighting to maintain my train of thought. "What about—"

"Let me ask *you* something. If your perfect husband waltzed into this place and demanded you go back. Would you?"

"I could have left—"

"But what if he had leverage?" Something in his tone makes my stomach churn ominously. "Like your sister. Or…your son?"

"Stop it!" I lunge for the side of the bed, but he tightens his grip, bear-hugging me to his chest. The more I struggle, the harder he grips me. Voice rasping, I choke out, "Why the hell do you like torturing me?"

"I'm *not*."

And that's the worst part. I can hear the pain in his voice as I go limp in his arms. He's hidden it well up until now—but Mischa Stepanov can only control his emotions for so long. And I don't want to think about why he's asking this now. Why, even as I struggle, he doesn't hurt me.

Why he won't let me go.

"I'm not," he repeats gruffly. "So answer the fucking question—"

"No!" I deflate as my voice echoes throughout the room, high-pitched and breathy. "I wouldn't go back. Never—"

"You want to know about me?" he says as if this is some twisted game of tit-for-tat. "My father disowned me. At first, I was too weak. Then too strong. Then too much like *them*." He chuckles darkly. "The Winthorps. My own father hated what I became—the same monster Anna saw. And Aljona. And Vanya…"

Suddenly, he shoves me aside and rises from the mattress. I watch him pace, the muscles in his back rippling with tension. "They were disgusted. They thought I was the corrupted one. But I am still alive, Little Rose." His eyes meet mine, shining with rage and anger and…pain. "I'm still alive. And them? Where are they?"

He storms from the room, leaving the silence to fill in the answer for him.

Where are they?

Gone.

The next morning, I visit the girl. Mouse. One night and she already looks better. Color paints her cheeks, and her eyes are open when I enter her room, tracking my every movement.

"Good morning," I say tentatively.

She blinks, but I notice her hands twitch over the surface of her blanket. She's alert, at least.

"I've brought you something to eat," I add, nodding to the tray I'm holding. Everything on it is courtesy of Vanya: cold porridge, bread, and ice water. "I'll leave it here."

I place the tray on the nightstand beside her bed. As I back away, she sits up and snatches the bread, breaking it in half. Watching her devour each morsel, I can't help but guess just how young she is. Ten maybe? Older?

Her frail, slight frame proclaims stunted growth, but her eyes are too bright for a younger child. Only God knows what she saw before the day Nicolai offered her up as a drug mule.

"Don't eat so fast," someone scolds from the doorway, making me jump. Dressed in gray fatigues, Mischa storms into the room, his arms crossed. "You'll make yourself choke. Are you a girl or a pig?"

He advances toward the bed and snatches the second half of bread from the girl's hand—but rather than flinch from him, she flashes a wicked grin and shoves the remaining bread into her mouth.

"Pig, then," Mischa says in disgust. He reaches out, ruffling the girl's ratty hair. His large palm covers nearly her entire skull, but she doesn't cringe at the contact. "Shame. Pigs can't learn to fight with knives. Not that you'll be getting any more lessons for a while—"

He breaks off and his entire body goes rigid. I must have made a sound. Shock flits across his expression as he spots me in the corner before a cold frown smothers all emotion. His hand leaves Mouse, curling into a fist as he turns for the door.

"Don't." I start after him. Almost against my will, my hand brushes his shoulder. "Stay. I'll go—"

Alarm steals my voice as he snatches my wrist, dragging me into the hall. Shadows obscure the corner he shoves me into. I can only make out the line of his jaw, stern and clenched. Without even seeing his face, I know he's angry. The man radiates rage the way some do their natural scent.

"I want to show you something," he says gruffly. "Tonight."

My mind goes blank. I'd been anticipating a scathing insult. Not a request. "W-what?"

He doesn't answer. Instead, he continues down the hall, leaving me to stare after him. Before descending the steps, he cocks his head, eyeing me from over his shoulder.

"You claimed before that you wanted answers. If you think you can stomach them, then be ready."

He comes for me at midnight, when the rest of the safe house has fallen silent. Dressed in black, he appears at the mouth of my room. Without glancing in my direction, he inclines his head. "Are you ready?"

"Yes." I lurch to my feet and enter the hall.

Without waiting for me to catch up, Mischa descends the stairs. In silence, we exit the house, entering the chill of night.

"Where are we going?" I whisper. Maybe I already know he won't answer—it's the act of defiance that matters. He can't order me around. I'm here because I want to be.

I half expect him to take me to the van—and predictably another far-off location where he makes a shady deal with a strange, imposing man.

My heart skips when he leads me off the path instead.

Amongst looming trees and the scuttling of night creatures, I find myself inching closer to him. Every footfall and sharp sound have me jumping, spotting specters in the dark.

"Here." Suddenly, he comes to a stop in a small clearing. Through gnarled branches, the moon looms above, casting barely enough light to see by. It doesn't help any that Mischa towers like a giant, drenching anything near him in shadow. "You have your questions? Ask them now."

"Why here?" I warily lick my lips. It's the perfect place for him to kill me once and for all, leaving my body where Robert could never find it.

He shrugs. "It's safe. Unless you've changed your mind—"

"Fine." I rack my brain for another question and come up with one easily. "Did I see Briar that night?"

He looks away. "And if you did?"

"Fine!" I turn, feeling blindly through the dark. "If you're not serious—"

"Let's hypothetically say that Briar Winthorp wandered from her brother, who offered to trade her life for yours. Does it matter in the end?"

My chest tightens. Could Robert really be so cruel?

Of course he could.

"Is she alive?"

He eyes me for so long that I assume he won't answer. "I'm not sure, but if he can't trade her, she's only a threat to his power."

I force myself to nod. "Fair enough."

"Any other questions while you're at it?" He's mocking me, but I eagerly take the bait.

"Tell me about my mother."

He shrugs, his expression suddenly distant. "You know most of what I know. She was taken by Sergei Vasilev, starting the war."

He's already told me this part of the tale. I don't know why it's still not enough. Maybe I'll always chase any hint of her I can—secrets and second-hand lies are all of her I'll ever have.

"Why?" I ask.

"Because your husband's father began flexing his muscle. Sergei decided he needed to be put in his place."

"So why continue this stupid feud if it was your *mafiya* who started this?"

"We didn't kill anyone, Rose," he snaps. "The Winthorps played dirty."

"But why keep it going for so long?"

He laughs. "Because it's all we know. Why do lions fight hyenas? It's life."

He makes it sound so damn simple. All of this violence and death. I think of Nikolaus, and Kostas, and Sergei.

Then I laugh brokenly, hating how hopeless I sound. "You're really okay with continuing this for forever?"

"Not forever." He reaches out, ghosting his palm along my cheek. "Just long enough."

I turn away, but my jaw burns in the wake of his touch. "So why keep me?"

"Do I really have to tell you again? What I want?" His hand captures mine, forcing me to face him. "This is what I want."

He doesn't give me the chance to resist. His lips descend over mine, his tongue invading. When I stiffen, his hand sinks into my hair.

"No." He draws back enough to nip my bottom lip between his teeth. "Don't fight it."

It. The way he tastes. How he feels. The longer he kisses me, the more my thoughts dissipate. He's worse than the drug Vanya gave me in the aftermath of my severed finger.

I can overcome an opiate, but not him.

"This," he breathes as my lips part further. "This is what I want. Little Rose, letting down her guard, dropping the act. You're mine." His hands cinch my waist, hungrily yanking me closer.

"S-stop!" Panting, I spring back, swiping at my mouth. Surprisingly, the kiss isn't what has my heart racing. It's a pathetic thought that should be the least of my concern. "I don't want to be your trophy—"

"Good. A trophy has no loyalty. It belongs to whoever snatches it at the end of a battle." His gaze rakes me over and narrows. "I don't want a token prize."

"So then what do you want?"

He throws his head back, exasperated. "Do not play stupid —because you aren't. You are not stupid."

"Maybe I need to hear it from you," I counter, breathless. "So just tell me—"

"Fine." He advances, backing me against a nearby tree. His fingers find my hair again, twisting in the strands of it. "Maybe I just like when you bite back. When you prove you're more than Robert Winthorp's pathetic little wife."

"Or maybe it's *you*," I suggest. "You're tired of being the wolf. I've seen you with Mouse. Even Vanya said—"

"Don't." He tugs sharply on my hair, yanking my head back. "Don't make pretty little assumptions you can't back up. You'll just hurt your delicate sensibilities, Rose—"

"But what if I need to?" It's a question I'm only brave enough to ask now. Not of him, but of myself. "What if I need to believe there's more to you than this?" I swipe my thumb across my scarred cheek and watch him eye the marks as well. "What if I need to believe there's more to you than a monster?"

"And why is that?" he demands, his voice low.

"Because…I don't want to crave a monster."

My cheeks sear at the confession, but it's too late. The words taint the air, spoken aloud, and I'm too exhausted to take them back.

He stiffens, suspicious as always. Narrowed eyes betray his first instinct: fight back. He surges forward, crushing me against moss and bark, and I tense, expecting an assault.

Anything but another kiss, deeper than the first. It's dangerous to let him in, but my body doesn't care. It rails against common sense, letting him invade and claim.

It betrays me in every fucking way.

Suddenly, Mischa pulls back, his gaze darting toward the shadows. "Shit," he hisses.

Dazed, my brain is slow to pick up on his unease. "What's going on?"

"Shh!" He slams his hand over my mouth, his body rigid. He's listening for something.

Or someone.

"Your husband might be more tenacious than I gave him credit for," he snarls into my ear. "We need to move. Now!"

Dirt and brambles crunch underfoot as we race through the dark. His grip on my arm is my only tether to stability, steering me forward.

The farther we go, the more disorienting it is trying to make sense of the swaying branches and uneven terrain.

"Stop!" Suddenly, Mischa drags me behind a tree. "Stay here. I'm going to see if we're being followed." He pulls away, slipping into the darkness.

In his absence, the noise of the forest echoes tenfold. Every scurrying creature and gust of wind is a rustling footstep or intruder.

"It's safe."

I jump as Mischa reappears between two trees and beckons me with a jerk of his chin.

"Come. It seems we have 'company.'"

We return to the house, where a black van is parked in the gravel driveway. For a second, I let my imagination play with the scenario that he finally decided to give up and sell me to Robert.

I'll find him waiting for me in the foyer, his smile smug.

Instead, Sergei Vasilev is there, casting a hulking shadow. "I've had some of my men help secure your perimeter. You're lucky I found your camp when I did," he says. "I had a feeling you wouldn't go far, and I don't mind extending my assistance. In return, I have only one request."

"Of course you do." Mischa's grip on my arm tightens. "And what is that?"

"To talk." He nods toward me. "Alone. One minute, no more."

"And if I refuse?"

Sergei laughs. "Don't be foolish, Mischa. Without my help, Robert Winthorp would already be knocking down your door. My resources have kept him at bay for now. Should I reconsider?"

Mischa grits his teeth. "You—"

"Mischa!" Vanya appears from the end of a nearby hall. "We need to talk."

"Fine, then. A minute, Sergei," Mischa says, pushing past him. "A minute."

"You look well enough," Sergei says in his absence, sweeping his gaze over me. "But you and I both know that any more of this reckless foolishness and you and everyone in this house will wind up dead."

"What do you want?"

"I want you to come with me," he says as if such a thing would be as simple as breathing. "See your ancestral home. Learn your real place."

I rub at my temples. It's surreal having him speak to me like this. There's no affection in his voice. Just desperation.

"Why should I?"

"Could you really keep your son safe here?" he asks. "With Mischa?"

Around me, the room spins and narrows as my mind goes blank. I finally notice something clutched between his fingers that I didn't before: a crisp, square envelope.

"W-What?" My voice shakes, so faint I barely hear it.

"This is proof." He shoves the envelope at me. "Proof that your son is still alive. And that only I can help you rescue him from Robert Winthorp."

I: (ONE)

ACKNOWLEDGMENTS

Mickey, thank you so very much for taking the time to help me perfect this draft. As always, your feedback and expertise have been invaluable. Thank you, Charity for applying the final touches on this draft.

Thanks so much to everyone who supported this draft along the way, including the many beta readers who provided encouragement along the way! Please keep in mind that this story includes dark, graphic and explicit content matter that is not suitable for readers under the age of 18—or for readers who are uncomfortable with the following subject matter: explicit sex, mentions of sexual abuse, and graphic depictions of violence.

My mother defined hell as a rose. One, she mused, with all the life sucked out of it. Its thorns had become knives, and the leaves swallowed up the stalk. Even so, underneath the violence, it was still beautiful.

I used to believe that philosophy was her subtle attempt at religion. But now, years later, I know what she truly meant.

Hopeless damnation isn't contained in a realm of fire and brimstone—but somewhere far more dangerous. It springs from your soul, growing on creeping vines, and claims your heart before you realize it.

In my mother's view, the worst torture couldn't be felt through pain, or death, or silence.

To her, hell was love—and it was every bit as insidious as a corrupted rose.

Mischa Stepanov has brutalized my body in ways I could have never imagined. My face bears his permanent mark, and he made me sever my own ring finger to feed his lie. He's toyed with me. Mocked me.

But this is the cruelest torture he's inflicted. His aim isn't to merely hurt me.

He's after my soul.

And his attack comes in the form of one sentence only he could deliver.

"I can help you find your son."

Even though Sergei Vasilev is standing before me, I know who's responsible for this. And I know that only lies lurk in the envelope brandished in his outstretched hand.

That's all this is: lies.

It *has* to be.

"You don't believe me?" Sergei's mouth twists into a contemplative frown. When I don't move, he raises the envelope higher, letting the ivory surface catch the dim light in the hall. "Fine. I'll say it again: I have proof that your son is still alive—"

"Please don't do this." I sound so hollow. Not angry. Not panicked. Just so damn tired. When he takes a step forward, I throw out my hand as if my trembling palm alone can ward him off. At least, for now, it does. "Please…"

"No?" A low hiss rumbles from his throat. A sigh? "I must admit that I expected you to receive this news differently."

"Did Mischa tell you?" I stare at my hands. The fingers twitch, aching to guard my ears against any more lies. "About my…*him*?"

"Mischa?" The inflection in his tone is convincing. He sounds confused—but I've already decided.

Only a man like Mischa would weaponize my darkest secrets against me. In fact, he'd relish in doing so.

"Well, he lied to you." I force a weak laugh as I scan the hall for my tormentor. Is he lurking there beyond the stairwell? Or maybe around the corner?

No matter the hiding place, he's somewhere close, savoring his victory.

"Mischa didn't tell me a thing." Sergei sounds too damn genuine. Smug, almost. He knows my captor better than I do.

"He's the only one I've told," I confess, hating myself for being so foolish. "No one else."

"Is that so?" Sergei surprises me by throwing his head back, and of all things, he…laughs. "Child, I've known about your son since the day he was born." When he meets my gaze, there is no amusement in his expression. Just unsettling insight that betrays a knowledge of so much more than I'm willing to accept. "In fact, I've known about *you* since the day you were born."

"How?"

I hunt his wizened features for any hint of a lie and come to one grim observation: He shields his emotions well. Better than Mischa. It's as if he can flick a switch, displaying only what he chooses to. And in this moment? His eyes reveal nothing.

"Your husband has hidden him well, your son," he says softly. "So well that my spies have gotten only a glimpse of him in four years—"

"How can I believe you?"

"You don't have to." He nods to the envelope. "You merely need to see for yourself."

He steps forward cautiously, giving me plenty of time to back away. When he's close enough, he presses the envelope into my hand and coaxes my fingers into curling over the square surface.

"I am the only one who can help you rescue him—"

"And Mischa can't?" Through watering, burning eyes, I watch his expression flicker—the briefest hint of irritation.

"Mischa rescue the son of his sworn enemy?" His doubtful tone reveals what he thinks of that scenario. "You and I both know that he could sooner chop the boy into pieces and sell him off to the highest bidder—"

"And you wouldn't?" God only knows why I'm even playing this game. The envelope in my fist burns. Every cell in my body warns me to let it go. I watch my nails flex over it, but the damn thing won't fall. Looking up, I meet Sergei's gaze directly. "Why would you even want to help me?"

"Because you are blood." His eyes flash, reinforcing the heat in his tone. "*He* is my blood."

Tears finally escape, obscuring my vision. When Sergei brushes his hand across my cheek, I can't even tell if the act contains genuine emotion or not.

"I want to teach you," he says. "You deserve a seat at the table, as my heir—"

"Your time is up, Sergei."

I stiffen at the sound of Mischa's voice.

He lurks near the mouth of the hall, paces away. When he spots Sergei's hand on my face, his eyes become slits. "I upheld my end of the bargain. Now, you can leave."

"I'll continue to provide my support," Sergei promises and he steps back—out of respect, not fear. "And if I'm needed, my men will know how to contact me. Goodnight."

I watch him push past me, toward the front of the cottage. His steps echo, slow and heavy, as if he expects me to take him up on his implied offer any minute.

But I remain silent, the perfect prey for Mischa to pounce on. His hand slams against the wall inches from my face, trapping me in place as he corners me from behind.

"Don't tell me," he murmurs into my ear. "I missed all the fun, didn't I—"

I push away from him and lunge for the stairs. Every step is a struggle, and by the time I reach the landing, I'm forced to hobble into the nearest room and slam the door behind me. Then I lean against it for good measure.

This small room contains only a bed and a rickety wooden chair in a corner—there's nothing to hide behind. I have no defense against the attack that I know is coming.

Sure enough, heavy footsteps rattle the floorboards in my wake.

"What did he say?" Mischa demands harshly through the door. He tests the handle once but doesn't push the door open. Yet. "What did he say?"

Closing my eyes, I try to ignore him—ignore everything. My psyche is a fractured mirror, and for so damn long, I've carefully hoarded the pieces, holding them in place with sheer determination.

Breathe…

Breathe…

"Fine, Rose. Play your little game of silence."

The walls themselves seem to sigh as Mischa retreats down the steps. He's angry. I'll pay for this later in the form of some insult or another.

I don't care.

His absence depletes my body of any ounce of fight and I slide to my knees. Through blurred vision, I scan the surface of Sergei's envelope. There are no markings on it. No hint as to its contents. My clenching fingers strain the thin parchment to the point of tearing it.

Then I throw it so hard that it bounces off the opposite wall.

"Ellen?"

Footsteps creep toward my door again. Not Mischa's, but someone slower, his pace uneven.

"It's me," Vanya says and I stiffen. Mischa probably sent him, utilizing another to do his dirty work. "Are you all right?"

"I'm…" In my mind, I envision those shattered pieces that make up who I am. To hold them together, I need to lie. Push back all remnants of the past. Suppress. Repress. Ignore. Ignore. Ignore.

I attempt to, but the pieces shatter further, and I can't protect myself from the aftermath.

"You knew Marnie Winthorp," I croak.

He's silent for so damn long. I try to imagine his expression, but I can't. He is an enigma, so different from the callous men I'm used to. Unlike them, Vanya has yet to lie to my face, or hit me, or deceive.

Which makes him more dangerous than a thousand Mischas combined. He's earned my trust on his own merit.

I can only hope I've earned his honesty.

"Did you?" I press to break the silence.

"Yes," he finally admits. His voice is so hollow that I barely recognize it. "I knew her."

"H-how?" Those vicious scenarios Mischa posed creep into my thoughts. *Brutalized. Kidnapped. Raped.*

I squeeze my eyes shut, desperate to fight the onslaught that I know is coming. But it's too late. More tears creep beneath my eyelids and spill down my cheeks in spite.

"You're crying." A gentle thud rattles the door as if he braced his hand against it from the other end. "Ellen…"

"Did you hurt her?" I ask, choking my sobs down. I can't seem to breathe again until his heavy sigh slips through the crack in the doorway.

"Never," he swears. "I would have never hurt her—"

"Did you hate her? She was your enemy," I point out. Before he can reply, I add, "Did…did you love her?"

Seconds of silence trickle into minutes.

"Tell me about her," I demand, changing tack again. "Please."

"She was brave," he says haltingly. "So damn brave. You wouldn't expect it, coming from a tiny thing like that. She was beautiful too…" The door bows against my back as if he's leaning against it from the other end. "So damn beautiful. I would never hurt her."

"But you kidnapped her," I insist. "Or your brother did, or…" I bury my face in my hands, digging my fingers into my temples. "It doesn't matter. You took her and then she escaped. But how? Why?" It takes everything I have to bite back the most important question of all.

Why did you abandon me?

"I don't know what you've been told," Vanya says, as gentle as always. "Some of it, admittedly, might be true. But some…" He sighs again and the wood creaks, protesting against more pressure exuded on it from the other side. I wonder if the damn thing will give way altogether. He'll break through.

Just as the hinges start to squeal, the pressure recedes and the wood jarringly snaps back into place.

"Just know this," he says thickly. "She was never my captive. Not for one second. And she didn't escape. I let her go—" His voice breaks, but he grunts, regaining his composure. "I let *her* go. Goodnight."

"Wait." I scramble to my knees and reach for the doorknob —but he's already gone and my eyes continue to overflow.

No man on Earth could fake the pain in his voice—or the raw honesty, either.

No matter the circumstances of their relationship, I don't doubt that he let Marnie go.

Or that *she* went back to Robert Winthorp, Sr. of her own accord.

Which means…*she* let me live as her dirty, unwanted secret.

And maybe most telling of all…

If Sergei wasn't lying, then she never even told my father about *me.*

CHAPTER 2

It feels like hours pass before I finally gather up the strength to stand and cross over to that crumpled envelope. I lift it carefully from the floor and wipe away the dust and grime newly coating that mocking white. Then I shove it beneath the bed's lumpy mattress and turn away, pushing it from my mind altogether.

Maybe I just don't have the heart to rip it into pieces like I should.

Or perhaps I just need it to serve one pathetic purpose: proof. Unlike Marnie Winthorp, I refuse to be used as a pawn, shuffled between players on the gameboard. From now on, I can only act on what I know. What I feel in my bones.

My past must stay dead.

I can't be manipulated again.

And it feels so damn good to leave that room, knowing that the only person driving my actions is me. Even as I sway unsteadily on trembling legs—at least I'm no longer Marnie's naïve mistake or Mischa's unwilling victim.

But as I wander the rickety hall beyond the staircase, I'm forced to admit one reality: I'm still a mouse trapped in a maze.

At least I'm not the only creature forced to jump through the hoops of this new world. Not far from the other room, I come across the one the little girl's lying in. My fellow Mouse, in the literal sense. Despite the late hour, she's sitting upright in bed, staring intently as a hulking figure attempts to spread jam on a piece of toast.

"Too much or not enough?" he gruffly inquires, holding his slathered slice up for input.

Unsatisfied, Mouse wrinkles her nose and shakes her head in a silent command. *More.*

"Fine." Sighing, Mischa applies another layer of jam. "Do you know how much sugar is in this shit? You're going to be bouncing off the walls—"

I must have made a sound, because he turns, breaking off. Oddly enough, my presence is acknowledged with only a grunt before he returns his attention to the girl.

"The old man says you can start walking around tomorrow," he continues, presumably referring to Vanya. "But I don't know… All this sugary shit and you might be able to *fly.*"

He relinquishes the slice of bread, which the girl promptly shoves into her mouth.

Looking at him, she cuts her eyes in my direction and Mischa copies her. Then he laughs.

"You watch your mouth," he scolds, running his palm over her scalp. "It's rude to call people names."

"And what is that?" I ask, stepping over the threshold.

Both figures turn to me and share another mischievous look.

"That's it," Mischa declares. My cheeks prickle with heat as he throws his head back and laughs more genuinely than I think I've ever heard. "Bedtime." He snatches the tray of bread and jam and places it on a table beyond her reach. "No more sweet stuff for you. You get too mouthy." He looks at me, still smirking, and my heart lurches.

Strip him of anger and he can appear human.

But like this?

He's a different man, glimpsed through the window of a rare second when he has no guard to maintain or façade to uphold.

But just as quickly, the hardened criminal returns and his smile transforms into a seething glare.

"I'll be back," he barks to Mouse before advancing on my position. "But first, Little Rose and I need to have a chat—"

I turn before he can finish and lead the way back to the room I came from while he follows. Rage lashes from him like a weapon. It slices at my skin, fighting to leave a mark —but my new armor is impenetrable, it seems: I've just stopped caring.

"What did he say to you?" Mischa demands as he barrels into the room, slamming the door. The violent thud echoes like a gunshot—and all I can do is laugh in its terrifying wake. "Something funny, I'm guessing?" He grabs my arm, wrenching me around to face him. "Did you two come up with some hilarious little scheme to—"

"Kiss me."

"What?" He blinks, his words ending in a shocked grunt.

I've startled him so greatly that he loosened his grip, but I don't capitalize on my new freedom. I endure him. Desperate, my nostrils flare for his scent and I choke it down with every breath—it's the only way to keep the dark memories Sergei unearthed at bay.

By dancing with another devil.

"Kiss me." I tilt my head back to meet his gaze fully, watching rage go to war with confusion. "Do it," I add. "Or was all that talk about wanting me just that? Talk—"

"Fine." He reclaims my shoulders, yanking me forward.

Our lips meet fiercely—teeth on flesh. Nipping. Tearing. Bruising.

But *I'm* the one doing the most damage. Like this, I can't think. He demands my sole attention, grinding his presence into my skin, forcing me to react. Breathe. Feel. There is no room for doubt, or pain, or anything else.

Just Mischa.

Luckily, consuming me is one task he doesn't hesitate to fulfill. His hands rake through my hair, teasing out any thoughts that don't contain him as he backs me toward the bed. Shoves me onto it. While I fight to catch my breath, he grabs my thighs, spreading them apart as his fingers come to tease me open.

"Look at me."

He's still fuming. Our conversation isn't finished yet—but he draws it out nonverbally instead. A searching thumb shoved inside me contains a futile plea he won't ever voice out loud: *How can I trust you?* Brutally, he repeats that refrain, thrusting inside me over and over as my toes curl. *How? How? How?*

All I can do is relax into the violence and compile my own primal answer. How can he trust me?

By letting me in. My tongue at first, sliding along his lower lip. Then my hands, sinking through his hair. Gradually, he removes his thumb from inside me and replaces it with something larger—and presents a more pressing question.

Can you ever trust me?

My body isn't sure at first. Tension seizes my muscles, paralyzing me. He's too fucking big—and though I've already taken him multiple times, this moment feels different.

The thin mattress is unforgiving. There's no resistance to each shallow thrust of his hips as tender flesh molds to his shape like clay. When he finally moves inside me, he goes too deep. So deep that it hurts, and the only way to soothe the ache is to close my eyes and surrender.

My traitorous body was made for him. The way he feels is almost too much for my brain to process all at once. Massive. Unending. *Gentle.*

I marvel at that fact more than any other. He braces his hand beneath me to keep my back from contacting the rough wood of the headboard, even though the act forces him into an awkward crouch. It's almost like he doesn't even realize he's doing it—shouldering the discomfort entirely on his own.

He's too busy tasting any part of me his tongue can reach. My shoulder. My throat. Soon, meaningless words meld with every wet flick of heat. "So beautiful…beautiful. So fucking good."

Sergei is a distant memory as long as I stay here in Mischa's arms, treasured and hated at the same damn time. My heart hammers into a frantic melody, matching the pace of his as our breathing slows and our sweat dries.

Eventually, he tries to pull back, but my limbs stiffen, keeping him captive for once. *My* prisoner. Unlike his increasing demands, I only want one thing from him.

Oblivion.

And for whatever reason…

He stays here, giving me a taste.

CHAPTER 3

"Did you really think you could fool me?"

I startle awake and find a shadow looming over me. With rough hands, it rips the blankets from my body, leaving me naked in the frigid air.

"So, *this* is your game," the specter growls, brandishing something in his fist.

A photograph? Whoever took it must have been only able to capture their subject from afar. In the dark, I can barely make out anything of substance.

Anything other than a small figure sporting a mop of brilliant blond hair.

My brain shuts down, refusing to connect the dots. It's like I'm sleepwalking, processing everything two seconds too slow. Mischa's anger. The unfamiliar boy in the photo. The torn remnants of an envelope sprinkled over the floor…

"No!" Reality slams into me all at once, and I lunge from the bed, snatching at the picture. "No!"

"Oh, *yes*." Laughing, Mischa steps back, dangling the photo beyond my reach. "Are you really that fucking stupid? What did Sergei promise you? A happily fucking ever after with your precious Robert and his goddamn spawn—"

"Stop! Stop! Stop!" I lash out with my nails drawn, striking any part of him I can reach. His skin is iron, reinforced by steel muscles, and each blow hurts me more than him. Regardless, I slap and punch and bite.

It's all I can do.

"Stop it!" Abruptly, he retaliates, grabbing my wrists. "Enough!" I can barely hear him above the rush of blood surging through my ears. "I said enough!"

"Why would you do this?" I've been shouting at him all this time. The same broken words, over and over. "Why? Why?"

My knees buckle, and he lunges, looping his arm around my waist. Even as I struggle, he remains the only force keeping me upright.

"Stop," he growls.

"Why?" His chest is the only refuge. My tears sink into the cotton of his shirt as I wrestle one of my hands from his grip and slam it harmlessly against him. "Why? I let it go… I didn't listen. I *can't* listen. Why? Why?"

"I'm sorry."

"Why? Why? Why—"

"I'm *sorry*! Do you fucking hear me?" He shakes me so violently that my head rears back and forth against my shoulders. When I go limp, he grits his teeth and something in his expression gives way. Guilt? "I'm sorry, all right?"

"Rip it up," I demand, squeezing my eyes shut. "Do it now. Rip it up!"

"Fuck… Okay!" He sighs.

But I can't breathe until I hear the telltale hiss of paper tearing. Suddenly, all the tension leaves my body, which sends me crashing to my knees.

"Hey!"

Fire engulfs me from above. I'm in his arms again, held stiffly as if he half expects me to continue attacking him. But all I can do is grip his shoulders, sinking my nails in.

"Don't ever mention him—never," I rasp. "Never. Never—"

"I won't." His voice drips into my ear, callously mocking. "I'll just talk about *you*."

Stung, I try to twist from his reach, but his arms tighten like a bear trap, crushing me to his chest.

"I'll talk about how good you feel when you drop the nun act." His mouth slips into the space between my shoulder and my throat, nuzzling the tender flesh there. "So good. Too good. I never taught you how to bite."

Against my will, my limbs relax, which leaves me at his mercy. In response, his fingers catch at my hair, sinking through the tangled strands, surprisingly gentle.

"And that mouth. I will teach you how to use that properly." His voice deepens to a merciless hum. "I'll have you on your knees every fucking day, Rose. But you're so damn selfish. I'll have to use mine first, won't I?"

He pauses but doesn't seem to expect an answer.

"I'm going to make you beg for it though," he muses, running his fingers along my scalp. "I'll make you beg… And we have all the time in the goddamn world. I intend to make use of every fucking second."

His threats shouldn't feel like a welcome reprieve. His grated, malicious tone shouldn't be enough to drive Sergei and his ultimatum away.

Violent lust shouldn't be a comfort.

But it is.

I wake up alone, splayed out on the floor with a musty pillow shoved beneath my head and a threadbare blanket draped over me. Chaos resonates from the hall, presumably what drew me awake. An attack?

My ears strain in an attempt to decipher the stomping footsteps and raised voices.

"Who said you could get out of bed?" Mischa's voice reaches me from beyond the door—but I'm not his victim for once. And he sounds different now from the harsh growl I'm used to. Almost…playful?

"Fine," he snaps. "You think you can handle it? Go get dressed."

Curious, I climb to my feet, bracing myself against the bedframe for balance. My dress is a crumpled heap tossed in a corner. Creeping toward it, I drag it on and advance to the door. Before I can reach for the knob, it's opened from the outside.

The intruder grunts, startled by the sight of me standing here.

He's changed into a fresh set of fatigues. In the shadows of the hall, his eyes gleam, flicking over me in a callous swipe. My chest constricts as I brace for an insult. Or maybe a cruel reminder of the night before?

Instead, he inclines his head and then advances down the hall, leaving me to follow. Seconds pass as I contemplate whether or not I should.

Playing with him is a dangerous game of hide-and-seek. My soul is the prize, and he's ruthless in his pursuit. Just when I think I've found a safe place, he pounces from the shadows, eager to rip me to shreds.

"Are you coming?" he wonders from the bottom of the stairs.

Only when someone whizzes past do I realize he wasn't speaking to me.

Mouse skips toward him, her hair in disarray. Wearing an oversized gray shirt as a makeshift dress, she looks younger than ever. The only clue of her injury is a slight stiffness in her left shoulder as she bounds down the stairs.

"Let's play a game," Mischa proposes when she appears at his side. His voice is louder than it needs to be. For my benefit, I suspect. He relishes in the fact that I'm spying. "How not to get shot or killed if we're attacked. You have five seconds to run and hide." He cocks his head and makes a shooing motion with his hand. "One… Two…"

Mouse takes off through the front door, navigating awkwardly over the uneven terrain beyond it.

"Don't go beyond the clearing," Mischa warns.

But three seconds later, he still hasn't followed after her.

Only when I'm halfway down the staircase does he finally jolt into motion and stroll into the pale dawn. God knows why I follow him.

It's cold out and my thin, filthy dress is no match. Mouse must be freezing as well, though Mischa doesn't seem bothered by the chill. His shoulders are set with determination—he's a man on a mission, apparently.

Paces away from him, I can no longer stay silent. "This is a cruel idea of a game."

"Can you think of a better way for her to learn?" he counters. "Or should she just cower in a corner the next time your husband's men come knocking?"

He looks over his shoulder, revealing the anger smoldering in his gaze. Maybe a hint of blame lurks there as well. I caused this.

Swallowing hard, I turn away from him and find myself eyeing the wooded clearing surrounding the safe house. The stone cottage might have been a family home once. A secluded haven possessing a flower patch, a small yard, and a rickety shed.

But now? It's a makeshift fort in a two-man war.

"Is it even safe to be out here?" I ask. "I don't see your men."

The trees looming a short distance from the house provide only minimal protection. There's no gate. No barbed wire. Nothing to slow a bullet or a trained soldier. I jump as underbrush crunches nearby and my heart hammers, spurring my unease. In every swaying shadow, I see danger. Movement. Robert.

"It's safe enough," Mischa boasts, suddenly closer. "And my men know how to hide, Rose. So don't get any cute ideas of running."

I hunch away from him, hugging my arms around my torso. "What is this place anyway?"

"Property," he snaps. "And, for now, any Winthorp spies should steer clear. Your good friend Sergei has ensured that.

Either way." He shrugs, scanning the area surrounding the clearing. "She needs to learn."

I bristle at the seriousness in his tone. "Learn what?"

"How the Winthorps play: dirty." He fixates on a distant part of the yard where, at first glance, I see nothing.

Then a glimmer of golden hair flashes between a thicket of branches.

"Bang!" Mischa bellows, letting his voice ring throughout the clearing. Startled birds scatter in every which direction, and I marvel at his confidence. Despite his mistrust of the older Vasilev, he truly doesn't seem worried. "I've found you. Try again."

A dejected Mouse limps from around the base of a tree, her lips pursed. My pity lasts only seconds before she disappears again.

But not for long.

"Pathetic," Mischa snarls a minute later. His new target is a monstrous pile of chopped wood. "You can't hesitate. Try again."

Sure enough, Mouse darts into sight and then races away.

For what feels like hours, he makes her hide before discovering her easily. Over and over. Behind brambles. Or trees, or sections of the house.

Finally, he advances toward another tree, huffing in exasperation.

"You're dead," he declares, yanking her from her hiding place. "You need to be more careful—"

"Mischa…" I watch my hand brush over his shoulder before I even register touching him.

"What?" He glares at my fingers and then follows my gaze toward Mouse.

She stands awkwardly in his grasp, huddled against the bark of the tree. In the pale light, it's easy to make out a silvery substance glinting on her cheeks. Tears.

I start toward her, but Mischa crouches on one knee and grabs her arm, turning her to face him.

"I've scared you, haven't I?"

The shift in his tone stops me in my tracks. The gruff soldier I know is replaced by…a man. One who sounds repentant.

"I'm sorry." He reaches out to smooth a stray piece of hair behind her ear. "But I don't want you to get hurt again. Do you understand?"

Swiping at her streaming eyes, Mouse nods. Her face is red, her mouth trembling. But her brave veneer is no match when Mischa coaxes her into his arms and stands, lifting her entirely.

"I *can't* see you hurt again," he repeats, his voice low, just for her. "So if I have to teach you to hide so that no one can ever get close enough, I will…"

His gaze turns distant, and I don't think he realizes what he's doing: holding the girl in his arms so tight that no one could ever rip her away. He isn't here but years in the past. With his sister, Aljona?

"I know." My heart pounds as I step forward, though I'm not sure why I intervene at all. "Let's play another game."

They both jump at the sound of my voice. Aware of their scrutiny, I stoop and pluck a wildflower from an unruly patch at my feet. Pale blue, its thin petals stand out in stark contrast against the gray, overcast sky above.

"This is the most valuable thing in the world," I say, holding it out to Mouse.

Still trapped in Mischa's embrace, she eyes it warily before finally clasping her fingers around the stalk.

"You need to protect it," I tell her. "Protect it with everything you have. And him?" I point to Mischa. "He's the monster you're guarding it from."

Mischa meets my gaze, his look long and searching. Finally, he releases Mouse and sighs. "You heard her. Go!"

The girl takes off, slipping between the trees.

In her wake, the silence is so oppressive, like a noose around my throat. I can't take it.

So like any prisoner sentenced to death, I meet my end with little fanfare.

"I forgive you," I say thickly.

Seemingly intent on his prey, Mischa doesn't even acknowledge I've spoken. But he's listening. His shoulders tense with every word.

"And you can sneer and shrug it off. But I do. I refuse to let my life be ruled by petty grudges—"

"Forgiveness." He grunts as if the concept is too foreign to understand. But, to my shock, when I glance at his face, I don't find a smirk. He merely sighs, running his fingers through his wild hair. "As you say, Rose."

"And I want you to know something." The wind carries my voice to him. I'm too tired to put any effort into the sound myself. I merely mouth the words and hope they escape the prison of my throat. "Something I've never told anyone else..." I tilt my head toward the breeze, letting it lick away the dried tears clinging to my skin.

Above, the sky looms a stormy gray. The swirling clouds could be trying to warn me, growing darker by the second. Or maybe the building tempest is just goading me on. *You've been broken already. What could be worse?*

"I don't know what love is," I admit. Out loud, it sounds so simple. So pathetic. "I don't know if I've ever loved Robert. I don't think I've ever loved anyone—not really. Not even my mother... I don't know what it feels like to worry for someone so much you can't bear to see them hurt. I don't know what it's like to..." I trail off. After licking my lips, I try again, but the words stick in my throat, so stupid. So raw. So desperate. I have to force them out. "I can't even mourn my own sister the way you can—"

"Are you calling me emotional, Little Rose?" He cuts his gaze in my direction.

"No. But…I'm jealous of you." I turn away from him as my cheeks catch flame. What am I even saying? "I don't know," I say. "I wish I knew what it was like…"

To be so rabid with affection, even as you rip apart anyone stupid enough to desire to get close.

"What it's like?" he asks.

I flinch as his hand latches onto the back of my scalp and steers me forward. Without warning, he presses me against the bark of a tree, stopping just short of grinding my face against it.

"So that you can manipulate me, Little Rose?" he pants against my shoulder. "Continue to spin your little web?"

I go limp, laughing softly to myself. Of course the bastard can't let his guard down for a second. Even in the rare instance when I try to lower mine.

"So that I can understand you," I gasp out to an ant crawling, inches from my cheek. It jolts and changes direction, scurrying away. "All I want is to understand you."

It's the only way I will ever beat him at his own game.

"Love?" Mischa echoes. He steps into me, fanning his hands out over my waist. "I'll tell you a little secret: It's pain, Rose. It's wanting someone so fucking much—but you don't know why. It's feeling them crawl beneath your goddamn skin. They're in your head. In your skull. Laughing at you.

Taunting you. You want to love?" He laughs and each unsteady cackle sears the flesh of my jaw. "I could fucking drown you in it—"

Nearby, a branch cracks, presumably snapped underfoot, and Mischa pulls away.

"I can hear you," he calls out to the creeping figure. Grabbing my wrist, he tugs me along as he picks his way between the trees. "Slow down," he warns, stopping short. He cocks his head, letting his ear pick up the slightest noise. "That's it. Get your bearings. I still haven't spotted you. Use this to your advantage. Don't panic. *Think*."

I strain my eyes, hunting for any hint of what he's sensing. The seconds trickle by painfully slow, but I don't catch a glimpse of her. Apparently, neither does Mischa.

"Good!" His laugh booms out proudly, a mark of approval. "*Very* good." He resumes his prowling stance and inches forward. "Now, let's see how long you can keep it up…"

We hunt for her long after the early morning stretches into the afternoon. If Mischa has more pressing business to attend to, he doesn't let on. So intent on his lesson, he doesn't seem to notice the passage of time.

Finally, he places his hand on my shoulder, motioning for me to stay back. Alone, he stalks to a nearby tree, barely making a sound over the brambles.

"There you are!" He lunges forward and reaches around the trunk. "Found you—"

His snatching fingers come up empty, however. He frowns at them, his eyebrows furrowing. Then, almost in comically slow motion, an acorn falls from a higher branch, hitting him squarely in the middle of his forehead.

He jerks back, looking up.

And at that exact moment, a grinning Mouse unfurls herself from a twisted thicket of branches.

Mischa's expression ripples, eerily stern. Then he laughs and claps his hands. "Good! Very good." Still clapping, he watches her climb down and then ruffles her hair. "Much better."

Mouse grins. Very carefully, she opens one of her fists, revealing the flower tucked against her palm. If she were one to gloat, I can imagine what she might say. *I win.*

"Show-off." Mischa's upper lip twitches, resisting the smile that transforms his mouth regardless. "Now, come. We should get back before Ivan starts grumbling."

Skipping ahead, Mouse leads the way through the trees, back to the house.

As predicted, Vanya greets us near the front door, his lips pursed. How long has he been watching us from afar? I can't tell.

Neither can I decipher if he recalls our conversation from last night. His gaze flits over me before settling on the figure prancing nearby.

"You're a mess," he grumbles to Mouse, beckoning her inside. "Come on. I'll get you something to eat, and then it's back to bed." To Mischa, he inclines his head respectfully. "The perimeter is still secure according to the men. Sergei wasn't lying. But…" He cuts his gaze in my direction. Then he shrugs, deeming me worthy to hear his concerns. "I don't like it. I say we move as soon as possible. It will be risky, but—"

"When haven't I been up for a risk?" Mischa finishes for him. "Make the preparations. We can move out in the morning."

"As you wish." Nodding, Vanya reenters the house.

I start to follow, but Misha grabs my wrist before I can slip past him.

"Wait. It's time for another game," he says, his voice grated. "I'm not in the mood for flower picking, so consider *yourself* the prize." He shoves me toward a section of forest. "So run."

I stagger forward, maneuvering as quickly as I can over the uneven terrain. There's no way I can outrun him. As my knees buckle, I haul myself behind the nearest tree and wait. Anticipation wracks my spine, heightening the hiss of every swaying branch and rustling leaf.

"Child's play," Mischa hisses, advancing at a lazy pace. He doesn't even try to hide the sound of his footsteps, which crunch sticks and undergrowth with every step. "If you make it this easy, then what is the fucking point?"

A million familiar sensations curdle in my stomach. *Caught. Trapped. Helpless. Hopeless.* Sighing, I lean against the bark, impatient for the inevitable.

Almost as if my hiding place is mocking my cowardice, something falls from a branch and lands at my feet. Small.

Round. An acorn. My eyes fixate on its brown surface as Mischa's advice to Mouse replays in my head: *Don't panic. Think.*

I can't outsmart him for long—but he's a wolf. Predators like him don't expect their prey to fight back.

"Found you," he hisses paces from my hiding spot. So smug in his capture, he doesn't attempt to hide his attack; a shadow rushing toward me warns the second he reaches out.

So I pivot in the opposite direction.

"Where are you—" His back is to me now.

I'm the wolf, and my attack comes swiftly: I lunge. Before I can reach him, he twists around with feline grace. But he's too late. Grunting, he's forced to catch me by the waist, but he can't defend from the palm I press against the center of his chest.

"Bang," I tell him coldly, meeting his widening gaze. "You're dead."

I expect him to shove me off. Or, better yet, leave me here in an exhausted heap. I'm so tired of fighting him at every turn.

But rather than let me go, he grips me tighter, moving his face near mine until they touch. Cheek to cheek. We share the same twisted breath.

"*This* is why you are more dangerous than the Winthorps and their army combined," he murmurs, digging his fingers into my hips for emphasis. "You are reckless. Nothing is sacred to you. You'll burn your enemies and yourself down in the same fucking blaze. Even the most sick, twisted bastards aren't that cruel."

An amusing thought comes to me, and I voice it near his ear. "Does that scare you?"

A harsh grunt catches in his throat. He sets me down but then captures my chin, forcing me to look up. His gaze bores through mine with a predatory accuracy. From this assault, there is no escape.

And I know now that his "game" has nothing at all to do with hide-and-seek.

"Look at me." His irises darken, a piercing, unsettling shade of black. "Tell me… Tell me how it feels when I'm inside you."

"W-what?" My cheeks catch fire at the crude request. Another sick joke? But no. His eyes are too open, meeting my probing stare unflinchingly.

"You heard me." He wants an answer, and my throat rasps as I try to compile one.

"It feels like sex—"

"No." His thumb swipes at my lower lip, dismissing the response. "Don't play coy. You were upset last night—but you came to *me*. I want to know why."

His expression shifts, and I catch a glimpse of the stranger I've only ever seen with Mouse. The exhausted man with shadows beneath his eyes. Worn lines distort the skin around his mouth, and his voice is so much clearer than the rough grumble I'm used to. Panicked, I realize it's his most lethal weapon, this guttural hum.

"Tell me—"

"Too much." I close my eyes against his judgment, but I can't seem to make myself stop talking. "You feel too big. Like all you want to do is rip me open, and there is nothing I can do to stop it. I…I don't want to stop it…" I sway as his grip loosens. But bit by bit, it tightens again, drawing me closer.

"Why?" he demands. "Tell me."

"When you kiss me… I can't think. And I don't want to."

I doubt he understands just how dangerous an admission that is. In my entire life, my only saving grace was my ability to think. Override my body's natural instincts. Endure.

Until now.

"It feels real," I whisper, horrified. "I can't ignore it. I can't suppress it. What you do to me feels so damn real—"

Moist heat rips my voice from me. His mouth—I've memorized the shape. It conforms to mine like nothing else, designed to overpower and subdue. Claim. One teasing brush of his tongue and my thoughts empty of anything tangible. All I can do is cling to him, pawing at his shoulders for purchase.

I'm vaguely aware that he's moving, backing me against the very same tree I attacked him from. Viciously, his hands sink into my hair, gripping tight as he draws back, breaking the kiss.

"I'll give it to him," he says, laughing in a broken, hollow series of grunts. "If you really are a skilled fucking spy—a trick… Then I have to hand it to him. I give in." His eyes meet mine again, unfocused and crazed. Truly insane. "You've fucking done it. He's won. I'm a pathetic fucking idiot. So here—" He grinds his pelvis into mine. "Savor your victory, Rose."

Savor. I run my hands down his chest, the planes of it rippling beneath the thin layer of cotton. In the darkness, I can't see the skin bared beneath as he wrenches it up over his head and tosses it aside. I have to feel every inch for myself.

Raw. Powerful. Broken and healed in some places, still wounded and sore in others. He lets me have my fill of tracing every inch of his armor. I barely even notice when his hands slip beneath my dress, ruthlessly turning the tables.

"You're so damn wet." He hisses that assessment even before his fingers dip between my legs, finding his boast to be true. "You *have* to be a fucking trick," he declares, breaching me with the pad of his thumb. "There's no other way…"

He doesn't elaborate. Once again, our conversation devolves into the unspoken. Grasping touches that convey more than words ever could. Slow, rasping breaths when he yanks his pants down and eases his way inside me.

My eyes flutter shut at the sensation.

"Tell me now," he snarls into my neck. "Tell me."

"You feel…"

He slows, panting against my throat. "Say it." Impatient, he thrusts again, utilizing his body like a battering ram.

I'm no match for him. "You feel so good," I whimper. "So, so good."

He groans, forging a frantic rhythm within seconds. Savor my victory, he told me, but there's no time. No chance. He overdoses me on his touch, taste—everything all at once.

"Beautiful Little Rose," he taunts as I shatter. "You win. You win. But I'll play your game: I'll drag you down with me. I'll destroy you—we'll both go up in flames."

And he breaks me, leaving me in pieces against the rough, unyielding bark.

But in the aftermath of him, I've never felt clearer.

And I've never felt more powerful.

We redress in silence and return to the house just as the moon rises to its highest point in the sky. Vanya still waits by the front door, watchfully eyeing the dark. As we slip inside, he casts us both a searching glance.

Once again, his gaze skims over me and settles on someone else.

"Mischa." He places his hand on the younger man's shoulder. "We need to talk—"

"If this is about leaving, I agree," Mischa says, shoving me through the doorway ahead of him. "We move out early. I'll take the lead. You pick up the rear and then we'll regroup—"

"That's not what I mean." Vanya sighs and I catch his gaze dart down the hall leading deeper into the house. "There is something—"

"What?" Mischa strokes his chin. "Are you worried about Sergei? Maybe we shouldn't inform the old man just yet. Not until we have a clear route."

"I have a suggestion." That voice…

My shock matches Mischa's as none other than Sergei appears at the mouth of the hall.

"Speak of the devil," Mischa growls under his breath. His grip on my arm tightens and I can feel the tension radiating off him in waves.

"Sorry to intrude," the older man says, though his expression reveals no ounce of guilt. He approaches us at a cautious pace, dressed head to toe in a practical black outfit that sets him apart from Mischa's filthy fatigues. "But I think it will be more prudent if a group of my men leads the way. Then you can follow. With Winthorp on the prowl, you should center your retreat around his biggest target."

"Oh?" Mischa raises an eyebrow. "And what would that be?"

"*Who*," Sergei corrects, turning to me. "Her."

"And let me guess. That biggest threat will stay with you?"

"No." Sergei shakes his head, raising his hands in a subtle sign of surrender. "I'll go with my men."

The two men eye each other, tension crackling between them.

"It's a good plan, Mischa," Vanya pipes up. He moves, positioning himself between his brother and his surrogate son. "I say we use his method and move out tomorrow night. That will give us time to plan a safe route."

"Fine." Eyes flashing, Mischa flexes his arm, dragging me closer to his side. "But she will stay with *me* and *you* will lead the way."

"Fair enough." Sergei nods. "As Ivan suggested, we can move tomorrow night, before the sun rises."

"Fine." Mischa releases me and barges deeper into the house, barking out orders.

Seemingly from nowhere, his men converge on the narrow space, pushing the limits of the cottage to their max. Once Mischa's plan is relayed in detail, they disperse to carry out their given orders and I can feel their leader's eyes on me as I make my way to the stairs.

"Wait."

I stiffen with one foot braced on the lower step. He takes his time coming up behind me. His finger teasingly ghosts my cheek before his entire hand pulls a lock of hair back from my face.

"Look at me."

He's frowning when I do, scanning my gaze. For what? I'm not sure. Only that the hunt for it hollows his features, and the line of his mouth is tighter as he turns away.

"Go run up to bed, Little Rose," he commands. "Maybe if you pray hard enough, the monsters will stay out of it tonight."

I obey, racing up the stairs. Once inside my small room, I find myself paralyzed by the sight of the rumpled bed, its blankets strewn all over the floor.

In the end, I brace my back against the wall and sink down to my knees, forsaking the comfort of the mattress.

The cold floor, with its covering of dust, is more welcome than any ounce of softness containing his scent.

Even if it means I suffer.

❧

A groan escapes my lips as I open my eyes to the dim glow of dawn filtering in through the room's only window. Already, I thoroughly regret my decision to forsake the bed. My legs throb when I attempt to stand, and I have to ease myself upright, using the wall like a makeshift ladder.

Sighing, I eye my filthy clothing and make a halfhearted trip around the room in search of anything else to wear.

So much for the new Ellen. Gone are my handpicked clothes, lost in the flames that consumed Mischa's manor.

Unsurprisingly, I find nothing here, which leaves only one other course of action to feel somewhat cleaner.

I steel myself as I approach the door and palm the knob. When I finally gather the nerve to push it open, I don't find any madmen lurking beyond it.

But I do discover a bathroom not far from my hideaway. It's small but contains a tub at least. Despite a circle of rust around the drain, the plumbing seems to be in working order.

After stripping my clothing, I climb inside and run the water as hot as I can stand it. Then I huddle in the center of the basin and struggle to find some semblance of peace. It's surprisingly easy. As the heat sinks into my limbs and licks away the grime on my skin, I rest my head against the rim of the tub and close my eyes.

A sudden thud cuts my reprieve short. The door opens, slamming against the wall, and the source of my unease enters.

I lurch upright, shielding my breasts with trembling hands. "What are you doing?"

Mischa scoffs, eyeing my body as boldly as if he owns every inch. "Don't tell me a haughty woman of your esteem plans to wear the same dirty clothing." He extends his hand, revealing a wad of material I didn't notice before. Fabric? He unfolds it for my inspection: a thick, gray shirt like the kind Mouse wore the other day.

But I doubt it will fit me as well as it fit her.

"Don't stick your nose up just yet," Mischa warns. Up until now, he was obscuring another garment behind his back: a pair of black pants. "I took these from the smallest man in my crew, but I doubt they'll fit you well enough. You'll just have to make do."

He tosses both garments onto the floor near the tub.

"Thank you," I croak, surprised despite myself. It's like he read my mind. Though maybe he can? He scans my features as easily as one would an open book.

"Thank me? For ensuring that you *don't* get the idea to walk around naked and tempt my men into doing your bidding?"

I scoff and turn my attention to my limbs. Steam rises from the basin of the tub as my legs redden in the heat.

"Doesn't it exhaust you?" I wonder. "Being so damn paranoid?"

A sound escapes his throat, but I can't decipher it. A laugh?

"Paranoid? I call it prudent." He turns from me and lifts his shirt over his head, tossing it to his feet.

My eyes scan his body appreciatively before I can help it. His tattoos gleam, melding with his healing scrapes and wounds. The man is a canvas of darkness and blood. If I believed in demons, I'd wholeheartedly insist he was one. Sin in the flesh.

"See something you like?" he wonders.

Licking my lips, I croak, "What are you doing?"

"Are you the only one allowed to be clean?" He braces his hands over the rusty sink and leans in toward the mirror, observing his reflection. Whatever he finds makes him turn away and fish a rag from beneath the sink. After sniffing it, he shrugs. Apparently, it's clean enough.

He wets it beneath the faucet and swipes at his face.

Watching him, I find that the only way to regain my composure is by utilizing the one weapon proven effective against him.

Speaking.

"You seem pretty calm," I remark as I stretch out my sore legs. "For a man whose home just burned to the ground."

He stiffens, and in the mirror, I catch his fleeting scowl.

"I've had many homes," he says simply. Setting the rag aside, he wets his fingers and rakes them through his tangled hair. "Unlike you and your Winthorps, I don't get attached to a pretty dwelling."

"But that place was different," I point out. "You called it by a name once. Pecavi?"

He ignores me, still combing through his hair.

But I can't fathom his indifference. "Your mother's things. Your sister's… Won't you miss them?"

He pushes back from the sink, but when he faces me, he doesn't look angry. "And do you miss *your* mother's things?" He eyes my neck.

I reach up automatically, clasping the tiny charm dangling against my collar.

"Don't," he scolds, and a curious thought makes me loosen my grip over my necklace. Have I insulted him? It seems I have. He's still frowning. "I've had plenty of chances to take it from you—"

"I never had anything of hers to hold on to before," I admit, referring to his previous question. "Not even a button or ring."

"Well, I'd give up a million *things*." He stoops for his shirt and pulls it on over his head. "Everything, to have more than a memory. And to avenge them, I will endure many fires and occupy a million fucking houses. Nothing ever changes."

It's a cold outlook. And a lonely one.

"So you don't cherish anything?" I ask.

"What's the point?" He shrugs and then jerks his chin to the running faucet of the tub. "Don't spend the day wasting away, Little Rose." He approaches the door and opens it, heedless of who might be walking by on the other end. "You need to be ready to move. Tonight."

"To another safe house?"

"You better hope so." He steps over the threshold, closing the door behind him. Regardless, his voice reaches me through the wood. "Because the only alternative is a

Winthorp prison. At least with me, your fashion choices differ from a ball and chain."

I listen to his steps retreat and hug myself as the water cools. By the time I finally climb out of the tub, I'm shivering. Thankfully, Mischa's clothing provides a decent amount of warmth, and the pants aren't uncomfortable. If I roll the hems a few times, they almost fit.

When I reenter the hall fully dressed, I can hear Mischa down below, marshaling his men to various tasks.

He claimed that property meant nothing to him, but I think it was a lie.

He's comfortable like this, living in transience. There's no stability to rely upon and nothing he could risk losing other than his life.

And if Mischa Stepanov seems to value one thing least of all.

It's himself.

CHAPTER 6

I spend the day lurking in the shadows of the property with no real purpose other than to bide my time. For lunch, I eat with Mouse, who barely acknowledges my presence.

While she may communicate with Mischa easily, any question I voice her way goes ignored.

Alone, I settle into the corners of the house, watching Mischa from afar.

Did he mean the words he groaned to me in the forest?

Or perhaps his more recent boast conveys his true feelings? *Nothing is worth holding on to for long.*

Though the man does seem to cherish his power. He wields it effortlessly, almost without realizing the control he has over people.

"Get ready," he says to me, noticing my silent observation once night has fallen. "Sergei will be here soon. His roaches are already scurrying around." He nods to a man standing silently among the quiet chaos of packing and coordination going on around him. Instead of fatigues, he's wearing black from head to toe and his build is sturdier than the agile men in Mischa's crew. "Keep an eye on him and his little friends," Mischa warns as I spot several other darkly dressed figures stationed at various points in the safe house.

"Spy on them?" I ask, but I'm intrigued despite myself. "Aren't they on your side?"

"Side." He scoffs, turning away. "Just tell me if they look too jumpy."

I'm bored enough to take him up on his offer.

Unfortunately, Sergei's men make for boring targets to spy on. They barely move even a step out of place. With a focused intensity, they observe Mischa's men as disinterestedly as I observe them.

Eventually, it becomes obvious that the scruffy outlaw leader is a much more interesting target.

I find myself creeping into the hallway just to keep watch as he directs the movement of vans in the yard and dishes out more orders. The shadows of the house paint him, highlighting the contrast of gold and darkness that make up his core.

Strip him of the scars and tattoos and he could have been a different man in another life. Someone honorable. A teacher sternly directing students? Or a police officer? It's terrifying how many possibilities could fit someone like him, armed with both authority and charm.

Redefining him consumes my focus—and I don't even notice someone beside me until it's too late. They brush past me and I jump, jarring my shoulder off the wall.

"Excuse me, miss," the figure says, placing a steadying grip on my forearm. "Are you all right?"

"I'm fine," I rasp automatically. Even so, my fingers rub at the back of my neck as I look up into the stern features of one of Sergei's "roaches."

"My apologies," he murmurs. "Let me make sure I didn't—"

"You can let her go," Mischa quietly insists from the entrance to the cottage. His eyes fixate on the man's hand until he releases me, and I smother a sigh. It's like he's hardwired to sense the moment any other dog might so much as sniff the air near his coveted prize. "Besides." He glances over his shoulder, frowning. "Your master is here."

Sergei enters the cottage a heartbeat later. He and Mischa lock gazes, trading a million warnings between them, I suspect. Together, they move into the sitting room off the hall. Someone left a paper map unfurled over the couch and Sergei points to it, stroking his chin with his opposite hand.

"Did you have a destination in mind?" he asks.

"West." Mischa positions himself near the doorway, his arms crossed. When I creep up beside him, he looks at me but says nothing. Returning his attention to Sergei, he adds, "I have a cabin there."

"Another safe house?" Sergei raises an eyebrow. "May I make a suggestion?"

Mischa grunts. "I doubt I can refuse."

"I suggest we regroup at my property. It's close. It's familiar, and I can supply more comfort to your guests than some shack in the woods."

"Fine," Mischa grates through clenched teeth. "We can go now. Gather your men. Lead the way."

"As you wish." Sergei exits the house, but paces down the front path, he calls back, "There is one thing we need to discuss, however…"

"Oh?" Mischa's eyes narrow, eternally suspicious, and I'm close enough to catch that. "And what is that?"

"Where is Ivan?"

Mischa purses his lips. "I had him scout ahead," he finally admits. "Why?"

"Because," Sergei calls, sounding farther from the cottage. "We need to discuss what he might do when I tell him about his daughter."

"Have you gone insane—" Mischa breaks off, glancing at me. "Don't move," he snarls before marching out to meet Sergei.

He shouts something. That's all I'm aware of as I approach the doorway in their wake, despite Mischa's warning. For some reason, I'm still swiping at my neck…but something's wrong.

My limbs feel heavy.

Too heavy.

My hand goes limp, falling to my side, and I sway, forced to lean against the wall for balance.

I can still hear Mischa growling something to Sergei paces away.

"Mi…" I try to speak. Cry out. Anything.

But with every attempt, I make less noise.

Until the world goes silent entirely, and I fall into a sea of black.

❖

I come to on a firm surface. The floor? No… The plush material beneath me isn't the harsh wood of the safe house. Have we moved already? My head throbs as I try to remember.

Mischa…

Sergei…

They were talking about Vanya—but anything after is an ominous blank. One fact I am aware of, however, is that the figure standing over me, reeking of cologne, is not Mischa.

My eyes fly open and I look up, scrambling into a crouch. Sluggish limbs rob me of any grace, and I have to brace both of my hands against the unfamiliar carpet beneath me to stay upright.

"You've been drugged, miss," the man says matter-of-factly. His face is strange. He isn't wearing the gray fatigues of Mischa or his men, either. In stark contrast, a crisp black suit differentiates him entirely. "The effects should wear off in a few minutes," he continues. "But to minimize any risk to yourself, I suggest you relax."

"Sergei," I rasp while blinking to bring the rest of our surroundings into clearer focus. We're in a room with one exit—and the man just so happens to be positioned closer to it: a door opened only to shadow.

The room itself is spacious, containing a lavish bed draped in red sheets and a wooden wardrobe. Rich burgundy wallpaper betrays a finery I've only seen matched in Mischa's manor as of yet. Is this place the property Sergei mentioned? My throat aches as I cling to that possibility—it has to be.

"Do you work for him?" I ask the man. "Sergei—"

"No." The reply comes from someone else who appears in the doorway like a phantom in a nightmare.

Chilling familiarity paralyzes me, snuffing any ounce of air from my lungs. As I suffocate, I dig my nails into my palms, hoping the pain jars me awake.

I'm dreaming.

I have to be…

"He works for me," the newcomer says, his voice a suave, polished tenor. "And he finally fucking earned his keep. Elle."

Dressed in black, my husband surges forward. He cut his hair in my absence, though it's styled in its familiar elegant coif. He's as tall as I remember, but his thin build casts less intimidation than Mischa's bulk. It's his bruised, swollen left hand that draws my attention the most.

And it's his eyes that make my heart hammer unsteadily.

Amber like fire, they brim with rage.

"You're safe," he swears, sinking to one knee. He reaches for me only to stop short inches from my face.

Because I'm filthy, reeking of dust, and the forest, and Mischa Stepanov.

CHAPTER 7

This nightmare doesn't end when Robert pulls away and stands. I'm painfully awake and aware of every ounce of freedom slipping through my grasping fingers.

This isn't a nightmare…

This is hell.

"She needs a bath," Robert declares, gesturing to my body. "And send for the doctor immediately."

"Yes, sir." As if conjured from nothing, a woman appears by his side. Her plain dress denotes her as a maid, and she obediently stoops beside me, helping me to my feet.

"And rest," Robert adds. His eyes sweep me over, brimming with rage I've never seen his aristocratic features manifest before. Hatred. Loathing. Fear? "I'll make them pay," he swears. "Those bastards will fucking pay."

Have they already been captured? I try to picture Mischa and Vanya in chains as my gaze returns to Robert's bruised hand. He holds it awkwardly, but judging from the greenish hue of his skin, I doubt it's a fresh injury.

Despite everything, I can't stay silent.

"Is he alive?" I force myself to ask. "Mis—"

"Stepanov?" Robert frowns and a familiar unease gathers in my stomach.

In so many ways, he's the same man I was taken from. But there's an aged quality to his gaze that wasn't there before. A darkness. Gone is his old childhood ring Mischa presented to me on a bloody platter as well. In its place gleams a new, more prominent piece of jewelry: the heavier insignia I've seen worn only by his father.

"I'll kill him," he swears, brushing the tip of his finger along my cheek—as much of himself as he can bear to taint. "I'll rip him to pieces. He will pay."

But he hasn't. Not yet. A painful emotion flutters in my chest as I sway, relying on the maid for support. I can't even find a name for it until Robert finally leaves the room, flanked by his henchman.

Maybe it's terror.

Or perhaps…

It's hope.

he maid bathes me without uttering a single word—but where Mouse's silence seemed stubborn at times, hers is deliberate.

There are no mocking taunts as she strips my clothing and coaxes me into the steaming tub of an ornate bathroom. There is no softness to her touch as she drags a rag over my bruised, swollen limbs. All in all, I'm treated mechanically, like a broken, battered object in need of restoration.

She doesn't even look me in the eye as she washes my hair and combs through the ragged strands. To her, I am merely a doll dressed in a gossamer nightgown and led back into the room I woke up in like a lamb to slaughter.

My breath catches at the sight of the bed. It's large enough for two people—and only one fact makes it possible to breathe again. Some things never change, and Robert Winthorp is a creature I've studied cover to cover.

As Mischa claimed, he never shared my bed. And he won't try to reclaim my body so soon. I need to be broken in first.

Still, it feels like I'm clinging to a child's prayer more than anything as the woman leaves, gently closing the door behind her.

Soon, another woman enters. The doctor, I assume from her crisp white jacket and studious bun. Without uttering a single word, she gives me a thorough, clinical examination. I shiver as her cold hands prod my inner thighs and healing scars.

Finally, she leaves.

And hopelessness washes over me, so vast and heavy that I'm sure I'll never escape it. Dangerous thoughts feed on the panic. *Do it now. Take the easy way out, like Marnie did.*

I can't go back.

I can't.

I can't.

Enough! I shake myself, lurching to my feet.

If Mischa is alive, I know the first conclusion he'd jump to: that I went back willingly. That I'm lying in Robert's arms right now, laughing over the idiocy of the monster who deigned to show me a glimpse that he might be something more.

He'd be smug, Mischa, the bastard. He wouldn't contemplate for a second that I would be pacing my gilded prison, aching to be anywhere. Dead. With him. Anywhere.

But my brain won't let me take that cowardly outlook for too long. It keeps returning to him. I see his face, those flashing eyes. They offer a challenge: *You want to prove me wrong, Rose? Then fucking run.*

I rush to the door and test the knob. It's locked.

Two windows, shrouded in scarlet curtains, are positioned on either side of the bed. I race toward one and draw the curtains back only to reveal the plywood nailed to it, obscuring any view. The second has been barred the same way.

Two additional doors lead to a closet and the bathroom. Apart from the bed, my only other piece of furniture is the wardrobe.

I'm trapped.

Tears well and escape before I can prevent their fall. I rub at them, but eventually, I wind up on my knees, against the wall, choking back sobs. They rip from me in dizzying waves, leaving my chest aching in the aftermath.

I barely hear the gentle murmur in between my gasping breaths.

"Shhh," a woman urges. "Shhh, love. It's all right. Shhhh. It's all right."

The words aren't directed to me, but that voice…

"Briar?" I whisper, pressing my ear harder to the wall. It must be thin enough that she can hear me, whoever she is. But the voice falls silent.

"Please. Briar, is that you?"

In a room that potentially isn't locked?

Desperate, I risk raising my voice. "Please answer me. Briar… Please."

But no matter how many times I call, she never replies.

CHAPTER 8

When the door to my cell opens again, I'm huddled on the floor, forced to scramble to my feet as Robert enters.

"Good news," he declares, his lips parted in a glorious smile. "The doctor believes your face can be saved."

He pauses and I can't resist habit driven in through years of obedience. Almost without prompting from my brain, my lips pry apart and I croak, "Th-that's wonderful—"

"With a few minor surgeries, you'll be your old self in no time," Robert agrees, still grinning. Then his eyes slide down to observe the rest of my battered limbs and his mouth flattens. "I've brought you something to wear, love."

He's flanked by a maid who approaches the bed and lays a dress across the foot of it. It's blue, made of silk, perfectly tailored. One of mine, I suspect, taken from my old wardrobe.

But I know for certain we aren't at Winthorp Manor.

"Leave us," Robert snaps at the woman, who scurries away.

She closes the door with a soft thud and my courage dies with it.

"My darling…"

I'm frozen as he advances and smooths his hands down my newly washed shoulders. For what feels like an eternity, his gaze roves from my injured face downward. With every inch traveled, his eyes narrow further.

In disgust.

I hope so. So fiercely that it hurts. He'll storm away and let me heal, too repulsed to try to reclaim what another monster has already messed over. I barely recognize the battered, bruised limbs revealed beneath the ivory cotton.

But then he fingers a lock of my hair, twisting the gleaming strands.

"You're still so beautiful." He sounds surprised by that fact. His flared nostrils inhale the air and his eyes flutter shut as he processes my scent. "I've missed you. The thought of you in that place…" He opens his eyes and I'm shocked to find that they're watering. Clearing his throat, he shakes his head and gently caresses my cheek. "It doesn't matter. You're safe now."

Safe. That word circles my skull as I resist the urge to cringe from his touch. It's such a vicious taunt. *Safe. Safe. Safe.*

"I will never let you go again," he swears.

My spine goes rigid when he leans in, but all he does is press his mouth across my jaw. Cold lips linger over Mischa's brand, imparting a sting I haven't felt since the wounds were freshly carved there.

"I'm sorry," he breathes against the scars. "I don't know how that little bitch—" Breaking off, he glowers at the wall. "Just know that I never intended for *you* to be hurt."

"Briar," I guess, treating her name with all the care of a live grenade. "Is she alive?"

"For now." His callous shrug catches me off guard. He and his sister had their own twisted rivalry, but I've never heard him refer to her so coldly before. "You don't have to worry about her. She's somewhere where she can't meddle, the little cunt. I don't know how she knew… It doesn't matter. She couldn't gloat for long."

But I remember her face as she appeared in the woods. My proud sister didn't look devious or triumphant then. She looked terrified.

"I have something for you." Robert returns his attention to me, placing his hand on my shoulder. "Something I should have returned to you a long time ago… What is this?" He swipes his finger along my throat and I don't register reaching up to stop him.

The necklace. That was what I was trying to protect. I realize that belatedly as white spots explode over my vision, and I regain awareness on my knees, tasting blood.

"I'm sorry. I'm *sorry*," Robert hisses as he and the rest of the room fade in and out of focus.

Dazed, I watch him shake out the fingers of his right hand and rub at the knuckles.

"I'm sorry. But why did you make me—do you realize what I've gone through without you? And this?" He brandishes a delicate chain between his fingers. My necklace. He must have torn it off, the source of his ire. "What the fuck is this?"

"Robert…" A sharp pain makes me swipe my hand across my mouth. In shock, I gape as my fingers come away red— an accessory as familiar to me as the dress on the bed is. Both compose my costume: a battered, caged bird.

"What?" he snarls, rounding on my position.

"It's my mother's," I murmur awkwardly while more liquid drips down my chin. "The necklace. I think it was my mother's—"

"She's dead," he snaps. Then he blinks and shakes his head, tucking the chain into his pocket. "I'll get you a new one, love. Would you like that? Something prettier."

A beautiful collar.

"But this? The fucking woman should have taken it. I'll have her beaten for this." He starts to pace, still muttering. "I don't want anything to remind you of that degenerate. He's fucked you, hasn't he?" His sharp bark of laughter chills my blood. "Of course he has. It's okay. I forgive you.

You survived and you're back now. You're safe. No one else will ever have you."

As his eyes glow a poisonous brown, all doubt is stripped away. *This* is the man I know.

Dread solidifies in my stomach, and nothing is clearer: If I stay in this cage, I'll never leave it again.

There is only one way out. It's the same dilemma I faced when assaulted by Nikolaus, and the tactic I used then is my weapon now.

Rebellion.

"Let me go."

He stiffens, frowning in confusion. "What did you say?"

I swallow, sensing the danger building in his narrow frame. His fingers flex, already reddening from his previous strike. "Just let me go," I whisper, cradling my throbbing jaw. "I can't live like this. Just let me go…"

"Go?" Uncertainty disrupts his rage. He almost resembles the boy he was what seems like a lifetime ago, mulling over the best way to get his point across to my ignorant brain. "Back to him?"

"Anywhere," I rasp. "I can't live like this anymore—"

"He's brainwashed you." He shakes his head, his expression crestfallen. "My sweet Elle—"

"No!" I meet his gaze, imploring him to listen. "I'm not brainwashed. I'm not broken. And he may be a degenerate, but at least... He knows what he is. And his name is Mischa—"

Bam! A monstrous crash resonates through the wall. From the other room.

"Fuck." Robert flushes red and I'm instantly forgotten. "That dumb bitch."

Whirling on his heel, he throws the door open and storms into the hall. I hear the click of another door opening nearby. The room beside mine?

"I'm sorry," a woman pleads a second later, but her voice is higher than Briar's could ever be. Plaintive. "It just fell. I'll clean it up—"

A sharp thwack muffles her cry.

"Can you not serve one goddamn purpose?" Robert hisses. I can picture him towering above a cowering figure as he wipes his stinging hand on the front of his suit. "You've ruined everything. Maybe I should sell you now? What else are you good for?"

The woman mumbles something unintelligible and another slap cuts her off.

"Enough," Robert bellows. "We'll return to the manor tonight and I will hire your replacement—"

"Please," the woman begs. "Not...not in front of him."

Him. Another man?

No. Those cries weren't hers I realize. They were too soft. Too high-pitched.

"*He* will learn," Robert snarls. "You see this woman? She is replaceable."

As he rages, I finally notice that the door to my room is open.

I could run. I *am*, staggering to my feet, lunging toward the doorway.

But I'm too late.

Robert appears before me, his expression flickering as he takes in my breathless stance paces from freedom.

Beyond him, a lush, carpeted hallway extends out of my view.

"You need more rest," Robert says while reaching for the doorknob. "Once we're home... Everything will be as it was. I promise." He smooths his hand over my cheek.

Then he leaves.

And I break.

I'm too hollow for tears. All I can do is breathe raggedly, my face pressed against the floor. Faint cries still emanate from the other room, echoing mine and cementing the chilling reality.

I'll never leave.

And even if Mischa comes after me, with Robert's resources, he would never make it through the front door.

"Shhh," the woman in the other room soothes. "Shhh. Please hush, my darling."

"Ama," the softer voice wails in response.

Who are they? *Mafiya* captives? New additions to his supposed sex trade?

Crawling to the wall, I rap my knuckles against it. "Ama?" I call tentatively. "Is that your name?"

Both figures fall silent.

"Please." Biting my lip, I try again, knocking even louder. "Answer me, please. I won't hurt you—"

"He'll hear you," the woman whispers frantically. "His spies are always listening."

My fingers tremble, leaving streaks of sweat over the wallpaper. Despite everything, one fact strikes me more than any other. I've dealt with plenty of Robert's favorite maids and whores—but she sounds like…*me*.

Her fear. The hitch in her voice. Those subtle clues prove to me that she isn't some recent captive. No, she's been under his thumb for much longer.

"We need to leave," I risk whispering. "I can't stay here. I won't."

I shut my eyes against a telltale burn, keeping any tears at bay.

"Do you know where we are?" I ask.

Silence.

Gritting my teeth in frustration, I turn from the wall and brace my back against it. "I can't stay here," I repeat, though more to myself than anyone else. "I'd rather die than stay here. I'll die…"

There are a multitude of ways I could usher along that inevitable ending. The bathtub would be the easiest option. I'd only need to find something sharp. It's Marnie's method, but maybe I finally understand how she must have felt. This oppressive, suffocating need to run.

I can't stay here.

"Hotel."

"What?" I turn to the wall again, pressing my ear against it so tightly that it hurts. "What did you say?"

"We're in a hotel," the woman replies hoarsely. "I think so… But an old one. One he owns. It's in the middle of nowhere. The windows are locked. There are guards in front of every door. There is no escape."

No… I squeeze my eyes shut and dig my nails into my palms so viciously that I break the skin. No escape.

Is that so? Mischa would taunt were he here. *You're just taking the easy fucking way out. You want to stay with him. Admit it.*

"Never," I snarl out loud. I sound insane—but it's all I have. Arguing with a phantom.

Helpless, I eye the ceiling and another grim plan forms: a makeshift rope with the bedsheets tied to a sturdy post. Hanging. Could I do it? In my morbid search, my eyes keep returning to a unique square-shaped cut-out closed off with metal slats.

A vent.

Cautiously, I lurch to my feet. Without something to climb on, it's too far out of my reach, and the wardrobe towers too high to stand on. Frantic, I race toward the bed, but the frame is solid wood, impossible to budge.

"Hello," I call to the other woman. "Is there a vent in your ceiling?"

"Yes," she whispers back. "But I can't reach it."

"Damn it." I fight against the panic building in my skull, warning me that it's futile. *Just give in.* "Is there anything heavy in your room? A table? Anything you can move or stand on?"

I hear a scraping sound like someone rising to their feet. Then soft, hesitant footsteps. Finally, I sense her return to the wall.

"Yes," she says. "There is a table."

"Good." It takes everything I have to keep my building hope from my voice. "If you stand on it, do you think you can reach the vent?"

More silence.

"Yes," she says nearly a minute later. "I…I think so."

"Thank God." I swallow hard, knowing that what I'm asking is more than anyone ever should of a stranger. But this isn't the time for pleasantries. "I need you to climb into the vent, Ama. If you come to my room, you can open mine. If you can bring me a sheet, anything like a rope, then I can climb. We can leave."

It's far-fetched. I know that even as the plan leaves my mouth. Far-fetched. Stupid. Futile.

But it's all I have.

"If we can make it out—no. I *know* we can make it. I know we can."

I hear nothing from the other end, but for good, I suspect. Ama's stopped listening.

But I can't stop talking.

"He'll kill you," I tell her. "He'll kill me too."

One day, eventually. I know as much with a certainty even Mischa's madness couldn't inspire.

"But I can't stay here. Not anymore. And you have a child with you?"

I hear a sharp intake of air.

"Yes," she admits.

"Then please…"

Silence falls again and I'm too tired to make another attempt. Instead, I curl onto my side and will my conscious mind far away.

It turns to Mischa, a fitting tool to compound on Robert's prison; before he can do it, I'll drive myself insane.

I can feel him inside me, my own devious, maddening parasite. *Is this how it ends, Little Rose?* he taunts. *With you on your knees, too pathetic to run? No. Get the fuck up. Try again. Run!*

Gasping, I pull myself upright, clinging to the wall for balance. My first few steps carry me in a pathetic circle. Then farther. Faster. Feeling along the walls, I test for any breaks. When that fails, I try moving the bed again. Then I retest the windows, running my fingers along the impenetrable wood. Still, I keep moving. Thinking. Trying —anything.

Everything.

I'll give in by the end. Robert will come for me before dawn. I know it.

But still, I resist the inevitable for as long as I can, even if it hurts.

Even if it leaves me too tired to fight back when my captor returns. Even if it leaves me exhausted and panting, I keep trying.

Eventually, I sink onto the bed, my face in my hands. Winthorp Manor looms, my virtual gallows. Once I enter beyond those gleaming walls, I know I'll never come back out. At least not as the woman I am now—Mischa's spiteful Little Rose.

Something tickles my nose and I jolt to awareness. There's no one around. My door is still closed, but cool air ruffles my hair…

Coming from above.

"Please hurry," a soft voice calls.

Looking up, I see the vent hanging open and a pale hand reaching from beyond like the madness only possible in a dream.

"All I have is a sheet," my rescuer says weakly. "It's secured to my waist, but you need to climb quickly."

As I gape, a tightly curled strip of ivory descends from the darkness.

I don't hesitate to grab it. But within seconds, I realize the full daunting nature of what my reckless planning requires.

I'm still physically weak, healing from multiple fractures and a severed finger. Climbing at all is hard—but without Mischa's ruthless strength to spur me on, it's damn near impossible. My feet dangle helplessly, inches off the ground.

It's hopeless…

Enough! I shake my head to clear it and reach higher. Then higher. Sweat beads on my forehead and pours down my shoulders, slicking my nightgown to my flesh. I'm moving too slowly. Any minute, Robert will return and this will all be in vain.

Fear of that outcome spurs me faster even as my muscles scream in protest. Closing my eyes, I focus on inching higher despite the searing pain. Higher. Finally, I lift my hand and my fingers strike a firm surface.

"I'll help you," Ama whispers and her hands grab mine. It's a struggle to pull myself the final distance, but finally, I'm fully inside the vent, panting on the frigid metal.

"We need to move," I say as Ama wrestles the vent closed after me.

She's pale up close, with long, dark hair shrouding her lithe frame. Behind her, an even smaller figure huddles out of sight.

"I don't think these extend far," she whispers. "They might be able to hear us through them."

My blood runs cold at the thought. *This is insane,* a part of me insists. I should climb down. Wait for Robert. If he finds us now, it will be so much worse.

"I think we can go this way." Ama tugs my hand and shuffles forward.

I follow, suppressing a cough as dust and grime catch beneath my fingers. I don't know how far we go before she reaches back.

"It's a dead end." Her voice shakes, racked with terror. "We have to go down."

Down leads into darkness glimpsed only through the slats of another vent.

"I'll go first." I lift the grate and reach for the coiled sheet still trailing from Ama's waist.

"I'm okay," she whispers as I hesitate. "Just…hurry."

I climb down, suppressing a groan as my muscles strain, pushed to their limit. Feet from the floor, my arms give way and I drop down, landing hard.

Bang! The solid thud echoes as my heart stops. Any moment, Robert or one of his men will come rushing. Seconds pass as the air sticks in my lungs.

But no one comes. Yet.

Scrambling upright, I race to get my bearings. Smooth tile flooring betrays that this isn't one of Robert's suites. Faint light enters from a single window, providing just enough context to the shadows to make out where we are: a room filled with towering metal squares stacked one on top of the other.

A laundry room?

"Is it safe?" Ama calls from above.

"I…I don't know," I admit. "But we don't have a choice."

I can sense her wrestling with the same indecision plaguing me. Finally, she sighs.

"I need to send my child down first." Fear distorts her voice, even more pronounced. Her child. She may as well have said her *life*.

"Okay. It's okay." I position myself beneath the vent and raise my arms. "You can lower him down."

Pale limbs pierce the dark, lowered with the utmost care. Ama's son is a thin, wiry boy with a mop of wild, blond hair obscuring delicate features. He stares down on me warily, his eyes massive in the dark.

"Do you have him? Please! Do you have him?"

"Y-yes," I croak, jolting back to awareness. As the child is lowered by his hands, I grab a metal folding chair and stand on it, grabbing him by the waist. Tiny hands paw at my shoulders, gripping tight until I climb from the chair and set him down.

By the time I look up, a slender woman has already unfurled herself from the ceiling to balance precariously on the edge of the chair. Observing her in shadow, I first think she's beautiful. Alarmingly so. Dark hair hangs down to her waist, shrouding a slight frame covered only in a thin, gray dress.

In contrast, the boy is wearing a crisp white shirt and pants that I can tell even in the dark are of expensive quality. He must be the relative of a Winthorp associate. One of Robert's business partners, maybe? The moment his mother descends from the chair, he races to her. "Ama!"

She lifts him, clutching him to her chest. "Now what do we do?" she asks, her face stricken with panic.

"We…" I scan the room and spot a door left ajar at the other end of it. A faint strip of light illuminates potential freedom. "We keep moving," I say, leading the way toward it. "We can't stop now."

CHAPTER 9

I would say that my life has been devoid of anything resembling luck thus far. Maybe the fates have finally smiled upon me, because beyond the laundry room, we find a stairwell extending down.

I lead the way, my heart in my throat, but at the base of the steps, propped open with a cinder block, is yet another door.

Fresh air tickles my nose, acrid and heavy—but it's too good to be true. I know that even before I hear the low, grating hum of a man whistling nearby.

"Shhh," I hiss to Ama, who goes still on the bottom step.

Inching forward along the wall, I spot the culprit of the sound. He's leaning against the outside of the building, blowing cigarette smoke into the open air. Dressed in a bulky shirt and jeans, he doesn't seem like one of Robert's men. A worker of this building perhaps?

I scan him more intently, deciphering what little clues I can. The sleeves of his shirt are rolled up enough to reveal a tattoo on his forearm: a gyrating serpent intertwined with a cross.

Frantic, Ama paws at my shoulder. "There's someone there," she breathes against my ear. "What now?"

My eyes go to the makeshift doorjamb, and once again, I channel Mischa. What was it he told Mouse? *You can't hesitate.*

"Wait!" Ama gasps as I slink forward. "What are you doing?"

I'm not sure. I can't let myself think it through, either. Quietly, I stoop for the brick and replace it with my bare foot. My leg trembles, fighting to support the door's weight as I lift the brick as high as I can—which is mere inches from the ground.

You want to die a pathetic little bitch? my imaginary Mischa goads. *Then go back. Let him inside you again. Be his whore again. His wife. His toy.*

Inhaling sharply, I force myself to focus. Luckily, the man isn't paying the doorway any attention. He doesn't see me creep between the sliver of open space, hefting the brick even higher. A single question crosses my mind: Could I really hit a stranger?

Kill him?

Yes…

No?

But as Ama said, Robert owns this building. Anyone here works first and foremost for him and the Winthorps. So I shut off the part of my brain urging me to retreat and count to three.

One…

Two…

Just as I tense to spring forward, the man turns and strolls up a concrete path in the opposite direction, still whistling. I give myself only seconds to recognize the change in fate before I shoulder the door open fully and beckon Ama through it.

The bracing night air greets us like a slap, cold and unforgiving. My bare feet register hard pavement beneath them, and the only real source of light comes from an orange bulb jutting above the door.

At least the man is gone from view—for now.

Beyond the narrow exit, a parking lot stretches across the entire width of a massive brick building. As Ama claimed, it's grand enough to be a hotel—but a reclusive one, used only by the Winthorps, I suspect.

Looming shapes betray a few vehicles. The nearest one is a massive white van. It's only as I race toward it that I realize I still have the brick in my grasp. In the darkness, I notice Ama eyeing it, and she clutches her son even tighter to her chest.

"Shh, my darling," she soothes as he starts to whimper. "Shh… Everything is fine—"

"We have to get out of here." I approach the van and tug on the first door I can reach. "Shit!"

It's locked. Just as I spot a car a few yards away, that guttural whistle returns.

"Damn it," I hiss. "We need to find—"

"Over here." Ama waves frantically from the other side of the van. "I think I've opened it!"

Sure enough, I circle around and find her propping open the door to the front seat with her hip.

"Thank God!" I slam the button on the console to unlock the rest. "Get in."

"Can you drive?" the woman asks fearfully as I claim the driver's seat.

I don't answer her. Once again, fate has chosen to both mock and reward me. The owner of this vehicle left the keys in the ignition.

As well as a knife on the passenger's seat.

A reddish liquid paints the surface and my stomach churns. I wrench the glove compartment open and find a wad of tissues, which I toss over the weapon for the child's sake.

Then I palm the steering wheel and try to breathe.

"Hold on," I warn as I rack my brain for every lesson Mischa taught me. Brake, I recall, identifying that particular pedal. Gas.

After that? Hope and prayer.

"I can do this," I murmur. Then I glance in the rearview mirror and my blood runs cold.

The smoking man has returned. Only now, he stands awkwardly, his neck craned, his hand positioned over his eyes like a visor as he stares in our direction.

"Oh God," Ama chokes out. "He'll spot us soon, if he hasn't already."

"We're fine," I insist.

But there isn't even time to panic.

Aiming my gaze on a clear path through the lot, I twist the key and slam on the gas. The van jerks beneath me, a living, untamable thing. I have to throw myself against the steering wheel to narrowly avoid hitting another vehicle.

"Careful!" Ama cries. "Please…"

Mingled with her voice is a softer whine that tugs at my heart.

"It's fine," I rasp.

Fortunately, the parking lot is surrounded by a stretch of desolate fields, and in the distance, a lone road leads to the horizon. I don't recognize this area—which only reinforces the fact that I barely know a world beyond Winthorp Manor.

I could be leading us to a dead end. A river. A lake. A cliff.

For a second, I can't suppress that panicked, pathetic part of me Robert Winthorp nurtured for so damn long.

What am I doing? I should return. Give in. Surrender.

But Mischa's voice is louder, drowning out all other thoughts in my head.

Run, Little Rose. Fucking run.

I drive for hours until the van slows to a crawl despite how hard I slam on the gas pedal. A straining groan issues from the engine with every attempt.

"We're out of petrol," Ama points out, her voice thin. Around a yawn, she warns, "We won't make it far on foot."

She sounds more realistic than pessimistic, but the point is the same: Without the van, it's only a matter of time until we wind up caught in the net of one monster or the other.

Suspiciously, I don't think we've been followed. Yet.

"They must not have noticed we're gone," Ama says as if reading my mind. I glance back and find her staring pensively from the window, stroking her son's hair. "But not for long."

I copy her, unnerved by the lightening sky. Eventually, I have no choice but to pull over onto the side of the road before the engine dies altogether. The surrounding countryside is eerily empty—something that I doubt is a regular occurrence.

Robert is powerful enough to keep certain roads clear at his leisure. All it takes is money pressed into the right hands to have traffic temporarily diverted, robbing us of any helpful passerby.

And blocking off the route of any potential rescue from a certain *mafiya* leader in the process.

"We can't stay here." I shoulder the door open on my end and step out onto shockingly cold gravel. A chilling breeze cuts through the thin fabric of my nightgown and reinforces the fact that I'm barefoot.

So are Ama and her son.

Just how far will we make it like this? Biting my lip, I smother the thought.

"Come on. We need to keep moving." I reach back into the van and grab the knife, holding it awkwardly in my damaged hand.

"We're ready." Ama moves stiffly, never letting go of her son for a second. Once out of the van, she faces me. "Where will we go…" She trails off, her eyes wide as she takes me in in the full light of day.

I know I'm staring at her as well.

She's alarmingly pale. So pale that she glows, but the pallor just enhances her beauty. And her smooth, unblemished skin only serves as a harsh contrast to mine: sliced and bruised and swollen.

"I don't know," I say as I turn away, shrouding as much of my face as I can behind my uninjured hand. "Come. Let's go."

"Ama!"

I look back and find the boy squirming in her arms.

"It's her," he says, pointing at me. His other hand claws at his neck and tugs a necklace from beneath the collar of his shirt. It's beautiful, if simple: a slender gold chain supporting a square-shaped charm. "The angel—"

"Hush, my darling." Ama turns his face toward her chest and shushes him until he goes silent.

My cheeks heat as I turn toward a swath of trees—the only coverage in view—and start walking, wincing as the uneven terrain tears at my bare heels. In theory, two women and a child shouldn't go far without being recaptured.

But, somehow, we reach the edge of the forest unaccosted. From there, it's a slow, painful trek toward nowhere. Brambles claw at my skin. Holding the knife, I'm weighed down as much as Ama. My exhausted, broken body can only go so far before my legs threaten to give out entirely.

"We…need…rest," Ama croaks in between panting breaths. Her arms quiver as she readjusts the boy on her hip. "Just for a moment—"

"We can't," I insist, even as my trembling hand clings to a nearby branch for balance. I feel it in the pit of my soul: If we stop now, it's over. "They've had nearly a day to hunt us down."

As I retrace our steps in my head, I realize how pathetically little we've traveled overall. Finding us will be child's play if they aren't encroaching on our position already.

And, God, I can sense them now: specters in every flickering shadow and rustling of distant leaves. I tighten my grip on the knife as much as possible, but with as weak as I am, I can barely brandish it higher than my knee.

Still, I stagger forward, grasping for another tree or branch. "We can't stop moving—"

"Someone's coming!" Ama cries.

Panic surges up my throat, robbing my voice, as my straining ears catch the same sound: the telltale crunch of footsteps expertly traversing the underbrush.

"N-no." Moisture floods my eyes, and it takes every ounce of strength I can muster to blink back the forming tears. "Hide," I spit toward Ama, but I don't check to see if she obeys.

Instead, I shift my focus toward putting as much distance between us as possible—and making as much noise as I can in the process.

I'll die rather than go back to Robert, but maybe I can ensure that I'm the only one forced to choose that fate.

And it seems our pursuer has taken the bait. His footsteps advance on me rapidly, growing less stealthy the closer he comes. Soon, I can hear him breathing. Panting.

I wait until I assume he's close enough to grab me. Then I pivot, lashing out with the knife. "Stay away from me!"

He grunts in shock, narrowly avoiding the blade. Then he grabs my arm and the game is over. Iron strength nearly takes me off my feet.

"Do you really think you can stab me, Little Rose?" he hisses.

I look at him sharply and blink. My eyes are playing tricks. Or maybe he's a joke conjured by delirium.

The figure before me certainly could be such a specter: a haggard-looking Mischa, his chin covered in stubble. His bloodshot eyes are honed like lasers, taking in my thin, beautiful nightgown and coifed hair. He opens his mouth, presumably to say something. A quip?

But I'm too tired to hear it.

"Mischa!" I throw myself toward him, and his arms encircle my waist. My face finds the crook of his shoulder and I breathe him in, relishing the heat and the way he stiffens against me—still so fucking suspicious. I can't humor him now. I try to speak, but all I can do is moan and go limp.

Something in my appearance keeps him silent. I'm in his arms within seconds, held tightly to his chest. His heartbeat plays a steady rhythm as he starts to move, racing through the underbrush. It's only now that I remember.

"Wait," I croak, bracing my hand against his shoulder.

"What is it?"

"There's someone else—"

"What?" He cranes his neck back and then goes rigid.

Following the line of his gaze, I see why.

Ama didn't run and hide after all. In the dim light filtering between the trees, she looks almost ethereal, her hair falling like a cloak. Wide-eyed, she gapes at Mischa. Then she sinks to her knees, still clutching her son to her chest. Her pink lips flutter, forming the same sound over and over, but it's wasted seconds before my brain can finally interpret it. A name.

"M-Mischa?"

The arms around me loosen, and I'm forced to stand, clinging to his shoulder for balance.

"No… You're dead." Mischa shakes his head, his expression pained. Broken. "No… *Anna?*"

"Oh my God!" Tears stream down Ama's face as she rocks herself, clinging to her son so tightly that the boy whines in response. "Mischa!"

He advances on her with slow, deliberate steps. Then, suddenly, he's on his knees, his arms thrown around her.

"Anna," he mutters. "I can't believe it. Anna."

And something pangs in my chest, so subtle that I barely register it before the feeling spreads, blossoming into full-blown shock that brings me to my knees.

Anna. Anna-*Natalia*.

His Anna.

She's alive.

Their reunion lasts for only a second before Mischa reluctantly stands and helps Anna to her feet.

"We need to move," he warns. But one look at her trembling body and his jaw clenches.

I was so focused on myself, but I wasn't the only one expending every ounce of strength I have. Her knees wobble, threatening to buckle any second. From her arms, the boy stares fearfully.

It's a miracle we came this far.

"Carry her," I tell Mischa. "I can take the baby—"

"No!" Anna hugs the boy to her, heedless of his plaintive cries. "I can keep moving. I can—"

"There's no time. Here—give him to me." Mischa reaches for the boy and Anna finally relinquishes him. Effortlessly,

Mischa swings the child around, setting him on his back. "Grab my neck," he commands, guiding the boy's tiny hands into position. "But don't you dare choke me."

Before Anna can protest, she's in his arms as well.

Meeting my gaze, Mischa inclines his head. "My men aren't far, but we need to run. Do you understand, Rose?"

I nod, and then he's gone at a lightning pace, picking through the underbrush with enviable grace. My lungs churn fire as I follow clumsily in his wake. There's no space in my exhausted brain left for caution. I throw myself forward without tact, my arms flailing for balance.

I'm loud and bumbling, and worst of all…

I'm slowing him down.

The fact that he's even in my line of sight at all betrays the lengths he's gone through to keep pace with me, despite being encumbered as he is.

"You need to keep moving, Little Rose," he taunts from up ahead, his breathing heavy. "Don't you fucking dare slow down. Stay with me… Stay with me!"

"I'm…trying…" It's a lie. Every last bit of energy I had has already been expended. Pure momentum drives me now. I'm losing speed, falling farther and farther behind. He's merely a speck now, bobbing on the horizon.

Carried by the wind, his voice reaches me. "Don't you dare give up. Move! Or do you *want* to get captured?"

Bastard. I keep going, if only out of spite. Gradually, his distant shape grows larger. Am I hallucinating?

No…

He's stopped.

Gasping, I scan our surroundings and realize why; we've finally reached a break in the woods. Up ahead, the trees give way to a narrow field marred by tire tracks.

"What now?" I croak to Mischa.

He pays me no mind. Stepping forward, he bellows over the landscape, "To me!"

As if on cue, several men rush forward to meet us from the underbrush. Their trademark fatigues reveal their identity: the *mafiya.*

One of them grabs Anna while another races toward me. Seconds later, I find myself in a van, hurtling toward an unknown destination.

"Where are we?" I manage to croak.

"Heading east," a man replies from the front seat. "We'll be in Sergei's territory soon."

Three others crowd the enclosed space alongside me, including the driver, their faces stern and focused on the road. I don't recognize a familiar figure among them—not even Vanya.

"Where is Mischa?" I ask, peering through the nearest window. Just behind this vehicle, I can make out the looming shape of another van.

Mischa, Anna, and the boy must be in another vehicle altogether.

Because otherwise…I'm alone.

Darkness shrouds the interior of the van when it finally comes to an abrupt stop. Consciousness is a battle I've fought to the bitter end. By now, my bloodshot eyes can barely open wide enough to make out my surroundings. Beyond the van, the vague outline of a structure looms, ghosted by moonlight.

Could it be Winthorp Manor?

Or was my escape more than a fantastical dream?

"Stay with me, Little Rose."

I jump as someone opens the door on my side. Cool air spills in and I find myself in familiar arms without warning.

"I've got you."

My head lolls against a muscled shoulder, a stern jaw the only focal point I can fixate on. God, he looks older, aged overnight. From this angle, the shadows beneath his eyes hollow his features, more defined than ever.

"Am I safe?" I ask, my voice a broken whisper. Despite everything, I'm curious as to his answer. Will he make the same boast Robert did once his pawn was back within his possession? *Safe. Safe. Safe.*

I wait for a mocking taunt, but he says nothing else as he carries me toward a grand structure that, at a glance, I can tell dwarfs even his old manor in comparison.

Sergei's property?

It's made of stone, at least four stories tall. The layout isn't as flashy as that of Winthorp Manor's. Regal and modest, it's more enclosed: a family home rather than a status symbol.

In the fading light, I make out a paved courtyard containing a small garden casting a mockingly sweet aroma as we pass. Up ahead, a massive door opens and from it rushes Vanya.

"Thank God," he says, spotting us. "You found her—"

"Papa?"

That voice stops him dead in his tracks, and I fear he'll collapse. Wildly, he scans the area before his gaze finally fixates on something beyond us.

"No," he croaks, his voice rasping. "No, it can't be…"

A hesitant step propels him down the stone path. Then another, until he's running across the courtyard. I turn in time to catch a slender figure limping toward him.

"Papa!" Instantly, she's engulfed in his arms and they sink to their knees, heedless of the paved stone beneath them. It's too raw of a moment to ogle for long. Too intimate.

I turn away, surprised to find Mischa staring resolutely ahead as well. Once we reach the entrance to the manor, he carries me into the grand foyer beyond it. Here, the mood shifts entirely as we're approached by a watchful Sergei.

"You found her," the older man says, eyeing me with a terse nod. "How?"

"Ask her," Mischa says, jostling me in his arms. "In fact, how fucking useful are you and your so-called expert intel?"

"Something happened." Sergei's eyes narrow imperceptibly. "Explain."

"No. How about you explain?" Mischa stops short of running into the other man altogether—for my sake, I suspect.

Trapped between them, I'm the only one who would suffer.

"For one," Mischa continues, "explain why, despite all your intel on the Winthorps, you've never mentioned that your *real* niece was alive?"

Sergei frowns. "What are you..." Then he turns to the commotion in the courtyard and something flits across his face so quickly that I can barely trace it. Shock?

Before I can be sure, he's already halfway to his brother and his niece.

"I thought you were dead," I admit to Mischa. I'm still in his arms, in a hallway, I think. Then a room. "I thought—"

"You need to sleep," he says, lowering me to a soft surface I assume to be a bed.

From the corner of my eye, I notice emerald-green walls, and a lavish canopy shrouds me from above.

"Go ahead," Mischa commands. "Get some rest. I'll be here."

"Oh?" A tired laugh trickles from my throat, much to my surprise. "To make sure I don't run away?"

Of all the times to joke…

This one lands flat.

"Yes." He scans my face, hunting for something. Searching. As my eyes drift shut, I hear him mutter, "Though maybe you shouldn't have come back after all, Little Rose. Maybe you shouldn't have come back…"

I wake up, aware of nothing other than the fact that I'm alone—and the most selfish, pathetic thought crosses my mind before I can squash it.

I want it to have been a dream: Robert. Anna.

Everything.

I want to wake up to an infuriated Mischa glaring over me while Vanya lurks worriedly in the next room and Mouse skips down the hall.

Seeing Robert at all, and finding Anna-Natalia, could have been just some vivid nightmare…

But I feel it: a cold sense of dread congealing in my belly like a lead weight. Something vital has changed. Positions have been altered overnight and nothing will be as it was.

I try to evade the inevitable by lying beneath the blankets for as long as I can. They're expensive quality, like the kind in Mischa's manor. The glimpses I have of the room as I toss and turn reveal an elegant, yet comfortable space with dark-green wallpaper and hardwood floors.

My bed is massive, shielded by a heavy, embroidered canopy: silver vines sewn over a rich forest green. When I finally shrug the blankets off and sit upright, I spot a set of neatly folded clothing on a polished wooden dresser in the corner. Across from it, a heavy chair is positioned near a wide window overlooking an expansive view of tailored gardens.

"We will regroup at my property," Sergei said what feels like an eternity ago. So this must be the place.

A world where Mischa Stepanov doesn't hold sway.

He didn't even keep his promise to watch over me. Straining my ears, I don't hear him grumbling or shouting nearby, either.

Cautiously, I try to stand only to gasp as pain ripples through my spine. Everything, down to my toes, throbs at the slightest attempt to bear any weight. I'm covered in thin scratches as well, though I don't need to look any farther than my torn, bleeding feet to know that I've pushed my body to its limits.

But the longer I stay in bed, the more that ominous dread in my gut grows. Limping to the dresser is the only way to push back that reality for as long as possible. The clothing I find is a pink dress with long sleeves. Courtesy of Mischa?

I picture him finding the garment he'd consider the most insulting. Robert's precious wife bundled in pink after being pried from his grasping hands. How ironic would that be?

I can't even look at the color without shuddering, so I set the garment aside and bite my pride back enough to open a drawer and snatch something new from it: another dress in a shade of blue.

Sergei keeps his home well stocked, it seems.

My search of the room thankfully turns up an en suite bathroom equipped with a tub large enough to submerge myself in completely. I run the water as hot as I can stand it and climb in. Washing Robert away a second time is a grueling, tenuous affair.

My battered limbs take ages to scrub clean. Once I've dried off and wrapped in a towel, I brush my teeth until my gums bleed. Then I use a bit of hand soap for good measure.

Dramatic in a sense. Or perhaps poetic?

He doesn't own me anymore.

But who does? When I finally gather the nerve to creep from my room, I feel rudderless. A careening ship without a captain, barely able to avoid the rocks waiting to dash me to pieces.

And this new landscape seems to contain plenty of pitfalls to stumble upon.

Sergei's home is a maze of ornate hallways, much like Mischa's Pecavi—only this place feels older. Colder.

Prestige seems printed into the very wallpaper and embedded in every portrait of a nameless figure I pass. A modest color scheme of dark green and silver creates a quiet atmosphere.

So quiet.

My footsteps echo, jarringly loud. Any minute, a snarling *mafiya* leader should appear from around a corner and snidely insinuate I have ulterior motives.

By the time I reach a grand, circular staircase, I've found no one. Here, at least, voices drift from nearby. I follow them to a small sitting room.

Inside it, Vanya is sitting on a leather chair, angled toward Anna. She's been washed and dressed in a clean black dress. In her arms, her son sleeps, held to her chest as she and her father speak in low, hushed tones. Suddenly, he reaches out, bracing his hand on her knee, and I can make out the glint of tears painting her cheeks.

Quietly, I turn away and continue past them. I have no idea how long this hallway goes or where it travels. Almost in a daze, I turn a corner and nearly trip over a small body huddled by the wall. Alarm lances down my spine and I jolt back reflexively, my arm outstretched.

But then I make out the figure's pale-blond hair and crouch beside her. "Mouse?"

She turns away from me. Her slight body heaves and she tries to shield her face with one of her hands.

"What's wrong?" A million horrific scenarios march through my mind. So many dark, twisted things.

She shakes her head. Then she brandishes her other hand, holding the trembling fingers up for me to make out the red substance painting each fingertip.

"Oh God. What happened?" I lurch to my feet, my heart racing. Is another attack imminent? "Is it your shoulder?" I ask her out loud. "We need to find Mischa—"

Mouse grabs my hand and tugs before I can take a step. *No!* She points to her belly and it takes my brain a second to put the pieces together.

"How old are you?" I ask, returning to a crouch.

She eyes me warily, mistrust glinting in her green irises. Only God knows how long she's had to survive like this, always on guard.

Finally, she raises all ten of her fingers. Then two.

"Twelve," I say, nodding. "All right. Come with me."

I don't know how to navigate back to my room, but with luck, I find a bathroom nearby and coax her into a shower. The brief looks I get of her body make my heart ache. She's twelve with the physique of a much younger child, though I doubt through natural means. How long has she been deprived of food, or comfort, or basic care?

"You don't have to be embarrassed," I tell her as she huddles at the back of the shower, hunched away from me. "This happens to every woman. My first time, I thought I was dying, but one of the older maids took pity on me and taught me about womanhood."

In crude, explicit terms, but it was a lesson nonetheless.

"You aren't dying," I add as shuffling sounds allude to her studiously scrubbing her body clean. "But you will have to learn to anticipate it. For now, we'll make do, but I'll see if someone can get you proper supplies. Would you like that?"

I pause in the slim chance she'll reply.

"Okay," I say as if she has. "No one else has to know."

Finally, Mouse reemerges, dripping wet. I help her dry off and then I leave her long enough to retrace my steps to the room I woke up in and retrieve the pink dress.

I return and find her rooted firmly where I left her, by the tub. Once she eyes the garment in my hands, she frowns and shakes her head.

"It's just for now," I insist, helping her put it on. "I'm sure you'll be back to climbing trees in no time."

Her wrinkled nose reveals her doubts about that.

When we finally leave the bathroom, she stays close to my side like a shadow. Hiding?

"We should find your room," I suggest. "Do you remember where it—"

"Here you are. The Mouse and Rose." Mischa seems to appear from the very shadows. He's still wearing a pair of filthy, faded fatigues. Either he's gone out again or he's still on guard, unable to relax even here. His eyes scan me in a ruthless sweep, settling on my face, then my hair. "You and I need to have a chat, Rose," he says, his voice uncharacteristically stern. "Preferably now."

"No." I have to clear my throat to find the traction to speak. "I'm tired."

It's like that first day all over again—trapped with him. My initial instinct is to run. I turn on my heel to do just that, but Mouse digs her nails into my wrist and yanks me back. She's surprisingly strong for someone so small. I look down and find her gritting her teeth as she inclines her head down the hall. Apparently, her room is nearby.

"Tired?" Mischa advances a step, his eyes narrowed, and unease washes over me. In an instant, he's switched from playful to guarded as only he can. His jaw twitches as if chewing over the words he plans to say next. Then he shrugs and continues moving, pushing past me. "Suit yourself."

The chill in his voice resonates down to my core. But before it can fully sink in, Mouse tugs me forward and I have no choice but to follow.

Her room is smaller than mine, but not far down. The layout of the floor curves—a giant oval centered around the staircase. Together, Mouse and I find a clean pair of underwear and a maid, who promptly supplies sanitary napkins.

"It should last for seven days or so," I explain as she throws herself onto a modest bed draped in yellow sheets. "The worst thing you'll experience is the cramping. You should learn to anticipate it, trust me. Mine should be due…" I do the math in my head and then bite my lip so hard that it bleeds. "Um…any day now," I croak. "Maybe I'll get to join in your misery?"

I try to smile, but her lips remain resolute in a flat, stubborn line.

"So you are twelve," I say, switching subjects. I wonder if Mischa knew that. Looking at her, I wouldn't guess her any older than nine or ten. "Where are you from?"

She looks away from me, her mouth wrinkling. Then she points to a portrait hanging above the bed.

"The ocean?" I guess, deciphering the clue from the framed scene of a stormy beach.

She shrugs and raises her arm before quickly extending it.

"There was fishing there?" I say, interpreting her miming.

She nods and then returns to her stiff, hunched position, looking at everything but me.

"Can you speak?" I know I'm unwanted here. But maybe she's preferable to the silence and thoughts of Robert and Mischa. Admittedly, a feral dog hungry for my blood would be preferable. "Or do you just choose not to—"

"She can."

I jump as the door opens from the outside, revealing Mischa behind it. He crosses his arms, oblivious as Mouse's cheeks turn blood red.

"How long were you standing there?" I demand.

"The girl can hear, so she isn't mute," he says, shrugging me off. "She can speak, but it's probably painful, and she wouldn't be able to say much, if anything at all. It's a trick that Nicolai uses to silence all of his drug mules. He gives them a daily dose of a chemical cocktail that causes permanent, lasting damage to the vocal cords if taken long enough."

Horror drains any irritation I may feel toward him. "That's horrible—" I break off as Mouse jumps from the bed and storms past Mischa, her hands in fists.

"What's wrong?" He reaches for her arm, but she easily evades him and dashes into the hall. Narrowed, his eyes cut toward me. "What did you say to her?"

"Me?" I scoff. "Maybe she's alarmed by the man who just rudely barged into her room and overheard a private conversation? How much *did* you overhear?"

"I don't know." Mischa frowns, stroking his chin. "Something about fishing."

"What do you know about her?" I blurt, staring at the space she occupied. In so many ways, she seems to fit that stupid nickname. A mysterious, scurrying creature.

"Not much," he admits. "Just what I managed to get out of Nicolai. She was sold to settle a debt."

And he callously threw her into his drug trade.

"Her story isn't as rare as you might think. In fact..." He looks up, meeting my gaze, and alarm jolts down my spine. I step back instinctively, but he's already advancing twice as fast. "Plenty of women find themselves caught up in the schemes of evil men. Isn't that right? Or at least that is the tale they want you to believe..."

He reaches for me, twisting a lock of my hair between his fingers.

"Stop!" I bat his hand away, and he cocks his head as if finally learning the answer to a puzzling question. "You should be with Anna," I croak.

"And where should you be, *Elle*?" he bites back. "How soon before I can expect Robert Winthorp knocking on the front fucking door, following the trail of crumbs you've left for him?"

My hand lashes out with no input from my brain. It's only as I feel the sting through my palm that I realize what I've done: I've slapped him.

And I don't regret one fucking second.

CHAPTER 12

"There she is…" Laughing, he lets the blow glance off him and leans in, forcing me farther into the corner. "What a shame you've dropped your grateful, jail-sprung act so soon. It was almost convincing—"

"And you?" I counter. "You should be with the love of your life, shouldn't you?"

God, I hate how nasty I sound. So damn bitter.

"Though," I choke out as my throat tightens, "maybe you wanted to tie up loose ends first? Don't worry. I can take a hint."

"What the hell are you talking about?"

"What you said," I insist. "According to you…I shouldn't have come back at all."

"What are you—" His eyes narrow and widen in quick succession. Then he laughs. "Oh, Little Rose. The next time you want to overhear my evil musings, maybe you shouldn't fucking pass out before you hear the whole thing? I don't think you should have come back because…"

"What?" I snarl.

"Because—" He grabs my wrist, yanking me against his chest. "Because I don't think I'll be inclined to let you go."

My heart stops. Muttered in such heated tones, the promise should be terrifying. And it is. So many nuances lurk in those words. Things a man like him could never say out loud.

And it's like the exhaustion and pain hit me all at once. I go limp. My arms are the only limbs I have control over and I throw them both around his neck.

"I've got you." He catches me, pinning me against the wall for support. "But if you're trying to choke me, it isn't working."

I'm too exhausted to form a comeback.

I break instead. Tears flood my eyes, and I sob like I never have in my entire life. So many years of pain and torment bleed from me. I can't slow the onslaught. My body trembles in the aftermath, and only now can I finally admit it. I've never been so terrified. So desperate.

I've never fought so damn hard before.

When my sobs finally subside, his fingers creep into my hair, and I finally register his voice murmured insistently into my ear.

"I've got you. I've got you. Let it out. Tell me what happened."

Between gasping pants, I manage to convey everything. The escape. Robert. Everything. But as the words leave my mouth, one thing remains clear: a nagging suspicion I've had since the second I crawled into the damn vent.

"It feels too easy," I admit as I draw back and swipe my hand across my face. "Too…clean."

"Hmm." Mischa strokes his chin, his gaze turned inward. "Like he let you go?"

"No." All I need to do is picture Robert to be sure of that. The man I know would never relinquish his toys, not even for leverage. "More like…"

"What?" His thumb grazes my chin, coaxing an answer from it. I shiver at the contact. Only he could master gentle and demanding in one gesture.

"More like someone planned it?"

But even that sounds too fantastical. The truth could be simpler: Living with Mischa has made me just as paranoid. No wonder he can't help but doubt me. In his world, everyone is an enemy or a potential foe.

Or a weakness waiting to be exploited.

"Anna," I rasp, turning my attention to the view beyond the window. A faint reflection taunts me regardless: his expression, suddenly guarded. "How is she?"

The softness that seeps into his mouth shouldn't make my chest ache. It shouldn't make me instantly scramble several steps away from him. His humanity—as rare as it is— shouldn't send a lance through my heart every bit as alarming as Robert's rage.

"She's…" He looks at the floor. Seconds pass and he can't seem to find a word to describe it: how a woman might feel after years of captivity, only to be miraculously found alive. "I thought she was dead."

Darkness creeps into his expression and just like that, he's hardened Mischa once more.

"They sent her 'body' in pieces. We had a burial. And all this time—" He runs his fingers along the stubble on his chin and sighs. "I said goodbye to her sixteen years ago. But if I knew, even a rumor, I would have broken down their fucking front door."

"I never saw her," I confess. And that's the terrifying thing. For sixteen years, Anna-Natalia was alive, presumably on Winthrop property, and I never saw her. I never heard any of the servants speak of her. Robert never so much as hinted…

And if a man could keep one such secret, only God knows what else he has in store.

"How could I have never seen her?" I'm shaking my head, and more tears threaten to fall. "I never saw her. I never saw—"

"Enough." He steps forward and I marvel at the sensation of being in his arms again. Of all the places in the world to seek refuge, his shoulder shouldn't be my chosen place to find it. I'm a parasite, leeching off his heat—and he lets me feed for as long as I need to.

At least until he wants something from me in return.

"I need to ask it." His fingers fan out down my back, running over the ridges of my spine. "Did he touch you?"

I know what he means. "And if he did?"

"Then he did." His grip tightens the moment I try to pull away. "I'd still want to know."

"Why?" I snarl. "Would that injure your pride? If I had to sleep with him? Would that make you feel like a pathetic, fucking—"

"I'd want to know," he growls into my ear so fiercely that I fall silent. "If he hurt you. If he touched you. I want to know."

"No…" I sigh, too tired to resist him any longer. "He didn't have to."

I felt violated anyway. In his presence, I was old Ellen again, and I know now more than ever that I can never be her. Not anymore.

"Is this the part where you vow to fuck me now?" I wonder, copying his gruff tone. "Erase him? Soothe your own ego?"

"No." His voice is so deep that it resonates in my bones. He isn't taunting me. "This is the part where you listen. To how we were somehow ambushed despite Sergei's protection. How I watched you get taken, and I knew then and there, even if you were a cunning little bitch who went back willingly. Even if it was all a game… Then you would have done your job too well, Rose, because I was going after you."

Only he could make such a heated confession sound more twisted than romantic.

"What happened?" I ask. "Robert's man said I was drugged."

From my hazy memories, I can't recall how something like that would occur. One moment, I was watching him from the doorway, and the next…

"All I know is you were gone and we were being shot at from the woods," Mischa says. "Luckily, Vanya had already moved out with the rest of the men, and I could catch up well enough. Sergei suggested he mount a rescue, but I went out on my own."

Which may explain why the leader looked more irritated than relieved when he arrived, his prize in tow.

"I didn't know where he kept you, though Sergei had a vague idea of the direction they went in," he admits. "Still, I expected to spend days tracking you down. But then…" He chuckles deep in his throat. "I find that you're already ten steps ahead."

"So what happens now?"

"Now?" He eases away from me, but his fingers slide along my hips, dragging out the contact until the last possible second.

When our gazes reconnect, I see a hint of that raw openness from before. But where, when Anna was mentioned, he looked softer—now, his bared teeth portray only ruthlessness.

"I'm going to destroy the Winthorps from the inside out."

"But why not just…" I trail off and let myself envision a fantasy world. One in which I could run away and no evil men would ever follow. I could live my life in peace, doing the things I've only ever dreamt of.

Find a home.

Make it my own.

Start a family…

But even in that beautiful fantasy, one fact cuts through everything like a thorn.

Robert would never let me go.

Maybe Mischa and Sergei are right in their own twisted way. There is only one method to ever fully eradicate the threat from the Winthorps.

Once and for all.

"Don't look so disappointed." Mischa swipes his finger along my chin. "I'll save your chosen prey for last. You can drive the spike through his neck."

I cringe at the imagery and brush my fingers along my jaw, tracing the remnants of Robert's last assault. "And if I don't want to?"

Am I talking to Mischa or myself?

"You want to," he replies regardless. "Oh yes. You fucking want to."

I turn away and head for the door. "We should talk to Vanya… Anna. Maybe she knows something about what Robert is planning."

Deep down, I know she doesn't. On her face, I saw the same doe-eyed expression I assume Mischa did the day he captured me. The stark, naked terror of a bird freshly freed from her cage.

Regardless, he says nothing, though I sense him behind me.

Vanya and Anna are still in the small sitting room. They're sitting as close together as they can, their hands clasped, their foreheads meeting. The boy is asleep on Anna's lap. When she spots me, she stiffens and her arms go protectively around him.

"Ellen," she says, her voice hoarse. "Is that your name? Ellen?" She looks to Vanya for clarification and he nods. "I want to thank you for—"

"Don't," I say thickly. "You don't have to."

"But I must." Sighing, she turns to Mischa. "I can't believe… I can't believe I'm really here—"

"Where did they keep you all this time?" he asks, his tone awkwardly gentle, as if he can't remember quite how to sound comforting. There's a hesitance in him he's never displayed, not even around Mouse. "They told us you were dead," he adds. "If I would have known, I would have done everything I could to—"

"I know." Anna eyes the child sleeping in her arms and strokes his hair. "They kept me at Winthorp Manor at first. I think so anyway. It's all a blur, those early days."

Her knuckles whiten as she fingers a blond curl and then smooths it carefully into place.

"They beat me at first. I thought they were going to kill me, but one day…" She breaks off as if reliving the memory. Her eyes widen and she removes her trembling hands from the boy and balls them into fists. "The older Winthrop. He came into my cell, and all he said to me was, 'My wife is the only reason you're still alive.'"

"Robert, Sr.?" Mischa asks, sounding to me as if he's miles away. "*His* wife?"

A torrent of blood surges through my ears as everything fades.

And all I see is her face.

"Marnie Winthorp," I say. "Her?"

"Yes." Anna nods. "I guess she made him keep me alive."

I blink rapidly, bringing more of the world into focus. The room. Vanya. Mischa. Both of them are staring at me. Watching me.

"They moved me after that," Anna continues. "I don't know where. It was isolated. They never visited much in those early days, but they didn't hurt me, either."

"One of their outposts?" Vanya asks Mischa.

The other man nods. "Most likely."

"I wasn't beaten or anything worse," Anna reiterates. She stares at nothing and I suspect she's speaking more for her own benefit than anyone else's. "They just kept me in a room alone, for years. So many years…" Tears well in her eyes, but she blinks them back. Her lips part into a breathtaking smile as she stares down on the boy in her arms. "If it weren't for him, I would have gone insane."

"What's his name?" Vanya leans forward and brushes his fingers along the boy's side. His wizened features soften for a brief instant and he looks years younger.

"His name?" Anna's gaze darts in my direction and then quickly flits away. "E-Eli," she says. "His name is Eli. Do you remember, Papa?" She croaks a watery laugh. "I always used to say that I would name my firstborn after—"

"Your grandmother." He smiles. "And a fine name it is."

"You said they didn't touch you." Mischa stands stiffly, staring into a past far beyond this room. "Then who is his father?"

"Mischa!" Vanya lurches to his feet. Anger brims over his face, darkening his eyes. For a brief second, he's transformed and I see an echo of the man Mischa claimed he used to be. "Don't." He shakes his head. "Not now."

"I-I'm tired." Anna stands as well, clutching the boy to her chest. He stirs, grumbling, and she cradles his head. "And I should put him down for his nap."

"I'll go with you." Stern-faced, Vanya stands between Mischa and his daughter like a guard, ushering her into the hall.

When they're out of earshot, I whirl on Mischa.

"Does it matter?" My voice comes out louder than I meant it to—I'm practically shouting. "Who his father is? Does that really matter to you? It's obvious she loves him—"

"That's not why…" He shakes his head as his gaze refocuses on me. "You said he kept you in separate rooms?"

Him. Robert.

"Y-yes. Why?"

"Nothing." He shakes his head and then storms into the hall. "It's nothing."

*I*n a day of reunions, I'm ready when Sergei finally comes for me. Like the darkness descending beyond the windows, he appears in the doorway of the small sitting room long after everyone else has left.

"Ellen. Did you sleep all right?" he asks, crossing the threshold. "Was the room to your liking—"

"I'm not taking your bait," I say, cutting to the chase. "If you want to tell me about my family, or my mother—fine. But I won't beg you to—"

"Understandable." He comes to stand beside me and gestures to one of the vacated chairs. "Shall we sit? Don't worry. I will not mention my *bait*, as you so put it. Whatever you ask, I am more than willing to answer."

I copy him warily, perching myself on the chair Anna occupied. It's still warm.

"How did you know my mother? I've already heard the abridged version from Mischa," I add. "But I want to hear it straight from you."

"Marnie Winthorp…" His eyes darken thoughtfully, and he cocks his head. "Should I say that I raped her? Tortured her? Beat her? I'm sure Mischa has filled your head with all sorts of sordid scenarios—"

"Just tell me the truth," I say tiredly. "I want… No, I *need* to hear it from you."

"Well, I never touched her. We never hurt her. If you don't believe me, you can ask Ivan."

"But you took her from her family," I point out. "From her daughter."

"Yes." He nods, turning his gaze to the window. "There was that. But you can rest assured that Ivan didn't force himself on her if that's what you're afraid of."

Hope forms a painful ball at the base of my throat. It's nearly impossible to speak. "How do you know that?"

He shrugs. "Because he loved her. More than I have ever seen him love anyone short of his own daughter. Even his first wife. While he cared for her, Marnie Winthorp had that man's soul in the palm of her hand."

It's strange, hearing it said so starkly out loud. I try to pair the two people I know: gnarled Vanya with beautiful, innocent Marnie. No matter how I arrange their imaginary specters, I can't see it clearly.

"But he let her go back to Robert Winthorp," I say.

"She was recaptured, yes." Sergei sighs. "You will have to ask him why he didn't rescue her, but do not doubt that he loved her."

"Did…" I swallow hard and force the question out. "Did he know about me?"

"I don't think so," Sergei admits. "But knowing my brother… I don't see him being content to let you grow up in that place."

A part of me wants to take comfort in that. At least until I recall how he was with Anna. Why go after one daughter when he clearly had another? One he raised and loved wholeheartedly.

"So what do you want with me now?" I demand.

Sergei holds out his hands defensively. "Nothing. I merely want you to learn about your family, the Vasilevs. Learn our ways."

I raise an eyebrow. "Even with Anna back?"

"Anna…" It's like he takes his time, mulling over the most polite phrasing possible. "Who knows what the Winthorps did to her. Is it really fair to ask her to helm so much so soon?"

"But I can?"

He doesn't reply. Instead, he settles into his chair and observes the ornate lawn visible beyond the window.

Moonlight ghosts the foreign landscape, making it seem more ethereal than real.

"I want you comfortable here, Ellen," he says after a moment. "I won't ask anything of you for a few days. Explore. Ask questions. Have the run of the entire manor." Grunting, he pulls himself to his feet and heads for the door. "How did you find your room?"

"Fine."

"Good." He meets my gaze with a searching look of his own and then steps into the hall. From it, his voice reaches me. "It was your mother's. I hope to see you at dinner. I've ordered my chef to prepare a banquet. A celebration of sorts, but I will understand if you prefer to have it brought to you instead."

I say nothing, listening to his steps retreat.

*M*ischa finds me in the dark. I sense him before his hand lands on my shoulder, painted silver by moonlight.

"You didn't eat." He tugs his grip, hauling me from the seat. "Come."

I let him guide me down the hall, but I'm surprised when we pass the room I recognize as mine and enter another alarmingly close to it.

At a glance, I know it's his. Only he would rebel against finery and comfort. He's stripped the bed of its fancy sheets, and his clothing lies strewn over the floor. Out of everything, the most alarming detail is the tray of food left steaming on a table in the corner.

Apparently, he hijacked the delivery meant for me and brought it here.

"Eat," he commands, nodding to the food. At the same time, he fishes something from his pocket and props a knee on the edge of the bed frame. With one hand, he balances the object over his thigh while manipulating a cloth in the other.

A few seconds pass before I realize what he's doing: polishing his knife.

Turning my back to him, I approach the table. Up close, I discover that not only did he take my tray, but a second one lies beneath a discarded gray shirt. He's barely touched the plump steak or vegetables on it.

I incline my head in his direction. "You didn't eat, either?"

He looks up and shrugs. "Banquets are not my thing."

Another glaring difference between him and Sergei. The older man seems to relish tradition, while Mischa…

Well, he prefers to stab what doesn't suit his preferences.

Near the table is a lone chair that I drag closer and sit on. I eat slowly to the soundtrack of the methodical motion of Mischa's polishing cloth.

Finally, the sound dies off.

"Sergei," he says as I pick at the remnants of food. "What did the old man say to you now?"

My hand stills, dangling a fork above my half-eaten vegetables. "What makes you think he has?"

He laughs. "Because you look like you've seen a fucking ghost. That's why."

I hear the thud of his boots striking the floor as he approaches me slowly. He savors the way I tense with every inch gained.

"And because… I'm not sure I trust him."

He lets the statement linger and I know he's gauging my reaction.

"Do you?" he asks when I remain silent.

I jump as he places his hand beside my half-eaten plate. "I don't know."

For all intents and purposes, the man seems genuine. But so could Robert Winthorp when he wanted to.

In this twisted game of men and money, I've learned that no one can be accurately judged at face value. Except…maybe Vanya.

"He's a cunning, sly old fox, Little Rose," Mischa insists against my ear. His breath fans my skin, erasing a chill I hadn't felt until now. "Maybe it's a family trait. But you've never asked: Why can Vanya barely stand to be in the same room with him? In fact, why would the man pledge his loyalty to *me* over his own brother? Think."

"Why?" I ask on cue. "Though I suspect you'll tell me anyway."

He chuckles, but there's a manic edge to the sound. This, I suspect, he's been itching to tell me for a long time.

"Do you remember?" he wonders, leaning in so that his lips graze my shoulder. I suck in a breath and curl my hands beneath the table to disguise how they shake. "That stupid boy you think you saw all those years ago? The one who saved your life, believing that you were Briar Winthorp?"

"You," I say hoarsely. "I saw you."

He crept into my room and urged me to hide. In the process, he gave me the mantra that saw me through years of torment. *Breathe.*

"But do you know why we were really there, Sergei and I?" He circles around my position and braces his hands against the table from the opposite end. "Ask."

"Why?"

"Revenge," he says simply. "We weren't aiming to merely whisk Briar away, oh no..."

His eyes darken in a way I've never seen before. It makes him look tired in a sense. A man who's seen a lifetime of horrors and hasn't forgotten a single one.

An ominous thrill runs down my spine as I brace my hands over the table's surface. "What were you going to do?"

His jaw clenches as if to reinforce the grim statement he utters. "We were going to slaughter the girl in her bed, Little Rose. Butcher her into pieces."

I wait for a laugh. A scoff. Anything.

As twisted as he can be, no man could be that cruel.

That evil.

But I wait in vain—he won't spoon-feed me this story.

I have to demand it. "Why?"

"As a warning and a lesson," he replies. "Don't ever fuck with the Vasilevs."

I can't disguise the shock distorting my features. My mouth is open, my eyes wide. Finally, I regain my composure enough to rasp, "That's…evil."

"Yes," Mischa agrees, surprisingly earnest. "And if anyone should have agreed with that plan, it should have been Vanya, right? It was *his* daughter we wanted to rescue—or avenge if we couldn't. He, more than anyone, should have been howling for Winthorp blood. But when he heard what Sergei planned…" He frowns, reliving the past. "He was furious. Livid. I didn't understand why, not then. But he threatened his own brother's life if he touched Briar."

For my mother? My heart feels too battered to consider it, so I bite the thought back.

"You agreed with Sergei?" I ask, assuming the obvious: Two men came to me that night, creeping through the shadows of Briar's room.

"I went with him anyway," Mischa admits. "I thought Ivan

was a stupid fool. Anna should have been his focus. Anna…" He grits his teeth and exhales harshly. "But when I saw her—you—I knew then and there which man I wanted to follow. Vanya may have been a fool, but…" He looks up and my heart pangs at what I find: something elusive but real enough that Vanya pledged his life to nurture it. "I've killed men before—with my bare fucking hands, even. But that was different. I couldn't… Not that."

"And that's why Vanya loves you," I interject. "He loves you like a son because he can see the good in you—"

"Or maybe I'm just a feral dog he wants to keep close." He flexes his fingers against the table's surface as if uncomfortable with that assessment. "Whatever his reasons, he left Sergei after that."

My mind spins, fighting to reconcile this new piece of information with what I know now. If Marnie saved Anna, why not tell Vanya? Could she really be so cruel as to allow his daughter to rot in a Winthorp dungeon alone?

But even so, she *did* save his child in the end.

And Vanya saved hers.

"Why didn't you tell me this before?" I ask, returning my focus to Mischa.

"Because of this." He reaches out, flicking his fingers accusingly along my jaw. "That look. Like you know me. Pity me. Tell me." He leans in close, letting his breath ghost my cheek. "Am I worthy of your pity, Rose?"

My reply comes automatically. "Yes."

He may be a brute and a monster and—at times—a psychopath. But his world shaped him this way. Somehow, someway, it hasn't entirely consumed him. Not yet.

"Wrong answer," he scolds as if it's a mortal offense. "You should be afraid of me, Rose. Deathly afraid. Shall I tell you why?" He boldly sweeps his gaze down to the high neckline of my dress and my skin prickles with answering goosebumps. "Because the things I want to do to you... They aren't very nice."

His hand shakes as he reaches for me again, batting another strand of my hair. In the process, he brushes over the place Robert hit me and I flinch. Instantly, he withdraws and something I'm not expecting flickers across his face. Guilt?

"I'll let you decide when I—"

"Tell me." I risk meeting his gaze when he stays silent and my belly clenches at what I find brimming there. Only the most primal terms in my arsenal can describe it: raw, naked lust. "Those things you want to do..." I reiterate before licking my lower lip. "Was it all just talk?"

"Oh?" He chuckles low in his throat, cocking his head. More than ever, he resembles a snarling wolf ready to pounce.

And in response, I bare my throat.

"I want to rip that hideous dress off you, for one." He casts my frock a glance of disgust. "Then I'll wash you. Count those marks and divots in your skin, make sure every hair is still there, just as I left it…"

My breath catches. "And then?"

"I'll remind you," he says. "How to scream the only man's name you're allowed to say in full. Do you remember it?" His eyes flash as my lips part.

"Mischa…"

The involuntary grunt erupting from his throat spurs me on.

"Mikhailovich…Stepanov."

"Good," he praises thickly. His knuckles whiten as he grips the edge of the table. "But that wasn't quite a scream…"

He rises to his full height and approaches me, skirting the barrier between us.

A million nuances in his posture stick out when they otherwise never would. The jerk of his throat betraying a hard swallow. The alarming gleam in his gaze.

How his muscles ripple, thrumming with ravenous intent.

I shudder in anticipation of his touch even before his hand cups my cheek and forces my head back. He eyes me like this, hunting my expression for something I'm not sure he finds when he draws me up to him and presses his mouth to mine.

The kiss is slower than expected. Like two stray animals reconnecting after an unexpected absence. Has their dynamic changed? They're unsure. Slow, searching touches become grasping exploration until they finally deduce what the other intends.

On his end? Corruption.

All at once, he pulls me from the chair and shoves me toward the bed. Seconds later, my dress is on the floor and he's on top of me, guiding himself between my legs. There is no slow, teasing buildup—just surrender.

And possession.

CHAPTER 15

I wake up in Mischa's bed alone. A new tray waits on the table in the corner, containing breakfast, judging from the smell.

Someone also left a pile of clean clothing at the foot of the bed. A smile tugs at my mouth as I inspect my options: a pair of jeans and a simple shirt.

But it's the color that draws my notice: a hated shade of pink. Maybe Mischa's opinion toward the hue has softened after all.

Once I'm dressed, I pick over the food—porridge, eggs, and toast—and then I slip into the hall, fully intending to take Sergei up on his offer.

But where Mischa mockingly goaded me to explore his own manor once, I suspect that Sergei has a different motive in mind, rather than to toy with me.

Now that I know it's where my mother slept, the emerald room takes on a different atmosphere. Admittedly, the plainness holds none of the intrigue Mischa's mother's red room did, and after twenty-four years, there shouldn't be much left to find.

Still, I swallow hard and push the door open, stepping inside as if for the first time.

Closing my eyes, I try to picture her here. Was the door locked behind her? Did she lie on that bed and pine for Briar?

It's no use. The Marnie I knew can only be conjured in the opulent finery of Winthorp Manor, draped in pearls and expensive clothing. I can't think of her as a captive or otherwise.

Maybe Sergei was lying?

But Anna wasn't. My mother saved her life. Would she go so far for a man she hated?

Thinking of it all makes my head throb, and I reenter the hall, closing the door behind me. I don't go far before commotion draws my attention to a nearby window.

Screaming?

My heart skips as I press my fingers against the glass. Is it another attack?

Thankfully, the reality seems far less nefarious.

A small boy runs across an emerald lawn, shrieking at the top of his lungs. Eli—and it doesn't take long before I spot the source of his peril: a monstrous pursuer giving ruthless chase. Blond hair differentiates them both from the dark green of the lawn. From this distance, they resemble two versions of the same figure: one young, the other battered with age.

Suddenly, the larger of the two lunges, snatching the boy from behind, and they both collapse into a heap on the grass.

Not far from them stands Anna wearing a faint smile of her own. To any casual onlooker, they would appear to be the perfect family enjoying a lazy morning. It's almost scary how well Mischa could fit into that mold when he wants to: caring protector. A father…

Watching them together should soothe the ache in my chest, but the discomfort only grows as I turn away.

Alone, I descend the stairs and eventually find my own way out to the garden through a back hallway.

At the center of a small, paved courtyard, Eli is now sitting near a plot of rose bushes, decapitating them while Mouse crouches in the dirt a few yards away.

"Hello," I croak as they turn to me in unison.

"Hello!" Beaming, Eli wrenches a handful of roses from the bush. He waves them absently, spraying blood-red petals over his once-white clothes. "Are you back from heaven for good?"

"W-what?" A startled laugh escapes my throat, surprising me. "I don't—"

"Eli!" Anna calls to him from paces away. "Come here, please."

He looks at me, his nose wrinkling, before he dutifully races toward his mother, leaving me with Mouse.

For once, the girl acknowledges my presence with more than resolute silence. I think I see her mouth twitch slightly. A smile?

She's holding a stick, digging persistently into the earth at the base of the bushes. The closer I come, her markings resemble something more deliberate. Letters?

DONATELLOVAN

She stiffens, noticing my attention, and strikes her stick through the letters, erasing them. Then she stands and darts to another spot of the garden.

Sighing, I turn away and notice Mischa and Anna nearby. A chill washes over me as I watch them. Her slender frame paired with his bulk creates a striking contrast.

They stand close together, speaking in hushed tones. Mischa reaches out, grasping her arm as his lips move fervently. Whatever he says makes her eyes widen and she shakes her head.

"Please, Mischa. Please don't—" She breaks off, noticing my approach. Her thin lips quiver as she forces a smile, but anyone could see the tears welling in her eyes. "H-hello. Excuse me."

She slips past Mischa and scoops Eli into her arms. "You're so filthy," she scolds him playfully. "Time for a bath?" Bouncing him on her hip, she returns to the house.

"She's protective of him," I say and I watch her go, if only to fill the silence. Though what mother wouldn't be, forced to raise a child among the Winthorps?

Mischa says nothing. He stares after her as well, his jaw tight. Then he shakes his head. "You," he declares, pointing to Mouse.

She startles to attention, smoothing her hands along her simple gray dress.

"You still want to learn?" He reaches into his pocket and withdraws a familiar object: his knife.

A slow, bright smile unfolds over Mouse's features and she races toward him.

"Fix your posture," Mischa snaps. "Stand tall—no! Straighter. Good." Like a drill sergeant, he guides her into the right stance and then carefully molds her fingers around the handle of the blade. "Every time you strike, you mean it," he tells her. "You may think a gun is more dangerous, but a knife is just as lethal, and bleeding to death is more painful than having your brains blown out. Trust me on that."

I find myself watching them as I lean against a willow tree. Overall, Mischa makes for a firm though gentle instructor. He corrects her mistakes but praises her accomplishments.

"Good," he says when she stabs at an imaginary foe. "Very good." He eases the blade from her grasp, sheathes it, and returns it to his pocket. "You pick up fast. Now, go. Let's see if you've gotten any better at hiding. If I can't find you before dinner, I'll pay you double."

She takes off, dashing across the gardens. The second she's gone, Mischa levels his searching stare in my direction.

"Tell me," he taunts, beckoning me closer with a jerk of his chin. "I know something is circling that little brain of yours."

"I'm thinking about her," I admit, going with one of the safer topics consuming my thoughts. "Mouse. I'm wondering where she came from. Did you know that she's twelve?"

"She is?" He glances in the direction the girl took off in. "I could always ask Nicolai if he knows more."

"She drew a name into the dirt," I add. "Donatello Van—"

"Vanici?"

From his tone, I sense a grim mixture of admiration and loathing typical for someone he considers a rival.

"A big player in the Italian mob. But I don't think he has a thing for children."

"Would that bother you if he did?" I ask.

He raises an eyebrow "Maybe. Or maybe I'm lying to avoid picking a fight you seem itching to have? Though it doesn't matter." He steps in close. "Don't get too comfortable. I don't plan to stay here long," he murmurs near my ear. "And when I decide to leave, I want you to be ready."

"You sound like we'd have to escape—"

"In any case," he grunts. "Be ready."

I blink, caught off guard by the honesty in his tone. For once, he lets me inside his head, and as chilling a proposition as it is, a part of me is more than eager to finally peek beneath his mask.

"Sergei is planning something," he adds. "After years of inaction, he's suddenly inserting himself into the fray. Something about it feels off. I don't know why yet, but—"

"Do you think he's dangerous?"

He exhales slowly, thinking it through. "I don't know. But the man is always one step ahead. I used to admire that about him, you know. Most men want to shoot their problems in the fucking face."

Himself included.

"But Sergei? He'll make that 'problem' wind up with a bullet in its brain, all without seeming to lift a finger."

"He knew my mother. But not in the way you think." I hesitate. How much of this can I trust him not to spit at me later, twisted into a mocking taunt?

His eyes give me no answers. I have to trust him.

"He kept her here," I add. "Vanya said… He told me that she wasn't his captive." I watch him carefully to gauge his reaction. Did he know that part of the story?

"Interesting." He observes the grand structure behind me, his gaze narrowed. "This place has been in the Vasilev family for generations. Who knows what Sergei has stashed here."

A sudden thought occurs to me. "Do you think Anna knew her, my mother?"

He shakes his head. "I don't know. Anna…" His lips part and close. Whatever he meant to say, he seems to rethink voicing it. Or not. "What do you think of her son?"

I flinch at the intensity of the question. "Her son?"

It's as if, until now, there was a wall in my head, blocking off any thought of Eli. With one question, Mischa breaks that barrier down.

"He's beautiful," I blurt in a rush. "So beautiful. I don't. I never—" I swallow hard, alarmed to find my eyes are watering. Before I can blink them back, tears fall. "I've never been around someone his age before…"

I'm being ridiculous. Furious, I swipe at my cheeks, smothering every bead of moisture into oblivion. Mischa merely watches me, offering neither judgment nor support.

"What about Anna?" I rasp.

Maybe changing the subject to her is my selfish way of turning the tables?

Or perhaps I just want to compound that aching, lingering pinch in my chest. Only now do I feel spiteful enough to name it. *Jealousy?*

"You loved her, didn't you?"

"I did," he admits gruffly. "I *do*. She's family."

"But as something more?" I'm acting childish now, no better than Eli or Mouse. Even so, I can't resist pushing him further. "Could you see yourself marrying her? Once the war with the Winthorps is over."

He strokes his chin. After a moment, he nods. "Yes. I could marry her."

I don't register cringing from him until he grips my shoulders, dragging me back.

"I could," he cruelly insists against my ear. "We'd have a couple of kids. Live in the fucking country somewhere. It would be perfect, Little Rose—except for one thing…"

My heart throbs as I eye the landscape behind him. If he wants me to respond, I don't.

So he answers for me. "Anna isn't a fucking hellcat."

"Bastard!" I lash out with the flat of my hand and he easily evades the blow.

"She's too sweet," he goads. "I don't think she could ride my cock the way you can—"

"You're disgusting," I spit.

But he's laughing and the sound affects me more than if he truly meant his boast. It's real and lilting, and he doesn't even seem to realize he's doing it: feeling something other than rage.

"Hmm." His tongue traces his lower lip. "I'd much rather see you bear my child. I could give you a few. Would you want that?"

"Never!" I thrust my chin into the air indignantly. "What makes you think I'd ever want your baby?"

"You're right." His face falls, and he lets me go. "Why would you?"

I gape as he pushes past me. By the time I recover from shock, he's already halfway to the house.

"Mischa!" I start after him, forced to run to match his pace. Of all the things to prickle through my nerves now, guilt shouldn't be one of them. "Wait!"

He makes me chase him into the foyer, ignoring me every step of the way.

"Mischa." I pant. "Mischa, wait—"

Suddenly, he stops short before the staircase and extends his hand toward me. *Quiet.*

Beyond him, I finally notice the two other figures already in the foyer, their voices raised.

"Are you insane?" a man demands. His tone radiates so much raw anger that I barely recognize it at first. Only as I follow Mischa's gaze do I realize *Vanya* is the one shouting. "Have you lost your goddamn mind, Sergei?"

"Have you, Ivan?" In chilling contrast, Sergei's tone is eerily level. "I'm doing what must be done to protect our name."

"Our name? Or your pride?"

"Why can't it be both?"

"Something tells me that this is more than a brotherly squabble," Mischa says, stepping forward.

It's clear from his positioning near Vanya just whose side of the argument he favors out of the gate.

"What's going on?"

"Have you told him? Your *leader*?" Vanya demands of Sergei. When the latter says nothing, he scoffs. "Of course not. Sergei has called a council tonight in a bid to reinstate himself as acting head. The Pakhan."

From Mischa's fierce expression, it's clear he doesn't approve of such a plan.

"Is that so?" he murmurs, deadly soft. "On what grounds?"

"On the grounds that you are too reckless to lead," Sergei says—but his gaze cuts in my direction. "Among other reasons. The *mafiya* needs stability if there is to ever be peace—"

"Peace?" Vanya spits on the floor at his feet. "You spout peace but forget the Winthorps—you're starting a fucking war within your own goddamn ranks!"

"Am I?" Sergei shrugs. "Perhaps. Perhaps not."

"In the end, this is just pointless." Vanya throws his hands into the air. "Tell him, Mischa!"

"Ivan has a point," Mischa says. "You may have your sway, Sergei, but I doubt that you could even muster enough support for a leadership change regardless."

"Perhaps." Sergei nods. "In any event, my main intent is beyond a respectful challenge."

"Oh?" Mischa says before Vanya can bite back.

"Yes. I'd like to elect a new head to the table—"

"Of course you would," Vanya interjects. "Have you learned nothing all these years? Or are you still so fond of your dirty tricks? Which fool have you groomed to be your whipped dog now?"

"Someone who has more say in ending this war than anyone," Sergei says, inclining his head.

"Oh? And who is that?" Vanya demands.

"The obvious choice: Ellen Winthorp."

"What?"

All three men turn to me, but Mischa's gaze draws my attention the most. He's guarded again in an instant—closed from me in a way he hasn't been since…

Never. Not even the first day, when he ripped off my blindfold and only saw an enemy.

"Ellen?" Vanya seems torn between laughing in disbelief and shaking his head. "With all due respect, what right does she have to sit at the table?"

"She was married to that family," Mischa says before Sergei can voice his own explanation. "She was married to its fucking head. She can have a say." He turns and mounts the stairs, leaving Vanya staring after him open-mouthed.

"M-Mischa—"

"I won't fight the appointment," Mischa declares over him. From the top of the staircase, he adds, "But don't expect me to roll over, Sergei. You want to play politics. We'll fucking play."

"Mischa…" With one last look at his brother, Vanya follows him, his steps resonating through the manor's very foundation.

Their absence drains the room of anger. Left behind is a mixture of Sergei's quiet observation and my own shock.

"What are you doing?" I demand, advancing on the older man.

His eyes flicker over my face, impossible to read. "I'm giving you a chance to state your case," he says. "Do you want an end to this bloodshed? Mischa may have the council stacked in his favor, but you possess one thing that neither he nor I have."

"And what is that?" I rasp.

He carefully tucks a piece of my hair behind my ear, heedless of how I flinch at his touch. "A voice," he says. "Your words alone have more impact than any political savvy. Remember that. I hope to see you tonight. If you don't mind, I've already taken care to have a dress delivered to your room."

He leaves, disappearing down a corridor at the other end of the hall.

In this moment, in the center of the marble flooring, I feel more like a pawn than ever.

And the game is already in checkmate.

CHAPTER 16

I must spend hours pacing this bare fucking room. Marnie's presence feels realer now more than ever. It's like she's mocking me sweetly from the grave: *What are you doing, my Rose? Do what I did. Give in…*

Stubbornly, I pace until the tapping of my footsteps drowns her out—but I don't catch the sound of the door opening until it's too late. My intruder is already inside, closing the door.

"You need to get ready," Mischa snaps, raking his gaze over my rumpled shirt and jeans. "Damn. Do you even have anything to wear—"

His eyes darken as he approaches the bed and inspects the dress Sergei provided. It's a deep navy with a bold neckline, made of silk. Mischa must approve of it, because he snatches the fabric in his fist and throws it in my direction.

"Put it on."

"Why?" I croak, letting the dress land in a crumpled heap at my feet. "Aren't you bored of having me used as a pawn in your twisted games? I know I am—"

"*Sergei* wants you as a pawn," he agrees. "But as for me… I want to see if you even have the balls to play the game. Lift your arms." He stoops for the gown and gestures for me to undress. "Hurry up. They won't take you seriously looking like some naïve innocent, Rose. I can assure you of that."

"How can I trust you?" Even as I voice the question, I stiffly lift the shirt over my head.

"You don't have to," Mischa counters. He steps in close and tugs on the clasp of my jeans himself. "Use your brain. A man like Sergei wants to manipulate you for his own gain. The only way to outmaneuver him is to outsmart him."

"And what about you?"

I'm naked now, painfully aware of how close he is. His breath bastes the flesh of my throat as he drapes the gown over my head and tugs it into place.

I watch him work, hunting his expression for a hint of conniving intent. "What do you hope to gain?"

He looks away. "Believe it or not, Little Rose, I only want the truth… Now, listen. Sergei will invite you to speak. He'll want you to argue against continuing the war with the Winthorps. But is that what you really want?"

Ending the war. The violence. The bloodshed. "Shouldn't that be what you want?"

"Of course." He looks me over—but whatever he sees makes him hiss through his teeth. "Turn around." When I comply, he positions himself behind me and I stiffen as his fingers sink through my hair, parting it roughly.

"What are you doing?"

"Improvising," he grunts in reply. "To answer your question: Of course that's what I want. But I'm not foolish, Rose. I know that wars rarely end with a handshake and goodwill. Someone tends to wind up with a knife in their back. I would rather this end in a hailstorm of fucking fire than…"

"Than what?" I demand when he falls silent.

"Than in checkmate." He continues to tug at my hair, arranging it with far more confidence than a man like him should have. Once finished, he spins me around and nods in approval. "With Sergei Vasilev at the head of the gameboard, I can't win this round, but you can. And *now*, you're ready."

He guides me into the bathroom and I catch sight of our reflections in the mirror.

"You're good with your hands," I grudgingly admit.

The woman standing before him is a stranger at first. Her hair has been expertly coiled into a knot at the nape of her neck. The navy of her gown highlights the blue of her eyes. For a second, it's like I'm staring into the past at someone else. The only difference is the prominent scar proclaiming my place in this war: fifteen.

"You look the part," Mischa admits.

My opinion differs. "I look like my mother."

"A player," he corrects. From him, such a term might be a compliment. "But now you need to decide what role you will play. And trust and believe, Little Rose—I won't go easy on you this round."

I flick my fingers along the silk skirt of the dress. "What do I need to expect?"

The last *mafiya* gathering I attended proceeded much like an outlaw court.

Where transgressions were paid for in blood.

But this meeting, with power on the line?

My brain shies away from envisioning it.

"Politics," he replies. "I trust Vanya with my life—but he is an optimist. If he truly wanted power, Sergei would already have it. For some reason, he seeks to use you." He brushes my cheek and scowls at his fingers. "Do you remember the man you saw with Nikolaus the night he attacked you?"

I swallow the memories back. "Yes. You brought me to him as well."

"Before I knew he was a fucking traitorous prick," he insists. "But he would have never had the balls to ally against me without sniffing something in the air. Rats are opportunistic, Rose. They only strike when it's to their advantage."

"So what do I do?"

His lips twitch, part grimace, part smile. "Be the daughter of a Vasilev—but never forget what leverage you have in your possession."

With that ominous warning, he steers me back into my room, and together, we enter the hall.

"When we reach the bottom of these stairs, we won't be allies," he warns.

But I marvel at his use of the word. Have we ever been so aligned? His tone didn't sound mocking.

"I didn't ask for this," I point out.

"And that's why you need to fucking fight." He snatches my hand, gripping tight, and I stare at our entwined fingers: his rough and callused, mine slim and pale.

With every step, we draw closer to the line he's drawn—once past it, we're enemies again.

But he takes his time.

And so do I.

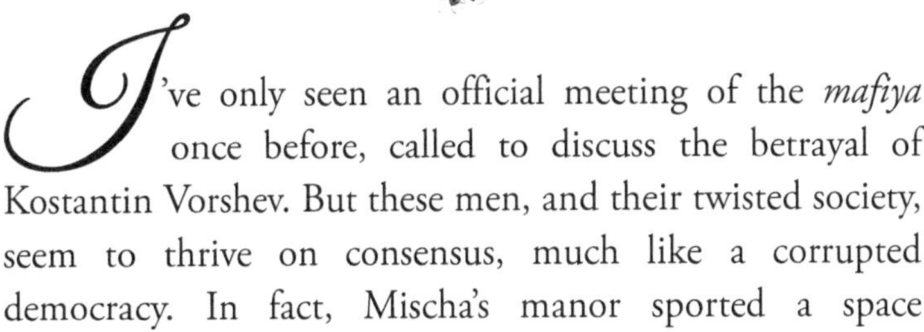

I've only seen an official meeting of the *mafiya* once before, called to discuss the betrayal of Kostantin Vorshev. But these men, and their twisted society, seem to thrive on consensus, much like a corrupted democracy. In fact, Mischa's manor sported a space designed for the sole purpose of hosting an enormous gathering.

Unsurprisingly, Sergei's home contains such a room as well, located at the rear of the house. It's spacious, its layout resembling a great hall. Wood-paneled walls create an enclosed atmosphere as marble flooring magnifies every footstep Mischa and I take over it.

In a grim bit of irony, I recall the pomp and circumstance that took place at Winthorp manor whenever a gathering was hosted there. Such an event would require months of preparation and organization—and if so much as a napkin color deviated from expectation, it would be deemed a massive failure.

In contrast, Mischa and his ilk seem to thrive on converging with barely an hour's notice.

Already, the room is partially filled with men and women gathered around a circle of eleven chairs positioned at the heart of the space. The impromptu layout evokes a sense of authority nonetheless. Those without power to their name seem to congregate on the outskirts, leaving a generous swath of space beyond the seating.

There doesn't appear to be a general consensus as to the dress code of this occasion. Some of the onlookers sport suits or dresses like mine. Others wear leather and jeans.

Dressed in his fatigues, Mischa approaches a chair slightly taller than the others, ornately carved. Meeting my gaze, he nods to one a few seats down. Warily, I approach the chair and perch myself on it.

Not long after, Sergei and Vanya arrive. The elder brother takes a seat across from Mischa, while Vanya stands beside his leader. As the room fills to capacity, Sergei rises, drawing all eyes to him.

Unlike Mischa, he opted for a black suit, expertly tailored to cast a subtle air of intimidation. He wouldn't belong at a Winthorp gathering—that's for sure.

"I've called a council for one reason only," he says, his voice booming to the farthest reaches of the room without the need for a microphone. "To put an end to this war. Mischa, while he may lead us bravely, will have us continue down a never-ending path of violence. Fortunately, I see another way to end this conflict."

"And how is that?" someone demands from the crowd.

"It's simple: We come to an arrangement with the younger Winthorp. Rumor has it that he is shrewder than his father ever was."

"Rumor?" Mischa scoffs. "Rumor has it that I dine on children for breakfast and bathe in their blood. Fortunately, at least *one* of those isn't true."

Uneasy laughter rumbles from those gathered, but the tension is palpable in the air. It's as if invisible battle lines have been drawn, apparent in the subtle body posture of those seated at the circle. Some eye Mischa intently, attuned to his every word. Others look to Sergei.

"The point is: I believe we should end this war now," Sergei insists.

"But we've taken a vote before," another man points out. "I doubt hearts have changed so quickly."

"Really?" Sergei glances at me and moves to stand in the center of the circle. "Then perhaps you'll listen to a voice other than mine? Ellen, would you join me?"

I swallow hard, choking a refusal down. My trembling legs barely seem capable of supporting my weight. As all eyes turn to me, it's a wonder I don't melt into a puddle.

One gaze burns more intensely than the others, however. He doesn't take his eyes off me for a second, even as Sergei stands aside, leaving me in the center of the circle alone.

My surroundings blur as what seems like a hundred faceless people focus on me.

"And who is this?" someone asks.

"She is Robert Winthorp's wife," Sergei says, receiving startled gasps. "I believe it is only fair that she should have a say in this conflict."

More murmurs rise from those gathered. "And what does she have to say?"

"Before we begin, *I'd* like to make a suggestion," Mischa cuts in. He sits casually in his chair, his arms crossed, but his eyes are fiercely alert. "As someone pointed out, we've already settled this matter via a vote. But as Pakhan, I'm willing to let her decision overrule any previous course of action. All opposed?"

A smattering of people dissent, but presumably not enough to make a difference.

"Then it's settled," Mischa says. He and Sergei share a searching look, but the other man makes no objection. "In fact," Mischa continues, "I say we go a step further: We give her a seat at the table with all the authority of an acting head."

"Are you serious?" someone scoffs.

"No."

"Out of the question!"

"Oh?" A flicker of emotion distorts Sergei's otherwise cold expression. Curiosity? "On what grounds would you make such a suggestion?" he wonders.

"It's simple." Mischa stands, and even the novelty of my appearance is no match as he effortlessly commands the attention of the entire room. "Not only is she the daughter of Robert Winthorp Senior's first wife, but she's also the bastard of Ivan Vasilev."

Chaos. A chorus of shouting nearly drowns out Mischa's calm, persistent baritone.

"Not only that. But she's the mother of Robert the younger's sole surviving heir."

I can't breathe. No matter how rapidly I suck air in, none of it seems to go into my lungs. It's ironic in a sense: Nikolaus broke my ribs. But Mischa shatters the pathetic organ trapped between them. Blood pools in my veins, stalled by an ineffective heart.

Though he did warn me: *When we reach the bottom of these stairs, we won't be allies...*

"Enough!" Someone grabs my arm, radiating gentleness. Vanya. "Mischa, what is the meaning of this?"

Either Mischa doesn't hear him or he ignores him.

"Silence!" The Pakhan raises his hand, radiating authority. "I have proof of my accusations, of course," he says once the clamor fades to a disturbed hum. His eyes scan the crowd and then land on one figure. Alarmingly, his gaze softens and my throat tightens even before he calls them by name. "Anna..."

A hush falls over the room as all eyes turn to the pale woman practically huddled in a corner. Shaking, she starts forward, tears streaming down her cheeks.

"Mischa, please," she gasps in between sobs. "Mischa, *please—*"

"Anna." His expression hardens. "Tell them. No harm will come to him, but you need to tell them. Now."

Trembling at the edge of the circle, Anna looks smaller than ever. A shadow of a woman, likely to fade into the ether with one wrong move. Vanya's grip tightens on my arm, but for whatever reason, he doesn't go to her.

"I…" She swallows hard and clears her throat. "I am Anna-Natalia Vasilev—"

"And for sixteen years, she was a prisoner of the Winthorps," Mischa finishes for her. "They kept her locked in a virtual cage while sending a stranger's body to her father. And what else did they make you do?"

More tears streak the woman's beautiful face and she staggers. One of the men near her lurches to his feet and lowers her onto his vacated chair.

"Four years ago, the younger Robert Winthorp brought me…"

"What," Mischa prods. "It's all right."

"He brought me a baby," she admits, her body heaving. "A newborn. He told me to raise him. There were other nannies throughout the years, but I've been with him the longest. I was told that his mother was dead. But when he got older, the story changed…"

"How?" Mischa crosses over to her and places his hand on her shoulder. "Tell them."

"He… He told him she was an angel, and that—one day, if he was good enough—he might bring her to see him."

It's a lie. It has to be a lie—no man could be that cruel. No woman could be *that* naïve. But horror renders me paralyzed regardless. I can clearly picture Robert performing every action described.

And it guts me to my core.

"A few months ago, he gave him a locket," she says hoarsely. "He said it contained his mother's picture." She looks at me. "*Her* picture."

"Is this the locket?" Mischa reaches into his pocket and withdraws a golden chain. From it dangles a square-shaped charm. God, I recognize it…

The chain I saw around Eli's neck.

"Yes." Anna hunches over herself, clutching her chest. "Y-yes."

The room descends into roars not even Mischa can overrule. A sea of voices and noise and grasping hands. I lash out, shoving my way through until I'm free of the press of people. Then I run until my shaking legs deposit me on the floor of a distant room and I'm alone.

But not for long. My pursuer betrays himself before he even finds my hiding place.

"Get up, Rose."

"Maybe this truly is just a game to you," I rasp, looking up and finding him in the doorway. "But this is my life!"

"A life you've been hiding from," he points out.

"How could you do that to Anna?"

"Anna?" He sounds harsher than I've ever heard him. "Don't fucking lie to me. You knew. You knew that child was yours the second you saw him. But you were afraid. Afraid to face the pain, and the anger, and the rage. I can understand that. But the time has come, Rose. You can't escape the truth forever."

"Truth?" I spit. "As if you give a damn about me. Admit it! All you wanted was to outwit Sergei and humiliate me!"

He blinks, and beneath the anger and rage, a suspicion gnaws away at the back of my mind: Maybe, for one brief second, the man feels some semblance of guilt.

But it's still not enough.

"I hate you for this," I spit, my voice breaking. "God, I hate you—"

"No, you don't," Mischa says. "You hate him. He manipulated and abused and lied to you for sixteen years. He turned your pain into a weapon, but now, you have the chance to do something about it. End the feud, or decide to run him into the ground. The choice is yours to make." He starts through the doorway, but near the threshold, he pauses. "But know this… Whatever you choose, I'll stand by it. If only to see you break the mold of a fucking pawn and finally play the game."

He leaves, and in his absence, I haul myself to my feet, using the wall as a crutch. My mind reels, and a million conflicting emotions wrestle for control of my heart. Too many to decipher all at once. I can't. My only course of action in this moment is to dry my tears and retrace my steps.

With effortless authority, Mischa and Sergei have regained control of the room, but the battle lines are even more defined. A virtual barrier splits the room in half. There is no question now as to who belongs to what side, save for two lone figures lingering on the outskirts of the hall.

One is Vanya, staring far away into the distance. Clinging to him is Anna. She looks at me, her eyes reddened and bloodshot, and quickly turns away, burying her face against her father's shoulder. He strokes her absently, and with every pass of his hand through her hair, the fractures in my soul deepen.

"Have you made your decision?" Sergei wonders from the circle.

"Yes," I croak. "But first… I need to say something." My gaze travels to Mischa and he stiffens, wary. "I've only ever known the Winthorps," I admit to the crowd, my voice growing in strength. "I was born in the manor, and for nearly twenty-four years, it was my prison…"

The hall remains silent as I finish my tale. It's almost funny how briefly my story can be summed up—barely a few minutes, I suspect. Yet every word has scraped the inside of my throat raw. I can barely suppress the horrors I've fought years to push back. They're conjured by my boldness in addressing them.

But in a sense, I feel lighter from having finally voiced them.

"I, more than anyone, should want to fight Robert Winthorp with every fiber of my being out of spite and revenge," I admit. "But that is not why I'm deciding how I am. It's because I know, deep in my soul, this will never end any other way."

"And your choice?" Sergei demands, his tone decidedly colder.

Mischa is watching me as well. Like always, it's nearly impossible to decipher him.

"I vote to continue the war," I say. "But not for myself, or Mischa, or any other argument."

I merely know the truth: There is no such thing as peace.

"Then it's decided," Mischa says, but I can't ignore the added harshness to his tone.

Neither he nor Sergei is pleased with my decision, it seems. Though admittedly for different reasons.

Sergei lost this round.

But Mischa seems unwilling to accept a victory.

"Council adjured."

Very few members disperse. Most crowd the center of the room, battling for an audience with Mischa or Sergei. I've only caused more chaos, but I don't stick around to see it unfold.

I push my way through the crowd and escape, racing down the hall, up the staircase, and into the barren room unofficially designated as mine.

Here, in the dark, I strip my dress and crawl beneath the bedsheets. The silence feels mocking after the deafening noise in the council chamber. My breathing scratches unevenly at the quiet—a fitting soundtrack for the creak of my doorknob being tested a second later.

"Please don't come to gloat," I plead into my pillow. "Please…"

Soft footsteps inch closer toward my bed despite the warning. They're far too soft to belong to a man, Mischa or otherwise.

"Mouse?" I lift my head and spot her slight shadow along the wall. "Are you here for Mischa?"

Unsurprisingly, I'm not given an answer. The mattress shifts as a lighter body climbs onto the end. Resolutely, they sit while I sob, offering no comfort or judgment.

Nothing at all.

I know that this conversation must happen, even before I wake up to an empty room and don my simple blue dress. Vanya is already lurking in the hallway near my door, his graying hair gleaming silver in the shadow.

When he sees me, he sighs and inclines his head for me to follow. Were I bold enough to claim a resemblance between us, it might be in our actions more than anything. We both dread the inevitable.

Vanya's chosen battleground is the small sitting room overlooking the gardens. Rather than claim one of the leather chairs, he leans against the wall.

"Your mother," he begins gruffly, "because I do not doubt that she was your mother…" Looking at me seems to hurt him. He turns away, raking his fingers through his hair.

"But I don't know what lies you were told. Or by whom. But I don't—"

"She never told me," I admit hoarsely. "Not about my father. I asked her about his identity once and...I was never brave enough to ask again."

"No," Vanya insists. I hear him swallow as if fighting to form words. "I can't be... She wouldn't do that—no." His eyes flash as they rake me over. From Marnie's blue eyes, to my brown hair, to my bare, battered feet. "She wouldn't keep something like that from me. Never. She wouldn't do that to me!"

Tears spill down my cheeks. "I'm sorry. I don't know how to prove it to you. I'm not sure if I even believe it myself..."

Of all the things to cross my mind, something Sergei said during one of our first meetings slithers across my thoughts. A name, uttered like a ghost's.

"Does the name Elena mean anything to you?"

"It was my mother's," he says absently. "She knew... My first wife demanded we name Anna after her mother and grandmother. I always boasted that my next child would be named after mine."

And maybe Marnie was more cunning in her deception than even Robert Winthorp knew. She named me Ellen, a subtle take on Elena—the name she only dared to call me on my birthday.

Along with another moniker.

"You called her Rose, didn't you?" I ask.

His face falls and I almost regret mentioning it in the first place. "Yes. I called her Rose. They were her favorite—"

"You gave her the necklace, too," I surmise. "The one Sergei gave to me. I know you've seen it."

"I have," he admits. "But it wasn't his to give. I never knew she left it behind…"

I can tell through his tone alone that he would have never retrieved it himself.

"I guess she enjoyed manipulating us both," I say.

Vanya looks at me sharply and steps away from the wall. With one hand, he parts my hair and cups my cheek. Then he wraps his arms around me, pulling me close.

"I knew from the moment I saw you who your mother was," he confesses to my shock. "I thought maybe she took another man under the nose of her husband."

Yet he still treated me with nothing but kindness.

"I would have deserved it. I let her go," he continues. "It damn near killed me, but when she left, I let her go. But if I had known… I would have never abandoned you. Never."

I don't doubt him, and deep in my soul, I know that Marnie didn't, either.

She knew a man like him would never throw his child to the wolves.

So she stayed silent.

But something in his tone sticks out, unwilling to fit in the puzzle Sergei and Mischa have forced me to put together.

"Left?" I pull back enough to meet his gaze. Instantly, I know he won't lie to me. Not now. "You make it sound like she had a choice."

In my own case, I didn't choose to return to Robert—and Mischa, for all his twisted jealousy, had been willing to come after me.

"Why did you leave her there?"

"You don't understand," Vanya says. He lets me go and moves to the window, bracing his hands over the glass. With his head bowed, it's easier than ever to see the pain—both emotional and physical—his body has endured throughout the years. "Marnie Winthorp wasn't taken, or kidnapped, or whatever story you've been told. She *chose* to leave her husband—"

"What are you saying?"

"The truth." He scoffs. "We didn't ransom her. She allied herself with Sergei. And with me."

Nothing in all of my twisted journey since being taken has affected me with the same hopeless sense of disorientation. Not Mischa. Or Nikolaus' attack. Or even the cruel reality that Robert may still be alive.

"She grew fearful of her husband. She wanted safety for her and her daughter. When she left, she tried to bring her as well, Briar, but something went wrong and the girl was left behind. Sergei perpetuated the rumor to protect her. In a way, I think he thought it served him as well, the image of a ruthless foe against the greedy Winthorp. But Marnie… All she wanted was a better life. A simple life."

"And you trusted her?"

He nods. "She gave us more than enough information to prove her intentions. She was smart, so smart. And so cunning. She could inspire a fish to live on land just by telling him to. Last night at the council…" He sighs wistfully. "You looked so much like her."

I try to reconcile this brave, bold woman with the fearful specter I knew who could show me affection only in secret.

I can't.

"She was an amazing woman," Vanya insists as if reading my mind. "Don't you doubt that for a second. She was."

"Then why did she leave you? If she was so afraid of her husband and so determined to live a better life, then why go back?"

He flinches. "Your sister. Every day without her pained her a little more. I knew that. And maybe I cared for her more than she did me. I could live with that. I *have* lived with that. But…" He looks at me and his gaze hardens. "She knew how to reach me, and if she so much as hinted about you—" He breaks off, grinding his teeth. "No Winthorp stronghold would have kept me out. She knew that. I loved that woman," he admits. "At least the woman I thought she was."

And maybe, in her own way, she cared for him.

"My name," I say. "I think she wanted it to be Elena."

He winces, gritting his teeth.

"I spent so long being afraid of who my father might be. But I never dreamed that he could be someone like you."

His mouth lifts into the semblance of a smile. "I am sorry you grew up in the way that you did," he says. "But I am proud to finally meet the woman you are."

I approach him, and he doesn't resist the hand I tentatively place on his shoulder.

"But there is still one thing I don't understand," I confess. "You say she wasn't your captive, but Sergei and Mischa seem to believe that she was."

"Mischa?" He cocks his head thoughtfully. "He doesn't know. I've never told him the truth. With Marnie gone, it was easier to maintain the lie. But Sergei?" His body goes rigid. "Sergei can be the staunchest ally you have ever had on your side. And he can also be more ruthless than every single Winthorp combined. I have never doubted his intentions, but you should always question his methods."

"Is that why you decided to support Mischa instead?"

"There came a time when Sergei crossed the line," he says. "He proposed a plan so despicable that I gave him only one option: step down or I would challenge him. So he did."

"He wanted to hurt Briar," I say. Butcher her, as Mischa put it.

"I should have gone with them," Vanya says. "Not only to stop them, but… Perhaps I could have stopped her."

My mother. Not long after that night, she did the unthinkable.

"But it's in the past," he says, pulling away. "There's no use in dwelling on it. All I can do is prepare for the future, and I will not make the same mistake again." He reaches out, ghosting his fingers along my cheek. Then he abruptly turns, limping for the door. "We will talk more later," he promises. "Later…"

I watch him go, unsure of what remains to be said.

Or perhaps it's painfully obvious: We both spent years seeing Marnie Winthorp as merely a victim.

When, all along…she may have been the villain.

My head throbs in the aftermath of Vanya's confession. Desperate for fresh air, I retreat to the gardens.

But all I find are shadows of the past.

Grim, overcast daylight paints the landscape in a silvery glow and I'm reminded of my comfortable prison in Winthorp Manor.

Was this how Marnie felt once freed from her own cage?

Overwhelmed. Exhausted. Terrified.

Rather than learn how to brave this new, dangerous world, she preferred the one she already knew and a more familiar monster.

But I always endured Robert. Understanding him beyond his surface brutality was a chilling prospect. He corrupted everything he touched, myself included. But as a childish bit of laughter reaches my ears, I'm forced to wonder just how far his taint has truly spread.

Up ahead, Eli runs across a patch of grass, his blond curls bouncing wildly. A watchful Anna hovers nearby. She calls to him and he giggles back, so oblivious to the darkness swirling around him through no fault of his own.

Darkness one man conjured purely out of selfish spite. I know he's behind me, even before his hand brushes my shoulder.

"We need to talk—"

"You put a target on his head." Fury distorts my voice. I doubt he can even understand me. "Even if he is—no. It doesn't matter. You've just made him the top prey of any sick bastard who thinks that he can use Robert Winthorp's son as a bargaining chip. Was humiliating me truly worth so much?"

"No one will touch him," he swears, and despite everything, I believe he thinks that. "And as for Sergei? You think *he* is the reason I'd hand the wife of my enemy a seat at the fucking table?"

The harshness in his tone makes me remember the role he and Sergei elected me to: a head.

"What does it even mean?" I demand as he comes to stand beside me.

"You have that power you crave, Rose," he coldly replies. "Enough to do way more than pout in the shadows if you wanted to. Not only that, but do you think I'd announce before the whole fucking world that I have access to not one, but two people Robert Winthorp would kill to reclaim? Leverage I have yet to use. Don't think it hasn't crossed my mind." He laughs darkly, revealing that it has. Multiple times. "But no. I didn't do it for him. I did it for *you.*"

"Me?" I scour the tightness of his jaw, searching for any nuance in his expression.

Downcast, his gaze reveals nothing.

"He has your eyes." His voice is so gruff that I barely hear him. His own eyes track the boy as he races around a bed of flowers. "And that bastard…he told him about you, did you know that? He taunted him with your picture. Told him you were dead. Though I'll admit it: I knew even before I saw him that he was still alive."

I stare at my hands, envisioning the life ripped from them four years ago. In such a relatively short time, he's grown into his own person. All without me.

Only someone like Mischa could clearly *anticipate* such a reality.

"How?"

"Because I know how Winthorp's sick, twisted brain works —that's how. He may have resented your pregnancy, but there's no way in hell he would deny himself of not one, but *two* people he could manipulate and control to worship only him. And to ensure as much, he'd keep you apart and use your own longing for each other as a prison. That is the kind of man he is."

He sounds far too confident in that assessment. In the pit of my soul, I know why: In another world, he might have done the same thing. The truly evil Mischa who would have killed Briar without hesitation and whom even Vanya couldn't save.

"And if Eli is my son?" I demand. "What will you do now? Lock him away if I don't support your stupid war? Threaten to sell him? No—" My heart won't let me even consider it. "I'll kill you if you do. I swear I will—"

"What I want?" He pulls ahead too quickly for me to keep pace. Like a storm cloud, he descends on the idyllic scene, heading right for the boy.

"M-Mischa." Anna pales when she sees him. "Eli," she calls, but the boy doesn't seem to hear her.

"It's all right." Once he reaches her, Mischa places his hand on her back. "It's all right."

She looks at me warily as Mischa tries to lead her down a path. Her gaze cuts to Eli.

"It will be all right," Mischa says.

They don't go far. Just far enough that Eli turns, confused to find me instead. His eyes cautiously meet mine, but he doesn't say a word. He merely continues to play, chasing specters in between the rose bushes. Cackling, he decapitates a bloom at random, scattering the petals at his feet like so many droplets of blood.

There is something so beautiful in his innocence.

So painful.

Tendrils of hope and fear encircle my heart, piercing and encasing it. Like vines studded in thorns.

My mother said that hell was like a rose—but that was the nicest way of phrasing it.

War, violence, and death can cause untold pain, but one emotion above all delivers the truest form of agony.

It slices you into pieces, but you can't help but relish every gaping, bleeding wound.

I once told Mischa I'd never felt love.

But that was a lie.

I've never stopped feeling it.

And now?

All I can do is watch its original source, oblivious to the passage of time.

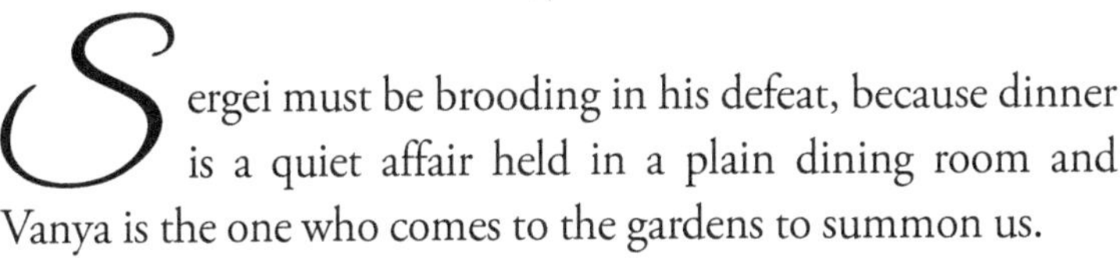

Sergei must be brooding in his defeat, because dinner is a quiet affair held in a plain dining room and Vanya is the one who comes to the gardens to summon us.

Eli skips to Anna, who bundles him in her arms, while Mischa lurks at the outskirts of our ensemble, watching me.

He doesn't stay long. After downing a glass of wine and a few bites of food, he stands and declares, "I'm going to train." On his way through the doorway, he points to Mouse and then Eli. "You two. Come and learn."

Both children scramble toward him in a stampede.

Anna starts to stand as well. "I don't think that's a good—"

"Eat," Mischa says. He grabs Eli and throws the boy onto his back while Mouse slinks past him, darting into the hall. "We won't be long."

Vanya stands as well. "I'll make sure no one loses an eye," he mumbles on his way out.

Finally, Anna sighs and meets my gaze. "I don't want you to think that I'm some evil, selfish woman—"

"I don't."

She inhales sharply and stares down at her hands. "He… He's all I have. I've spent four years devoting every waking moment to him. And now…" Her eyes meet mine accusingly. "You're a stranger. How can I just abandon him? I'm the only mother he's ever known."

I say nothing.

"I knew you weren't dead," she says after a moment. "Even though Robert insisted. I knew. I just thought you were some rich, careless woman who didn't want him. Maybe thinking as much made it easier to hate you. I couldn't feel sympathy for that woman. It *did* make it easier. I could give him everything if his mother never wanted him in the first place."

"I don't expect you to stop loving him," I rasp, my throat tight. "I don't—"

"You just want to know him," she says. "Deep down, I know that. But I can't help feeling like…" She chokes a sob back and tears at her hair. "Like I've woken from a nightmare, but everything I've ever had now belongs to someone else. Honestly, I'm not sure if I prefer the nightmare."

She's referring to more than just Eli. Vanya? And Mischa.

"I don't think I can ever stop seeing him as my son."

"You don't have to," I say in a rush. "But I want… I want to learn to see him in that way too."

Marnie hid me from the world. Maybe she was ashamed of who my father was. But I know now that I refuse to do the same. There is no mistaking that Eli has parts of Robert.

But, as Mischa pointed out, he also contains pieces of me.

"I don't want to take him from you," I admit to Anna. "I couldn't."

"And it isn't my place to deny him his mother," she replies, smiling weakly. "Even if I wish he could stay mine forever."

In awkward silence, we pick at our food. Finally, Anna reaches across the table, brushing her hand over mine. "You aren't hungry?"

I look down at my untouched plate. "I don't think so," I say.

"I see…" She eyes me for so long that I'm not sure whether to question her or leave. Finally, she sighs. "Robert wasn't a terrible father, per se. In fact, I don't think he even knew how to be one. He kept his son well-fed and protected, but he never held him. He never soothed him when he cried. He saw him rarely… Mischa?" Her gaze turns wistful and darts toward my stomach. "Misha would be different. Anyway, I think I'm going up to bed."

She gingerly gathers up her plate and I copy her. Together, we ascend the stairs, silent creatures, victims in this brutal war.

We've both lost an untold amount as collateral.

But in a twisted way, we've gained more than we could ever have imagined as well.

Of all the places in the world, a cold, foreboding fortress should be the last one would expect to find children shrieking through the winding corridors, chased by a specter whom I can only discern from their giggles is the worst kind of monster.

The kind whose identity is alarmingly easy to suspect as I rise from my bed and get dressed in a pair of jeans and a loose-fitting top.

I leave my room only to be nearly run over by Mouse. Grinning, she skirts past me and rounds a corner. Not far behind is Eli, cackling madly. Bringing up the rear is a stranger. A care-free laugh booms from his chest as he moves slowly, ensuring that every footstep echoes like thunder.

"I can hear you," he growls as the children scatter deeper into the house. "You better run—"

His wicked grin falls flat the moment he spots me, and the illusion is shattered.

"Rose." Drawing himself to his full height, Mischa inclines his head toward my room, a subtle command. *We need to talk.*

After everything he's put me through, I should run. I start to, but he's beside me in a second. His fingers interlace with mine, locking tight when I try to wrench away. He all but shoves me into my room before quietly closing the door.

"As much as you love to play the victim, I won't let you this time," he warns. "You can hate me if you want. But don't you dare skulk around like a fucking prisoner—"

"Then how should I act after having my personal drama exposed to your fucking society?" I ask, jutting my chin into the air. "You tell me."

He chuckles under his breath. "Like this," he admits. I shudder as he brushes his hand down my shoulder. I was on guard for violence—not this. "A haughty little bitch. One who may have a point—"

"A point? Maybe I should lead by example?" I suggest, shrugging him off. "I'll share my own little secret in private, without an audience."

"Oh?" He cocks his head as his expression darkens. "Let me guess: Robert Winthorp still has your soul and it was never really mine to claim? A bit anticlimactic, Rose, but not entirely unexpected—"

"No." Balling my hands into fists is the only way I can keep from hitting him. "I… I think I'm pregnant."

He blinks and that mask he wears so doggedly around me cracks. "Are you sure?" His gaze lowers to my stomach. "Is it mine?"

I slap him—but his question didn't trigger the action. It's how he asked it. Hesitant and coarse, as if he wasn't sure of the answer.

And, for once, his confusion isn't played as a joke.

"Who else's would it be?"

He frowns and I understand.

"Fine." I throw my hands into the air, forcing a cold laugh. "It's Robert's. I threw myself at him after being dragged back into my old cage. Does that make you feel better? Now, you have three pieces of 'leverage' to use against him—"

"Stop it." He grabs my arm, but the touch lacks any malice. He merely uses the limb as a leash, keeping me close. "Tell me."

"Does it matter to you so much?" I demand, exasperated.

"Maybe I just need to hear you say it?" His voice deepens, radiating a warning. "Is it mine?"

"Forget it." I shake my head and laugh again. I sound insane. Maybe I am. He's finally driven me past the brink.

"Forget all of it. It's not like someone like you could ever be a father anyway."

He recoils. "And what kind of woman would willfully deny her child one?" His voice chases me as I lunge for the door and throw it open. "A selfish bitch, though why am I surprised?"

"Don't," I whisper hoarsely as my steps falter in the doorway. "Don't you dare."

I brush my hand against my chest, a weak protection against an impending assault.

Like any wolf, he doesn't just bite.

He aims to maim.

"It's in your blood," he hisses. "Like mother like daughter."

I run, racing past a corner where giggles emanate. Panting, I leave the house and venture beyond the outskirts of the woods, vanishing beneath the trees.

Sergei Vasilev owns miles of land. I walk until my legs ache and I can't go a step farther, but I have yet to approach a barrier or land marker. For all of Mischa's hatred of the Winthorps, what makes his world any different? The secrets are the same, as are the twisted lies. Which man's story is more accurate. Sergei's? Or Vanya's?

Hunched against the trunk of a tree, I can't decide. My heart warns me to trust one man more than the other. Vanya. But that muscle is a fickle fucking thing. It hurts now when I think of Mischa, but not in the way that it should. I need to hate him. Despise him. Anything but parse over the agony I saw lurking in his expression.

Like I was the one who hurt him despite the man doubting me at every turn.

But so what if he does? It's growing increasingly apparent that everyone in my life has only ever seen me as a tool, or a burden, or a secret to hide. Never as a living, breathing, bleeding person with a soul of her own.

I should just run. Disappear into the ether and leave the war and its casualties behind. My heart pangs as I think of Eli, but he already has a mother. Yes. I shift to my knees and feel along the tree bark for a branch to help me stand.

I find one, but it breaks off the second I apply pressure and falls onto my shoulder, lashing at my cheek. Laughing, I ignore the slight pain and curl into a ball.

I could fade here instead. Just let the world go on without me.

As if it would be that easy.

I hear them first: footsteps crashing through the undergrowth. Then his voice rings out, more grated than ever.

"Fuck... No, fuck!"

I open my eyes as he staggers toward me and snatches the branch away.

Frantic, he grabs my shoulders. "Can you hear me? Rose? Can you hear me?" He brushes the hair back from my face and sways when he sees me staring back.

"I'm fine," I admit.

"Thank God." He stands, helping me to my feet.

"I'm going back if that's what you're worried about," I say, starting in the direction I assume the manor is in. "I don't require an escort—"

"Fine. So it's Robert's." He grabs me from behind, sliding his hands to my waist. "You can even name it after him. I don't care."

The heat in his voice eats away at any anger I feel. All that's left is just…pain.

"Don't you ever doubt me like that," I say hoarsely. "Never."

"I won't," he swears into the skin of my throat. "I won't… But you don't leave."

I blink rapidly and swallow, fighting for air. "I want to trust you, but every time I try… You attack me."

"Something in me won't let me believe you, Rose," he admits. "Even if I want to. I can't. If I let you in, you'll hollow me out. You'll rob me of everything I have left, and I need to fucking fight. Or I'll be like—"

"Vanya?" I ask.

His arms tighten, giving me his answer. "He told me a story once," he says gruffly. "When I asked him why he gave up so fucking easily. Why he let me take the reins, even though the only reason anyone followed me and not Sergei was because of him. He became a shadow of who he was, Rose. Maybe for the better, but…he was still broken."

"What did he say?"

"He told me about a woman he knew." He sounds distant, as if he's relaying some sordid fairytale he hasn't deciphered yet. "A woman who showed him what love was." He laughs and I doubt it was a cherished lesson. "He said it was like a rose. Beautiful, but painful. The thorns dig deep. They cut through you, but a part of you still won't let it go."

"Is that the real reason why you call me Rose?" I ask in a thready whisper. "To mock me?"

"To warn myself," he replies. "I always fucking knew… You'd cut me into pieces."

"I want to trust you." My hand goes to my stomach before I can help it. At the moment, it's flat, seemingly empty. "I need to trust you. So stop pushing me away every time I try."

"I will… But I need you to promise me—right fucking now." He turns me to face him, his eyes like midnight. "You won't ever use this against me." He gestures to my belly. "That you won't ever turn against me."

My lips part, but it's a promise I'm not brave enough to make just yet. All I can do is take his hand, intertwining my fingers with his. "Learn to trust me and I won't ever have a reason to betray you."

"Trust." He leans in, mulling over the word like it's a foreign concept. "I'm sure that includes many avenues we can build on. Thoroughly. Maybe we'll live out that fantasy yet."

My cheeks flame as I recall his vision of the future: me, giving him multiple children.

"But first…" He draws back suddenly serious. "I'm going to drive the nightmares from your skull. For good."

Meaning Robert Winthorp and this stupid, petty war. Did my mother know the chaos she'd leave in her wake with such a simple lie?

As Vanya stated, Mischa doesn't even know the extent.

"How?" I ask.

He hesitates and I can see the war within himself playing out across his features. Hatred and desire. Finally, something wins. "We're going to cut the serpent off at its head."

In other words: kill Robert.

"When?"

"Soon." He stares off into the distance. "Fairly soon."

"And when it happens, you'll tell me?"

"Yes." He looks down, meeting my gaze. "I'll tell you, Little Rose. As promised, I'll even let you twist the knife."

Mischa seems to think I hate Robert—enough to want him dead—but I'm not sure if that's the case. Can you hate someone who merely exploited a willing victim?

Everything he did was never forced—even the supposed death of our child.

I just never questioned. Like a good doll, I merely accepted every explanation he deigned to toss my way.

You can't blame a wolf for devouring a doe.

But you can blame a monster cunning enough to deceive his prey. One who enjoys watching his victims squirm in anguish. After all, the wolf only seeks to sate a primal urge, but the monster?

He desires control above all else. Power.

And, for whatever reason, the only man to come to mind in that context is Sergei.

He finally makes his reappearance as Mischa and I return to the manor as the first hints of darkness creep along the horizon.

"I need to speak with you," he says, meeting us at the edge of the gardens. Though he speaks to us both, his eyes remain fixated on me. "In private, if you please."

"Why?" Mischa demands. He steps forward, effortlessly inserting himself in between us. "Is there something you can't say in my presence, Sergei?"

"No," the man says calmly. "But I am sure there are some things that Ellen would not like discussed. Even in front of you." He turns and beckons me with a nod. "I'll be in the drawing room off the foyer."

Mischa starts after him, but I place a hand on his shoulder.

"I'll be fine."

When I enter the manor without him, I can sense his ever-present hesitation. Once again, his paranoia will fester. Can he truly trust me?

I can't bring myself to look back and gauge which emotion wins out.

Instead, I force my shoulders back and navigate my way to Sergei alone. Sure enough, I find him in a large room lined with bookshelves. He's standing near a row of windows, glaring out at the dimming sky. It's easy to see the resemblance between him and Vanya now; they share the same contemplative, brown eyes and stern expression. But where Vanya radiates an exhausted neutrality, Sergei is always alert. Always watching.

"That was a remarkable performance the other night," he praises, but I suspect that the compliment is more grudging than genuine. "You reminded me so much of—"

"Marnie?" I interject. My arms go around my chest. It's instinct. A subconscious guarding against the cold shift in his posture. He's standing taller, angled away from me.

It's like he knows the topic on my mind before I even voice it.

"Why didn't you tell me that she wasn't taken? She *willingly* left the Winthorps."

"Ivan told you that?" he scoffs dismissively. "Always the romantic—"

"So then what is the truth?" I'm too tired to disguise the pain in my voice. "Just tell me."

"Fine." He faces me, crossing his arms as well. "You deserve to hear it. Your mother wasn't the naïve innocent that rumor and legend have turned her into. She was a cunning, intelligent, and—I'll say it—ruthless young woman. The elder Winthorp forced her into marriage—did she tell you that?"

I lick my lips, unsure of just how much I should reveal. I'm on a different playing field than the battles I've fought with

Mischa. There are no petty tricks or scathing insults to dodge. Sergei reminds me of a tactician, already twenty steps ahead, one wrong move from instant checkmate.

"She didn't tell me much about her family," I admit.

In reality, she told me nothing.

"Oh?" A satisfied gleam flits across his gaze, but the instant I place it, it's already gone. "Do you know that the Winthorps liked to dip into the sex trade? Your mother was one of those unfortunate girls, plucked from obscurity, destined to be sold to some rich, old baron. Unfortunately, Robert Winthorp took a liking to her first. She was undeniably beautiful…" He trails off as if staring into the past, seeing her, this lovely, doomed creature. "But she was far smarter than the bastard gave her credit for. She tricked him into believing she loved him despite the circumstances of their meeting. So he married her. Worshipped the ground she walked on, and gradually, she convinced him to grant her more and more freedom until she could enter and leave the manor as she pleased."

In some ways, the woman he's described sounds more like Briar than Marnie: cunning to her own advantage.

"So why did she come to you?"

"Me?" He raises an eyebrow. "No, she went to *Ivan*. He was the liaison between the *mafiya* and the Winthorps."

"They did your accounts," I recall from what Mischa told me—but he never mentioned that *Vanya* oversaw that little arrangement. "In return, you protected their investments."

"Yes." His eyebrows furrow. Is he surprised I know as much? "Marnie went to Ivan with a proposition: She would tell him everything she knew about the Winthorp business if he rescued her and her daughter."

"So there was no kidnapping." I can't tell if the hitch in my voice is due to shock or relief. "The whole start of this war was based on a lie—"

"Not quite," Sergei corrects. "Winthorp was growing bolder. He planned to attack us eventually and control our territory himself. By warning Ivan, Marnie thought she was saving his life. She was also sly enough to ensure she got something out of it."

Could the mother I knew truly be that selfless? And simultaneously selfish?

"So then what happened?" I prompt.

"Ivan came to me with her plan and I agreed to use my resources to assist in her escape. But, in the end, Briar was left behind."

Something pinches in my chest. Jealousy? I know it's selfish to feel it now. But a cruel part of my mind eagerly points out the glaring facts I want to ignore. Marnie sacrificed her freedom for Briar, but in return, she doomed me to a lifetime of hell. Did the fact that Vanya was my father make it easier for her to live with such a choice?

Maybe, as Mischa believed, her love had been a lie.

"How was she recaptured?" I ask, returning to the topic at hand.

"I don't know." Sergei meets my gaze, but I can't discern a single emotion from his expression. "When she had a child roughly nine months later, I suspected that you were Ivan's."

"So why didn't you tell him?"

He stiffens and eyes the knuckles of his hand. One by one, he curls each finger into a fist. A ring glints from one of them: silver, sporting the visage of a coiled serpent.

"Tell him what? That the woman he loved turned her back on him? That she would rather raise his bastard among the Winthorps than send her to her father? How could I tell my brother that?"

My chest tightens with the weight of such a twisted dilemma. I couldn't imagine making a decision at all—but I've had twenty-four years to live with the consequences of his.

"So you left me there."

"With your mother," he corrects. "And when she died... I didn't know your circumstances were as dire as they were. How could I?"

But something in me won't accept that answer. "You told Mischa that I was the continuation of your line." At least before Anna was found. "You said you knew about me since the day I was born. For someone who seems to care so much about your family, you have an odd way of showing it."

"And I deserve your anger, yes." He nods. "I deserve your mistrust, even. But for a second, think from your mother's point of view. She kept you from your father, but perhaps that, more than anything, reveals her true thoughts of Ivan? Perhaps we were her pawns all along? After all, would you return your son to Robert Winthorp?"

"Don't." I cut off his scenario with a sharp wave of my hand. "Don't you dare mention him. I never had a choice in how he grew up."

"And if you could have done things differently?"

My heart breaks. "I would have never left him alone. Never."

Even if it meant putting on a charade with Robert.

"And maybe your mother felt differently than you in that respect," he says. "But now that you have been reunited with your son, what choice will you make?"

I grit my teeth at how effortlessly he's managed to turn the tables. "Why do you care?" A suspicion creeps into my brain as if on cue. "Could it be because he's the Winthorp heir? If Robert dies…"

Then Eli could stand to inherit it all.

"Maybe you should ask Mischa the same question?" Sergei steps forward and brushes his hand along my cheek. "It's not my place to poison you against him—"

"You couldn't," I counter, but my voice falls flat. A weakness he doesn't miss.

"I would caution you to carefully consider your circumstances. I didn't kidnap Marnie Winthorp. I never brutalized her or made her a martyr, but can Mischa say the same?" His thumb grazes my branded cheek for emphasis. "There are some lines even I won't cross. I wouldn't use your child against you, and when you realize that, we can further this discussion."

He moves past me for the door, but before he crosses the threshold, I call out, "You claim you wouldn't use children, but what about Briar Winthorp?"

"Briar." He stiffens with one foot still in the air. "What about her?"

Something in his tone makes me blurt my words out with no ounce of tact. "You were willing to have her killed when Anna-Natalia was taken. Weren't you?"

It sounds so evil when paired with Misha's supposed crimes. Ruthless.

But Sergei doesn't flinch. "What could I possibly gain from the death of a little girl?"

Without giving me the chance to ponder that, he leaves.

On the surface, he has a point.

But the answer doesn't take long for me to settle on. What could a man like him gain? Nothing material, perhaps. Not money or Winthorp prestige.

But I know firsthand what the death of a child could do to a woman.

You could break her irreparably.

You could change her loyalties.

And perhaps the cruelest aim of all: you could punish her.

CHAPTER 21

$\mathcal{M}$y room is a quiet refuge after my conversation with Sergei—but not for long. The second I lift my dress over my head, I hear the door open.

Cool air drifts in, ushering heavy footsteps. Alarmed, I cover my chest with my hands—but maybe the act is for show. Because I can identify my intruder by his scent alone.

"You don't look very pregnant," he declares, eyeing me up and down. "And I would like to think that I would notice."

"Is that so?" I turn away from him, eyeing my reflection flung over the window. "I haven't menstruated since I've been with you," I admit, smoothing my hand along my abdomen. "And…I just know."

His steps echo as he comes up behind me. "And now?" he wonders near my ear. "Do I treat you like a glass doll? No more sex?"

The scary part is how earnest he sounds. Curious.

"Would this really stop you?" I press my hand against my flat stomach as if shielding innocent ears from his answer.

"Maybe," he admits, surprising me. "But that doesn't mean I can't touch you. Watch you." He grabs my waist, guiding me against him. "I think I could enjoy that."

Closing my eyes, I let my head fall back against his shoulder. "I hate the way you toy with me." I sound pained. Desperate.

"I hate the way you tempt me." In retaliation, he runs his finger beneath my rib cage. Then he guides me to face him. "It's like you're a witch." He laughs bitterly at his own descriptor as he startles me by sinking to his knees. "It's the truth. You make me feel things, Rose… Devious little things. I've wanted to kill men before, but never like what I want to do to you."

"Oh?" I shiver as his fingers brush the backs of my knees, urging me closer.

"Yes." He nods, but against me, the motion feels more like a caress. "I want to destroy you. Devour you."

"You sound like you want to hurt me—" I break off as his lips ghost my abdomen and flutter over my hip bones. My knees tremble. For stability, I sink my hands into his hair.

"Painfully. That's how I crave you," he whispers. "There is no sanity. No logic. When I'm with you, I crave every fucking thing I spent years telling myself I never wanted."

Mischa Stepanov deny himself anything? "Like what?"

"More," he admits, fanning his hands over my belly. "More than the *mafiya*. More than crushing Winthorp. You make me consider a life beyond it all. And I never wanted to before."

Because this violence and conflict are all he has.

"But I'm going to watch your belly swell, Rose," he promises between heavy breaths. "I'm going to watch you grow with my child. And…" He looks up, meeting my gaze. "And maybe I'll change my mind."

"About what?" I say, barely able to breathe.

He looks down and rests his forehead against me. "About it all. Maybe we could leave Winthorp behind. Runaway to that tiny strip of the world I know you've dreamt about. The place where violence and death can't follow you. Only those worthy of sharing such a paradise with. Anna, and Vanya, and Eli, and Mouse…"

"But you can't," I whisper, dashing the fantasy before it can unfold.

"Because this is who I am," he agrees, but for once, it's not a boast. "And one day you'll take your pretty eyes, and your baby, and your sweet little cunt, and you'll leave me, Rose. Men like me don't keep women like you for very long. Ask Ivan."

"Shut up." I curl my fingers in his hair and pull until a growl revs in his throat. "Just... Just tell me that you want me."

"Want," he chuckles and stands, trailing his lips up my torso the entire way. When he reaches my lips, he claims them, groaning at the taste. "I need you, Rose—but not like your precious husband did. You don't keep me sane, or human, or anything like that." He kisses me even deeper, guiding me into his arms. Against my parted lips, he says, "You make me *think* after years of hating, and killing, and feeling. I can finally fucking think."

And he makes that simple fact sound more powerful than any other commodity I've known men to chase.

Including any amount of money.

I wake up in Mischa's arms, but my first instinct isn't to squirm, or endure, or count down the seconds. I turn the tables instead and observe him in the pale light of dawn streaming in through the window. He's deeply asleep, lying on his back, with my body crushed to his side. Even unconscious, he's possessive.

I can't stop myself from touching him when he's like this. He's handsome while peaceful, irresistibly so. For a second, I toy with the idea of what his child might look like. Perpetually angry, with a head of wild hair? Would they have his dark eyes as well? Or maybe blue, like Eli's...

Sergei's warning intrudes on the innocent thought: Does Mischa intend to use him for his own gain?

I pull my hand away and it's like flipping a switch. Mischa opens his eyes, homing them on me. He shifts and captures my wrist, resettling my hand over the tattooed flesh above where his heart resides.

"See something you like, Rose?" he wonders, his voice husky.

"What do *you* see when you look at me?" I ask. "A pawn? A willing victim? Or is it leverage—"

He sighs and releases me. "Someone hasn't been paying attention."

I wait for him to shove me off and storm away, but he doesn't move. Neither do I. With my face against his chest, I can hear his heart beating. The steady, gentle thrum is my translator for whatever his face doesn't express. He may be wearing a shadow of a scowl, but he isn't angry.

He's…content. Such a strange concept that I have to feel it rather than observe. In him, peace is expressed in slow, heavy breathing and muscles that twitch only slightly when I run my fingers over them.

"Maybe I need to hear you say it out loud?" I counter, using his saying to my advantage.

"Hmm." He hums low in his throat and then looks down on me from across the scarred, tattooed planes of his chest. "Out loud… How about: Robert Winthorp begged for you the second I realized you weren't Briar? He offered millions to have you back. He even offered to trade his own sister. Then he killed his father with his bare hands. By then, you weren't of any use to me but as bait, so what reason would I have for keeping you?"

I mull over the question, trying to view the world as he does, where everyone has a price tag—even little girls who are intentionally silenced in order to play a role in some criminal enterprise.

"You could want to use me as a sex slave?" I venture to guess. "You did threaten to sell me."

He scoffs. "I beat Kostastantin Vorshev within an inch of his life—not because he was a lying cunt, selling me out to Winthorp. No… Because he touched you. He hurt you." He reaches out, dragging his fingers along my cheek. "I kept Mouse—not that I would ever sell her back to Nicolai—but I kept her here because she reminded me of you. You look at me the same fucking way: like you're waiting for the moment I'll pull out my knife and run you through." He laughs, but it's a hollow, empty sound. "And if you're worried about him. Your son…" He tilts his head back, eyeing the ceiling. "There is Robert Winthorp in him. I can see it. He can be ruthless when he plays." He laughs, and it's real this time. "He declared 'war' on the roses in the garden and decapitated an entire bush of them. That boy is definitely a Winthorp."

I stiffen, but not out of fear. It's the first time he's said that name with something other than hate lacing it: admiration?

"But he has more of you. His eyes. His laugh. As young as he is, he isn't afraid to show compassion or guilt. I think he'll grow up just fine, Rose."

I look away, blinking rapidly. "Thanks to Anna."

"No." He guides my chin into the palm of his hand, forcing me to meet his gaze. "Anna may be part of it, but some of it is you."

"And do you think you can use him in ways you're unwilling to use me?" I have to ask him.

He sighs. "I should be. I'm sure Robert would pay just as much or even more to have him back. But I'm a selfish fuck, Rose." He sits up, bringing me with him, and pushes the covers back. "He isn't going anywhere."

My heart swells, sensing the ruthless promise contained within that boast.

"Thank you," I rasp.

"But he's not the only reason you're worried," he suspects. "I've seen you watching me and Anna together."

I bite my lip, but the pain does little to counteract the flood of fire searing my cheeks. "You loved her. I can understand that—"

"I still do," he says. "But not how you think. We grew up together. In some ways, we were more like siblings than anything else. And if something more might have come from it..." He shrugs and slides his arm from around me.

Before I can mourn the loss of heat, his hand captures mine. "We will never know."

Letting me go, he stands and grabs his pants from the floor. "But, now, I need to ask *you* something. Sergei put that suspicion into your head. Didn't he?"

I briefly consider denying it—whatever is brewing between the two men, something warns me that it isn't good. In the end, I nod. "He said you might have 'plans' for him."

Mischa scoffs. "I might have plans… Do you trust him?"

The hostility in his tone stings. "I-I don't know—"

"I don't." He pulls his shirt on and starts to pace, speaking to me from over his shoulder. "The night you were taken— from right under his fucking nose, I might add—he put on a grand show, Sergei. But something was off."

I sit straighter, bracing my feet on the floor. "What do you mean?"

He could be giving in to paranoia, but I can't ignore my own suspicions. As much as I try to deny it, our escape was too damn easy.

"I know the man," Mischa says, frowning as he dissects his thoughts. "I know when he's worried. I know when he's afraid. But that night, he wasn't."

"What are you saying?"

"I'm saying: Watch the man for yourself. Listen to everything he says, and use that smart brain of yours, Rose."

He taps his finger on his forehead for emphasis. "I'd say I'm not a very complicated man. I plan directly and go for the jugular. But Sergei plays mind games. I warned you once and I will warn you again: He was the most effective and ruthless leader the *mafiya* had. Don't forget that. Now, get dressed." He tosses something to me that I barely manage to catch: my plain dress. "I want to show you something."

Whatever he aims to show me requires intruding on the small sitting room where Anna is cuddling with Eli. He's nestled on her lap while she hums a song and runs her fingers through his hair. Spotting us, she stiffens.

"I can go," I blurt, but she shakes her head.

"No." She stands and gingerly sets the boy on the floor. "Mischa." Her voice breaks, but she swallows and tries again. "I'd like to go for a walk, please."

"Of course." Mischa extends his hand to her and guides her to the doorway.

Looking back at Eli, Anna forces a pained smile. "You stay here, my darling. I'll be just a moment, all right?"

Eli shrugs, wringing his fingers.

As they leave, I sit on the chair beside him. "My name is Ellen," I say. Of all the ways to begin this conversation, it's the only one to come to mind.

I wonder if Robert ever told him as much.

To my surprise, he nods solemnly and digs something from beneath the collar of his crisp blue shirt. His locket. Mischa must have returned it to him. With his tiny fingers, he pries it open and holds it up for my inspection.

I barely recognize the woman staring blankly from a small color photo. Angel, he called her? More like a ghost. Her blue eyes are lifeless, her face unblemished. I can't even recall a time such a picture could have been taken—it's as if my entire life before now has been a blur. Snippets of clarity in the midst of a nightmare.

But him…

I never forgot him, no matter how hard I tried.

Gingerly, I brush my finger along his cheek. It's plump, sporting twin dimples and a ruddy redness. The boyish attributes soften the reality of his slender neck and elegant nose—Winthorp features.

Even now, a part of me half expects him to fade beneath my fingertips—this is all some cruel fantasy.

But he doesn't.

Beaming, he points to a pile of objects strewn over the floor instead. Someone found him makeshift toys: a spoon, a small ball, and a porcelain figurine far too delicate to have been intended for use by a child.

"Watch," he commands. Flopping onto his stomach, he smashes the spoon against the ball.

And I observe him for what feels like an eternity, my eyes watering.

Robert kept me caged for years, and despite Mischa's insistence to the contrary, I don't think I hate him for it. I can't.

Because as cruel as he was, I *let* him use, and control, and manipulate me. I made myself numb to every bit of abuse and fed myself the lie that survival was worth it.

But this? My throat aches as I picture what life could have been like just for a second if I had Eli. I would have looked upon his innocent face and maybe I would have seen through the bars of my narrow cage for the first time. I would have known that no future was worth suffering an existence where he would see his father as a monster and his mother as a victim.

Holding Eli back then, I would have woken up from the dazed, nightmarish life Robert had accustomed me to.

And he knew it. Just like Mischa manipulates his own pawns across this ruthless gameboard, Robert maneuvered me and his own son as well. All in the name of leverage, and power, and winning.

But this is one game I can't excuse him for playing.

And this crime deserves more than death as a punishment.

a nna and Mischa return far too soon, with Mouse in tow. Eli jumps to his feet when he spots the younger girl, and the two promptly dash into the hallway, playing a makeshift game of chase.

"Outside," Mischa bellows and the children heed his command with him grumbling in their wake.

"Shall we make sure no one loses an eye?" Anna asks. For once, her small smile seems genuine.

Together, we enter the gardens and find the children darting between the trees while Mischa stands guard nearby. From here, his stern shouts are easily discernible.

"You have five minutes to hide. After that…I will be taking prisoners."

My heart swells while I watch him. Even if I still have doubts about his plans for me or Eli, I know one thing more than anything else: He'll make a good father.

If this war doesn't consume him first.

So lost in thought, I barely hear Anna say, "It feels so strange to be out in the fresh air again."

I turn and find the wind whipping her hair behind her as if in emphasis.

"Visiting the gardens once every few days was a rare treat," she says.

My heart pangs. I recognize the wistful note in her voice. Once upon a time, I might have said the same thing.

"I'm sorry," I tell her. "If I had known…"

I'm not sure what I could have done. Warned Mischa at least. He could have rescued her sooner.

"Don't," she says softly. "In a selfish way, I almost wish I had more time with…" She shakes her head and clears her throat. "Mischa told me what Robert told you. That Eli —*Robert*—was dead. And as horrible as it sounds, I almost wish you *had* abandoned him. I would feel less guilty."

"You shouldn't. He's beautiful. And Eli is a wonderful name." Watching him, I'm struck by a sudden realization. Perhaps *this* is what Mischa wanted to show me: a young boy with wild, blond hair traipsing boldly through the edge of the forest.

There is no mistaking the hints of Robert Winthorp peeking from his features. His nose. His mouth. The calculating way he eyes his target—Mouse—before pouncing on her without warning. But he's quicker to laugh, and his impish grin reflects no ounce of malice.

Robert Winthorp may be his father, but he is his own person.

And I have hope that he will be different.

For better *or* for worse.

Mischa runs the children ragged until they barely have the strength to make it to the upstairs sitting room before collapsing into respective corners.

"I'll get them some water," Anna suggests. Smiling, she hustles toward the stairs.

Funnily enough, even Mischa looks winded. He pants while meeting my gaze and rakes the sweat-soaked hair from his face. "What are you thinking behind those judging little eyes, Rose?"

I turn away, spotting Eli curled on his side, deeply asleep. Across from him, poor Mouse is struggling to keep her eyes open. The dirt and mud streaking their faces are clues as to the kind of "games" they were playing.

"I'm thinking that you have a very strange idea of playtime."

Knife fighting, war drills, and escape lessons.

"And what should we be doing instead?" Mischa asks, crossing his arms. "Playing with dollies and tea parties?"

"Maybe."

He frowns. "Maybe it's you that has a strange idea of playtime."

"If all you teach them is violence and war, then all you can see in their future is violence and war," I explain, gesturing toward Mouse. She's fully asleep now, huddled against the wall, but her posture remains tense. Guarded. As if she expects an attack at any moment. "And maybe it's naïve, and foolish, and stupid, but…"

"What?" he prods when I fall silent. I look over, surprised by the stern tilt to his jaw. He's curious.

"I think it's braver to imagine a future for them in which their only fear is pouring the tea wrong or wearing an outdated dress to dinner. Is that so wrong?"

Maybe it is—shallow in a sense.

But while I always resented Briar's vain upbringing, there was a comfort in it that I envied more than anything.

She never had to evade her father's men or jump on the first offer of security thrown her way. She never saw safety as a commodity worth trading her soul for.

"I don't want to fear for them." I brush my hand along my stomach before I can help it. "I'd rather *hope* for them."

"And what does hope lie in?" he counters, though I don't think he's mocking me. His tone is way too soft. "Piano lessons and etiquette classes?"

I shrug. "Maybe. Or in someplace where they can feel safe. A home. One they don't have to worry might be invaded—"

"Rose." His posture shifts and he becomes the imposing soldier once more.

I turn to the doorway and see why. Sergei stands there, flanked by Vanya.

"Sorry to interrupt," the older man says. Dressed in black, he radiates an authority even Mischa reacts to by gritting his teeth. "But something has come up that may draw your interest."

"What is it?" Mischa demands.

"Since Ellen decided our course of action, I think I may have the perfect opportunity in mind for you to fulfill it."

Mischa stiffens. "Fine. But then she can hear the details as well." He gestures toward me with a wave of his hand.

"Of course." Sergei extends his arm in a silent invitation to follow. "I don't object."

"I'll stay here," Anna suggests, appearing beside her father. Her eyes go to Eli and she smiles. "If I can wake them up, I'll send the children off to bed."

"Fine." Mischa shoulders past me and enters the hall. "Let's hear it, then."

"As you wish." Sergei pulls ahead and descends the stairs. Leading the way, he approaches the larger drawing room off the foyer.

Mischa and Vanya form a guarded audience along the wall while Sergei stands in the middle.

"After the unceremonious death of his father, Robert Winthorp has had to shore up support among the old man's allies," Sergei says. "Some of them, admittedly, are wary about an untested upstart. I know for a fact that Robert is on his way to one of those men as we speak. Unfortunately for him, I have my men staked along the route as well."

"So an ambush," Mischa surmises, stroking his chin. Raw hunger for revenge sinks into the line of his mouth, tilting it at the corner. His eyes, however, remain mistrustful. "And what is your plan?"

"Simple," Sergei replies. "I'll provide support. You and your men can have your prize. I won't interfere."

"Oh?" A tense few seconds pass as Mischa rattles off various logistics at a rapid-fire pace.

When.

Where.

How.

Sergei has an answer for every one.

Finally, Mischa sighs and drags his fingers through his hair, raking the strands back from his face. "So when do we go?"

"Now."

As if on cue, a man appears in the doorway. Though he isn't wearing the crisp, black ensemble most of Sergei's men do, I don't recognize him as Mischa's, either. Plain jeans and a short-sleeved tee-shirt set him apart, as do a few scattered tattoos down the length of his arms. One in particular draws my interest: a serpent coiled around a cross.

"This is one of my best scouts," Sergei says, drawing my attention back to him. "He will be your liaison as we bring up the rear."

"You won't be with us?" Vanya asks.

"I think it's for the best if Mischa takes the lead in this instance," Sergei replies, eyeing the younger man thoughtfully. "I wouldn't want to interfere."

"But shouldn't we call another council? Discuss this with the other heads? Request support—"

"You worry too much, Ivan," Sergei interjects.

"Does he though?" Mischa cocks his head as if a sudden thought occurred to him. "It isn't like you to be rash, Sergei."

"Rash?" The man strokes his chin. "Or prudent? After all, the best way to catch your enemy is off guard. However, I will concede to convening with the heads. It's unusual to meet so soon after a council—"

"But we'll make an exception," Mischa says. His eyes cut in my direction, impossible to read. "Little Rose should learn the true ways of the *mafiya*."

"Infernal politics," Vanya grumbles.

"Though necessary," Sergei says. "What say you, Mischa?"

"Fine. I'll arrange a *banquet*." He puts a mocking twist on the term. "For tomorrow night. From there, we can discuss our next course of action."

Both brothers nod in unison. "Agreed."

"Good." Mischa pulls away from the wall, but on his way out, he grabs my arm, dragging me after him.

In silence, he leads me past the staircase and into another room. One that, I assume, was chosen at random. It's spacious, but instead of portraits on the walls, this one sports weapons locked behind glass. Knives. Guns.

It's like being inside Mischa's brain.

"So what do you think?" the man in question murmurs against my ear. "Should we trust the charming Sergei Vasilev?"

He grunts when I don't give him an answer—but I'm still stuck on his use of that dangerous term. *We.*

"Tell me, Rose—"

"I don't know," I admit. "But you don't."

His mouth tightens as if his first instinct is to deny it. Then he shrugs. "You saw something. When Sergei's muscle came in. Your face changed."

"What?" I recall the unfamiliar man, picturing him clearly in my head. "I don't…"

"What?" he demands as I feel my face pale. "What is it?"

"I think…" My blood runs cold as I picture his tattoo. A serpent and cross. I've seen it before just once. My eyes widen as I meet Mischa's intent stare. "I think he's the man I saw outside of the hotel. When Anna and I escaped."

"What?" Mischa's eyebrows furrow. "No, it's…"

"Insane," I agree, my voice hoarse. "I must have seen it wrong."

"No." He sighs, gritting his teeth. "It's fucking devious and calculating. No wonder the bastard wasn't worried."

He apparently had a man on the inside.

"Do you think he's working with Robert?" Even as I voice such a suggestion, it sounds too fantastical to consider.

"I don't know," Mischa admits. "What was that spiel of yours about hope again? Maybe the raw, honest truth is that there is no such thing. You can delude yourself into thinking as much in a moment of weakness." He drags a finger along my cheek. "But then you find a knife in your back."

"Are you trying to warn me?" I ask, though I'm honestly not sure if I'm brave enough to hear the answer.

"Maybe," he admits. His breath ghosts my lips and I realize just how close he is: towering above me with a hairsbreadth between us. "Or maybe you've already realized that." He nods to my abdomen and the hand I have protectively braced there. "Either way... It's time for you to play some games my way."

"Like how?"

His nod beckons for me to follow as he crosses to the other end of the room. Two leather chairs are positioned at opposite corners. Mischa claims one for himself, leaving the other for me.

"Sit," he commands while he does the same, letting his bulk strain the confines of the leather.

The casualness is all for show, I suspect. When I meet his gaze, it's honed like a razor, deadly serious.

"So what will we play?" I force myself to ask.

"A history lesson." He props his elbow on his knee and then perches his chin atop the same hand. "The most dangerous game of all. Navigating a room of murderers and cutthroats —while gaining something from it at the same time. Let's say that Sergei is a snake, and that he's planning something..." He clenches his jaw, and his knuckles are white over the armrest from gripping it so tightly. "Then the only way to beat him is to anticipate him. Outmaneuver him. Outsmart him. Do you think you have what it takes?"

I eye him from head to toe, unnerved by what I find now. An unguarded Mischa offering up more secrets.

Forget the knife. *This* is the most dangerous weapon in his arsenal.

Trust.

"Do I? I don't know," I admit, supplying an answer before he can. "But I can learn. So teach me."

"Good." He smiles and a part of me squirms in anticipation. How strange it feels to finally be included in one of his schemes. "First, a bit of advice. Men like Sergei are patient. They can get inside your head and outwit any plan before you even come up with it. How do you defeat a man like that?"

"How?" In a way, dealing with him has given me the answer. I don't think Mischa realizes how similar he is to his old mentor. And the few times I've ever fought back against him have been born from the same place. "You can't plan," I say, frowning.

Mischa raises an eyebrow, but he doesn't interject even though I've just contradicted his entire argument. "Oh? How, then."

I shrug. "You just have to react. Intuitively."

Like starving yourself out of spite due to an insult.

Or attacking someone, claws drawn, when they expect you to surrender.

Desperation is the only tactic that can't be outmaneuvered.

"There is no way to outwit someone like that," I say, meeting Mischa's probing stare. "You can only retaliate."

"Hmph." He chuckles deeply, but there's no mocking in his tone. Admiration instead? "*Now*, you are thinking like a member of the *mafiya*. So tell me, Rose: How do you plan to react to him?"

*M*afiya history lessons seem more like horror stories. Murderers who command respect through their gruesome deeds. Drug smugglers. Politicians who deal in lies. The insights haunt me all night, circling my brain until morning comes.

Mischa plans his "banquet" with little fanfare. It's almost insulting compared to something one might have found at Winthorp Manor in its heyday. There are no four-course meals planned or tables draped in finery. In fact, the meal itself seems secondary to the true main course: intrigue.

"There," Mischa says against the nape of my neck. "Watch them. Do you remember your lesson?"

We stand positioned near a window overlooking the front of the manor. The setting sun reflects off a row of black vehicles lined up in the courtyard like children's toys.

One by one, various figures exit them.

"There's Boris Lynchkoft," Mischa remarks, referring to a balding man in a tight suit being ushered from a limo by two men who I assume are bodyguards. "And he…"

"Runs a drug trade," I rasp, recalling my "history lesson." "He isn't loyal to Sergei per se, but he doesn't like you, either."

"Good. And him?" He points to a different man exiting a dark sports car this time, flanked by even more muscle.

"Andrei Zagitov," I say. "He launders money through a shipping operation he owns. Also a somewhat neutral party. Him, along with Alexi Somodorov," I add, nodding to a different man strolling up the stone path to the manor's entrance. With a head of silver hair, he's the oldest man of the bunch. "He controls mercenaries and makes up the last party whose alliances you're unsure of."

"Very good." Mischa flicks his thumb along my chin, guiding my face toward him. In his eyes, I see something that may be amusement. He isn't scowling for once, either. "You may be able to play the game yet, Rose. But…" He cuts his eyes down to my dress—one of the few from the wardrobe in my room—and frowns. "Not like this."

"Oh?" I smooth my hands along the cotton skirt. "I never knew you had such an interest in fashion."

"Fashion?" He scoffs. "It's presentation. The wolf can't show up to the den dressed like a sheep."

"I didn't know you were poetic, either," I remark dryly.

"You don't know a lot of things about me, Rose. But I do have a feeling that Sergei won't supply you with a dress this time. At least not one fit for a wolf."

He takes my hand, leading me back through the upstairs level of the manor and into my room.

Sure enough, a dress is waiting for me, draped over the end of my bed.

But I doubt Sergei had a hand in choosing it.

"I guess wolves wear red in your world?" I croak, breathless.

Mischa cups my waist, guiding me back against his chest. "*This* wolf," he murmurs near my ear. "She is cunning and sly, and she bathes in the blood of those foolish enough to trust her." I stiffen, but he brushes his lips along my throat, negating any insult his words may contain. "Put it on."

With him on my heels, I approach the bed and run my fingers along the garment: a silk gown composed of a stunning shade of scarlet.

"It's beautiful—"

"Here." Mischa helps me shed my dress and ease the new one over my head.

Spotting my reflection in a nearby mirror, I certainly don't look like my mother.

Or Briar.

I'm someone new, clothed in blood red that highlights her healing wounds and injuries. Paired with the man beside me, I don't resemble a captive, either.

"Your necklace." Mischa runs his fingers along my neck, highlighting the absence of my rose charm. "It's gone—"

"Robert took it." I brush my fingers along the hollow spot as my heart pangs. The one thing I may have had of Marnie's, lost. "But I'm sure that means nothing to you. Mr. 'there is no point in getting attached to things.'"

"You're right," he agrees. "Only a fool would ever think there was something meaningful in some worthless trinket."

My face heats, but the second I try to pull away, he grabs my shoulder. I jump as something tickles my collar. When I look down, my eyes go wide.

"So consider me a fool, then," he grumbles while manipulating a slender, golden chain in one hand.

I gape as he fastens it around my neck. It's longer than the other one, sporting a delicate charm that takes my breath away: a rose in full bloom.

"It's lovely," I whisper, brushing my fingers along the charm. "I don't know what to—"

"Enough."

I sense him lean into me, his mouth in my hair, his breathing slow and heavy.

With my free hand, I reach back and find one of his, clenching tight. My body relaxes into him, fitting neatly within the rugged contours that make up his bulk. When I feel a telltale hardness against my hip, I press against him, drawing a groan from his lips.

"No." He pulls back, sliding his hands down my thighs until the last possible second. "If you tempt me now, we'll be late…"

I turn and find him eyeing me from head to toe, his eyelids lowered.

"*Very* late." When he bites his lip, I know he's mulling over that very possibility, weighing the pros and cons. Then he sighs. Apparently, politics trumps all else.

Even sex.

"But. First, my wolf needs to bare her teeth." He positions me with my back to him and runs his fingers through my hair. Within seconds, it's arranged into an elegant coil.

"And now what?" I ask as he observes his handiwork, finally satisfied.

"Now, we enter the den." He extends his hand and captures one of mine. "But, this time, we remain as allies."

*I*f I am a wolf, then Sergei resembles a bear. Approaching him head-on would be suicide, and the man relishes in his obvious strength. Once again, we're gathered in the grand hall. The marble floors magnify every sound, making those of us here—fifty at most—sound like hundreds.

Sergei holds court near the back of the room, surrounded by those of the council I recognize as having supported him at the last gathering. A black suit helps him cast an imposing aura damn near everyone succumbs to—Mischa included.

His grip tightens over my forearm, keeping me close to his side. Then he seems to realize his reaction and gradually loosens his grasp until we're standing apart entirely.

"This is an arena you'll have to navigate on your own, Rose," he murmurs as if reading my mind.

Childish panic goads my heart into beating faster. "What happened to us still being allies this time?" I demand, eyeing his clenched jaw. "Changed your mind already?"

"No. But every wolf needs to learn to hunt." His hand brushes my lower back, providing subtle reassurance while nudging me forward. "So hunt."

Before I can turn around, he's gone, slipping to the back of the room to strike up a conversation with a figure not mentioned in his "history lesson."

Alone, I spot Sergei already mingling with two of my three targets. The only remaining figure to approach happens to be the most intimidating enigma on my list, per Mischa: Alexi Somodorov.

He stands, eyeing a portrait hanging near the center of the room, his back to all other inhabitants.

Supposedly this man is second only to Sergei in terms of sheer ruthlessness. He murdered plenty of Winthorp associates, adding to the victim tally of this twisted war.

I approach him slowly as fear gnaws away at what little resolve I have. Hunt, Mischa told me.

But in what instance?

My role is nothing more than a formality. What power could a battered wife and illegitimate bastard truly command among such men?

"Look who deigns to grace me with her presence?"

Startled, I realize I've drawn even with Somodorov already.

He acknowledges my presence with a hiss, his eyes casting me a dismissive glance. "Robert Winthorp's whore."

I swallow hard as fire paints my cheeks. A part of me bristles at the insult, and I know what Mischa would do if he overheard: flex his muscle. Demand obedience.

But I am not him.

Tilting my head back, I meet the man's gaze directly, forcing him to maintain the eye contact far longer than comfortable. After all, only a coward would dare look away from a whore.

"I guess that means I know him better than anyone," I counter, surprised by how little my voice wavers. "Doesn't it?"

The man grunts and returns his attention to his painting. It depicts an ancient battlefield, where blood and mud churn in a sickening mass beneath fighting soldiers.

"I suppose so. But make no mistake, girl. I am not one of the besotted fools who think you may have some worth. Mischa called this little party for a reason. What?"

"No reason," I admit. "I simply wanted to learn."

"Oh?"

"I wanted to see for myself if any of you men truly have anything more to offer the world than someone like Robert Winthorp?"

His eyes flash and I know I'm on dangerous ground. Mischa relies on brute strength, Sergei on cunning, but what kind of combatant am I?

Neither, I'm realizing.

My strength may lie in something between the two. A skill that only a "whore" might possess and be willing to wield to its full potential. Something within my grasp, even now as Robert waits for me beyond these walls and secrets threaten the fragile security around me.

I excel at utilizing desperation.

To an artform.

"Tell me," Somodorov demands. "Why the hell should I entertain a child who got her say by fucking the head of the table? What could you possibly offer me?"

"It's simple." I copy him, observing the painting as well. In a way, it's a physical manifestation of our conversation. Mindless and static, mainly for show. The outcome is already set in stone: an eternal stalemate. "I can't offer you anything. Yet. But I think you know better than I do how alliances can change and that power can shift on a whim."

"Oh?" He laughs deep in his throat. "I don't have time for this—"

"Let me put it this way." I raise my voice just enough to stop him in his tracks. "You control mercenaries, correct? Who stands to lose more if the war with the Winthorps is over?"

"I have more important matters than Mischa's squabbles," the man scoffs.

"Fair enough. But then who might stand to see you as a threat if Robert is gone entirely? I don't think Mischa would care, but what about someone who may want to ensure they keep control of Winthorp estate themselves?"

He frowns and I instinctively brace. I'm on a tightrope. One wrong move and the consequences will be swift and brutal.

"Are you even suggesting what I think you are?"

"Of course not." I innocently incline my head. "But maybe your thoughts go in the same direction as mine? Some men would do anything to maintain their power. But a whore? All she would want is…peace."

Beyond his shoulder I find Mischa, watching us, his face unreadable.

"Excuse me." I slip past Somodorov, my heart pounding.

"I see you went for the most dangerous prey out of the gate," Mischa remarks once I reach him. The gruffness of his voice contrasts the odd tilt to his mouth betraying an emotion he's trying to resist: admiration. "He must like you. Alexi tends to stab what offends him." He eyes my throat, finding it unscathed. "What did you say to him?"

"Nothing," I rasp. "But I'm not sure I want to be a wolf for very long."

Not because I'm scared.

But because…

Toying the line between caution and power, I enjoyed every second of it.

I enjoyed it way too much.

We move to the manor's expansive dining room, where the heavy atmosphere should lessen somewhat. However, when Sergei claims the head of the table, his stern expression reveals that this setting is yet another battlefield.

This line of fighting is a lot simpler, however.

A vote.

"Do we take our chance now?" he wonders, glancing around the table brimming with guests. "Or squander it?"

He looks to Mischa, but for once, the younger man seems reluctant to take the reins of the conversation. He sits sideways on the chair beside mine, his hand on his chin.

"I vote yes," another man pitches in from Sergei's end of the table. "I say we put an end to this now."

"Agreed," another man says.

"Fine." Mischa looks up, meeting Sergei's gaze directly. "I may have the final say, but old Sergei…he would never lead us astray."

"Then it's settled. We move out tonight."

"Tonight?" The question comes from Somodorov. "Launch a full-scale operation on Winthorp with just a few hours' notice? That seems hasty, Sergei."

"Or intuitive, he will be returning from his meeting," the other man corrects. "As Mischa stated, would I suggest a plan I didn't think would work?"

"I guess," Somodorov says, "but still. I think we—"

"We should vote," Mischa says over him. He lifts his hand, displaying the callused palm. "I say yes."

I bite my lip to disguise my shock. Has he changed his opinion so soon? Around the table, various sounds of agreement or dissent are voiced, but within minutes, a consensus is clear.

"Then it's settled," Sergei says. "We strike tonight. A small contingent. My men and Mischa's—"

"What about mine?" Alexi interjects.

"I think a smaller team is better," Sergei says. "We can be discreet until it's time to strike."

The men on his side of the table grumble in affirmation of that plan.

"Fine." Mischa stands and heads for the doorway. "We'll leave at midnight." Before he exits the room, his eyes cut to mine, brimming with a silent invitation to follow.

When I finally track him down, he's in the upstairs sitting room with his back to me. From another room, giggles erupt and I marvel at the innocent contrast to the grim discussion that took place below. Mouse and Eli are in their own universe, blissfully unaware of the danger brewing around them.

And I'd give my soul to keep them there.

"I don't trust it," Mischa admits as I advance on his position. "And I know you don't, either." He reaches out, grasping my hand. "But you can't show it. Not to him and not now."

"This doesn't sound like you." Cocking my head, I place my hands on my hips. "Mischa Stepanov, biding his time?"

His lips quirk almost too quickly to catch. "Maybe your pretty little words are stuck in my brain," he counters. "Peace. Fighting Sergei out in the open certainly won't achieve that. It would split the *mafiya* right down the fucking middle and start an even bloodier war than the one with Winthorp. If he is a fucking liar, I need him to prove it on his own."

Even if waiting kills him.

"You're right." I brush my hand along his shoulder, feeling the muscle flex at my touch. "There is a lot I don't know about you."

And maybe it's not a bad thing.

"But," I add, "if you don't confront him now, then when?"

He looks away, eyeing the world beyond the windows. "When the timing is right."

"And until then?"

He rakes his gaze down the length of me, tracing the plunging neckline of the dress. His fingers cinch a handful of silk, and it's no match, easily giving him enough leverage to lift it over my head.

"Mischa!" I gasp as he tugs me against him, fully naked. "Anyone could come in," I whisper, painfully aware of the faint giggles betraying a world beyond this room. As his mouth comes to nuzzle my throat, the danger feels farther and farther away. "We can't—"

His lips capture mine, silencing my protests. Grunting, he spins me around, pressing my body against the window. The thin sill provides just enough stability to support me as he draws back, tugging on the fastenings of his pants.

Seeing him bare in the dim light shouldn't be enough to make all logic dissipate from my brain. Straining and swollen, he's breathtaking. My fingers reach for him before I can help it, easing a groan from his lips.

"Be a different animal for now, my wolf," he murmurs, sinking inside me on a single thrust. "Something quiet," he grates as his eyes flutter closed. He groans again, his throat cording as he starts to move. "A sheep?"

I'm too breathless to mount a comeback. Each thrust is rough, plunging as deep as he possibly can without hurting me. This isn't for pleasure.

It's a promise.

A plea.

A demand.

"Mine," he grunts against my ear in time with his next punishing thrust. "You're mine, Rose. Say it."

"Yours," I breathe into his sweat-coated skin. My fingers trace the line of his throat, tracking the sharp inhalation he takes. "I'm yours… And you're mine."

He grunts in acknowledgment, bucking his hips. The full weight of my ownership strikes me deep, far beyond where he could reach.

"Mine," I say as he stills inside me.

But if all goes wrong…

For how long?

Darkness has fallen beyond the windows by the time Mischa finally carries me to his room. It's a miracle we weren't caught by prying eyes. Or a curse. The longer I have him like this, the more reckless directions my thoughts travel. Lying beside him, I find it easy to imagine a future far different than any I would have envisioned before.

A world where I'd live by his side and no one would dare intrude on our peace.

Strangely enough, I think he's imagining the same thing as he absently strokes my back. But there is no denying the reality waiting for us beyond these walls. We both stay stubbornly awake until a knock on the door draws him away.

"Vanya," he says, greeting the figure on the other side of the door.

"We're ready," the older man replies. "Everything is in place."

"Good." Mischa looks back at me and inclines his head.

Reluctantly, I creep from the mattress and redress beside him in the dark.

Together, he and Vanya descend the staircase while I follow. Sergei is waiting below, joined by several of his men.

"We should go now," he suggests as we approach. He's traded his posh suit from the meeting for a plain black sweater and slacks.

Frowning, Mischa inspects him and shrugs. "Fine. But first…"

He turns to me, and I stiffen as he reaches out, cupping my cheek. The brief affection isn't like him—especially with several startled eyes tracking his every movement. Oblivious to them, he tugs me in close, giving me no chance to resist as his lips boldly brush mine. At the same time, his hand slithers between us, unseen by the two men, and he presses something firm against my palm. My fingers automatically close around the shape and I tuck it behind my back as he deepens the kiss.

His teeth nip me, a brutal reminder of his prior warning: *Be on guard.* Gasping, I return the favor with a nipped message of my own: *I will.* Beneath my fingers, the item he gave me is easier to interpret. A weapon with a sturdy, leather handle.

"Ahem." As if from far away, Sergei clears his throat. "I don't mean to rush…"

"I'm ready." Mischa pulls back and heads for the door.

My cheeks flame as I catch Vanya staring, his gaze unreadable.

"Don't wait up, Little Rose," Mischa calls as the men approach the front door of the manor.

Sergei and Vanya flank him on either side while the rest take up the rear.

"Ellen?"

I turn and find Anna at the top of the stairs.

"Is everything all right?" Her wide eyes focus on the object I still have tucked behind my back. From this angle, only she can see it: a knife. It's too small to be Mischa's usual weapon but lethal enough, I suspect.

Facing her, I maneuver the object to keep it from sight. "Everything is fine." I smile even as my heart hammers in my chest.

For the first time, I look down and observe the knife fully. It's thinner than his blade and therefore easier for me to wield. That fact makes my stomach sink; he got it for me especially.

He planned for me to *need* it.

Or he could be giving in to his usual brand of paranoia. Yes. I nod along with the pathetic logic as Anna gapes at me from the top of the staircase. Everything, from his history lessons to his hostility toward Sergei, was a gross overreaction. If the former leader is right and they are able to capture Robert, then the meaning of the knife could be more subtle—a mocking reminder of everything I've sacrificed without Robert: blood, soul, limbs…

Even so, maybe I'm not ready to be a widow after all.

"You look like you've seen a ghost," Anna says as I finally ascend the stairs to her.

A ghost? Or a serpent. Sergei's soldier's tattoo reappears in my mind: a snake entwined with a cross. The more I think about it, the surer I am. He was the same man we saw the night we escaped from Robert.

"Ellen?"

When I meet Anna's gaze, I can tell she's worried. "I'll help you put the children to bed," I tell her, forcing a smile.

Together, we turn to the sitting room and usher a drowsy Mouse off to bed while Anna carries Eli.

At the threshold to her room, she grabs my arm. "Something's wrong, isn't it? I can see it in your face."

"No," I start to lie. Then I bite my lip and eye the blade in my grasp. "Keep an eye on him," I warn her, nodding to the boy sleeping against her shoulder. "And take this."

She stiffens when I press the blade against her palm, exposing it completely. "W-what is—"

"Hide it on you always," I insist, cutting her off. "And if anyone tries to take him… Use it."

"Who would take…" Suddenly, she swallows and then nods. "I understand."

I don't sleep. I stand and pace, wringing my hands together mercilessly. Around me, the old house creaks and sways, bustling with Sergei's men. Finally, after what must be midnight, I hear the sound of clamor coming from the foyer.

I race down the staircase, and Sergei is already at the bottom to meet me. Alarm lances through my chest as I spot the mud on his clothes. For once, ruffled hair and filthy hands ruin his usually polished façade.

But his bloodshot eyes stop me dead in my tracks, even before he says the words my brain takes ages to process.

"I'm sorry… But we failed."

"Oh," I croak. It's the only thing I seem capable of saying.

"Ellen…" Frowning, Sergei takes a step forward, his hand outstretched. "Mischa and Ivan…they're dead."

CHAPTER 25

I thought the day I lost my mother taught me what pain was. Even losing Eli the first time. My heart shattered, but I could still bear it and pull myself from the darkness.

I could make myself numb to reality and cushion myself within the bars of my cage.

But now…there is no more hiding and no shelter from the truth.

Even hearing it said out loud—the fact that Mischa could be gone—makes everything go black. When sensation returns, I'm on my knees, wrapped in the arms of someone whose silent sobs rack my body.

But I just stare blankly, eyeing a spot on the wall as Misha's voice echoes in my thoughts on a constant loop. *Be on guard. Be on guard.*

Don't trust him…

"I'm sorry," Sergei says, but something in his voice makes me bury my face into Anna's shoulder and obscure my expression from him. "We tried to recover the bodies, but it was too late. I'm sorry."

Anna continues to sob.

But I just listen. Mischa said that the night I went missing, Sergei put on a good show, but something was off. And I can hear it in his voice now.

He isn't gloating.

But he isn't devastated, either.

He's merely resigned.

And I feel that gnawing, consuming paranoia itching at my psyche, keeping true grief at bay.

He knows more than he's letting on.

And I can't fall apart now.

So, biting my lip, I lock the pain away. I keep the tears at bay, and I guard my heart against anything that might threaten its fragile surface.

Even if it kills a part of me.

nna brings me to my room, her arms protectively around me. "Do you need me to stay with you?" she asks, choking her own sobs back. Blazing with concern, she scans my face and eases stray bits of hair from it. "I can—"

"No." I shake my head and turn from her, clinging to the door for balance. "Stay with Eli."

Once alone, I run my fingers along my face, surprised that there aren't any tears there to wipe away.

I wait long enough to hear Anna's steps retreat. Then I reenter the hall and descend the stairs. Unsurprisingly, I find Sergei alone in the drawing room, his back to me.

"What happened?" I demand hoarsely. "Tell me."

"It was an ambush." Turning to me, he sighs, raking his hands through his graying hair. "Winthorp must have anticipated our arrival. I did everything I could—"

"How did they die?"

He cocks his head at my tone, but finally, he unhooks his jaw. "We were separated," he says. "Unfortunately, when Robert's men retreated, I knew that—"

"That your man had done his job?"

"Ellen?" His eyes widen and narrow in rapid succession as my heart pounds a frantic rhythm against my rib cage. "I'm not sure I understand what you mean…"

"You let Robert take me." It sounds insane. I'm not even sure it's the truth—not until I see his expression harden. My heart solidifies into a throbbing, aching mass. Mischa was right. "Not for good," I add, still putting the pieces of my suspicion together. "You planned on retrieving me again. You had a man planted there and an easy route for him to enter my room via the vents—"

"And why would I do that?" he interjects, crossing his arms. The simple motion highlights just how large he is compared to me. A wall of muscle and power I have no chance at withstanding.

"Why?" I echo hollowly.

On the surface, such a plan makes little sense. But Mischa taught me well. I do what he would: view the situation from a different angle. I let my paranoia run rampant.

"Because I was never your true target," I blurt. "I'm still valuable to you, but one person could strengthen your position more than Robert's illegitimate wife. His son." My throat aches as I think of Eli, blissfully unaware of the games being played with him as a pawn. "You tried to bribe me into seeking him out myself. Maybe you would have revealed your plan then. But I refused. So you needed another method. For whatever reason, you knew that Robert would keep me near him. I just don't understand why."

"Why?" He faces me directly, his mouth thoughtfully tilted. "He's an easy man to manipulate—once you understand him."

"Robert?" I risk venturing a guess. "I think your goal was always to get control of Eli."

"He's the heir," he says simply. "Without him, Robert can't shore up support. Eventually, his empire will crumble around his fucking hands—"

"Then why didn't you say something!" My voice rings out, bleating and broken. It's a weakness. One I desperately try to regain control of, choking any hint of tears back. "Why all the secrecy and the lies?"

"And concede it all to Mischa?"

I jump as he advances toward me and brushes his hand along my cheek. Stripped of any feigned gentleness, his touch burns: callused flesh and brute strength.

"Mischa, the impulsive, violent fool who would run this enterprise into the ground?"

"You killed him." I fight any lingering tears back and force myself to meet his stare. This is the one truth I won't let him avoid. "Didn't you?"

"No." He sighs. Disappointed in that fact? "I didn't. But he is dead. I can assure you of that."

"And Vanya?" Again, my voice breaks. Gasping for air, I can't disguise the pain in it any longer. "Mischa was your rival, fine. But your own brother?"

"Ivan was an accident," he admits, turning his back to me. Even so, guilt radiates from his hunched posture—which only confuses me further.

"An accident?"

"Yes! Don't look at me with hate in your eyes," he snaps. "I loved him, even when he betrayed me. I was the only person who ever looked after him."

"Like with my mother?"

He should laugh at the insinuation. It's too petty to even consider. But he shoots me a look that chills my blood. It gleams with the malice he managed to conceal until now.

And I can easily discern the truth.

"You lied to him about her," I whisper in horror. "Didn't you?"

"Your mother..." He laughs darkly, failing to hide the loathing in his voice. "She was a haughty little bitch. She had Ivan wrapped around her finger. She put ideas into his head. Made him question what he shouldn't."

"Like you," I surmise. "She didn't trust you."

"No." His mouth flattens into a thoughtful line. "I suppose she didn't. Ever since I ordered my men to leave her precious whelp behind."

He says it so coldly that one could miss the true cruelty implied.

"Briar." I fight to keep the disgust from my tone. "You used her as a bargaining chip. Didn't you?"

On paper, he had a powerful weapon against the Winthorps in the form of Marnie to use against Robert Sr.

But he still needed leverage to control the woman herself.

And a mother would do anything for her child.

Even if it cost her the man she loved.

"I don't think Ivan ever believed her suspicions." He frowns and then shakes his head. "No. He would have killed me if he knew. But Marnie grew more devious. The time came when I knew she would run off with him and my—the Winthorp money."

"So you tricked her," I say. "Vanya thought she went back willingly, but that wasn't the case."

He nods as if finally admitting it all is freeing to him. Cathartic. "I promised her Briar. Then I told Ivan she left." The wry twist to his mouth could be guilt. Or smug satisfaction. "It broke his heart, but it had to be done—"

"All so that you could maintain power."

"For the good of the Vasilev name," he growls, his voice booming. "Ivan was too worried about sticking his cock in a pretty woman and siring more children. But *I* had the mantle of the *mafiya* on my shoulders. I had our family name on my shoulders—"

"But you abandoned your own family," I hiss. "She told you about me. Didn't she?"

"She tried to reach Ivan," he says. "I managed to intercept her messages, though I don't think she realized that. She pleaded for him to come for her. Then she primarily pleaded for you. In her words, even if he didn't love her…" He laughs again. "She begged him to take you."

My eyes burn, watering as I imagine Marnie. Her face. The pained way she looked at me. How she held me the few times she could. My pathetic, faithfully acknowledged birthdays…

All this time, I thought I was the source of her pain—but I wasn't.

Her heart broke for *me*.

"You made her think Vanya abandoned her," I say thickly. "And you left her to rot."

"I did what was best for Ivan." But from the grit in his tone, I doubt he believes that lie himself. "The fool would have gotten himself killed. Besides, he had Anna-Natalia—"

"Until she was taken," I point out. "But rather than rescuing her, you went after a child." A sudden thought churns my stomach. "Was hurting Marnie your real intention for wanting to kill Briar? Punishing her?"

"Are you really that naïve?" His eyes flicker and I instinctively take a step back. For the first time, the true Sergei Vasilev peeks from beneath his charming mask. Not a vengeful brute like Mischa, but something far more dangerous.

A cold, calculating tactician content to wait years to see his plans bear fruit.

No matter the cost.

"We spun Marnie's little excursion to our own benefit, but Winthorp retaliated much harder than I expected. I'm sure Mischa told you about what happened to his family? Imagine countless more gruesome tales, and widows, and pain. Not to mention what we thought happened to Anna."

"You saw my mother that night, didn't you?"

"I did," he says. "And knowing what I do now, I should have spit in her face."

"You're a monster! She learned better than to trust you. In her eyes, Anna was better locked in a Winthorp dungeon than anywhere near you—"

I don't even see the slap; it happens so fast. Then I blink, realizing I'm on my knees and Sergei is standing above me.

"I see you are like your mother in more ways than one. Eric!" He raises his voice and a man appears in the doorway. The one with the serpent tattoo. "Miss Winthorp is tired," Sergei says, waving a dismissive hand in my direction. "Please show her to her room."

The man approaches me and grabs my arm, hauling me to my feet. As he steers me to the door, I look back at Sergei. "Are you going to give me back to Robert?"

It's my obvious fate: With Eli under his control, he no longer needs me.

"No," he says. "But I will *sell* you back to him. Long enough to serve as a distraction while I put the pieces into play to obliterate his standing completely. Mischa wasn't as stupid as he pretended to be, but he was a fool," Sergei says. "He didn't realize that men like the Winthorps can't simply be butchered out of existence. With their money and prestige, it takes a slow, methodical approach to ensure their demise. I need to infest his holdings from the inside out and crumble the house of cards from the very foundation."

In some ways, it's a more gruesome end for Robert than a bullet would be.

"So what now?"

For a second, I think he won't tell me as his man drags me over the threshold. Then he holds his hand up and the man stops.

"I'll tell him that Mischa flew into a rage and killed the boy. I can offer you to him—for a price. And while he enjoys you in your current condition, I will solidify my alliances and then burn the manor to the ground when he least expects it."

Presumably with both Robert and me inside it.

Swallowing hard, I ask, "And Eli?"

"I'll ensure that he remains the sole inheritor of the Winthorp estate," he says. "Then I'll train the boy to take his rightful place as my successor. Maybe that will give you solace. He'll learn the Vasilev way, just as I did. Goodnight, Ellen."

The man, Eric, ushers me up the stairs and into my room. Once the door closes, I hear the lock engage.

And I can't help wondering if, before he sent her back to the Winthorps, Sergei made this room my mother's prison as well.

Robert was a cruel captor and Mischa a ruthless one—but Sergei is methodical. When my door opens in the morning, his man enters and places a tray of food on my nightstand.

It's not a bowl of gruel or the stale bread of a prisoner's rations. Though the scrambled eggs and porridge could easily contain a lethal powder. So could the orange juice or the steaming mug of tea.

Maybe he wants me to suspect as much. A part of me bristles at the paranoia.

But even Mischa let his guard down around Sergei.

I can't afford a single mistake.

So I ignore the tray and sit on the bed with my back to it. Closing my eyes, I think.

If Mischa were here, what plan would he compile? Something reckless and violent, no doubt. Though maybe that's the only way to counter methodical planning—brute strength.

Had I his knife, he'd probably urge me to stab the next person to bring me a meal. Stab Sergei afterward. Run.

But I know, even as I let the fantasy play in my mind, that my method needs to be different. Desperation is what Sergei expects. As Mischa claimed, a man like him is already one move away from checkmate.

The only way to beat such a foe?

Play a different game.

As my mind parses over every potential escape, I barely hear the door open.

"You haven't eaten," Sergei remarks with feigned surprise. "Maybe you'll find your lunch more palatable?"

Ignoring him, I eye the wall as he replaces the trays, and finally, he leaves. Newer smells tickle my nose in his wake. Soup? It's no matter. I close my eyes and focus on a game— but one far simpler than the elaborate chess match I grew up in.

The same one I can hear Mouse and Eli playing right now, innocent of everything else.

Cat and mouse.

And the most effective chases require only bait.

And sheer desperation.

851

When the tattooed man returns with my dinner tray, I stand and face him.

"Take me to Sergei," I command, meeting his startled gaze directly. "Now."

He frowns, but I suspect that Sergei warned him that I might make such a request. Without hesitation, he turns and beckons with a jerk of his chin. "Come but stay close."

And don't you dare run.

I follow him down the hall and nearly sigh with relief when we pass the sitting room. As if conjured by a miracle, Anna, Mouse, and Eli are already inside it.

"Ellen?" Anna lurches to her feet. Her eyes dart to the man in the hall, but there's a grim resignation in her gaze. Years with the Winthorps haven't made her naïve. "Are you all right?"

"I'm fine." I force a smile. "Mouse?"

The girl sits hunched on the floor beside Eli. I don't doubt she's already picked up on the inevitable shift in the atmosphere as well. Her eyes are sharp as they meet mine, as guarded as always.

Still smiling, I make my voice deliberately soft. "You and Eli should play a game. Remember the one you and Mischa played?" I pray to God that she understands. "This time, he is the flower." I point to Eli, who wrinkles his nose.

"I don't want to be a flower—"

"Hush, darling," Anna scolds. She tracks the silent communication between me and the girl, biting her lower lip.

"Wouldn't that be fun, Mouse?" I say, hoping the fear isn't apparent in my voice. "A game?"

With her as silent as always, I can't gauge her reaction. It's like Mischa gave her lessons in masking her emotions as well as knife fighting. Finally, she nods.

"Come, miss," the man prods. His hand brushes my lower back—a warning.

Reluctantly, I follow him down the stairs and across the foyer. Instead of the drawing room, he leads me to a different space, closer to the staircase: a study. Inside it, Sergei is sitting behind a desk, studiously eyeing a pile of documents.

"Can I help you, Ellen?" he wonders without looking up.

"I wanted to know when you were sending me back," I demand. "Because you are, aren't you?"

"What an odd coincidence." He shuffles his papers and finally looks up. "I was just about to make the arrangements. You'll return to your husband tonight. I was merely waiting for confirmation."

My stomach sinks at his cold, mocking tone. "C-confirmation?"

He slides something across the desk toward me. My eyes process the item in pieces: silver blade. Leather handle.

It's a knife, long and battered. Recognition shreds my heart. It's *Mischa's* knife. Only now, blood streaks the surface its owner strived so hard to polish.

"No…" My breath catches on a moan as I sink to my knees. At the back of my mind, I never believed he was dead.

But this…

Logic goes to war with blind faith, utilizing my heart as their battlefield.

Alive.

Dead.

Alive.

Dead…

"That is one matter of business handled," Sergei says. His callous tone is a harsh anchor, grounding me amid the wave of grief threatening to drown me.

I can't lose focus now, and Mischa's old mantra returns to haunt me. *Breathe!* I inhale raggedly, and through a screen of tears, I watch Sergei stand and rummage through a drawer.

"Now for the other." He looks at the man behind me. "Retrieve the boy—"

"No!" I lunge to my feet, but I barely go a step before a hand latches onto my arm from behind, locking me in place. "No! Don't you dare touch him!"

Oblivious to me, the tattooed man ascends the stairs. Seconds later, he returns—but my knees buckle with relief.

He's alone. He doesn't have Eli.

"The woman said they are 'playing'," he tells Sergei.

I fight to smother any reaction I might reveal, despite how my heart hammers. Mouse listened. I can only pray that she can stay out of sight long enough.

"Playing?" Sergei wrenches me around to face him. Whatever he sees makes him grunt in appreciation. "Make sure he's found."

"What do you want with him?" I risk asking. "He's a child. He's too young to inherit anything regardless—"

"Is that so?" His jaw clenches. He doesn't want to tell me, and I half expect another slap. But he sighs. "By tomorrow, I'll have him in Moldova, nestled away in a family compound—"

"Why?" I place my hand on his shoulder imploringly. "Why not let him stay with me? His mother—"

"Why?" He smooths his hand along my cheek. "And let you plant foolish ideas in his head?"

Pain bites into my jaw as his nails flex against the skin, robbing any kindness from the gesture.

"So that you can mold him the way you've twisted Mischa—"

"Let go of me!" I cringe out of his reach. "Don't touch me!"

He releases me so suddenly that I trip and fall to my knees. Then he sinks into a crouch and meets my gaze. "You haven't asked, but I know you've considered it: How could I let you go back if you could easily tell Robert all you know?" He raises a brown bottle that I didn't realize was in his grasp and shakes it. "Mischa has an associate who likes to use unwitting innocents as drug mules. To keep them silent, he had some unethical physicians concoct a poison that paralyzes the vocal cords, rendering the victim unable to speak." He cuts his gaze to Eric. "Hold her."

The man grabs me from behind. I struggle, but it's no use. Together, the men pry my lips apart and Sergei pours the liquid down. It's bitter, like copper. Or blood.

The second it hits my tongue, I put all my energy into choking, spitting out every drop.

"Swallow," Sergei demands. His hand encircles my throat, squeezing until my eyes water. When he finally releases me, I instinctively swallow, gasping for air.

Fire sears down my esophagus. Any noise I make comes out hoarse and broken.

It's like he struck a match inside me and chased it with gasoline.

"Get her in the van," Sergei commands loudly enough to rise above my wheezing.

The man grabs me, dragging me to my feet. My eyes stream as he ushers me from the manor and unceremoniously shoves me into the enclosed space minutes later. I scramble to get my bearings and reach for the door, but it's already locked. I'm in the back. I feel around for an emergency lever or anything I can use as a weapon, but I find nothing.

Seconds later, the van begins to move, pitching me forward. To protect myself as much as possible, I curl into a ball and try to steady my breathing. My only hope is that Mouse got Eli away. Just long enough…

For what?

It terrifies me that I didn't think that far ahead.

But now…

I have to find my own way to keep them safe. Even if it means dropping to my knees before Robert. Even if it means selling my soul in the process.

I'll do whatever desperate, dirty thing required to prevent Sergei from getting the upper hand.

But in the meantime, he has the last laugh; all I can do at the moment is suffer and wait.

We must travel for hours. By the time the van finally stops, I can't tell how far we are from Sergei's property. It's still dark out. In the early morning hours, I'm guessing. As the door opens from the outside, I tense.

"Come on." The man, Eric, grabs me and drags me from the van before I have a prayer of mounting an attack.

I blink to make out our surroundings as a gravel-like substance irritates the soles of my bare feet. The moon illuminates snatches of bushes and looming shadows—but a familiar stench makes my heart lurch. Fresh roses.

Like the kind that bloom on Winthorp manor.

Before I can be sure, Eric unfurls a strip of cloth from his pocket and wraps it around my eyes, snagging pieces of my hair in the process. Then he shoves me forward over uneven terrain that quickly gives way to a smooth, firm surface.

The air here feels thinner. Colder. A basement or garage?

"Be careful with her," a chillingly familiar voice commands from up ahead. "That's close enough for you. Let her go."

Grunting, Eric releases me, and I hear his footsteps echo as he retreats.

I'm left shaking, tears welling behind my blindfold. My body quakes down to my core, resisting the confines of my old cage as the doors to it figuratively slam shut. I'll never escape before it's too late. Eli and Mouse are already recaptured. So much for my so-called teaching. I'm just a pathetic doe, always on the run. I'm trapped. Forever…

Enough. Gritting my teeth, I bite any sobs back as heavy footsteps approach me. The time for self-pity is over.

Mouse.

Eli.

They consume my concern. To save them, I'll do anything.

Even if it means placating Robert. He's the one approaching me, his steps unsteady over what I sense is concrete flooring.

"Elle…" Soft fingers swipe at my cheek in their search for my blindfold, undoing the knot—but that's as much as he'll allow himself to touch me. "Are you hurt?" Robert scans me from head to toe. His finger hesitates near the corner of my mouth.

Licking the area, I taste blood.

"She's bleeding," he says before swallowing in distaste. Anger distorts his expression, and my heart pangs as I catch the subtle resemblance between him and Eli. They both can't hide their emotions for long, and now? Robert is murderous. "You bastards will pay—"

"R…" I try to speak. "Rob—"

"Sir!" A louder, masculine voice cuts me off. A man dressed in a black suit brushes past me and leans toward Robert, murmuring something into his ear.

"Damn it," Robert hisses, his hands clenching into fists. "Put her with the other one. They won't look for her there."

Before I can react, the blindfold is drawn over my eyes a second time.

"This way, miss." Someone grabs my arm and steers me in a different direction.

I strain my ears, desperate to track any other figures nearby or any clue as to my surroundings.

"Mr. Winthorp will see you shortly," the man adds. "You'll be home soon enough."

Home?

Rather than elaborate, the man leads me forward until he comes to an abrupt stop. I stiffen as he tugs at my blindfold, removing it. Frantically, I blink to make my vision come into focus: vast darkness. A heartbeat later, a door closes behind me.

I'm in a room. That much I can tell.

I feel along the nearest wall in search of a light switch. Despite flicking it, no light comes on. Eventually, I wind up sinking onto a carpeted floor with my back to the wall.

Only now do I realize I'm not alone. A slender figure creeps through the darkness toward me.

I stiffen, but they're too slight to do much damage, almost as tiny as Mouse.

"Hello?" a woman whispers, her voice familiar.

The closer she comes, the more of her I can clearly make out as cold recognition robs me of any urgency for a precious few seconds. Bright, familiar curls drape her shoulders. Her pale skin gleams in the darkness, and her huge blue eyes glisten like mirrors, reflecting my own terror back at me.

"Ellen?" Briar whispers. Her hand brushes my shoulder and she jerks it back as if burned. "Is that you?"

I can't speak, though my throat isn't the cause. In a relatively short amount of time, I've gone through so many wild emotions when it comes to my sister. Nearly twenty-four years of devotion have been reduced to a grim uncertainty.

Did I ever really know her?

Did she ever even love me?

All this time, I thought I was Marnie's dirty little secret she hid in shame. Now, I know the truth—she loved me enough to risk her life for me, countless times.

And she loved Briar enough to gamble her freedom.

And ultimately forfeit it.

"I don't know what's happening," my sister whispers, demanding my attention. "I don't…" She breaks off, her mouth flat. "I know you hate me. I… You don't understand what it's like. The wedding, and Father, and—none of this was supposed to happen!" Her voice shakes. "When Robert volunteered to lead the wedding procession to the airport, I knew." She laughs bitterly, shaking her head. "I knew there was a reason. But I didn't… I just thought if he were planning something, he'd get a big fucking shock if I outsmarted him for once. I didn't think you'd be hurt." She runs her fingers along her uninjured cheek. "Or maybe I did. Maybe I knew something bad would happen and I wanted you gone."

Hearing her admit as much out loud stings—far worse than I could have anticipated. Old wounds sear over my psyche: that constant fear of being unwanted. Of never fitting in.

Of being a burden.

Despite everything, I risk irritating the sore flesh of my throat to ask, "Why?"

She shrugs. "I spent my entire goddamn life being compared to you. Perfect Ellen. Sweet Ellen. Servants. Friends. Robert…even Mother loved you more. Maybe I wanted to know what it would finally be like if you were gone and I was just Briar without the more appealing shadow."

She sounds so young. So…desperate. Any hatred or resentment I may have felt disintegrates. Now? I only feel pity.

"Ellen, please say something!"

In silence, I reach for her hand, curling my fingers around her thin, trembling ones. Then I lean my head against the wall, close my eyes, and try to gather my strength.

Because this war isn't over yet.

It hasn't even started.

*M*ouse. *Eli. Mouse. Eli.* It's the only mantra I have left worth clinging to. *Mouse. Eli…*

Faint thuds jar me from my reverie and I stiffen, lurching into a crouch.

"What's that?" Beside me, Briar scrambles to her feet. "Something's happening," she whispers, dragging me upright as well. "Did you hear that? I think the guard is leaving! I don't know what's going on."

But I do. Distant shouts allude to only one kind of danger.

Sergei.

Damn. I start searching the room, cursing myself for not having done so sooner. How could I be so damn pathetic? No matter, the time for self-pity is over. There's a window in the corner of the room. I scramble toward it and attempt to open it.

"It's locked," Briar whispers, creeping to my side. "There're guards nearby too—"

I turn away from her and stop at a sideboard table. There's nothing on it but a lace doily and a vase—a metal statue. I grab it, pushing any doubting thoughts back. Then I turn to the window and slam it against the glass with all my might.

Glass rains down with an alarming crack as it gives way. Heedless of the pain, I knock away any loose shards, creating an opening barely large enough to slip through. Warm liquid drips between my fingers, but I ignore it.

"Come," I croak to Briar. God, speaking even that little hurts. Despite everything, a vain voice inside me wonders if the damage is permanent.

How ironic: I find my voice, only to die silenced.

"What now?" Briar asks, eyeing the makeshift opening.

I grit my teeth, grounding myself to the present. Now? If we're lucky, the guards aren't already on their way.

We're on a lower level, I realize with a sense of relief that nearly barrels me over. A carefully manicured terrain stretches out: flower beds, and paddocks, and enclosed paths. Even in the dark, I recognize it: the west gardens. Meaning we must be imprisoned at, of all places, the guesthouse.

Of Winthorp Manor.

"What now?" Briar asks again.

"Climb," I croak, shoving her forward.

"Ow!" She whines, struggling to maneuver her limbs through the opening. Finally, she disappears and her soft groan alludes to the fact that she made it safely below.

I scramble after her, feet first. Glass bites deep, and more alarmingly, hot liquid coats my limbs. When I let go of the sill, I grunt, landing hard on an earthen surface. Bolting upright, I grab Briar's hand and run, heading toward the back of the property.

But we're already too late.

Briar screams as a smattering of gunshots pierce the air dangerously close. Once again, Sergei lied to me; he won't even give Robert the chance to enjoy our little reunion.

He'll kill us all first.

"What's going on?" Briar squeals.

It's a good question. From this part of the estate, the only way forward cuts through the expansive gardens between the guesthouse and main manor. The whole damn manor could be on fire for all we know.

Heading there at all would be foolish.

But it's the only way out. From the garage, I could steal a car or a van and find my way back to Sergei's manor. I could find Mouse and Eli on my own.

Deep down, I know it's a stupid, foolish plan.

But I spent sixteen years living my life in the safest way I knew.

"We need to hide!" Briar rasps. "This way—"

She tugs me toward the farthest gardens, but I break away.

"Ellen!"

"Hide," I hiss to her. Then, shrugging aside her attempts to pull me back, I take off toward the main manor.

Idiot! I imagine Mischa shouting. *Hide!* Running toward danger is the stupidest thing I've done.

Reckless.

Selfish.

But, in war, there are no true winners. Here, in the sanctity of the Winthorp stronghold, Sergei has the advantage.

And he can't win.

My breaths rip from me as I run, plowing my bare feet over the cool grass. It's surreal in a sense, being inside my old cage as it's attacked from within. The beautifully tended flowerbeds of Winthorp manor create a mocking backdrop to the figures, dressed in black, streaming across it, wielding weapons.

Mischa made his name through his combat prowess—but Sergei can apparently muster the same amount of manpower.

He hasn't brought just one henchman to ensure his victory —he brought an army.

They cut boldly through the heart of the property, heedless of any Winthorp men who may be out on patrol.

I stick to the outskirts. Up ahead, the breathtaking façade of my childhood home stands, bathed in moonlight. The fighting started here, it seems.

Breaking glass and more gunshots allude to the battle raging within.

And every fiber of my being warns me to run. Hide. My heart pounds as I search for clarity among the shadowy figures battling on the terrace. I see nothing but sparks as guns fire and glass shatters.

I have to keep moving. As the clamor and violence rage around me, I deafen myself to everything but the sound of my ragged breathing. Then I set my sights on the detached building housing all Winthorp vehicles and inch my way toward it.

Mouse. Eli. Mouse. Eli...

"Ellen!" Someone grabs my arm, spinning me around.

A scream crawls up my throat before I even make out my captor's face, gleaming in the moonlit dark. I was so focused on the garage that I didn't even realize I'd passed the west end of the Manor entirely.

Here, it seems, Robert and a contingent of bodyguards have made their last stand. Fitting, since they create a makeshift barricade before the guesthouse and the prisoners he had locked inside it.

"What are you doing out here?" Robert demands. He cuts his gaze to a uniformed guard standing beside him, his face white with rage. "It's no fucking matter now." He grabs my arm, dragging me forward as he approaches a black van, flanked by two more bodyguards. "I'll keep you safe," he swears. "Once we're away from this fucking place, I'll never let you—"

He breaks off, his eyes wide, staring blankly ahead. His lips move, but no words come from them.

Just blood. Splatters of it speckle my cheek as he goes limp and falls backward, his mouth frozen in a startled O.

I can't scream.

Can't breathe.

In an array of beautiful, terrible noise, several quiet pops echo one by one, and the rest of the men around me go down in the same way.

Shot.

Dazed, I turn around in time to catch the killer, aiming his weapon at me. He's alone—I register that first as my brain tracks his approach in slow motion. His gray hair catches fire in the moonlight, making him seem more ethereal than human. A demon, his teeth bared in rage.

Panting, he says something my brain can't process and then aims the gun directly over my heart.

"Ellen, look out!"

Blond hair gleams in the air as a slender figure dashes from the front of the manor. Briar. Startled, Sergei turns toward her and the world explodes with a monstrous sound. *Bang!*

Acrid smoke tickles my throat as my ears ring in the aftermath. I can taste death; it comes *that* close to claiming me. But, as I stagger a few steps back, I realize I'm unscathed.

He missed…

But I wasn't his target. Paces away, a limp, blonde figure lies motionless on the lawn.

"No!" Even as I scream, there isn't time to think. React. Mourn.

Sergei's already whirling in my direction—but he doesn't expect the second I lunge.

There's no way I can overpower him. Stunning him is my only goal as my hand grapples with his. The gun swishes wildly in his grasp, pointing at me. The ground.

"Shit!" Finally, he drops it entirely.

But I don't have long to feel triumphant.

"You bitch!" He grabs my throat, wrenching my feet off the ground.

In vain, I strain and kick and flail until he trips, crushing me to the ground. Panic flares as the air leaves my chest. I brace my hand protectively over my stomach and fight for leverage to slip from his grasp.

"You little bitch," he grunts, tightening his grip. "I knew the moment I saw you that you were like her," he hisses. "Marnie Winthorp. Meddling and foolish—"

"I…saw…through you," I manage to croak. "Just…like… she did…"

Blood rushes through my ears, drowning him out. Closing my eyes, I focus every ounce of strength I have into kicking. Clawing. Biting. But he's no easy foe to overpower.

His angry growls seep into my ears as every attempt I make to resist has less and less impact. "Just…like….that fucking…whore…"

Suddenly, he stiffens, impossibly heavy. Crushing me…

"Ellen?"

The faint shout triggers a sharp pang through my chest. Hope? I open my eyes as unseen hands roll Sergei off of me. Gasping for breath, I blink up at the figure in question, braced to fight. A haggard face stares back at me and I shake my head. I'm dreaming.

Still, I indulge my insanity. "V-Vanya?"

He's holding a knife. Blood streaks the tip and my brain takes a pathetically long second to put the pieces together: the weapon, the unmistakable shape of a larger body lying beside mine.

Swallowing hard, Vanya flexes his free hand without looking away from me once. "Come with me." He hauls me to my feet, and into his arms.

"Briar…"

"She's alive." He jerks his chin toward a man racing past us, Briar in his arms.

But she wasn't the only potential victim.

I crane my neck, hunting for the awkward shape lying on the ground nearby. "Sergei—"

"Don't look." Vanya grabs my chin, forcing me to face him. "Come. Come!"

"How?" I rasp as he approaches the main manor. "How?"

It isn't long before someone lunges from the dark to meet us and I have my answer.

A tattered scream rips from my throat. First, from fear. Then, as the moonlight plays over the planes of the attacker's face…

Air wheezes from my chest as any words I mean to say die as a gasp. I'm dreaming. I have to be. But even my imagination isn't so vivid.

I could never recreate the grated cadence of his voice.

"You're shaking, Little Rose," he scolds as I scramble from Vanya's grasp.

I'm falling. My knees give way, but he catches me, looping an arm around my shoulders. "Mischa—"

"Did he hurt you?" he asks near my ear. "If he touched you, I swear to God, I'll kill him."

I shake my head, hoping it conveys my meaning: I don't matter. Inhaling deeply, I try to speak. "He has…" My voice is a thin, broken mockery, barely discernable.

"It's all right," Mischa snaps. He angles my face toward him and I can't stop myself from tracing the rugged features.

My hands shake so badly that my nails catch his flesh. I have to be hurting him, but he doesn't so much as flinch.

He doesn't fade away beneath my fingertips, at least. His heat is a cushion against the chill encasing me. I can feel his heart hammering through his rib cage, as his arms cradle me, firm and gentle all at once.

"You're dead," I whisper, cringing with the pain it takes to say even that little. "Dead—"

"I would be," he says softly, for my ears only. "If it wasn't for your friend Somodorov." He chuckles as my eyes widen in shock. Gingerly, his thumb teases the corner of my mouth. "Apparently, a certain whore made him rethink his alliances. He intervened during Sergei's ambush—"

"Mischa," Vanya calls. "We need to move. Now."

"Mouse and Eli," I say, forcing the words from my raw throat. "We need—"

"They're safe," he says. "We went there first, but you were already gone. Mouse had him hidden." He laughs gruffly, shaking his head. "I almost didn't fucking find them. But then we came for you."

Which is why Sergei had to move up his timeline by attacking so soon.

"Mischa!" Vanya jerks his chin toward a van idling in the main courtyard. "We need to move."

Mischa grits his teeth. "Sergei still has his allies," he says as he hastens me toward the van.

From the pain in his tone, I know that his worst fear is now a reality.

The *mafiya* has split down the middle.

And we've just ushered in a new war.

***

"We're here," Mischa says into my ear.

Dazed, I blink my eyes open and my heart jolts in my chest. Of all the places to find looming beyond the van, Sergei's manor wasn't on my list.

"It's safe," Mischa says as I stiffen. "We drove off his men. No one else would dare attack it now—"

"It's *my* home," Vanya says gruffly from the front seat. Reaching back, he grabs my hand and squeezes reassuringly.

"Even those loyal to Sergei wouldn't dare strike here. Not if they want to keep breathing."

The coldness in his tone bolsters the threat and I have no doubt he'd follow through. I'm not sure how much of Sergei's rant he overheard, but something in his gaze is different. Harder. Pained.

Maybe I'm selfish for wanting to ease it the only way I know how.

"She…loved you," I rasp as Mischa exits the van and pulls me into his arms. "My mother. She—"

"I know," Vanya says hoarsely, his eyes downcast. His hands are in fists, the knuckles stark white against his tanned, callused skin. "I know."

Mischa pulls me away before I can say anything else. This conversation will have to be continued later.

"Stay with me, Little Rose," he warns, his voice rumbling in his chest. "Don't you dare close your eyes. Stay with me."

He's not worried about any life-threatening injuries, I suspect.

For once, Mischa Stepanov is more direct than anything else.

Stay with him.

Without Robert.

Despite the end of the Winthorp war.

Despite the *mafiya*.

Stay with him, in spite of the targets on all of our backs.

Trust in him....

But not for survival, or security, or any other lies I could feed myself.

Stay with him because I want to, even if it means fighting for every scrap of peace.

Even if it means never finding it at all.

My mother was wrong. Hell isn't a rose. Hell is love. The agony of blind desire. Trust in the face of inevitable destruction. The acceptance of death to protect the breath of another.

Even so, under all the violence, it's undeniably beautiful.

In lieu of fire and brimstone, my Hades contains a small garden overflowing with roses. A gothic manor serves as its austere backdrop, but just a few weeks of childish laughter have eased the darkness lurking in its shadows.

A beautiful blond boy runs screaming through the gardens, chased by a silent girl with golden hair.

And my devil stands beside me, frowning at the display. "What are you doing?" he bellows. "Run her down!"

Heeding his advice, Eli changes tack, tackling Mouse to the ground.

"More military games?" I ask, raising an eyebrow. "Anna will kill you if Eli winds up with another bruise, you know."

"They need to learn," he counters. "One day, he might be thankful for surviving a battle with *just* a bruise."

I sigh internally at the reminder. Sergei's death created a void several of his allies have jockeyed to fill. There have been no outright attacks—yet. But the prospect keeps Mischa up at night and worry has deepened the lines around his mouth. Just as the thought crosses my mind, he spites me by flashing a wicked grin.

"Besides…the piano lessons start Tuesday."

"You're not serious." As I gape, the line of his mouth softens, just a fraction of an inch.

Even now, nearly a month after Robert's death, he gives me only snippets of what lurks beneath his mask. Just enough to reassure myself that this demonic creature is still human.

"I don't know… Maybe they should be able to play music before stabbing the first bastard to piss them off? My children won't be pampered runts," he adds, his tone harsh. "But table manners couldn't hurt, either."

"*Your* children?" My throat rasps.

Turning away from me, he steps forward, drawing Eli and Mouse's attention. "You." He jabs a finger at Eli and the boy startles to a stop, blinking. "And you." He nods toward Mouse. "Do you think you have what it takes to be Stepanovs?"

The two share a look and then nod solemnly in unison.

"Good. You." Again, he points to Eli. Then he moves toward a nearby rose bush and plucks a blooming rose from a stem. He rips a petal from it and then sinks to one knee, pressing the petal against Eli's forehead. "You are now Eli Mischovich Stepanov."

The boy watches him with all the reverence of a knight being anointed by a king.

"As for you." He beckons Mouse closer, frowning. "You need a real name. Will you tell me yours?"

She eyes him and then shakes her head, and I can't help wondering about her past. Despite the chaos, Mischa went to Nicolai about her, demanding answers, but all the man could tell him was that she had been sold to him.

Sold by a man named Donatello Vanici.

I'm not brave enough to wonder what she endured before then—and I can't blame her for not wanting a reminder.

If it weren't for Eli, I'm not sure I'd ever want to be reminded of the creature I used to be, either. Even Briar seemed too ashamed to face our shared past. Not long after we regrouped here at Vasilev Manor, she disappeared. So did one of the few Winthorp soldiers to survive Sergei's assault and defect to Mischa's *mafiya*. Maybe, in her own way, she thought we were even.

I saved her life years ago.

She saved mine.

"What about a new name?" I suggest.

"Something better than Mouse," Mischa seconds, ruffling her hair.

The girl wrinkles her nose. Then she points to one of the trees at the back of the property.

"Tree?" Mischa asks, incredulous.

"Willow?" I say, making a guess of my own.

Smiling, she nods.

"Fine. Willow it is." Mischa rips another petal from the rose in his hand and presses it to her forehead. "Willow Mischovna Stepanova."

"What about this one?" I ask, stepping forward. My hand cradles my belly and Mischa promptly sinks to one knee, pressing a petal against my abdomen.

"This one…" He frowns, mulling it over. "Mischa Junior."

A laugh escapes me. "And if it's a girl?"

He shrugs. "Mischa Junior."

I roll my eyes as he stands, drawing me close. His lips flutter over my cheek, imparting a million promises he can't say out loud.

Danger swirls around us—maybe it always will.

But, this time, we'll face it, two wolves with nothing to fear.

Side by side.

Hey there!

Thank you so much for reading! If you enjoyed the story, please leave a review and recommend the book to any friend you think would love this twisted world. You'd have my eternal gratitude. Even a short sentence goes a long way!

Then, come join the rest of us dark romance lovers in my Facebook Group where you can get snippets, sneak peeks of upcoming books and even help vote on aspects of future novels.

Come to the dark side:
https://www.facebook.com/groups/lanasbeautifulmonsters/

WANT MORE STUFF TO READ?
Join my newsletter and get a **free book**! Plus, you get to stay updated with any new releases, random giveaways and exclusive sneak peeks!
https://www.lanaskybooks.com/newsletter

Other Novels: https://lanaskybooks.com/

Dark, Twisted Romance

Join my newsletter and get a **free book**! Plus, you get to stay updated with any new releases, random giveaways and exclusive sneak peeks!

https://www.lanaskybooks.com/newsletter

Lana Sky is a reclusive writer in the United States who spends most of her time daydreaming about complex male characters and parenting her Cockapoo Joey. She writes dark, twisted romance across several genres. Her titles include everything from mafia romance to vampires.

facebook.com/AuthorLanaSky

twitter.com/lanasky101

amazon.com/author/lanasky

pinterest.com/lanasky101

goodreads.com/lanasky

instagram.com/lanasky101

bookbub.com/authors/lana-sky

www.ingramcontent.com/pod-product-compliance
Lightning Source LLC
Chambersburg PA
CBHW060740210726
48292CB00012B/10